Noctis Rising

Blood & Magic, Book 1

A.L. Richards

Bottled Chaos Publishing

Contents

Copyright		VI
Dedication		VII
Content Warning		VIII
Playlist		IX
Rules of Noctis		XI
Prologue		1
1.	NOTHING SAYS "WELCOME BACK" LIKE A DEATH THREAT	5
2.	LET'S TAKE THE CREEPIEST ROUTE POSSIBLE	21
3.	BAD NIGHT, WORSE MORNING	39
4.	IS THIS A TERRIBLE IDEA? I THINK IT'S A TERRIBLE IDEA.	55
5.	SOULS FOR SALE. NO RETURNS.	63
6.	DO NOT MAKE EYE CONTACT	89

7. ABANDON ALL HOPE, YE WHO ENTER HERE   107

8. CONGRATULATIONS! YOU ARE THE CHOSEN ONE! TRY NOT TO DIE.   131

9. SET THE PLACE ON FIRE AND RUN-STANDARD OPERATING PROCE-DURE   153

10. THE CHURCH OF BAD DECISIONS WEL-COMES YOU   173

11. PEOPLE WHO KNOW TOO MUCH SEL-DOM LIVE LONG. LET'S CHANGE THAT.   193

12. SOME MONSTERS WEAR FRIENDLY FACES   215

13. WOW. BETRAYAL. GROUNDBREAKING.   227

14. THANKS FOR THE KNIFE, IT LOOKS GREAT IN MY SPINE.   245

15. SOMEONE'S GONNA DIE, AND IT'S NOT GONNA BE ME   263

16. THERE ARE THINGS WORSE THAN DEATH: LET ME SHOW YOU   287

17. TIME TO DISASSOCIATE LIKE A QUEEN   297

18. OH LOOK, THE DOG HAS LORE   309

19. TEAM TRAUMA, ASSEMBLE   333

20. PLEASE HOLD WHILE WE FUCK EVERY-   359
    THING UP

21. DEATH CULTS AND CHILL   379

22. I DID NOT CONSENT TO AN ASCENSION   403
    ARC

23. GUESS WHO'S SOUL BONDED NOW?   423

24. NOT QUEEN, BUT THANKS FOR ASKING   439

Epilogue: THIS IS WHY WE CAN'T HAVE   456
NICE THINGS

Rose Tea With Honey   461

Also by A.L. Richards   462

About the author   463

Acknowledgements   464

For my Viking,

Whose strength anchors me, whose love shields me, and whose unwavering presence has made me braver than I ever thought I could be.

And for my Valkyries,

The fierce daughters I was gifted by fate. May you always know the power of your voices, the fire in your blood, and the legacy of warriors who choose love over fear, again and again.
This story is as much yours as it is mine. You are my home, my battle cry, and my greatest adventure.

Content Warning

Noctis Rising contains mature themes and intense situations that may be distressing to some readers. These include:

Violence and graphic injury

Psychological trauma and emotional abuse

Death, grief, and mourning

Horror imagery, including body horror and eldritch elements

Mind control and loss of bodily autonomy

Religious fanaticism, cult dynamics, and manipulation

References to familial trauma

Brief mentions (non-graphic) of suicidal ideation

Kidnapping threats and abduction scenarios

Panic attacks and emotional breakdowns

Blood, bones, and ritualistic magic

Non-graphic references to systemic oppression

Explicit sexual content

Reader discretion is advised.

Playlist

"Atlantic" — Sleep Token

"Neon Grave" — Dayseeker

"Just Pretend" — Bad Omens

"Hallucinations" — PVRIS

"Is It Really You?" — Sleep Token, Loathe

"crawl" — cloudyfield

"Phantom" — Nightcall

"The Summoning — Sleep Token

"Circle With Me" — Spiritbox

"The Ghost of Me" — Nightcall

"Good Enough" — Evanescence

"Take Me Back To Eden" — Sleep Token

"Bad Timing" — Blindlove

"My Immortal" — Evanescence

"Running With The Wolves" — AURORA

"Carry You" — Blindlove

"Sun Killer" — Spiritbox

"Chokehold" — Sleep Token

"The Reckoning" — Within Temptation, Amy Lee

"Armageddon" — Blindlove

"A Haven With Two Faces" — Spiritbox

"Silver Swarm" — Thornhill

"Damocles" — Sleep Token

"Pale Moonlight" — Dayseeker

"Doomed" — Bring Me The Horizon

"Homesick" — Dayseeker

"Birds and the Bees" — Blindlove

.

Rules of Noctis

1. To name is to bind.

2. Magic flows to memory.

3. Rewrite the self, and risk becoming unknown to fate.

4. Power taken leaves a scar. Power given leaves a bond.

5. Take only what is freely offered. Define your terms carefully.

Prologue

Brianna: *You could have had a quiet life. Chosen a different man, a different fate.*

Rhiannon: *I could have chosen cowardice, too, but it never suited me.*

Brianna: *No. You always preferred the blade to the shield. Even as a little girl.*

Rhiannon: *And you always preferred to speak in riddles when clarity would do.*

Brianna: *Clarity is a luxury the clever rarely enjoy. She's dreaming, you know.*

Rhiannon: *Of course she is. Her father carved dreams into her bones before she even had a name.*

Brianna: *So you named her Selene, after the moon. The light in the dark.*

Rhiannon: *Because one day, she will need to become it.*

Brianna: *Or burn chasing it.*

Rhiannon: *She won't burn. She'll blaze. There's a difference.*

Brianna: *You're sure? Even with his blood in her veins?*

Rhiannon: *Especially with his blood. She'll turn it into something he never expected.*

Brianna: *She already has your eyes. Your temper, too.*

Rhiannon: *She tried to hex the bathwater last week.*

Brianna: *Did it work?*

Rhiannon: *The tub exploded.*

Brianna: *(laughs) That's a yes, then.*

Rhiannon: *A loud one.*

Brianna: *She's going to be dangerous.*

Rhiannon: *She's going to be magnificent.*

Brianna: *You really think she can change it all? The legacy? The chains we broke, and the ones still hanging?*

Rhiannon: *Not alone.*

Brianna: *So she'll need her people.*

Rhiannon: *She'll build them. One by one, strange by strange, loyal by loyal. We're giving her a head start there.*

Brianna: *She'll have to learn to trust.*

Rhiannon: *She'll have to learn to lead, and to walk away when it hurts. She'll have to learn to survive the kind of love that doesn't ask permission.*

Brianna: *Will she forgive you?*

Rhiannon: *If I do this right, she'll never need to.*

Brianna: *And if you don't?*

Rhiannon: *Then the gods help the ones who come for her.*

Brianna: *There's no peace in this. You know that, don't you?*

2

Rhiannon: There's her. That's more than peace. That's purpose.

Brianna: She won't be easy.

Rhiannon: She's mine. I'd be offended if she was.

Brianna: She'll inherit your sharp tongue and sharper instincts.

Rhiannon: And your patience for prophecy and pettiness.

Brianna: He'll come looking for her.

Rhiannon: Let him. The day he finds her is the day he begins to lose.

Brianna: You always did play a long game.

Rhiannon: Not long. Just inevitable.

Brianna: Then let it begin, daughter.

Rhiannon: It already has.

CHAPTER ONE

NOTHING SAYS "WELCOME BACK" LIKE A DEATH THREAT

Serena

S OME MORNINGS, YOU JUST know the universe is going to punch you in the face.

My mornings were usually quiet. Riot would curl at the foot of the bed until I dragged myself up, cursing the day before it started. I'd make a pot of extremely strong coffee, microwave whatever hadn't gone fuzzy in the fridge, and try to forget that my family name was one people whispered in terror. I'd grab my laptop, take a look at my planner, and start work. This morning was no different.

Until it was.

Riot had already knocked over his bowl, ears flicking in irritation because I didn't fill it fast enough, when I heard the thump on my back doorstep. I rubbed my eyes, trudging toward the door in my worn pajamas, coffee mug in one hand, the other already flipping off whatever asshole left garbage in front of my stoop again.

Only it wasn't garbage.

It was a death sentence cosplaying as marketing.

I found the flyer on my doorstep like a dead rat left by an ungrateful cat—deliberate, unsettling, and a clear message that someone out there wanted my attention. It was printed on thick, expensive card stock, the kind that said, "We have money and don't mind wasting it on things like sending ominous mail to people who would rather not be found."

Afterlife Insurance, it read, in bold, too-eager letters. *Guaranteed Protection from the Unseen and the Inevitable. Premium Coverage for Souls at Risk. No Contracts. No Questions. No Second Chances*.

Because the biggest problem with dying was the paperwork, obviously.

Beneath that was a sigil I hadn't seen in years, one that had no business being anywhere near my very carefully constructed new life. My stomach did an unpleasant little flip, the kind that usually preceded an urge to either throw up or burn something to the ground. I stared at it, unblinking, hoping it was just a coincidence. Maybe after all these years my family had stopped looking for me and gone into the fine business of insuring the eternally damned.

I'd never been that lucky.

The shadows in the alley behind me felt heavier than usual, pressing in like they knew something I didn't. That was the problem with hiding from things that went bump in the night. When you spent enough time pretending to be normal, you found yourself believing it, right up until a little reminder like this showed up on your doorstep, smelling of secrets and old debts.

I flipped the flyer over. Nothing. No name. No polite little tagline like, "We've missed you, Serena! Come back soon!" It didn't need one. I knew where it had come from; if the topic hadn't been clue enough, it was addressed to my name. My real name: Selene ap Myrddin.

I knew a summons when I saw one.

Sighing, I pulled out my phone and dialed a number I'd hoped to never need like this again. The line rang twice before someone picked up. "Yeah?"

"Moshi," I said, gripping the flyer tight enough to crumple it. "You have some explaining to do."

There was a pause, a beat of hesitation so slight that most people wouldn't have noticed it. I wasn't most people, and I did.

"Serena," Moshi said, voice smooth and easy. "Long time."

"Not long enough."

"Is there a problem?"

"You could say that." I glanced at the sigil again, my fingers twitching. "I thought we had an understanding. I thought you were good at keeping people from finding me."

"I am," he said.

I barked out a laugh. "And yet here I am, with a very unfriendly calling card in my hand."

"And like you, I'm real interested in how they did it." Another pause. A slow exhale on his end. "Where are you?"

"My doorstep."

"Not safe."

"No shit, Moshi. I figured that out when I saw the damn sigil." I hesitated, the phone pressed to my ear, my other hand curled into a fist, crumpling the flyer.

It had been five years since anyone had used that name. Selene. Five years since I'd built Serena Morrigan from the bones of a girl who should have died. A girl who'd almost *wanted* to die.

I wanted to scream, to burn the flyer and pretend none of this was real. Riot was already pacing. He knew what I knew; Noctis never stopped hunting. It only waited until you got soft.

Another silence. Then, quieter, "You should come in."

I closed my eyes, pressing my free hand against my forehead. "Moshi—"

"You know the rules, bella. If someone's found you, it's not gonna stop here. You come in, we talk, and I help you fix it. Or, you can stay out there and wait for whoever left that pretty little message to show up in person." He took a breath. "This wasn't a threat, Serena. It was a promise." Another just-a-beat-too-long

8

hesitation, then, softly, "A threat would give you the option to refuse."

I could hear the tension in his voice. He was worried. That he was taking me seriously should have reassured me on some level, but it absolutely didn't. If Moshi was actually worried, then things were every bit as bad as I thought.

I glanced up at the bruised sky, the edges of the day creeping in. I didn't have a choice, not really.

"Fine," I muttered. "I'm coming in."

"Smart girl. You know the place. 8 pm." The line went dead.

I sighed, stuffing the crumpled flyer into my pajama pocket. "Yeah, we'll see how smart I actually am."

And with that, I stepped off my doorstep and back toward a world I had sworn I'd never return to.

Moshi picked the kind of bar where people went to forget they existed. Dim lighting, peeling leather booths, the scent of stale beer and the sound of bad choices hanging in the air like an old curse. The bartender looked like he'd survived three exorcisms and still had demons left to drink away, and my boots made a ripping noise as they stuck to the floor.

Moshi was waiting in the back corner, sipping something dark and expensive, looking as sharp as ever. He'd always been a man who made you feel safe first, only to realize your mistake later. He wasn't flashy. Wasn't loud. Somehow, though, he was always the voice of reason in the room. He was the one everyone ended up listening to without ever realizing they'd stopped speaking.

He looked the same as he had five years ago. Ageless in that quiet, uncanny way that made you wonder if he'd ever really been young. Medium-golden skin, smooth and unblemished, like even Noctis didn't dare mark him. Not a single scar, not a line out of place. His glossy black hair was slicked back with just a hint of strategically scattered silver at the temples, like time had passed him by with reverence. He didn't age; he curated.

His eyes were deep brown and warm at first glance, but they held the kind of stillness that made your instincts itch. Nothing ever flickered behind them: not guilt, not excitement, not regret. All you saw was the careful calculation of a professional liar.

Or not, if the truth served him more.

Moshi didn't deal in favors. He dealt in facts. If Noctis had a black market for truth, he was its gatekeeper. People whispered he had a gift, something rare. Not prophecy, but a knowing. A sense. He could tell the difference between a useful lie and a dangerous truth before a single word left your mouth. That was what made him terrifying, and what made him a purveyor of one of the most valuable things in Noctis.

He was lean, tall, and always perfectly dressed: tailored charcoal coat, subtle silver ring, boots that never scuffed. He didn't wear armor, but he'd never needed it. His weapons were suggestion, silence, and that razor-sharp smile he wore like a signature.

Even his scent was carefully chosen: bergamot and cardamom, softened by old paper and something just barely arcane. It lingered after he left, like a ghost with excellent taste.

"Serena," he greeted, motioning for me to sit. "Thought you'd bring backup."

"Didn't think I needed any," I said, sliding into the booth. I lied; my backup was in my car, and I was sure he knew that. I motioned to the bar around us. "You take me to the nicest places. Talk to me."

Moshi sighed. "I did some judicious reaching out. I was hoping it was a coincidence. It's not. Someone's put your name back in circulation."

Before I could respond, a shadow loomed over the table. Not just any shadow, but one shaped like six feet plus of bad decisions wrapped in a leather jacket.

I looked up and froze, caught in his gravity. He was built like someone who knew exactly how much damage a body could take before it broke, because he'd tested it. Broad shoulders. Arms that carried heavy muscle. Scarred hands. I had no doubt he carried a lot more scars that you couldn't see. His dark

11

brown hair was cut short, a military-cut jawline covered in a well-groomed beard, and dark hazel eyes that held no patience for bullshit. This was the kind of man you crossed the street to avoid, unless you were the kind of idiot who liked playing with fire. I'd been accused of a lot of things. Never arson.

"This her?" Gabriel asked, voice low, rough. Like he didn't have time for me or my problems, but somehow, here he was anyway.

Moshi nodded. "Serena, meet Gabriel Cade. He's going to get you back into Noctis."

I arched a brow. "Oh? And does he come with a return policy?"

Gabriel's mouth twitched, not quite a smirk. "You couldn't afford me, Red, so don't worry about the return."

Oh, I already didn't like him. This was going to be fun.

I leaned back, crossing my arms. "I don't like mercenaries, Moshi. They're expensive, and they tend to get messy."

Moshi sipped his drink. "He is expensive, but that's covered. The messy part I can't help with." My glare could have melted iron.

Gabriel pulled out the chair across from me, sat down, and leaned forward. Everything in his posture said this was a man who didn't take offense to much, but he still noted every insult. "Good thing I'm not a mercenary."

I cocked my head. "What are you, then?"

"I'm a problem solver," he replied in that just-this-side-of-bored tone.

"Funny," I said, "because right now, you just look like a problem."

Moshi pinched the bridge of his nose. "Can we not do this? Please? I already have a headache, and you two just met."

Gabriel tilted his head, considering me. "Fine. Let's talk about why you're worth my time."

I exhaled sharply. "Let's start with why you're worth mine."

This was going to be a disaster.

"Why am I worth your time? Because when the Noctis wants someone," Gabriel said, leaning forward, "it doesn't stop until it's drained every last drop of everything that you are. You, Red, are positively hemorrhaging time."

Something in his tone made my skin prickle. Not fear, I'd left that behind years ago, but recognition. He knew things. Dangerous things.

"I don't need a bodyguard," I said, keeping my voice steady. "I need answers. And maybe a small arsenal."

Gabriel's eyes never left mine. "You need both. And I'm the only one offering the package deal."

Moshi cleared his throat. "Serena, listen to the man. Gabriel's one of the few people who's been to the Glass Menagerie and walked out with his sanity intact."

That caught my attention. The Glass Menagerie was a labyrinth of mirrors and madness, a place where reality folded in on itself like origami made of nightmares. Nobody went there voluntarily, and sure as hell nobody came back whole.

"The Glass Menagerie," I repeated, tasting the words like poison. "No one walks out of there without leaving something behind. What exactly were you doing there, Mr. Problem Solver?"

Gabriel's expression remained unchanged, but something flickered in his eyes, something that put me in mind of a well-hidden scar. "Solving problems. And I didn't say I walked out whole. Just sane."

"Debatable," Moshi muttered into his drink.

"And why were you spending time in that particular cesspool of Noctis?" I took a drink of the surprisingly smooth Scotch in front of me, letting the burn focus the chaos in my head. Moshi did have excellent taste in liquor.

Gabriel's expression remained impassive. "Because if I'm going to solve a problem, I have to go to where the problem lies." He looked at me, more closely this time. "I go where I'm needed."

I felt the power stir inside me, an old familiar ache that I'd spent years suppressing. The lights above us dimmed slightly, and Moshi shifted nervously.

"Easy, bella," he murmured.

Gabriel reached for Moshi's drink and took a sip without asking, grimaced, and turned to face me dead on. "The way I see it, you've got three options. Run again, which clearly isn't working. Face whatever's coming alone, which will get you killed. Or, work with me, and together we might just get this dealt with once and for all."

I leveled his gaze with my own. "Work with you," I echoed, my voice flat. "And just how many people who've 'worked with you' are still breathing?"

He didn't smile. "All of them. At least they were breathing when I left them."

"That's an impressive claim." I wasn't bullshitting. It was.

"It's not a claim. It's a record."

I stared at him, trying to read beyond the mask of indifference he wore so well. "What exactly do you get out of this arrangement? Because men like you don't do charity work."

Gabriel's mouth quirked into something that wasn't quite a smile, and he glanced at Moshi, so quick I almost didn't catch it. "Let's just say I have a vested interest in keeping Noctis from getting what it wants."

"That's not an answer."

"It's the only one you're getting right now."

The tension between us crackled like static electricity. I could feel Moshi watching us, calculating, always calculating.

"Time's running out, Red," Gabriel said, his voice dropping lower. "That flyer wasn't just a message. It was a beacon. I'd bet folding money they know exactly where you are right now."

As if on cue, the lights in the bar flickered. Once, twice. The ambient noise seemed to recede, like someone had turned down the volume on reality itself. The air grew thick, charged with something that wasn't quite electricity.

I recognized the feeling, and it signaled nothing good.

"We need to move," Gabriel said. "Now." The relaxed, indifferent man I'd been talking to was, in the space between heartbeats, changed into a soldier ready for violence. He was on his feet, his movements fluid and precise. Those sharp hazel eyes were trained on the shadows in the corner of the bar, shadows that had begun to writhe and stretch, taking on shapes that had no business existing in this reality.

Moshi drowned his drink in one swift motion, sliding out of the booth. "Back exit. Through the kitchen. I'll distract them."

My head snapped around. "Moshi..." I started, but he cut me off with a sharp gesture.

"Don't get sentimental now, bella." He straightened his cuffs. "It's bad for business, and it doesn't suit you." He reached into his jacket and pulled out what looked like a hand grenade, if hand grenades were made of twisted silver and bone and hummed with a frequency that made my teeth ache.

I wanted to argue, but the shadows were moving faster now, coalescing into forms that made my eyes hurt to look directly at them. Not human, more like the *idea* of a human filtered through the lens of a nightmare. Too many limbs with too many joints and faces that shifted like smoke and blood. Recognition twisted my stomach.

"Collectors." Those twisted forms could only belong to the Bone Lords' favored enforcers.

Gabriel's hand closed around my upper arm, his grip firm but not painful. "Kitchen. Now."

The rational part of my brain knew they were both right but something broke in my chest at the thought of leaving Moshi to face these things alone. I wanted to argue, but the forms were moving faster now, and the temperature in the bar had plummeted, frost creeping across the sticky tabletop. Moshi looked at me. "Go, Serena! I've got this."

The world tilted as Gabriel dragged me through the bar and into the kitchen. We shouldered past bewildered staff frozen in place like mannequins caught in a moment that wasn't quite real. Their eyes were glazed over, their mind's defense against witnessing the impossible. Time stretched like taffy in Noctis's proximity, and I envied them their oblivion.

"They're not just collectors," I said, my voice tight as we burst through the back door into an alley that felt far too narrow. "They're high ranking. The bone masks—did you see them? Shifting patterns." I huffed out a laugh. "They sent their best."

Gabriel didn't slow, navigating the urban labyrinth with unsettling precision. "I noticed. Your father's people must be feeling sentimental."

"They were never really 'his people', and they shouldn't be feeling anything. I ki—"

A sound like tearing silk erupted behind us. The alley wall rippled like water, and a figure stepped through, a figure in a bone-white suit with too many angles, its face a shifting mosaic of tiny skulls that clicked and chattered.

"Hello, daughter of Myrddin," it said, its voice like glass breaking underwater. "You've been missed." My stomach lurched, and I felt the blood drain from my face.

Gabriel shoved me behind him with one hand, the other pulling a matte-black gun from his waistband. Something about it made my teeth clench. Not standard, then.

"Collector," Gabriel acknowledged coldly. "You're way out of your jurisdiction."

The thing's laughter rattled like dice in a cup. "There is no jurisdiction when it comes to reclaiming what belongs in Noctis."

"I don't belong to anyone," I snarled, feeling power surge through me, hot and familiar, but before I could shape it, send it out, something hit the Collector square on the back, sending it flying face down onto the pavement.

The blue-and-gray blur that had exploded from the shadows with a snarl tore into it without hesitation, teeth sinking into that too-long neck where the mass of tiny, chattering skulls tried to rearrange into something resembling a face. Gabriel sighted down his weapon, trying to get a clean shot.

The Collector shrieked. The sound wasn't natural, like metal dragged across metal. It fractured into a garbled, multilayered scream that didn't come from one mouth but from dozens. The shockwave of that scream hit us, the pressure knocking me and Gabriel sideways. My head cracked against the alley wall, pain exploding behind my eyes. I heard Gabriel grunt as he hit the brick beside me. I reached up with a shaking hand to wipe away the blood that was now threatening to trickle into my eye.

Riot snarled in answer, driving his weight down harder, on the thing beneath him, but still it wouldn't die. It bucked violently, slamming my dog against the bricks with bone crushing force. Riot yelped, an awful, sharp sound, and staggered back. Black ichor smeared his side, causing his coat to smoke. The Collector rose, twitching as if reassembling itself from fractured logic, limbs cracking into place at impossible angles.

Gabriel raised his gun, fired once. Twice. A third time. Sparks flew from bone plating, but the thing kept coming. Power surged beneath my skin, begging to be used.

I didn't. I couldn't.

Riot lunged back in. This time, he went for the legs, tearing through one with brutal, grinding force. The Collector screamed again—higher, harsher—and spoke as it fell:

"She is unfinished. We will come again. She will be unmade."

Its body cracked down the middle like a mirror splitting from the center. I threw an arm up too late; bone shrapnel grazed my cheek, leaving a stinging burn in its wake. Riot didn't let go until the thing collapsed entirely into a heap of steaming fragments.

For a moment, nothing moved. The alley was silent. Too silent.

Then the shards began to *curl,* little pieces of bone twitching like they weren't ready to be done.

Gabriel stepped forward and crushed the largest one beneath his boot. He turned to look at me, but my eyes were on my dog.

"Riot," I breathed, dropping to my knees.

With a shake of his head, he limped his way through the debris and over to me. I buried my face in his fur, ears still ringing, gut knotted that he'd gotten hurt protecting me. It wasn't the first time. "Good boy," I whispered. Gabriel tugged at my shoulder.

"That noise is going to attract more of them. Move."

CHAPTER TWO

LET'S TAKE THE CREEPIEST ROUTE POSSIBLE

Gabriel

THE NIGHT SWALLOWED US whole as we ran, the scent of frost and iron thick in the air. My boots hit the pavement in steady, even strides, but my mind was a storm. I should have walked away the second Moshi introduced me to Serena. Too much fire, too many secrets, and the target on her back might be enough to make me regret every step I was taking right now. Hell, I was starting to regret it already.

But here I was, running through the streets of Seattle toward a place I swore I'd never set foot in again, making sure she stayed alive. It had been a solid year since I'd been in that godforsaken city, and I'd wanted to keep it that way. The worst part of it was I wasn't even sure why. Some misplaced sense of obligation? A debt I never owed but felt responsible for anyway? Or was it something worse—something I didn't want to name?

Dealing with Noctis hadn't always been this haunted. It used to breathe differently; it had still been sharp and dangerous, but with edges I could see coming. This? This felt feral, like something had gone wrong in its bones and nobody noticed until it started smiling with too many teeth. You didn't see it coming until it started spilling over into a Seattle dive bar.

I remembered the sound the streets used to make when it rained. The way the slick neon reflections would turn the gutters into rivers of melted color. I remembered the quiet screams tucked into the alleyways, the ones that weren't always human. The ones I ignored. The ones I answered. The ones I'd caused.

I remembered what it felt like to matter there. I remembered how the power of being important made you safe, until it made you a target. That city knew me, and when we got there, it would know I'd returned.

"Keep moving," I said, low and firm. She didn't need the reminder, but I gave it anyway. Maybe for my own sanity, because if I didn't keep talking, I'd start thinking, and thinking was the enemy right now.

"Supplies," she gasped, keeping pace beside me. "We need supplies before we go under."

She wasn't wrong, but stopping meant risk. It meant giving Noctis time to catch up.

"Not my first rodeo, Red." I exhaled sharply. "I'm taking us someplace to gear up."

She shot me a look. "Does it involve anyone trying to kill us?"

The corner of my mouth twitched, but humor had no place here. "Only if you can't behave."

Her snort told me exactly what she thought of that.

We slid through the labyrinth of the city, dodging the places where the shadows stretched too long, the alleys that whispered invitations to step inside and never leave. Noctis was always like this: hungry. Restless. A place that never let you go once it had you, and right now it was flooding into this world at a frightening rate. I'd spent years digging my way out, and now I was sprinting straight back in.

The street was quieter than I remembered, and it made the hairs on the back of my neck stand up. We weren't in Noctis, not yet, but there were plenty of places where it bled over on a good day, and this was anything but a good day. I led us to a narrow doorway beneath a dying neon sign: **Vex's.**

"Vex?" Serena asked, skeptical.

"Old contact." I knocked once. Twice. A pause. Then a third knock, off-beat. Code. "We can get what we need here."

The door creaked open, revealing silver eyes that gleamed from the dark. Vex's lips curled like she was already bored. "Well, well," she purred. "Look what the cat dragged in. Cade, you're either desperate or stupid."

"Little of both," I admitted. "We need gear. Fast."

Vex tilted her head, gaze sliding to Serena. Her smile sharpened. "And you. You're carrying a storm in your bones."

Serena crossed her arms. "You selling or stalling?"

Vex laughed, stepping back. "Oh, I like her."

I sighed through my nose. "Are we doing this or not?"

The shop smelled of dust and ozone, stacked to the ceiling with things that should never see daylight. Magic thickened the air, clinging like oil. I ignored it, zeroing in on what we needed: weapons, first aid, maps that didn't lie. The essentials for staying alive in a city that liked to kill for fun.

Serena ran a fingertip over a curved dagger, testing its edge. "Any chance you've got something that works against Collectors?"

The room stilled. Vex's amusement evaporated. "You're not kidding, are you?"

Serena met her gaze head-on. "We're going into Noctis."

Silence. Then Vex let out a low whistle. "Hell of a death wish."

I slung a bag of supplies over my shoulder. "Can you help us or not?"

Vex sighed, muttering something before disappearing into the back. When she returned, she was holding a vial filled with something that shimmered like liquid silver. "This will buy you five minutes against a Collector. No more. Very probably less."

Serena caught it, frowning. "What is it?"

"A last resort."

"Five minutes," she echoed, like she was tasting the weight of it. "Better than nothing."

"Just barely," I muttered. Vex tilted her head, studying us. The boredom had slipped from her expression, replaced by something quieter. Something sharp.

"You really are planning to go into Noctis." Not a question. A reckoning.

Serena didn't blink. "We're not gearing up to go whale watching."

A pause stretched between the three of us. The silence in that little shop grew thick and knotted with tension, vibrating between people who'd seen too much and hadn't flinched at the sight. Vex leaned in, resting her elbows on the counter. Her silver eyes caught the low light, glowing faintly. She addressed me. "You're going to need more than blades and bandages down there. Noctis is… starving. It remembers her."

"It remembers a girl alone. She's not alone now," I said flatly.

Vex's gaze flicked to me, unimpressed. "You think loyalty's enough? You think that city won't peel it off your bones like skin from fruit?" She looked back at Serena. "There's an old name moving in the dark. People whisper it when they think the walls aren't listening."

Serena's lips thinned. "Don't say it."

"I'll say what I damn well please," Vex snapped. Then, quieter—softer, even—"The Vesper's active again."

I felt rather than saw Serena stiffen beside me. She didn't speak. Didn't breathe. Vex noticed. Of course she did.

"You've crossed paths," she said. "Explains the jagged edges." Serena said nothing.

"The Vesper, they hunger for stories. Faces. Names," Vex continued, her fingers drumming against the countertop, the sound oddly rhythmic. "And yours, darling? Yours is a collector's piece."

I took a slow step closer, my voice low and cold. "You offering advice, Vex, or just enjoying the sound of your own funeral rites?"

Her smile was all teeth. "Call it a freebie, Cade. Now, we all have our limits, and you've reached mine."

She pushed a small, dark cloth bundle across the counter: a pack of iron-tipped stakes wrapped in old velvet, a faded sigil stitched at the corner. "Take these. They won't kill a Collector, but they'll slow it down. Pin it long enough to get clear."

Serena hesitated, then took them. "Why help us?"

Vex's expression turned distant. "Because I've seen what's coming, and I'm not interested in dying slowly in a place that thinks mercy is a myth."

I clenched my jaw. I didn't like unknown variables, but I liked the Collectors even less.

Vex leaned against the counter, arms crossed. "I'd wish you luck, but it won't do you much good down there."

Serena looked back, face solemn. "I don't believe in luck."

I touched her elbow, steering her toward the door. "Time to go." I tossed a wad of bills down on the counter, nodded at Vex, and we were gone.

We hit the street running, doubling back toward the bar until we could slip into the truck I'd stashed a few blocks away. Serena barely got the door closed before I gunned it, weaving through the streets with a precision that came from years of knowing exactly when to be somewhere, and when to disappear. Her dog had jumped in as soon as she'd opened the door, sliding into the seat behind hers. He looked like an Australian Shepherd, but the way he'd taken down the Collector, the way he kept himself beside her without her having to say a word? No way was he—Riot, she'd called him Riot—a normal dog.

"We need more than magic," she said, stuffing the vial into her coat. "We need clothes, food; you know, things normal people use."

I sighed. She was right, and that meant a detour.

Somewhere between the desperation and the silence, we ended up in the hell of a 24-hour fucking super mart.

Nothing like end-of-the-world shopping under fluorescent lights to really hammer in the deep cosmic fuckery. The contrast made me grind my teeth. Serena peeled off down the hygiene aisle like she'd done this a hundred times, like apocalypse prep was just another item on her to-do list.

A woman in pajama pants and clogs side-eyed me when I grabbed a couple of boxes of protein bars and a hand axe from seasonal camping. I had a go bag in the truck, but I could still stand to pick up a few things. I stared her down until she decided her coupons were more interesting. I hated this part: the pretending we were normal, just two people gearing up for a weekend in hell.

When I met up with Serena at the self-checkout, she was tossing a t-shirt onto the stand, behind a couple bags of jerky, a bright pink thing with gaudy silver letters.

FIFTY SHADES OF FABULOUS.

I stared at it. Then at her.

She raised a brow. "Problem?"

"Didn't realize we were leaning into the 'disguise' thing this hard."

She grinned. "I like options."

I shook my head, tossing socks, sweats, and hoodie in the cart next to her remaining purchases, along with the protein bars and axe. While she fiddled with the checkout, I looked at what she'd chosen. Jeans, some underwear, a couple of T-shirts, thankfully in more muted tones. There were also a few toiletries, a first aid kit, and a bag of Halloween candy. I raised an eyebrow at the last.

"Planning to bribe the Bone Lords with chocolate?" I asked.

"Noctis doesn't do candy," she said. "Which is exactly why I'm bringing it."

There was something in the way she said it, like defiance wrapped in sugar, a live grenade with glitter on the pin. It caught me off guard.

I scanned the candy without comment. Let her keep a little normal; God knew we wouldn't see much of that where we were going. However, when she wrinkled her nose at my boxes of protein bars, I spoke up. "You know, you'll thank me when we're stuck in a sewer with nothing to eat but rats and existential dread."

"We have Kit-Kats," she countered. "The jerky is for Riot." Hilarious. I muttered something under my breath about regretting all my life choices up to this point and finished scanning our items. No time for arguments.

"What, no comment?"

I snorted. "I'm not about to die in the middle of a goddamn Supermart, Red." I looked over, and she was smiling, but her eyes held something raw.

By the time we were back in the truck, Serena had pulled the pink shirt on over her old one, looking entirely too smug. I focused on the road, trying not to think about the fact that I was driving toward Noctis with a woman who had a bounty on her head and an attitude to match.

Riot huffed in the backseat. Yeah. I agreed with him.

"Next stop, Noctis," I muttered, gripping the wheel tighter. "Hope you're ready."

"As I'll ever be, after I swore I wouldn't go back."

I kept my eyes on the road. "Plans change."

Her voice was quiet. "People don't."

The silence between us crackled with things we couldn't quite find words for. Riot whined softly from the back seat, pressing his muzzle against Serena's shoulder. We hit the outskirts of town just as the moon slipped behind a bank of clouds. Perfect timing; the veil between worlds was always thinnest when light itself couldn't decide where to land.

I pulled off onto a service road that shouldn't exist, the truck's headlights carving twin paths through mist that coiled like living smoke. The road to Noctis wasn't marked on any map, but I could feel it, pulling at us like a black hole. The closer we got, the more the world around us seemed to thin. Reality flashed from the edges, the sky overhead bleeding into colors that didn't exist, warping as the walls between the worlds wore down.

Riot whined in the backseat, and as I glanced back at where he sat with his nose pressed to the window, his reflection showed something other than the Australian Shepherd he appeared to be, something with too many teeth and eyes that burned blue as Saint Elmo's fire. I blinked, and it was gone.

I cleared my throat. "He's not just a dog, is he?" I looked at him, and his ears flicked forward even though he didn't meet my eyes.

Serena's mouth quirked. "Asks the man driving us into a parallel dimension."

"Fair point," I conceded. "But I'm right."

"No," she said, quietly. "He's never been just a dog." She took a deep breath and continued. "There were nights I'd wake up screaming, tangled in my sheets, soaked in sweat, and Riot would be there. No barking. No panic. He'd just lay with me until I calmed down." She reached back and curled her fingers into his ruff. "He's more than a companion. More than magic." He nuzzled into her hand, and she smiled. "He's mine."

What could I say to that?

I squinted into the fog. "Not much farther now." I pulled the truck into the tree line and killed the engine.

The tunnel entrance loomed before us, a gaping maw of absolute darkness. I'd seen it before, minutes and a lifetime ago, and it hadn't gotten any more inviting. This wasn't a tunnel you'd find on any official blueprint from the city; it was more a gash in the landscape. Its concrete facade was cracked and sagging, as if it were pulling away from whatever was on the other side.

I reached into the back, grabbing my go bag. Serena had wedged hers under her feet, and she pulled it out, shoving her purchases into it, slipping her arms into the straps. She tilted the seat forward for Riot, and he jumped down, his nails clicking against the pavement. In the eerie silence, each sound seemed amplified. He stared at the tunnel entrance, hackles raised.

"He doesn't like it," I observed.

"That's because he's smart." She reached down to run her hand over the top of his head and he settled, pressing close to her leg. "You know the drill. Keep your eyes to the front, don't slow down and don't stop, no matter what you hear."

I nodded. There were things that prowled the tunnels, and they were always hungry.

She fell in beside me. We stepped into the tunnel, and the world changed.

The darkness wasn't just the absence of light; it was something alive, swallowing light and heat and any semblance of hope you might have had when you walked in. The walls twisted, writhing as if the concrete itself was panting. They glistened with something that wasn't water, something that looked infected, and the air smelled fetid and wet.

We'd walk what felt like north for five minutes, then take a turn that should have taken us west, but suddenly we seemed to be heading back the way we'd come. The minutes felt like hours, and the ground beneath our feet became increasingly spongy. Our footsteps had been echoing, but they became increasingly muffled, like walking on raw meat, and other sounds started to make themselves known.

"Keep moving," Serena murmured, her voice barely audible over the whispering that was getting louder. "Don't listen."

But I *was* listening; I couldn't help it. The voices were insidious, slipping past defenses I'd spent years building. The tunnel was hungry; that was the only way to describe it, like it wanted to peel us apart and see what we were made of. Riot pressed against my leg, and his solid warmth was grounding. I didn't trust animals much: too unpredictable, too instinct driven. But this dog? He knew things, and right now, he knew I was close to the edge.

They knew things, too, the things in the tunnel, or pretended to. That was the danger; half of what they whispered were lies. The other half was worse, because it was true.

I heard my mother. A voice I hadn't heard in decades, soft and sharp at once, the way it always was right before the belt came out. *You could've been better, Gabriel. You were supposed to be better.* My boots squelched against something that moved when it shouldn't have, and I didn't dare look down. The air thickened, wrapping around my throat with invisible fingers.

The dog pressed harder against my leg.

Gabriel, they hissed, voices layered, mismatched, out of sync like a broken tape. *You're still one of us. Come home.*

Gabriel...you left us to die...

My sister's voice. Jason's voice. Perfect in every inflection. I stumbled, just for a second.

Serena's hand found my wrist, her grip hard enough to bruise. "Gabriel. Focus on me."

The voices grew louder, a cacophony of accusations. My team, dying in the sand half a world away. My sister, begging me

33

to come home before it was too late. Faces I'd tried to forget, all calling my name with perfect clarity.

"Cade!" Serena's voice cut through the noise, sharp as a blade. "Look at me!"

I dragged my gaze to hers. Her eyes were fierce, luminous in the darkness, twin points of emerald that somehow outshone the whispers. Riot pressed against my leg, a solid weight that anchored me.

"It's not real," she said, each word precise and measured. "It's not them."

I forced myself to focus on her face, on the biting grip of her hand on my wrist. "I know," I gritted out, forcing one foot in front of the other. "Just keep moving."

The darkness laughed in reply.

The tunnel contracted around us, the wall pulsing like a living throat. Riot growled, and the sound vibrated through my bones as we pushed deeper. His eyes flashed that eerie blue again, and his shadow didn't match his movements.

"We're getting close," Serena whispered. "The transition is starting."

I could feel it, feel reality stretching thin, plastic wrap ready to tear. The air grew heavy with the scent of ozone and something ancient. The air buckled and spat us out.

And we were standing beside the sidewalk inside Noctis.

Noctis wasn't a place so much as it was a wound in reality that had festered and grown sentient. Buildings loomed, their architecture defying every law of physics I'd ever known. Windows pulsed with light, occasionally blinking like watching eyes, and the street hummed with vehicles of every possible description, driven by people that weren't always people. The sky, if you could call it that, hung low and bruised, perpetual twilight cast everything in shades of indigo and purple, streaked with the neon that blazed from the shopfronts and clubs along the way. The air tasted like ash and copper, and the streetlights burned with a greenish flame that didn't illuminate the sidewalk as much as it emphasized the darkness around it.

Some structures grew up and sideways at the same time, collapsing inward like they'd gotten tired halfway through. Others spiraled, reaching for a sky that never quite agreed on where to stay. The ground shimmered under our boots as if it resented being stepped on. People moved like smoke, or didn't move at all, just stood with eyes too wide, too black. The miasma hit harder here, curling under my tongue like a warning I couldn't swallow. A woman brushed past us, except she didn't. Her face turned to follow me even as her body kept walking. Her smile lingered, stretched too wide.

Serena stiffened beside me, fingers brushing my wrist for the briefest moment. Just a brush. A spark of silent agreement: We move. We don't stop.

I took a moment to get my bearings, feeling the weight of the city pressing on me. I hadn't been born here, but I'd been here enough to know this place, and nothing I knew was good. The fact that it knew me back wasn't something I wanted to think about right now.

"Home sweet home," Serena murmured, but there was no warmth in her voice. "Try not to stare. It's rude."

I forced my gaze away from a woman whose skin seemed to be made of stained glass, fracturing the light around her into kaleidoscopic patterns. All of her skin, since she wasn't wearing a single stitch of clothing. "Been awhile," I replied, shifting my pack higher on my shoulder. "Some things have changed."

"And some things never do."

I scanned our surroundings, trying to find my bearings. "Which district are we in?"

"Looks like Lowtown, near the Crossroads." She angled her head, listening to something I couldn't hear. She seemed calm, but the way she twisted her fingers in Riot's fur betrayed her nerves. He stood close, and when I looked carefully, his form seemed to shimmer around the edges. His shadow stretched longer than it should have, occasionally flickering with what looked like an extra limb. "The Veil Market should be three blocks east, if it hasn't moved. That's probably our best bet for information." She started to move off, and I grabbed her wrist, stopping her.

"I hate to tell you this, but you can't just waltz into the city. You're being hunted, remember?"

Her face darkened. "I know what I'm doing, Cade."

"You're the Necromancer's Daughter," I said, voice low enough that only she could hear. "Every person in Noctis knew who you were. Five years is a long time away, but not long enough for these people to forget your family—or you." I dropped her arm. "We need to get out of sight and plan our strategy from there. The Bone Lords have eyes everywhere, and right now you might as well have a spotlight on you and a 'Welcome Home' banner stapled over your head." I looked around again. "If this is Lowtown, I've got a safe house not far from here."

"A safe house." Serena's voice was flat. "In Noctis."

"Believe what you want," I said, scanning the street with practiced precision, "but standing here is suicide."

The streets of Noctis pulsed with a sick vitality, crowds parting around us like water around stones. Some of the faces weren't faces at all, just suggestions of features, dark hollows where eyes should be. I caught Serena watching a man whose skin rippled with symbols that crawled across his flesh like living tattoos. When he turned to look at us, his irises were clock faces, the hands spinning wildly.

"This way," I said, nudging her toward a narrow alley between a pawnshop advertising *Memories Bought & Sold - We Pay Top Dollar for Childhood Trauma* and what appeared to be a butcher shop with a disturbingly human leg hanging in the window.

God, I hate this place.

CHAPTER THREE

BAD NIGHT, WORSE MORNING

Serena

T HE SAFE HOUSE WAS little more than a rusted, graffi-ti-covered outbuilding wedged between crumbling fac-tories, its metal door reinforced with bolts and etched with protective runes. Hidden in a back alley the city had tried desperately to forget, the space was imbued with an ancient magic that seemed to pulse in the very air, an aura strong enough to sting your skin like a burn. The moment I stepped inside, I felt the traces of long-ago spells, lingering like shards of shattered glass. They were designed not only to deny access, but to make intruders rue their boldness.

Gabriel shut the door behind us with a firm thud, the clang of the lock sealing away the chaotic night. Riot's nails clicked sharply against the cracked concrete floor as he prowled around, nostrils flaring as if sniffing for deceit in every dark corner. I rolled my shoulders, trying to shake off memories of countless hidden eyes tracking my every step. For now, we were alone.

I surveyed the room in detail: yellowed maps taped haphazardly to cinderblock walls, an array of well-worn weapons neatly arranged on a scarred wooden table, a kitchenette against the wall near the door. A door beside that hopefully led to a bathroom, and there was a bed pushed up into the far corner, the mattress bare, blankets folded on the foot. Definitely bare bones, but a man like Cade didn't need luxuries; he had curated his existence around the relentless practice of staying two steps ahead of death. I knew that intimate dance all too well.

Gabriel's gaze remained fixed on me, sharp and calculating, his silence filled with questions. Breaking the tension, I hefted my bag onto a threadbare couch and commented, "Not bad." Across the room, Riot slumped near the door, his body still humming with a feral alertness. "I was expecting worse."

Leaning casually against the scarred counter, Gabriel folded his arms with a slight smirk playing on his lips. "I do so live to exceed expectations," he countered.

Pulling my boots off, I lifted my feet onto the couch, wrapping my arms around my knees. "So. Safe house. How did you come by this?"

"I was owed a favor a few years ago," he replied, moving to the kitchenette and opening a rickety cabinet. He extracted a bottle of amber liquid and two mismatched glasses. "The kind of favor you collect when you've pulled someone from the wrong end of a ritual at the hands of The Order of the Eyeless Benediction."

I watched him pour two fingers in each glass, noticing how the liquid seemed to catch the light. He continued, "They don't own this anymore. Neither do I, officially. It doesn't exist on any map, magical or mundane. I've got a few of these places around the city."

"And the wards?" I asked, accepting the glass he offered. "Those felt pretty potent, and you said you've been gone awhile. Takes a lot to keep that kind of thing powered up." Our fingers brushed, a fleeting contact that sent a current racing up my arm. His eyes caught mine for a heartbeat. Two.

I lifted the mismatched glass to eye level. It had a cartoon ghost on it that said "BOO, BITCH" in faded purple script.

"This is what you pour Irish whiskey into?" I deadpanned.

Gabriel didn't even blink. "You're welcome."

I glanced at his glass. It was lime green with a smiling jack-o'-lantern wearing sunglasses.

"What exactly is your aesthetic here? Goth Halloween garage sale?"

"Apocalyptic practicality," he replied, taking a sip. "Besides, these glasses are warded."

"Against what?"

"Bad vibes."

I snorted and shook my head. "If this place is warded against bad vibes, how the hell are either of us still inside?"

He smiled, but it didn't quite reach his eyes. "Occupational immunity."

I laughed, the sound startling me. "And the wards?"

"Expensive." He answered simply. "Worth every drop of blood they cost."

I arched a brow. "You paid in your blood?"

He took a sip, face impassive. "I didn't say it was my blood."

He left me with the whiskey and moved through the room like a ghost with a mission, all quiet, practiced angles and focus. His hand brushed the wards near the door, his fingers following the shape of the glyphs carved into the frame. I watched him from the couch. Maybe he didn't know I was watching, or maybe he just didn't care. The wards shimmered under his touch, reacting to the trace of blood still bound to the sigils. That was how Noctis worked; it didn't need belief, just sacrifice. He stood there for a long moment, staring at the door like he could make the city stay out through sheer force of will.

"You expecting company?" I asked, my voice rougher than I intended.

He didn't turn around. "Just making sure we survive the night."

"You realize that might be a fool's errand here, right?" His silence was answer enough.

I gingerly sipped my drink, surprised to note it was a quite decent Irish whiskey. "We need a plan."

Without a hint of resistance, Gabriel replied, "That's true. The Bone Lords won't sit idle. They've already dispatched the Collectors after you. They need you alive, because let's be honest, if they wanted you dead, they'd have leveled that bar back in Seattle as soon as they knew you were in it. The question I have is why?"

Each word from him settled heavily in my chest. "Because I'm the only one left," I confessed in a low voice, the admission edged with both defiance and sorrow. Riot, tuned in to my emotions like he always was, rose from his place at the door to hop up on the couch next to me, laying his head on my arm.

Gabriel tilted his head, his eyes narrowing with a curiosity he wasn't able to hide completely. "Left of what, exactly?"

I turned to face him squarely, my own eyes challenging him to look away. "My father's children. There are...were...dozens of us. Maybe more. He bred us like a breeder breeds pedigree puppies, trying to produce the perfect offspring. Most of us never survived beyond childhood." I gulped a mouthful of my drink. "But I did. When I was born, I had inherited everything dear old dad had been trying to create, and more."

A slow, understanding expression softened his features; not shock or fear, just a grim acknowledgment born from years of seeing the dark veins of Noctis.

"Let's back up for a minute. I know the Necromancer, or at least I know of him. All of Noctis did. He was the closest thing to royalty that this city had." He took another sip of his drink, kicking long legs out in front of him. "What I never actually knew was WHAT he was. What his power was. There were rumors. Rumors that he was a god in every way that mattered."

"Rumors," I echoed, a bitter smile curling my lips. "There are always rumors in Noctis. The whispers that follow you down twisted alleys, the stories that make even the Apostles of Ruin check under their beds at night." I drained my glass in one swallow, welcoming the burn. "My father collected those rumors like trophies."

"And which ones were true?" Gabriel pressed, leaning forward to refill my glass.

I ran my fingers through Riot's fur, drawing comfort from his solid warmth. "All of them. None of them. The truth is always worse than the stories." I huffed out the skeleton of a laugh. "The stories are merciful in comparison.

"Necromancy is just the word they gave it, but it barely scratches the surface." I ran my finger around the rim of my glass. "He could manipulate life force: transfer it, store it, bend it to his will. He could pull the vitality from a room full of people with a gesture and use it to heal fatal wounds, or to grant temporary immortality. Take it, give it, reshape it. But that was just the beginning."

"And what exactly did you inherit?" he pressed, though a hint of uncertainty lingered in his voice.

"Oh, I inherited all of good old dad's genetic goodies," I said. "And more." I pulled my hand from Riot's fur, hugging my knees close to my chest. "I can do things," I admitted. "Things that would make the Bone Lords themselves barter away their treasured collections for a taste of it. Reality...bends for me, when I let it. When I *command* it."

Gabriel's expression didn't change, but I noticed the subtle way his body tensed, the slight shift in his posture that betrayed his wariness. Smart man. He should be wary.

"Reality manipulation," he said, rolling the words around like he was tasting them. "That's not something to advertise on a business card, even here." He poured himself a refill. "I've seen practitioners who claimed they could do that. Most ended up as smears on the pavement or drooling in an asylum somewhere."

"That's because they were trying to use something that wasn't theirs to command," I replied, my voice soft but edged with something sharp and brittle. "It didn't belong to them. They weren't born to it."

He studied me with those penetrating deep hazel eyes. 'And you were."

It wasn't a question, but I replied anyway. "And I was."

The following silence stretched out, and the room suddenly felt smaller, the walls inching closer with each beat of silence between us.

"Show me," Gabriel said finally.

I laughed. "That's not something you ask casually, Cade. It's...it's like asking someone to juggle live grenades in your living room." I shook my head, copper hair falling into my eyes. You don't understand what you're asking."

"I think I do," he said, his voice level. He set his glass down deliberately, the soft clink echoing in the silence. "I've seen supernatural shit all over Noctis for years. I've seen men melt into puddles of screaming flesh when they tried to control power that was beyond them. I've watched reality fracture around beings who couldn't contain what they channeled."

"And yet you're still asking."

He nodded. "I'm still asking."

I toyed with the end of a curl, considering him. There was something refreshing about his directness. Most people here spoke in riddles and half-truths, weaving webs of deception because it never occurred to them to do otherwise. Gabriel just sat there, waiting, his eyes never leaving mine.

"Fine," I said finally. "Something small. And you stay where you are."

I unfolded myself from the couch, placing my glass on the floor. Riot shifted, watching me with eyes that glowed in the dim light. With deliberate movements, I stepped into the center of the room, flexing my fingers at my sides. The concrete floor was cold beneath my socked feet, and I let that anchor me.

"The simplest way to explain it is that reality has seams," I said, my voice dropping to something just above a whisper. "Most people never see them. Some sensitive types might feel them occasionally; déjà vu, strange coincidences, those moments when you could swear something moved in your peripheral vision. The moments when time seems to skip like a scratched record." I raised my hands slightly, palms up. "But me? I can see them all the time. I can see where they're stitched together. And I can pull on them."

The familiar tingle began in my fingers, snaking up my arms and down my spine. "They're everywhere," I continued. "Most people pass by them every day, never knowing how close they are to unraveling the whole damn world." I turned my palm over, letting a glimmer of power dance across my fingers. "It's not completely like thread and needle. It's not neat. It's more like scars. Stress fractures in the skin of the world, repaired over and over."

Gabriel stayed silent. Good. Most people tried to jump in, tried to fill the air with noise. He didn't.

"Some witches see ley lines," I said. "Some read fate threads. Me? I see the seams. The fractures. The thin places where reality didn't quite stick the landing." I tilted my head. "You ever walk into a room and forget why you went in there?"

He blinked. "Sure."

"That's not a glitch in your memory," I said. "That's the room not remembering you."

His shoulders tensed.

"Reality tries to mend itself. It forgets us when we start pulling. The wrong tug at the wrong seam, at the wrong time? The whole patchwork unravels and starts to bleed."

I drew in a steady breath, letting my awareness expand beyond the confines of my skin. The air around my fingers began to shimmer like heat rising from sun-baked asphalt. I focused on a patch of empty space between us, finding the almost invisible thread that connected possibility to reality.

"What most people don't understand is that everything is connected," I murmured, my voice taking on a hollow quality that wasn't entirely my own. "Life and death. Matter and void. What is and what could be."

With a delicate twist of my wrist, I pulled.

The air between us rippled, then parted like a curtain. Through the tear hung a perfect, shimmering apple suspended in midair, its ruby skin gleaming as if freshly polished.

I hated how easy it still was. How the magic responded before I even gave it permission, like it had just been waiting for me to crack. It always came fast, like breath, like blood. At least, calling on it here, while I was calm, I had some control. When the trigger was pain, or fear, or fury, it just rushed out. Water crashing through open floodgates. My mother had called it instinct magic; my father had just called it useful. He'd discovered all sorts of ways to trigger it.

Magic like mine wasn't free. It burned hot and bright and loud, but it took from me every time. Sometimes just a headache, or a nosebleed, maybe a fractured memory. Sometimes, when I pushed too hard, it hollowed me out so deep it felt like something else might move in to fill the void, and I was terrified of what that something else might be.

I didn't avoid it because I was afraid of power.

I avoided it because I was afraid of what came *after*.

Gabriel's expression remained carefully neutral, but his eyes widened fractionally. His fingers tightened where they rested on his knees as he leaned forward. "Is it real?" he asked, his voice deliberately level.

"As real as anything else in this room," I replied, the words coming out strained. Even this small demonstration sent tremors through my muscles; I hadn't done this in a very, very long time. "Reality is more malleable than most people think. I just...persuade it."

"May I?"

I nodded once, my concentration still focused on maintaining the tear. He approached slowly, circling the floating fruit with the careful precision of a man who'd survived by taking absolutely nothing for granted. I let the apple fall into my hand and held it up to the light. It looked real. Felt real. It was even cold, from wherever I'd pulled it from.

This wasn't about the apple. It was about the fact that I could still do it, that I could reach into the between of possibilities and bend it to my will. Gabriel didn't say anything, but he didn't have to. His stillness spoke volumes.

"You're scared of me," I said flatly. Still, he didn't answer. "Good. You should be." Riot sat beside me, curled tight, body tense. Gabriel didn't blink; he just stared at the apple in my hand like it might detonate. It wouldn't be the craziest thing I'd ever seen happen.

Slowly, Gabriel reached out and grasped the fruit, and once he had it in his hand, I let the seam close. "It isn't an illusion," I said softly. "I didn't conjure it or teleport it. It was always here, in a way, just in a possibility that hadn't been realized until I pulled it through."

Gabriel turned the apple over in his big hands, examining it the same way I imagined he might inspect unexploded ordinance. He brought it to his nose, inhaling its scent, before taking a slow, deliberate bite. The crisp sound echoed in the quiet room as juice glistened on his lips.

"Sweet," he said finally. "With a hint of something I can't place." His eyes never left mine as he chewed thoughtfully. "Where, exactly, did this come from?"

I sank back on the couch, suddenly exhausted. Even small manipulations took their toll, and I was very out of practice. "From a possibility. Maybe there was once an apple tree outside this building. Maybe someone was meant to bring fruit here tomorrow. Maybe in another reality this was always an orchard." I shrugged, trying to hide the tremor in my fingers. "The possibilities all exist simultaneously. I just make a choice about which reality manifests."

He cocked his head, taking another bite. "That was barely flexing your muscles, wasn't it? You're rusty, but this was just a drop in the well of your power." When I nodded, he cocked his head and looked more closely at me. "What's it like?"

I tilted my head back to rest on the lumpy back cushion. "The first time I ever used magic, I didn't even know what I was doing. I was seven. Terrified. Hungry." I gave a bitter laugh. "My father sometimes trained me more than raised me, like you train a pet. He found food to be an excellent motivator." I took a breath, then another. "He left me in a room full of bones and said, *Show me what you are.* I don't remember making a conscious choice; I just remember the bones knitting themselves into a bird, with feathers made out of shadows. Then he smiled, and I knew I'd done something wrong, because I'd done something he'd liked." I rolled my head to face Gabriel and opened my eyes. "Maybe that's why I hate using my power so much. Every time I do, I see his face."

I could see him measuring. Calculating. "What are the limits to your power?"

I smiled ruefully. "If I really wanted to show off, we'd need a much bigger room. And probably insurance."

I let my head loll back onto the couch and closed my eyes. My pulse was still skittering under my skin like a moth trapped in a jar. I hated how unsteady I felt. My fingertips tingled with aftershocks, and I could still feel the seam I'd pulled open, like a thread snagged on my spirit. Too much. Even that tiny act felt like it weighed on my soul. I could already feel the edges of depletion, like the burn from holding a match too long. If I pushed again before I was ready, the magic would push back. Hard.

"I'd promised myself I wouldn't do this again," I murmured. Gabriel didn't say anything, but I could feel his gaze on me, steady and unreadable.

"The last time I pulled something through," I said, barely above a whisper, "it wasn't an apple."

His posture shifted. Just slightly, but I caught it. I pressed my palms flat against my thighs, grounding myself in the feel of the couch beneath me. "It was a person, or it should've been. I was trying to save them."

"And?"

"I got pieces," I said. "A ribcage. Half a face. Screaming that didn't have a mouth to come from."

The hum of the safe house wards pulsed against my spine. I didn't look at him. I couldn't.

"I don't do magic anymore," I said finally. "Not like that. Not unless I have to."

A long pause. Then, Gabriel's voice, low and rough. "You didn't *have* to tonight."

I finally looked up. "Didn't I?"

I leaned my head back, Riot pressed close against my hip. The wards hummed in the silence, a low, constant reminder that even now, Noctis hadn't stopped watching. My fingers still trembled, but I curled them into fists, holding tight to the truth I couldn't unsee: I hadn't shed my power. I'd just been afraid to claim it. And now that I had taken that particular thing out of the box, there was no putting it back.

CHAPTER FOUR

IS THIS A TERRIBLE IDEA? I THINK IT'S A TERRIBLE IDEA.

Gabriel

S ILENCE FELT WRONG IN a city like Noctis, an absence of sound that wasn't so much peaceful as it was a breathless pause before inevitable chaos. I sat on the edge of the chair near the table, facing the couch. The core of the apple Serena had pulled into existence was still in my hands, and I turned it over in my fingers.

Serena lay curled on the couch while Riot sprawled on the floor beside her. She slept with a wariness that hurt to see, as if sleep itself were an enemy. She rested as if it were a vulnerability, every moment offering the promise of betrayal. I saw it in the way she drew her arms close, legs folded inward as if bracing for the impact she expected to shatter her already fragile defenses.

The silence of her troubled sleep spoke more clearly than words ever could.

I should have walked away when Moshi introduced us. I knew the price of entangling myself in other people's consequences, and yet here I was, watching her sleep like some sort of reluctant savior. Like the guardian I'd once been.

I'd buried that version of myself years ago, or tried to, along with everything he stood for. Guardian. Protector. Fool. I'd watched good men die believing they could make a difference. Watched kids barely old enough to shave bleed out in the dirt because some higher up had decided a line on a map mattered more than lives. When you finally come face to face with the fact that you've been used as a pawn by men whose only concern is power? It corrodes you from the inside out, turns you into something brittle. I'd given up on having a life that included things like hope a long time ago.

She hadn't, though, and that fact awed me. Curled on a couch in the heart of a city that shouldn't exist, hunted and haunted and somehow still managing to look like hope personified. Fire-forged, sharp-edged, and yet fragile in a way I didn't know how to fix.

I hadn't planned to do anything but get her in and get her out. That was my mission. That was the responsibility I'd accepted a very large amount of money to shoulder. I hadn't meant to *care,* but the truth was that somewhere between the first glance and the first time she said my name like it meant something, I stopped being her bodyguard and started being something else. I didn't have a name for what that something was yet.

Whatever it was, though, it had teeth. It had gravity. I'd stood on battlefields that hummed with prophecy, walked through places soaked with the blood of old gods and forgotten wars, but I'd never felt anything like this. Like the universe had been holding its breath waiting for us to meet, like I'd been built with a lock I didn't know existed until she looked at me like she held the key. There was something ancient in this, something that didn't care about logic or timing or that we were both broken in ways that didn't come with glue.

We'd already collided, and anything, everything else would bend around that moment.

I still had questions. I still needed answers, because without those answers I was flying blind, and I needed to be ready.

That's the thing about consequences. They don't care if you're ready for them or not. They just come, relentless. They'd keep coming for her, and for that damn reason I couldn't yet put a name to, I wasn't ok with letting that happen. I tossed the apple core onto the table and leaned back, my chair creaking in protest.

I wasn't ok with letting them break her.

Outside, Noctis held its breath. The city had a way of rearranging itself when you weren't looking, like reality was a deck of cards it liked to shuffle while you blinked. I could feel the wards hum against the edges of the room, their magic old and uneasy, as if even they weren't sure they were enough anymore.

The floor beneath me vibrated with something not quite mechanical, not quite alive. Noctis didn't sleep, and it sure as hell didn't rest easy.

Riot's eyes flickered open at the sound, two perfectly blue orbs that held far too much intelligence for a normal animal. He regarded me with what I could only describe as wary assessment. He let out a soft chuff, something between a warning and a sigh.

"Don't start," I whispered to him. "I'm not getting attached."

His ears flicked back, his posture suggesting he found my self-deception amusing. Then again, I was talking to a not-dog in a twilight realm where reality bent like warm taffy, so who was I to judge what constituted normal behavior?

"Yeah. I don't believe that, either." I reached down, my fingers ghosting near his fur. "You ever wonder if we're just the punchline in someone else's joke?"

Riot tilted his head, ears twitching in silent agreement, maybe. Could be mockery. Hard to tell with him.

I rubbed the back of my neck. "Not that I expect you to answer, it's just... you ever get the feeling that this place is waiting for us to slip? That it wants us to?"

Riot stood, gave himself a long stretch, and sat next to Serena, laying his head on her hip like the world couldn't touch her if he was there. I envied him that certainty.

I sat and watched her breathe, but as the shadows crept farther into the room, they brought memories with them. Sand. Relentless, unending heat. The weight of a rifle in my hand. Blood, metallic and thick in the air.

A tiny whimper yanked me back, and I leaned forward. Serena's brow furrowed, a dream tightening her expression into a frown. A sound slipped from her lips, a whisper, choked and sharp. "Don't..." She curled tighter, one leg twitching like she was running. "I said no..."

I moved closer, hating the way the words sliced through the quiet. I'd seen battle cries and dying gasps, but nothing haunted me like that soft note of *please,* even though she hadn't said the word. Whatever haunted her dreams, it wasn't just memory. It was prophecy, maybe, or something deeper. Something trying to call her back to a place she'd clawed her way free from.

I didn't let her go there. It wasn't taking her tonight.

I exhaled sharply, shaking off the past that dragged at me for the present I couldn't abandon. Standing slowly, I crossed the few steps to the couch. Riot watched carefully; I knew he was analyzing my every move, and I made sure to keep my motions steady. I'd seen what he was capable of, and I wanted no part of it.

She was too exhausted to wake, too worn down from running, too depleted from using the very power that defined her. I slid one arm beneath her knees and the other around her shoulders, lifting her slowly. She weighed less than she ought to, and as she stirred against me the warmth of her breath across my collarbone mingled with the cold certainty that I was already too far in. I'd carried bodies like this before. Dead weight. Men who didn't make it. Women who'd lost too much blood to hold onto their souls. Children with vacant eyes and bullet holes where laughter should've lived.

But she was *here*. Warm. Breathing, even if her skin was too pale and her body was too light. She was still fighting. Every breath she drew was defiance.

The last time I carried someone with this much care, I was twenty-three and dragging my squad leader out of a burning compound. He'd died in the chopper. I still dream about the look in his eyes: hope, trust, and the slow, terrible realization that I couldn't save him.

I hadn't let myself remember that day in years, but something about the way she clung to life, the same way he had, ripped the memory wide open.

I couldn't lose someone like that again.

Gently, I laid her on the mattress, tugging a blanket over her. She remained asleep, and my presence seemed to have calmed her dreams somewhat. She didn't immediately curl back into a protective ball, and her face relaxed from its frown.

She looked so fucking young.

The clicking of Riot's nails on the concrete made me turn, and I watched him jump effortlessly to the bed, laying his head on her stomach. His eyes locked with mine again, and for a moment, something passed between us. Not quite approval, and not quite trust, but acknowledgment. A silent measure, as if weighing whether or not I was worthy of the burden we both carried. We were soldiers in the same war now, whether I wanted to admit it or not.

"You're not supposed to be on the bed."

He deliberately stretched, his gaze unblinking. The message was clear: *try and move me.*

"Fine," I muttered. "One night. I'll take first watch."

I returned to the couch, settling in for the long stretch of night ahead.

I closed my eyes for half a second.

When I opened them, the shadow in the corner of the room had moved. Only slightly, maybe an inch. But it hadn't been my imagination.

Riot's ears flicked back, his head lifting slowly from Serena's stomach. His body was still, but his eyes were locked on the place where the dark had thickened. He wasn't afraid, but he was aware.

I reached for my weapon without a sound. The city didn't sleep. Neither did its monsters.

And neither would I.

CHAPTER FIVE

SOULS FOR SALE. NO RETURNS.

Serena

G ABRIEL WATCHED ME SHOVE the last warded charm into my boot with something close to disapproval.

"You sure this broker of yours is going to be there?" he asked, voice low, arms crossed as he leaned against the wall of the crumbling stairwell.

"She'll be there," I muttered, tightening the strap on my pack. "Mira Dusk likes secrets, and she likes rare currency even more."

I didn't say what kind of currency. He hadn't asked yet.

Riot shifted by the exit, ears flicking as the veil between worlds hummed just beyond the door. I checked the trigger rune drawn on my palm. My demonstration last night had set it to tingling.

I had to be careful. I couldn't pull from a well that was already half dry.

That was the other thing people never tell you about magic like mine. You don't just have it; you have to feed it. When it runs dry, it doesn't come back with a nap and some orange slices. Every cast drains something; energy, willpower, memory. There had been days after a hard spell where I hadn't been able to open my eyes or hold a steady thought.

The longer I went without rest, the more the magic fought back. Warped. Twisted. Turned on me.

That was what terrified me.

Not that I'd use it.

That one day, it might use *me*.

"This still feels like a bad idea," Gabriel said.

I shot him a dry look. "We're in Noctis. That's the default."

He didn't laugh, but he did offer a hand to pull me up. I took it, ignoring the flicker that passed between us like static. It wasn't attraction, and it wasn't trust. It was something older, like a thread pulling tight across the Weave, as if fate had already taken sides and was waiting for us to catch up.

I cleared my throat. "I've got two backup exit routes, a signal flare that only Riot can hear, and enough hexed salt to ruin a small village. I think we'll manage."

Gabriel raised an eyebrow. "Just the essentials, then?"

"What can I say?" I shouldered my pack. "I travel light."

The Veil Market was where you went when you needed something that wasn't supposed to exist.

Gabriel and I stood at the threshold of the market, the air thick with the relics of ancient magic and the acrid residue of regret. The entrance pulsed, neon light bleeding out in an array of colors that made the human brain want to run screaming and crying its eyes out. The door wasn't so much a door as an idea, a boundary where tangible reality dissolved into the surrealism that Noctis insisted was possible.

In Noctis, the impossible was the rule, not the exception.

"You sure about this?" Gabriel asked again, his eyes scanning the shadowed nooks where figures hunched, lurking like ravenous carrion birds poised over their next meal. "This place is like the breeding ground for bad ideas."

"Perfect, since we seem to specialize in those," I replied, pulling the hood of my stolen hoodie down further over my forehead. I'd nabbed it off a line, a baggy thing that was so stained I was afraid I was going to catch something I couldn't get off with scouring powder and steel wool. I hefted my pack further up my shoulders, the weight somehow reassuring. Beside me, Riot's presence was a steady constant, his ears twitching in response to the muted, unseen whispers that always seemed to echo here.

Gabriel exhaled a slow, measured breath, his silence speaking volumes. Smart man, that one. I'd never admit it to him, though. With a sigh, I triggered the rune and stepped over the threshold.

Inside, the Market bustled with a dissonant static, a cacophony woven from bartered souls, whispered scandals, and desperate exchanges. Shadows wove in and out of the stalls, detached from any physical tether, and the occasional scream drifted up and out. A vendor whispered to a customer, their face shifting subtly, features refusing to settle into one form. Nearby, a cart of bottled memories hummed in eerie synchrony, their vendor watching with ink-dark eyes.

"What specifically are we here for, Red? Are we just window shopping for worst case scenarios?"

I looked over at him. "We need to know who put the contract out on me. There's a broker here who deals in just that kind of information."

His expression remained neutral, but I noticed the subtle change in his stance, the minute twitch of his fingers near his sidearm. "You think they'll just hand that information over?"

"No," I confessed, "but I have an offer that might just loosen their tongue."

We moved quickly, slipping past a stall where a hunched figure whispered to a mirror, its surface distorting as though it were arguing back. We rounded the corner and came to a halt before a stall draped in deep crimson fabric. The stall's owner was already waiting.

Mira Dusk wasn't human, not anymore. Her skin shone like polished obsidian, her bottomless eyes a void that drank in the dim market light. Her lips curved in a smile too sharp to be anything but a weapon.

"Selene," she purred, voice like silk drawn over a dagger. "I expected you sooner. The dead don't usually linger this long before coming to me."

The air around us cracked, like a seal breaking. I didn't move; it wasn't my name itself, it was the way she said it, each syllable carved into my bones.

The Weave tightened.

Gabriel tensed at my side, his hand dropping to his weapon, but I ignored him. "That name is not yours to speak."

Mira didn't blink. "The city remembers. I only gave it voice."

"I need information."

"Oh, darling, everyone does." Mira waved a lazy hand, her wine-dark nails catching the light in a way that made my stomach lurch. "But not everyone has the currency to pay."

"I do." I reached into my pocket and produced the vial, etched in runes so old the glass shivered faintly, resisting the air around it. Inside, a silver mist swirled, slow and deliberate, as if sentient. "The last breath of a saint."

Mira's expression didn't change, but I saw the way her pupils contracted and the faintest hitch of breath belied her cool indifference. "A saint," she mused. "Not just any breath, then."

She held out her hand.

I didn't move. "Not until I have what I came for."

Mira's smile widened, predatory. "You think I take things on faith, Myrddin?" She clicked her tongue. "It could be mist stolen from a corpse. Condensed fog in a bottle. I deal in certainty, and you, of all people, should know better than to expect blind trust."

Shit.

She wasn't wrong. Mira wouldn't just take my word for it; she wasn't stupid, and this wasn't a pawnshop transaction. I could feel Gabriel shift from one foot to the next beside me, tension rolling off him in waves, but I exhaled slowly and reluctantly uncorked the vial.

The breath curled outward, a single wisp of silver vapor escaping before I sealed it again. It drifted through the air, weightless, searching.

Mira inhaled deeply, her black-hole gaze going momentarily glassy, as if she were tasting something only she could perceive. Then, just as fast, she snapped back, licking her lips as if savoring a rare delicacy.

"Interesting," she murmured. "Authentic. And valuable."

I braced myself.

"But not enough."

"What?" I ground out. "This could buy you favors from the oldest of the Bone Lords, Mira. It's worth more than..."

"I know exactly what it's worth." Her smile turned razor thin. "I also know what *your* life is worth. The question is: do you?" She leaned forward, the darkness in her eyes pulling at the air between us. "Tell me, Necromancer's daughter—what are you willing to bleed for this?"

I swallowed the acidic burn of frustration. "Name your price."

"The breath and a memory," Mira said, in her silk-over-steel voice. "One of yours."

My fingers curled into fists. "Absolutely not."

"Then you walk away blind, darling, and if you think the Bone Lords will grant you more mercy than I will, I suggest you start running."

Gabriel moved beside me, but I barely registered him. My mind churned.

One memory.

Mira didn't deal in simple theft. If I gave her a memory, she'd own it. It wouldn't just be forgotten. It would belong to her. She could sell it, use it, weaponize it against me.

I had no choice, but that didn't mean I had no options.

Slowly, deliberately, I reached into my pack and pulled out a small, silver charm, etched with symbols of remembrance, of loss. A piece of magic meant to preserve what it held. I let it settle in my palm before choosing a memory and pushing it into the charm. The silver began to glow softly.

"You get this one," I said, voice tight. "No negotiations."

Mira's fingers ghosted over the charm, her smile slow, victorious. "Oh, I do love when you give in, darling."

"Go to hell," I muttered.

She laughed, pocketing the charm and plucking the vial from my hands with obscene grace. She studied me for a beat longer than necessary, head tilted just enough to unnerve. "You've grown teeth since last we met, darling," she murmured. "Your father would be so proud."

"I'm not him," I said, the words colder than I meant them.

"No," she agreed, her smile tightening. "He would've burned this place down before trading anything of himself. You? You know when to bend. That makes you infinitely more dangerous."

I didn't answer.

Her gaze flicked to Riot. "And you're still dragging that beast behind you, I see."

"He drags himself," I said. "He just happens to like me."

Riot let out a low, unmistakably offended huff. Mira's smile deepened.

"Careful, Myrddin. Sentiment is the quickest path to ruin." She turned toward her stall. "And ruin already has your scent."

She leaned in, breath cool against my ear. "Your hunters, sweet girl? They are not merely whispering your name. They are screaming for your blood."

I swallowed. "Why? What exactly do they want with me?"

Mira purred. "The Bone Lords want their heir back."

My pulse stuttered. "They think I'd take his place?"

She scoffed, drumming her nails on the counter of the stall. "Who knows what they think, darling. However, they're not the only ones in the hunt for your delectable self."

My stomach dropped. "Who?" I demanded.

"The Hollow Vein," she continued, "because they want to see you shattered. Sources are saying that one of them has detained a seer, a person plagued by visions that are anything but convenient when it comes to you, Serena."

She cocked her head, looking at me closely. "The Bone Lords would give anything to have you back in their possession," she added, eyes gleaming like something predatory. "They want you alive, but whether they want you whole? That's anyone's guess. The Hollow Vein?" Her mouth twitched. "They tried to keep their motives to themselves, but nothing stays completely hidden for long." She took a breath, then continued, her voice soft. "They don't want to kill you, not exactly. They want to erase you. Unwrite you."

I stiffened. "Why?"

"Because you're a fracture," she replied. "Living proof that the Weave doesn't always obey. You're not a puppet, not a prophecy. You're a possibility, and the Hollow Vein doesn't tolerate uncertainty." Her fingers drummed the edge of her stall. "They believe the world was never meant to remember. That stillness, that emptiness, is purity. They want to hollow out the cycle itself. No death. No rebirth. Just the quiet."

I swallowed hard. "And if they win?"

Mira's smile vanished. "Then the threads collapse. No futures. No names. Just silence, screaming under the surface."

I swallowed the lump in my throat, my voice barely above a whisper. "Where do I find what I need to know? Where do I find out what they're planning?"

Mira's teeth flashed in a smile that would have given a shark pause. "Why, the Glass Menagerie, darling. At least, that's where you'll find what they have on you. As for the whereabouts of the seer, that's information I do not possess."

Gabriel exhaled sharply, a low, dangerous sound of both frustration and grim acceptance. "Well, shit."

That was about the size of it.

The universe has apparently decided that it wasn't enough for my day to be merely terrible—it needed to be completely catastrophic.

"The Glass Menagerie," I echoed, feeling my stomach drop like I'd just stepped into an elevator shaft. "Because of course it couldn't be someplace reasonable. A park. Maybe a Starbucks."

Mira's obsidian fingers danced over the vial, her void-like eyes drinking in the light from the swirling silver contents. "The Keeper has acquired many things of value lately. The information on you is merely the latest addition to a growing collection of inconvenient truths." With that, she turned and walked into her stall, dismissing us.

"The Keeper doesn't take kindly to uninvited guests," Gabriel muttered as we pushed our way back through the Market's twisted pathways. "Last time someone tried breaking in, they ended up as a particularly interesting display piece. Still screaming, from what I hear."

"You said you'd gotten in before, and out," I accused.

"And I have, but I went in on an invitation. Not *my* invitation, but still an invitation."

"Then we'll just have to make sure we're invited," I replied, ducking beneath a canopy of writhing shadows that reached for my hair with greedy tendrils.

Gabriel's laugh was sharp and humorless. "And how exactly do you propose we manage that? Send a polite RSVP?"

I stopped abruptly, causing him to collide with my back. His hand darted out, instinctively steadying me, warm and solid, and I let myself have that comfort for one tiny fraction of a second. "Not exactly, but I know someone who might be able to get us through the door without us ending up as part of the permanent collection." I turned to look up at him, finding his expression dark.

"I don't like the sound of that."

"You're not gonna like the reality of it either," I said, navigating past a vendor selling bottled nightmares, dark, viscous liquids that vibrated with the terror of their donors. "We need to find The Vesper."

"The one who steals faces?" Gabriel's voice dropped to a dangerous whisper. "Absolutely the fuck not."

I set off again. "I'm not actually suggesting we hand me over," I clarified. "Just...dangle the possibility."

Gabriel stiffened. "The Vesper," he said again, like the very taste of the name might poison him. "You don't ask that kind of favor unless you're willing to lose something vital."

"I know."

He shook his head. "I once knew a guy. Name was Jaro. Smart, tough, walked out of a firefight with half his guts in a bag. He made a deal with The Vesper to buy his daughter's name back from a soul auction."

I stilled. "And?"

Gabriel's mouth twisted. "He came back without a face. No skin. No eyes. Just a voice. Said The Vesper didn't like his smile."

I swallowed. "They like mine."

He stared at me. "Red—"

"I'm not offering my smile. Just...a taste."

He looked away, jaw tight. "One day, you're going to stop trading pieces of yourself like they're currency."

"I'll stop when I stop needing leverage to survive."

"That's playing with fire, Red," he growled, stepping closer. "The Vesper doesn't do anything out of the kindness of their heart, and The Keeper doesn't let things go once he's got his hands on them. This is a buy one get one of bad."

I looked at my boots as I walked, feeling the weight of everything on my shoulders right then. "I'm already being hunted by two of the most dangerous factions in Noctis, Gabriel. How is this any worse?"

"Because The Vesper doesn't just want something from you. They want to BE you. There's a difference between being hunted and being consumed."

I had no good response to that, so I kept moving. The Market's twisted pathways breathed around us, the very air sticky with malevolent intent. A woman with fingers that branched into delicate twigs offered us bottled starlight. A man whose skin was peeled back and pinned to reveal the clockwork beneath hawked seconds stolen from dying breaths.

I ignored them all.

"I'm tired of running," I said finally, my voice steady despite the churning in my gut. "I need answers, and at least some of them are in the Menagerie." Gabriel's hand closed around my upper arm, pulling me to a stop and spinning me to face him.

"You are not expendable, Serena."

Something hot and unfamiliar flared at his words, but before I could respond, a growl from Riot broke into hearing. He shifted, putting himself between us and the shadows to our right.

"We've got company," Gabriel muttered, reaching into his jacket to pull a blade from his waistband.

The temperature around us plummeted, and the ambient sounds of the Market—the haggling, the whispers, the occasional scream—collapsed into silence. The shadows twitched. Twisted. Peeled themselves from the walls.

Hollowborn.

They moved like liquid wrongness, their bodies stuttering, glitching, folding in and out of themselves. Not people, not anymore. Just husks, empty vessels filled with whatever hunger the Hollow Vein had given them. Skin like stretched wax, smooth and unfinished, with featureless faces. There was only a gash where a mouth should be.

The first one lunged with unnatural speed, a smear of darkness slicing through the air. Gabriel barely had time to twist aside before its clawed hand raked through the space where his throat had been.

I shoved my hand into my boot, fingers closing around cold iron. Too slow.

Another was already on me.

Its fingers latched onto my arm, needle-sharp and ice-cold, sinking through fabric, through skin, through bone. A wave of sickness surged through me, an icy burn spreading through my veins as it tried to pull something out of me. My breath hitched, my knees buckling.

Then Gabriel's blade rammed through its chest.

A high, shrieking wail ripped through the corridor, the thing convulsing as black ichor sprayed across my arm, the scent of burning rot filling my nose.

"Move," Gabriel growled, yanking me upright just as two more Hollowborn came surging toward us.

The corridor was narrow and far too tight; a claustrophobic wall of bodies pressed in, shifting like oily, unnatural static.

They were herding us.

Riot snarled, his hackles spiking like quills, his teeth elongating into something more wolf than dog. He launched at one of them, his body a silver blur of teeth and fury, knocking it back against the wall, and the Hollowborn screamed as Riot's jaws closed around its throat, a sound something like fear.

The Hollowborn didn't go down clean. It clawed back, talons raking Riot's shoulder and leaving a deep gash. Blood flowed from the wound, and Riot yelped, staggered—but didn't stop. His jaws clamped harder as he shook his head, for all the world like a terrier killing a rat. I saw the way his limbs trembled, though.

The others hesitated.

Gabriel barked, "Push left! Riot's opening a lane!"

Gabriel didn't just fight. He orchestrated. One blade already gone, he ducked beneath a swipe and drove another knife into the soft joint of another Hollowborn's hip. Before it hit the ground, he yanked the blade free. "Two more!" he shouted, catching Riot's eye and jerking his chin. Riot veered right.

Gabriel grabbed the downed Hollowborn by what passed for its hair and smashed its face into the wall hard enough to crack stone. "You good?" he snapped without looking at me.

"Working on it," I gritted out.

"Work faster."

I twisted, ducking beneath one Hollowborn's clawed lunge, slicing the blade I'd pulled from my boot upward into its gut. The blade connected, but so did its claws. One carved a shallow line across my ribs. Not deep, but enough to sting. I gasped, the cold from its touch sinking into my skin like poison.

Magic surged instinctively, too fast, too sharp. It flared through my body uncontrolled, burning out like a short-circuited wire. My head spun. My fingers went numb.

"Behind you!" Gabriel shouted.

I dropped just as a claw sliced the air above me. Gabriel's blade struck downward an instant later, a clean arc that severed the thing's arm at the elbow. It didn't stop coming.

I staggered back, the corridor tilting around me. Shadows clawed at the edges of my vision. My magic surged, unbidden, crackling at my fingertips, and then sputtered. I'd used too much, too fast, and I didn't have it in me to pull from again. My battery was dead.

My dagger slipped from my grip.

The Hollowborn closest to me grinned, that too-wide mouth splitting open. It stepped forward—

A knife appeared in its right eye, the hilt wobbling. The blade didn't kill it, but it staggered. And that was enough.

Gabriel drove his remaining knife into another, but the blade caught, stuck, flesh sealing around it like living tar. His expression barely flickered before he ripped the entire thing free, dragging out a chunk of whatever passed for the thing's insides.

I ducked as fingers like curved bone swiped inches from my face, so close its passing stirred my hair.

They pressed in from all sides. We were going to get buried.

One lunged for me, but I was already moving, twisting beneath its reach. My dagger met soft, pulsing flesh, slicing upwards, parting it in a wet, sickening rupture. The Hollowborn looked at me with that ruined face and hissed, "You were never meant to leave. You were meant to unbecome."

Then it screamed, and I drove the blade deeper.

The Hollowborn convulsed, screeching, but I barely had time to brace before another slammed into me from behind, knocking me hard into the wall.

Pain flared, sharp and white-hot. My vision blurred. A wet laugh filled the corridor, like something choking on blood. My head snapped up. Another of them was speaking.

"She isssss not meant to leave." It reached out, a tracking rune glowing in its hand. The Hollowborn's mouth twitched wider, stretching into a grin too large for its skull. I barely had time to react before its fingers stabbed into my ribs, curling, twisting. That freezing burn seeped into my bones, something inside me giving way.

My vision dimmed.

No. Not like this.

I scrabbled for my pack, reaching inside. My fingers closed around the glass vial I'd gotten from Vex.

"Close your eyes!" I gasped.

Gabriel barely had time to react before I slammed the glass into the ground.

The vial shattered, and light exploded; a raw, searing detonation of white fire, tearing through the Hollowborn like paper. Their wails splintered into the air, bodies unraveling like shadows in a storm.

Silence.

My breath came in ragged gulps, hands shaking. Gabriel's blade was slick with black ichor, his breathing controlled but shallow.

Riot padded to my side, his fur still shifting in unnatural waves, his teeth too sharp, too long.

Gabriel looked at me, assessing. Then, with a nod, he murmured, "Nice trick Vex gave you."

I nodded, but my hands were still trembling, blood sticky down my side. Riot was bleeding too, rivulets dripping onto the stone. The smell of what we'd done hung in the air like burned circuits and spoiled meat. I exhaled, forcing a weak smirk. "I figured if it would work on Collectors, it might work on them. I was saving it for a special occasion, though."

Gabriel's eyes scanned the corridor and the street beyond, ever vigilant. "We need to get out of here. That light show will have attracted attention."

He wasn't wrong. Displays of power were like blood in shark-infested waters here. I whistled softly to Riot, who padded back to my side, his form still flickering between canine and something altogether more primal, something with too many teeth and eyes that burned like cold blue stars.

"Thank you," I murmured, running my fingers through his fur as it settled back into its familiar pattern. The residual energy from his shift prickled against my skin like static electricity.

Gabriel watched, his expression unreadable. "You know, one of these days you're going to have to tell me exactly what he is."

"He's Riot," I said simply, as if that explained everything.

We emerged from the service corridor into a street that reeked of things best left unidentified.

"Is it clear to go back to the safe house?" I asked. "We need food, and to clean up, and we need to formulate our next move."

Gabriel stopped, eyes calculating. "Up," he said finally, nodding toward a maintenance ladder. "Veil Market rooftops are a maze, but they're less patrolled than the ground level." He looked at Riot. "Will he let me put him on my shoulders to get him up there?"

"He will if I ask him to," I replied. "He's not afraid of heights."

The rooftops of the Veil Market were, like the rest of Noctis, something out of a nightmare, all twisted spires and impossible angles that seemed to fold in on themselves. Riot had allowed Gabriel to drape him over his shoulders and I had to admit, his careful climbing while keeping my boy safe sent a surge of gratitude through me.

Once we were on the roof, Gabriel set Riot down with the care of someone handling a priceless relic. Riot shook himself out, bob tail flicking once before he trotted off to do his perimeter check.

Gabriel turned, breathing hard, a smear of black ichor across his jaw. "You okay?"

I nodded. Then winced. "Okay adjacent."

He moved closer, brushing a finger against my ribs. I hissed and slapped his hand away.

"That," he said dryly, "is not okay."

"'Tis but a flesh wound," I muttered dryly, settling onto the edge of the roof. Noctis sprawled below like a fever dream, all glinting metal and too-bright lights, like the city couldn't decide if it wanted to dazzle or devour.

Gabriel sat beside me, stretching his legs out. His proximity was warm. Steady.

"We got lucky," I said after a long moment.

"Maybe," he said. "But we fought like hell to earn a little luck."

I didn't reply. Didn't need to. We sat in silence for a while. Not the charged, tense kind, but the kind that sat in your lungs and dared you to breathe around it. Gabriel leaned back, stretching out with one knee up, and pulled a crumpled protein bar from his jacket. He tossed it at me without looking. "Eat something."

I caught it on reflex. "Is this your version of pillow talk?"

"If you think that fight was foreplay, we need to revisit your dating history."

I snorted, peeling the wrapper. It tasted like chalk, but it gave me something to focus on besides the way my hands wouldn't stop shaking.

"You good?" he asked eventually, not pushing, just... asking.

"No," I admitted, and the honesty surprised even me. "I'm tired, my ribs are bruised, and I can still feel where that thing tried to icepick my soul."

He gave a grim nod. "That tracking mark they had? It's gone, by the way. That flare took care of it. So, at least we don't have to add that to our list of things to avoid."

"Good," I murmured, chewing. "Hate the idea of being someone's blinking beacon."

"You're more than that," he said, then shook his head like the words slipped out before he meant them to.

I glanced sideways at him. "I know."

It wasn't cockiness. It was survival.

But knowing and believing? That was a razor-fine difference, and after Mira's little parting shot, that difference was starting to ache.

They're screaming for your blood. Her voice echoed in my head like a siren. *The Bone Lords want their heir. The Hollow Vein, too.*

I traced the ridge of a broken tile with the tip of my boot, heart thudding dully. "I keep thinking," I said, softly now, "about what happens if they win."

Gabriel looked at me. "They won't."

"You don't know that."

"No," he agreed. "But I know you. And I've seen what you do when someone tries to cage you."

Riot huffed, ears twitching where he lay curled at our backs.

"And if they do?" I asked. "If I lose?"

Gabriel turned to me, his expression serious. "Then I go down with you."

The words hit like a blade slipping past all my armor.

"Idiot," I whispered.

"Probably," he agreed.

I took a deep breath, knowing what I was about to offer was a sacred thing in Noctis. *To name was to bind* was something we were taught as children here.

"My name is Selene ap Myrddin." He turned his head, eyes wide. "I'm telling you because I want to. Not because anyone took it. I want you to know the truth of me."

He held my gaze for a long breath, then dipped his head. "I'll never use it unless you ask me to." And just like that, it was mine again.

I didn't answer, just leaned my shoulder into his. I let my head rest against the steady rise and fall of his breathing, and let myself believe, for one moment longer, that I was more than the sum of the people trying to tear me apart. Maybe he was proof that the Weave could tie something soft to something sharp and still call it balanced. He shouldn't have mattered this much, but Noctis didn't care about time. It cared about resonance.

"Tell me more about The Vesper," Gabriel said as we picked our way across a particularly treacherous section where the rooftop simply dissolved into mist at the edges. "I know the bare bones; I want to know why you think they can, or would, help you."

I sighed, ducking under a low-hanging arch made of what looked like fossilized spiderwebs. "The Vesper collects identities the way some people collect stamps. Only instead of putting them in albums, they wear them."

"And they want yours."

"Who wouldn't?" I flashed him a smile that didn't reach my eyes. "Daughter of the Necromancer, heir to powers that shouldn't exist. And this ass. I'm quite the prize."

Gabriel didn't laugh. His eyes remained fixed on mine, searching for something beneath the flippancy. "This isn't a joke, Red. If what is said about them is true, The Vesper doesn't just take faces. They take everything. Memories, abilities, connections. They hollow you out and wear you like a suit."

"I know what I"m doing," I said, softer this time. "The Vesper wants to be me, but they can't take what I won't give. That's the loophole; they can only claim what is freely offered."

We reached a flat section of rooftop where someone had inexplicably placed a garden of black roses that wept crimson tears. The scent was intoxicating, and vaguely narcotic. I steered us clear.

"You know what makes The Vesper so fucking dangerous, Red?" Gabriel's voice was tight. "They don't just hunt you. They wait for you to offer something without realizing you did. That's the rule here, right? You can't take what isn't freely given.

That isn't about etiquette, Serena. It's how the city breathes. How The Weave holds. You take something that isn't offered, and Noctis *will* answer. The Vesper waits for loopholes, listens for you to say something careless. To forget to set the terms. If you leave the door open, they won't knock. They'll walk right through wearing your skin and won't even thank you for the hospitality."

"I know that, Gabriel. 'Say yes with your whole heart, or don't say it at all'. I learned that in the cradle. The city doesn't care if I understand the terms, if I wasn't specific. I know every deal is a trap unless I'm careful." I sighed. "I know how to be specific with my offer."

"And what exactly are you planning to offer if they agree to get you invited into the Glass Menagerie?" Gabriel's voice had that dangerous edge again, the one that made my skin prickle. I cleared my throat.

"The Vesper and I have…history. We made a deal once, back when I was still trying to survive in Noctis long enough to find a way out."

"What kind of deal?"

"The kind that keeps you alive when you're desperate," I replied, my tone sharper than intended. "I promised them a favor. They've been waiting to collect ever since."

We'd reached the corner of the alley that led to the safe house, and before I could swing myself to the rusty ladder that led to the street level, Gabriel grabbed my wrist and turned me to face him.

"What exactly is the favor, Serena?"

I pulled my wrist free, but didn't step back. The heat of his body was a stark contrast to the perpetual chill of Noctis, and there was a part of me that wanted to lean into it.

"A glimpse," I said finally. "One hour in my skin. Not possession, more like, I don't know, riding shotgun. They get to experience what it feels like to be me, without taking complete control."

Gabriel's jaw clenched so hard I could hear his teeth grinding. "That's playing with fucking fire, Red."

"It was that or die."

"And now you've given them an opening to get what they really want."

"Maybe," I admitted, swinging onto the ladder. "But they're bound by the rules of the exchange. They can't take more than what's offered."

Gabriel swung Riot up onto his shoulders again. "Rules can be bent. Especially in Noctis."

CHAPTER SIX

DO NOT MAKE EYE CONTACT

Gabriel

I SHUT THE DOOR behind us, the heavy bolt sliding into place with a metallic finality. The city outside still stirred, restless and full of unseen eyes, but for now, we were secure. Riot prowled the perimeter, sniffing at the corners before settling near the door, ever watchful. Serena, for her part, was moving through the space, seeking the bare comfort and momentary security it offered.

She shrugged off her coat and tossed it onto the chair in the corner, exhaustion evident in the way she carried herself. When I looked at her, she managed a smile. "Longer day than usual, yeah?"

I huffed out a breath. "We're setting new records."

She snorted, but it lacked its usual bite. The day *had* been long, full of running, bleeding, and narrowly avoiding becoming another cautionary tale in the underbelly of Noctis. I busied myself checking the wards, fingers brushing over the sigils carved into the doorframe. They were still intact. Strong, but strength had a way of fading when tested enough times.

"You should clean up," I said without looking at her. "Water's hot if you don't take too long."

She hesitated for a fraction of a second before nodding, disappearing into the bathroom. The sound of running water filled the silence, and I opened the cabinet over the cooktop, pulling out some MREs. Not exactly gourmet, but survival rarely cared about taste. The familiar process of heating them kept my hands busy while my mind tried to wade through the mess we were in.

The Bone Lords knew she was back; that hadn't been a surprise. The unwelcome addition to the party was that the Hollow Vein was hunting her, too. And me? I was standing in the center of it, trying to calculate a way out.

The bathroom door creaked open, and I glanced up, only to find myself abruptly regretting it.

Serena stood there, barefoot, wrapped in nothing but a threadbare towel that clung to wet skin. Copper hair, still damp, curled over one shoulder, droplets tracing slow paths down her collarbone, disappearing beneath the fabric.

Her skin was littered with faint scars, ghosts of past fights, past escapes. A fresh bruise was blooming along her collarbone.

Another angry mark darkened the soft line of her hip where the towel barely covered. I shouldn't have cared. Should've let my mind keep ticking over exit strategies and worst-case scenarios. Instead, anger coiled tight and hot at the sight of it, at the proof that something had managed to hurt her. Not rational, or useful, but there all the same.

She was exhausted. Scared. And somehow, in the midst of all of that, she was still breathtaking. Not because of the way she looked, even though she was stunning, but because she was still here. Still fighting.

My throat tightened, and I forced my gaze back to the MRE in my hands. "Water still works, then."

She didn't respond right away, but I could feel her amusement. Then she blinked, glanced down at herself, and made an annoyed noise. "Forgot these." Grabbing a change of clothes from her bag, she turned and disappeared back into the bathroom before I could say anything, shutting the door behind her.

I let out a slow, controlled breath, my grip on the MRE finally easing, and I found a couple of mismatched plates so at least we weren't eating out of the packaging. I had heated one for the fur ball, too, and I set it down near the door where he'd been camped out like an early warning system.

I handed her the food when she returned, now dressed, and sat down on the bed. She joined me, cross-legged, and we ate in comfortable silence. She ate efficiently, finishing everything on her plate without a single comment about the less-than-ideal taste, and rose to put her plate in the sink. She picked up Riot's, polished clean, and added it to the sink.

"I hope that doesn't upset his stomach. He can already peel paint."

Shit, I hadn't thought about that, but the dog had to eat, and we hadn't exactly grabbed a bag of kibble on the way in. He'd survive. I got up, grabbed a pair of sweats and headed to the bathroom, dropping my plate off as I went. "I'm gonna grab a shower; why don't you try and get some sleep?"

She didn't argue, just climbed beneath the blankets and exhaled, scooting so that her back was to the wall, knees pulled up so that she was curled into a little ball. Riot jumped up, fitting himself into the space behind her knees, head on her hip, eyes on the door. He looked at me for a second, and I knew what he was saying. *I've got the watch.*

The water was lukewarm at best, and I wasn't inclined to linger, but I'd learned a long time ago not to take the opportunity to get clean for granted. I pulled on my sweats and headed back into the room, settling into the space next to Serena. I thought she was asleep; her eyes were closed and her breathing was even, but once I got myself settled, she spoke.

"The Whispering Vault isn't exactly on a map," she murmured. "Getting to them means taking the train."

I sighed. "Fantastic."

The trains in Noctis weren't like trains in the regular world. They didn't run on diesel or electric tracks. They ran on need, on fate, on desperation, on bargains struck in the dead of night. Some cars were filled with people who had long since forgotten where they were going. Others were empty, save for shadows that flickered too fast to be reflections. Then there were the ones that swallowed passengers whole, never to be seen again. The only destinations they deigned to serve were ones that nobody sane wanted to visit.

We stood on the elevated platform, watching the ghostly shapes of the trains materialize from the perpetual twilight fog. The station itself was all corroded metal and faded grandeur, ornate architecture that had been left to rot for centuries. A woman in a Victorian mourning dress stood perfectly still at the far end, her veil moving against a wind that didn't exist. An old man with clockwork eyes that clicked as they turned sat hunched on a bench, muttering differential equations that solved questions no one had asked.

Serena stood close enough that I could feel the heat of her, her shoulder occasionally brushing mine. She'd dressed for trouble in jeans, a black shirt and her leather jacket. She'd pulled her mane of hair back in a tight braid, and she had her pack slung over one shoulder. Riot, as always, stood within reach of her hand.

"Tell me we're not taking the Red Line," I muttered, rubbing at my temples.

She sighed. "We don't have a choice. The Red Line is the only way to The Vesper."

The Red Line wasn't just dangerous. It was a test. You didn't board it; you entered it like a gladiatorial contest. The train decided who made it to their destination and who simply disappeared. Even in Noctis, people gave it a wide berth unless they had no other option.

"It'll arrive soon," she stated, voice pitched low. "We need to be in the fourth car."

"The fourth car," I echoed. "The one with the windows that bleed when you try to look outside?"

"That's the third car," she corrected, shifting her weight from one foot to another. "The fourth one is where time moves differently."

"Well, that makes it so much better."

Her lips quirked, but the smile didn't reach her eyes.

A distant whistle cut through the fog, high and sharp, more scream than sound. The platform trembled beneath our feet, dust and fragments of tile skittering across the ground. Riot grumbled, pressing close to Serena's legs, and I had to say I didn't disagree with him.

The Red Line emerged from the mist like a hungry serpent, a collection of gleaming scarlet cars that shone with a malevolent light. The windows were dark, not reflecting the dim light of the station but absorbing it, creating pools of absolute darkness. Steam billowed from beneath it, carrying the scent of copper and ozone and rot.

"Remember," she said, "don't make eye contact with anyone inside, don't accept anything offered to you, and whatever you do..."

"...don't fall asleep," I finished. "Not my first ride on the Nightmare Express, Red."

Her fingers brushed against mine, a fleeting touch that spoke volumes. "This is different. The Red Line knows what you want. It'll try to offer it to you."

The doors slid open, and we stepped inside.

The inside was deceptively ordinary, with faded velvet seats, brass fittings tarnished with age, and a floor of polished wood that gleamed in the dim light. A woman with hair like spun glass sat halfway down the carriage, eyes unblinking, while the child next to her played cat's cradle with hands that had too many fingers, the string forming impossible geometric patterns. Neither of them looked at us as we entered.

I put my hand on the small of Serena's back, guiding her to seats near the door. The cushions hissed when we sat down, like they were exhaling. Riot squeezed in behind her legs, his body vibrating with tension.

"Four stops," she whispered, her voice barely audible above the train's unnatural hum. "We get off at the fourth stop, no matter what we see or hear." The doors snapped shut, and the train lurched forward.

Shadows stretched and contracted along the walls, and the sudden acceleration pushed us back into those hissing seats.

"How long?" I asked.

Serena's fingers tapped against her thigh, counting something I couldn't see. "I'm not sure. Time doesn't work right in here, remember? Could be minutes. Could be hours."

I nodded, settling in for whatever passed for a journey on this transit system from hell. The lights flickered and dipped, and the shadows that appeared didn't match the objects that should have cast them. The woman with glass hair still hadn't moved, hadn't blinked, but her child's fingers were now weaving patterns that hurt to look at, the string between them forming shapes that shouldn't exist in three dimensions.

"Care for a drink, sir? Madam?"

A porter materialized beside us, his uniform pristine. His face was pleasant enough, but his smile stretched a fraction too wide, and his eyes reflected nothing.

"No," I said firmly, not meeting his gaze.

He lingered, that terrible smile unwavering. "Are you certain, sir? We have exactly what you desire."

Serena's hand clamped down on my wrist, and she fixed him with a look that I'm positive knocked the ambient temperature down a few degrees. "We're fine," she said, voice like steel.

He nodded. "As Madam wishes," he said, and moved on, his footsteps making no sound as he receded down the aisle.

I realized I was holding my breath, and I slowly released it. Serena's grip on my wrist loosened, and she went to move her hand, and I grabbed it, lacing our fingers together. I just—I didn't want her to let me go. She didn't argue, just let me nestle her fingers between mine, her thumb absently rubbing the pulse point in my wrist.

"He'll be back," she whispered. "They always come back. Three times they'll offer. Three times we refuse."

"Stop one approaching," announced a voice from nowhere and everywhere at once. The train began to slow, and the world outside the windows turned from total blackness to a landscape of twisted spires, the sky above them the color of an old bruise.

"Not us," Serena murmured, eyes fixed on the floor, the hand I wasn't clutching fisted in Riot's fur.

I kept my gaze away from the windows, focusing instead on the warmth of her hand in mine. She had long, elegant fingers, I thought, tipped with short, oval nails she'd painted in a soft pink. The varnish was starting to chip; that little mundane detail focused me, but I still shivered when the doors slid shut with a sigh that sounded too much like relief. We lurched forward again.

Twice more the pattern repeated; first, we firmly denied the porter's offer, then we stopped at places that weren't places populated by people who weren't necessarily people.

The train slowed, but this time the lights flickered wildly, plunging us into darkness for several long seconds before returning. A quick glance showed me that the glass-haired woman and her impossible child had vanished, leaving only a tangle of string behind on the seat.

"Last chance," came the porter's voice, though he was nowhere to be seen. "We have exactly what you need. Your heart's own desire."

The whisper slithered against my skin like cold fingers at the nape of my neck.

Gabriel.

My sister's voice.

I went rigid. The train shouldn't have known of her. Shouldn't have been able to mimic the rasp in her throat, the way she used to say my name like a warning.

You left us to die.

A male voice now. A memory. A lie. A trap.

I clenched my jaw, breathing through the sudden surge of nausea. But the train wasn't finished. I saw them—Jason, my team, caught in that last moment before the world swallowed them whole. Blood in the sand. The smell of burning.

Step inside, the whisper crooned. *Undo it. Just one step, Gabriel. Bring them back.*

I swayed.

And then Serena's grip on my hand. A sharp, grounding pressure, her thumb skimming my wrist, deliberate and steady.

"No," she said, her voice cold, absolute. She pulled me forward, and I followed, my breath coming too sharp, too unsteady.

Riot was already at attention, hackles raised. Hand still clenched in mine, she led us out of the door and onto the platform. She squeezed my hand, just a whisper, but I held onto it like a lifeline.

This station was unlike the other, more cathedral than terminal. Vaulted ceilings disappeared into darkness, supported by columns carved to resemble twisted human spines. The platform itself was polished obsidian that reflected our faces back at us, but with subtle distortions: my eyes were too dark while tendrils of Serena's hair that had escaped her braid were moving as if underwater. The train itself didn't linger, pulling away with that same unearthly whistle. "Charming place," I muttered, scanning our surroundings.

Serena's hand was still in mine, her grip firm. "The Vesper's territory begins here. We need to follow the stairs down." I followed her gaze to a spiral staircase set off to the side of the room.

The obsidian stairs spiraled down like the inside of a nautilus shell, each step emitting a soft chime when our feet touched it. No two notes were the same, creating an eerie melody that echoed through the darkness below. I kept Serena slightly behind me as we descended, my free hand hovering near my weapon. Riot padded silently ahead, his hackles still raised, ears and nose twitching.

"You're still holding my hand," Serena observed quietly.

I didn't loosen my grip. "Problem?"

She was silent for several steps, the chimes filling the space between us. "No," she said finally. "It's comforting." As if to add weight to her words, she squeezed my hand.

I cleared my throat. "So, The Vesper. You said you still owed them a favor, but are they what you'd call a friend?"

Serena snorted. "Not exactly. More like a professional acquaintance."

"The kind that tries to kill you, or the kind that just overcharges?"

"The kind that knows things," she said. "The Vesper trades in truths and lies, memories and secrets. They collect identities like others collect art. With that comes information; they get access to everything that person is, if they're not careful."

As we moved through it, The Vault didn't just whisper. It *watched*.

The air turned syrupy as we descended, heavy with pressure that didn't touch the skin but settled in the bones. Every breath felt like it had to claw its way through memory to get out. The corridor pulsed faintly underfoot, and the reflections on the mirrored walls weren't ours. Not really.

I kept Serena close, my fingers tightening on hers now and then. Not because she needed it, but because I did. Because I knew what this place would do to people who walked in alone.

A voice laughed behind me. I didn't turn. That laugh had been dead for years. I'd buried it with the rest of my team.

"Eyes forward," I muttered. "Don't look at the glass."

Serena nodded once, jaw tight. Riot let out a low, uneasy growl, fur on end. Even he didn't like it here, and the mutt usually treated death like a chew toy.

The corridor split into impossible angles, seven paths that bent in on themselves like someone had folded space with a shaky hand. My skin prickled.

"Which one?" I asked. Serena considered each corridor, finally settling on the third one to the left.

"That one."

"You sure?" I asked.

"Nope," she replied, and started walking, letting the stairs carry us into the branch.

The staircase finally ended, opening into a vast chamber that seemed to bend and breathe around us. The walls were covered in mirrors of varying sizes and shapes, each one reflecting a slightly different version of reality. In one, my reflection wore military fatigues stained with blood. In another, Serena's hair was bone white, her eyes black pools that swallowed light.

"Don't look too long," she warned, tugging me forward. "These mirrors show possibilities, not truths, but you don't want to give one of them the chance."

The floor shifted subtly with each step, like walking on water where the surface tension refused to break. Sometimes our footsteps preceded the steps, sometimes they followed a beat too late. Riot stayed close, occasionally growling at reflections only he could see.

I glanced at one of the mirrors, and my reflection pressed a hand against the glass, leaving a smear of blood. I snapped my eyes away, refusing to give in.

I didn't care what was hungry. I wasn't going to be its dinner today.

The silence turned viscous, like the room had inhaled and then forgotten how to breathe.

"Selene ap Myrddin," came a voice, beautiful in the way that a honed blade was beautiful. "Or do you prefer Serena Morrigan these days?"

I felt her stiffen beside me. Not visibly—Serena didn't rattle easy—but the shift was there. It was there in the sudden stillness of her breath, the faint tremor that passed through her fingers, still laced with mine.

That name, her real name, hit her like a bullet, the memory a weapon.

I moved instinctively, adjusting my stance and positioning myself half a step ahead of her without making it obvious. The

Vesper's words weren't just a greeting. They were a scalpel, testing the edge of an old scar.

Serena had shown nothing outwardly. She wouldn't give them the satisfaction, but I felt the damage, anyway.

Selene ap Myrddin.

It echoed like something sacred. Or cursed.

The light brightened, enough to reveal we'd entered a chamber. At the end was a high-backed chair fashioned from twisted glass and bone, held together with sinew, facing away from us. As we approached, it slowly rotated, revealing its occupant.

Neither male nor female, their form shifted subtly with each breath. The face was a beautiful blank canvas, features rearranging themselves in slow, hypnotic patterns.

"Vesper," Serena greeted. "It's been a long time."

"Five years, four months, and seventeen days," The Vesper replied. "And you've brought company to my vault, Selene. How delightful."

"It's Serena now."

The Vesper made a sound that might have been a laugh, or might not. "Names are such fragile things. So easily changed, yet the essence remains. You may call yourself Serena until the stars burn out, but your blood knows differently." They turned to me. "And you—you've carried so many names. Son. Brother. Soldier. And now...what? Lover?" I heard Serena's slight intake of breath at that, but that was something to unpack at another time.

I didn't answer. Not because I didn't have one, but because that question wasn't meant to be answered in the presence of anyone but the woman at my side. I kept my position slightly ahead of Serena, not liking how The Vesper's eyes lingered on her. Those eyes shifted color with each blink - blue, violet, gold, black—never settling, never revealing.

"I need information," Serena said, her voice steady despite the slight tremor I felt through our still-joined hands. "I am here to settle what I owe you, and to offer payment up front for what I need."

The Vesper smiled, and the room bent around it. "A price must be paid of you both," it said. "You know how this works."

Serena's fingers were still in mine, and I felt the tension tighten. Not fear. Not exactly. But reluctance. She knew the rules here, maybe better than I did.

"I'll pay it," I said.

The Vesper tilted its head toward me, eyes shifting color in a slow ripple. "Very well, Gabriel Rhys Cade. What memory will you trade?"

I didn't hesitate. "Kandahar. The night before the last mission. The campfire. The sound of laughter."

The Vesper rose from their chair and approached, reaching for me with a hand that wasn't a hand, just light and shadow and ache. It touched my temple, and I felt something soft tear loose inside me. A warmth I hadn't realized I was still carrying burned out.

Serena watched, lips parted, expression unreadable.

Then the Vesper turned to her. "And you, daughter of Myrddin?"

She hesitated. A beat. Two.

Finally, she said softly, "There was a day. A park. Sunlight. Riot running ahead of me. I laughed, and I believed I might be free."

The Vesper took it.

Her shoulders dropped, just a little, and she swayed like the floor had tilted under her feet.

And I felt the absence of her laughter like the world had gone a shade dimmer. I'd seen her fight monsters. I'd seen her take hits that would level anyone else, and keep going. But losing that memory? That hurt her more than anything that ever made her bleed.

When good memories were few, each one was so very precious. I could relate.

The Vesper stilled, inhaled slowly. "Bright. Bitter. Rare.". For the first time since we entered, their form stopped shifting. The blank canvas of their face held just long enough to feel unnatural.

"Your names are knives," they said at last, and the chamber echoed with the weight of it. "Do not forget which way they cut."

Beside me, Serena's jaw tensed. She didn't blink.

"The Vault remembers you, Selene," the Vesper went on, voice quieter now. "And something older than the Vault remembers, too. Something that does not forgive."

Their attention turned to me next, and every instinct I had flared to life.

"You, guardian."

The title coiled like smoke.

"You will not die clean. You can't, when love is the reason you fall."

I said nothing. I didn't need to. Serena's pulse fluttered against mine for one beat and then steadied.

The Vesper smiled, slow and sharp. "The storm has already begun. Let us discuss your need, heir, and then we will settle what you still owe."

CHAPTER SEVEN

ABANDON ALL HOPE, YE WHO ENTER HERE

Gabriel

S OME IDEAS ARE INHERENTLY bad. Some ideas are downright suicidal. Apparently, some ideas can land you in the Glass Menagerie with an eldritch entity riding shotgun in your partner's body.

This was that kind of idea.

I tightened my grip on my self-control as Serena—no, not Serena—turned toward me, her eyes flickering with too many colors at once, an aurora of disjointed hues that ebbed and flowed.

I hated it. I wanted to see her deep green.

The Vesper settled into her skin like they belonged there, but I could see the *wrongness* in the way they held her, the way they made her body move, like they were remembering all the nuances of how to be human. I hated it. I hated that we needed this.

"Don't look at me like that, guardian." The voice was Serena's, but not. It held a cadence that didn't belong, a weight of too many voices layered into one. "You act like I'm going to break your favorite toy."

I gritted my teeth. "Not a fucking toy, Vesper."

The Vesper, wearing Serena's skin like a well-tailored coat, smirked. "Ah, I see. Something more precious, then." They looked down at themself and frowned. "Hm. This will never do."

As I watched, the air around them shimmered, their clothes morphing like ink bleeding across fabric. The worn leather jacket and practical gear Serena had been wearing dissolved, replaced with something else entirely: a long dress the color of a starless night that fit like it had been sprayed on. High-necked, long-sleeved, viciously elegant, and utterly indecent in the way it left Serena's back entirely bare, the fabric stopping just below the dimples of her heart-shaped ass. It was a deliberate choice, meant to unnerve, to distract, and it worked, far more than I liked.

I clenched my jaw. "Is that really necessary?"

The Vesper stretched, arching Serena's spine like a cat luxuriating in its own skin. "You wound me, Cade. I thought you appreciated aesthetics." When I glared, they sighed. "There IS a dress code. As her...employee...nobody will notice you, but her? Her they will see."

I dragged a hand down my face. "The point of this was to get her in *without* being recognized, not put a fucking spotlight on her."

"Oh, don't worry. No one sees her like this but you." The Vesper's eyes glinted with amusement. "To others, she's merely another beautiful shade in the crowd. You only see the truth because you know what's happening."

I muttered a curse under my breath, forcing my gaze away before my brain could process the sheer audacity of it. "This is a tactical disaster laughing while it waits to happen," I said tightly. "You might as well have painted a target on her ass."

The Vesper laughed, a sound that made my skin crawl, and turned toward the Menagerie. "Let us go."

I didn't move right away. My boots stayed planted, my eyes on hers. Theirs. My mind couldn't make peace with the contradiction of the creature in front of me. They wore her body, wielded her voice, but they moved like something that had only read about humans in a book and decided to try one on for fun.

"Is she still in there?" I asked, my voice low.

The Vesper's gaze slid back to mine, and for a moment, just a heartbeat, I thought I saw something flicker behind it. A pulse. A tremor of recognition.

"She watches," the Vesper said simply. "More than you think. Less than you want."

"Fuck you."

The Vesper's laugh shimmered like crystal breaking. "So protective. It's almost sweet."

I stepped forward, jaw tight. "If you so much as scratch her..."

"What, you'll kill me?" they purred, stepping in close enough that I could smell the sweet-rotting perfume curling off their skin. "You can't. Not here. Not while I wear her so perfectly."

My fingers twitched near my weapon. Not that it would matter. "You don't wear her perfectly," I said. "You can't. Because you don't understand her."

That earned me a slow blink. "And you do?"

I didn't answer.

"She chose to let me in, Cade. Do you think she did that lightly?"

"I think she did it because we were out of options. Don't make the mistake of thinking it was trust."

That tilted smile was back. "Doesn't matter. She let me in. Which means, in some twisted way, you both need me. Let's not forget that."

I shoved past her—no, *them*—my nerves fraying at the edges. My grip on my temper was razor thin, and if I let it slip, even for a second, this thing would know.

And worse? It might enjoy it.

The walk to the Glass Menagerie was silent but heavy with tension, the kind that wrapped itself around the bones and settled deep in the gut. Noctis watched, as it always did, the streets pulsing with something just shy of sentience. The further we moved through the city's twisting pathways, the more the world seemed to shift under our feet—reality bending in preparation for where we were headed.

Ahead, the Menagerie loomed like a bad omen. It didn't have a single fixed form. From one angle, it was an opulent Victorian mansion, windows gleaming with candlelight that shouldn't exist. From another, it was a museum, its grand marble entrance flanked by pillars etched with screaming faces. Then, with a blink, it was something else entirely, an organic mass of architecture, its structure wrong in a way my mind refused to fully comprehend.

I hated this place.

The Menagerie didn't wait to be approached; it reached. The air around it vibrated like a plucked string, sending dull, nauseating waves through my skull as we neared. The closer we got, the more the world around us bled into its illusion, colors muting, angles distorting. It was like being drawn into a painting that hadn't yet decided what it wanted to be.

Each step felt longer than it should've, and not just metaphorically; the ground didn't behave. I looked down once and regretted it. My boots sank half an inch into cobblestones that undulated beneath me like water trapped under glass. I could feel the Vesper watching me out of Serena's eyes, amused.

"I always forget how tactile your reality is," they said conversationally.

I didn't answer. The Menagerie had begun to morph again, the museum-fronted horror flickering into a towering cathedral, black spires twisting like bones toward a sky that churned too fast. A second blink and it was a rusted carnival gate, grinning skulls replacing the lion-headed statues.

"This place is a wound," I muttered.

The Vesper's voice was amused. "It's a mirror. You just don't like what it shows."

I stared up at the latest manifestation: a tree. Vast, dark, leafless, its branches made of writhing, jointed limbs, its roots twisted into skulls. I could swear it had grown taller since I'd last blinked.

"This is where nightmares go to breed," I said. "You sure you remember the way?"

"I never forget," they replied. "Not this. Not anything."

They started walking again. I hesitated, then followed.

Behind us, the tree blinked out of existence.

The Vesper walked ahead of me, their steps sure, their borrowed body moving with the kind of grace that made my skin itch. Serena's effortless stride was wrong when used by this creature. The muscles in her back moved with each step, her skin glowing with a soft luminescence. She had a tattoo down the length of her spine, a stylized series of moon phases, and I tried, and failed, to focus on the ink rather than the skin underneath it.

I exhaled slowly through my nose, tearing my eyes away from the supple flex of Serena's spine, putting my focus instead on the entrance as it shifted again, this time into a towering wrought-iron gate, flanked by two marble figures that might have been statues. Might have been something else entirely.

"The Menagerie knows we're here," I said quietly.

"Oh, it knew the moment we set foot in its district." The Vesper rolled Serena's shoulders like a cat preparing to pounce. "Now it's deciding whether we're guests or acquisitions."

Riot let out a low, warning growl, the fur along his spine rippling unnaturally. The shadows at the gate flickered, shifting like something was watching from behind the veil of illusion.

I checked my weapon out of habit, knowing full well that bullets weren't going to do much in there. "Then let's not keep it waiting."

The Vesper tilted their head, those too-wrong eyes narrowing. "Try not to get too attached to what you see inside, Cade."

And with that, we stepped through the gates.

The Vesper led, their presence slithering through the defenses like a whisper in the dark. Wards that should have flared up at our approach simply dimmed, the sigils curling in on themselves in submission. I didn't like that. It was too easy, and nothing in Noctis came without a price, usually one you didn't want to pay.

The hallways were solid mirrors, but they didn't reflect; they contained. Cases set in front of them bled ink onto the polished floor, pooling under the memory jars placed three deep. Every footstep echoed with someone else's voice. Riot growled, not wanting to step past the first arch. I didn't blame him.

This place wasn't sacred. It was *scarred,* stitched together with the kind of magic that remembered you.

The moment we crossed the threshold proper, the air changed and became heavy. Still. Like stepping into the belly of a beast just before it decided to digest you. My fingers flexed. I hated how fucking helpless I felt.

Inside, the Menagerie was worse than I remembered.

People, if you could still call them that, were suspended in crystal cases that pulsed and breathed, their bodies locked in endless, repeating moments. A woman frozen mid-laugh, her lips stretched wide but her eyes screaming. A child reaching out, fingers forever inches from the toy he'd never touch. Some were whispering, their words an unbroken chant that burrowed under my skin.

The Vesper moved through this nightmare with an air of unholy appreciation, like we were strolling through a legitimate art gallery instead of a prison full of stolen lives. They trailed Serena's fingers along the edge of a display case, and I swore I saw the imprisoned figure inside flinch away: a man suspended in a crystal teardrop, his body continuously dissolving and re-forming, mouth open in a silent scream.

We passed another case, and I stopped cold.

It was her.

Or not her, but close enough. A red-haired girl, maybe twenty, her expression locked in panic. She was turned sideways, half-falling, like she'd been shoved. Her hand was outstretched in a gesture I knew too well, pushing someone else away. Her mouth frozen in the start of a scream. The resemblance was gutting.

Riot let out a whine low in his throat, pressing closer to my leg.

The Vesper glanced back and saw it. "Not her," they said, too quickly.

"What the fuck is this?"

"She tried to be," The Vesper shrugged, as if that explained everything, and moved to the next exhibit.

I couldn't tear my eyes away. There was something scribbled across the crystal from the inside, like fingernail gouges. Repeated over and over again. *Not her. Not her. Not her.*

I looked away before I could throw up.

A few steps later, there was a child. A boy, maybe six, covered in soot. He was singing a lullaby, over and over, his voice warped into a slow dirge. His mouth moved, but his eyes were bleeding. I turned my head.

"I thought I'd seen horror," I said under my breath. "But this...this is different."

"It's the Keeper's art," the Vesper murmured. "His definition of legacy. A thousand truths, stolen from time."

"Don't call them truths."

"They were. Once."

There was one last case before we turned into the final hall: a woman floating in zero gravity, hair splayed like a halo, her belly swollen in mid-pregnancy. Her hands clutched her stomach. Tears hovered on her cheeks, suspended in time.

"Fucking stop," I said.

The Vesper stopped walking.

"I don't want to see any more. I don't want *her* to see any more."

They inclined their head. "Then close your eyes, Cade. But the Menagerie will not stop for you."

I walked faster, Riot beside me, his hackles stiff, the space between us tight. The walls here breathed, and every breath felt like judgment. As we moved on, our progress was noted by...something. It might once have been human, but was now a writhing mass of eyes that all turned to watch us.

The Vesper strode ahead with eerie confidence, barely sparing them a glance. I moved in their wake, keeping close, watching every flicker of movement from the shadows that stretched too long. They hummed appreciatively. "The Keeper has been busy. Three new acquisitions since my last visit."

"You're a regular, then?" I kept my voice low, eyes scanning the shifting corridors ahead.

The Vesper's smile was all wrong on Serena's face. "Let's just say we have a professional understanding."

"That's not reassuring."

They laughed. "It wasn't meant to be."

We had to find the archives before this place devoured what souls we had left.

Time stretched and frayed as we moved deeper, the layout shifting when I wasn't looking. My head pounded with the effort of keeping track of our route. The Vesper led us unerringly, until suddenly, they stumbled.

The Vesper's borrowed body straightened with a liquid grace that made my skin crawl. Those eyes, Serena's eyes but not, locked with mine, the colors swirling like oil on water.

"The archives are just ahead," they said, voice dipping lower. "But there's a problem."

Of course there was. In Noctis, there was always a catch. I kept my voice steady. "What kind of problem?"

"The kind with teeth and a fondness for collecting souls." The Vesper's smile stretched wider than Serena's face should allow. "The Keeper has added a new layer of protections. What you seek sits behind wards that even I cannot slip through undetected."

My hand moved instinctively to the modified Glock at my hip. "So what's the play?"

"The play, dear Cade, is that I create a distraction." The Vesper's fingers traced along Serena's collarbone in a way that made me want to snatch them away from touching her. "While you slip through the narrow window I open."

"Fuck that. We stick together."

"How adorably human." The Vesper stepped closer, and the scent that wafted from Serena's skin was all wrong, too sweet, like flowers strewn on a corpse. Serena was all spice and vanilla, her sweetness tempered with fire.

"You are NOT using her as bait!" I growled, stepping closer.

"No, I'm not. The Keeper has spent centuries studying my kind, hoping to claim one for himself. His wards are... precise. Not just repelling intruders, but designed to dissect them, unravel them piece by piece. If I walk past these wards as I am, I become his next experiment, and her along with me. But an echo? That he will chase without danger to myself or her."

I narrowed my eyes. "That wasn't the deal. You stay with her until we get out." I hated them being in her, but without them, she was revealed. Fucking dammed if you do, dammed if you do more.

"Circumstances change." The Vesper stretched Serena's fingers, examining them like newly acquired trinkets. "Our time grows short, and I've no intention of being trapped in this flesh when the Keeper comes calling."

A cold weight settled in my gut. "You knew this would happen."

"I suspected." The Vesper shrugged with Serena's shoulders, the motion too fluid to be human. "Information is never free, darling, and aid comes at a cost."

Before I could respond, something moved in Serena's expression, a flicker of green breaking through the oil slick of her eyes. "Don't you dare fucking leave her now..."

"Too late," The Vesper purred. "I can feel him sliding through the walls of his domain like a spider, sensing vibrations on its web." Serena's body convulsed once, her back arching at an impossible angle, her mouth opening in a silent scream as wisps of smoke poured from her lips, nostrils, even the corners of her eyes. Her clothes morphed back into the utilitarian outfit she'd been wearing before as the smoke coalesced into a vaguely humanoid shape. "Go now, darlings, and get what you came for. The Keeper will only chase me for so long."

Serena collapsed into my arms, her body shuddering as she reclaimed herself. For a terrible moment, her eyes remained unfocused, pupils blown wide as she gasped for air. I held her tighter than I should have, one hand cupping the back of her head.

"Breathe," I whispered. "They're gone."

She pushed away, swaying slightly, but standing on her own. "Fucking double crossing...". She coughed, her voice raw. "I knew they couldn't take more, but I didn't expect them to take less."

"We can have a bitch fest about them later, but for now I think they've given us the best chance we've got," I said, glancing at the darkening corridor behind us, watching The Vesper's smoky form slithering into a separate hallway. "We've got maybe minutes at best. We're on purchased time, and the Menagerie wants a refund."

A door loomed ahead, lined with carvings of faces stretched in silent screams. I pushed it open, and the Keeper's archives swallowed us whole. I stopped, something hitting my brain so hard it knocked the wind out of me. "Red...did we kiss in here?"

She blinked. "What?"

I shook my head, trying to clear it. "I remember..."

"You remember what it put in your head. The Menagerie doesn't just keep records. It rewrites."

Inside, the shelves curved in spirals, stacked with books that wrote themselves as we passed. The air hummed with restrained knowledge, thick enough to choke on. I didn't waste time reading the titles. We had almost no time before the Menagerie stopped hunting The Vesper and started hunting us instead.

Serena moved with renewed purpose, though she was still unsteady, her fingers trailing along the spines of books that seemed to lean into her touch. Riot kept pace with us instead of roaming the perimeter of the room; he knew that staying close made us a smaller target. The archives pushed around us, an organic library that breathed—and watched. Files arranged themselves into patterns that shifted when I looked away, and drawers opened and closed of their own accord. "Fuck me," I muttered.

The ghost of a smile touched her lips before she turned back to the shelves. "Maybe later," she murmured. "If we survive this."

"That's certainly motivation," I said, trying to keep my tone light as my heart hammered against my ribs.

"Here." Her fingers stopped at a drawer that looked no different from the others, at least not to me. The moment she touched the handle though, sigils flared to life across the surface, cold blue flames twisting themselves into arcane shapes. I moved closer, ready to pull her back, but she shook her head. "I know these," she said, almost to herself. She took a deep breath, and spoke a name into the silence. "Selene ap Myrrdin."

The drawer hissed open, releasing a plume of frost that crystallized in the air before fading away. Inside lay a single black folder, its edges shimmering with what looked like liquid light. Serena's hand trembled as she reached for it, her fingers hesitating just above its surface.

"This is it," she whispered. "Everything they know about me."

I kept my eyes on the doorway, the hair on the back of my neck standing up. Something was coming. "Grab it and let's go."

She snatched the folder, clutching it to her chest as if she was afraid it might dissolve. The moment it left the drawer, however, a low, resonant tone began to reverberate through the archives. The sound crawled inside my skull and made itself at home.

"Shit," I growled, drawing my weapon as the room shifted around us. The shelves began to undulate like the ribs of some massive beast taking a deep breath. "Time to go."

Serena clutched the folder tighter, her gaze darting to the exit that...

Fuck.

The Menagerie *shuddered*, walls twisting, corridors folding inward like a dying creature trying to keep hold of its prey. The door that should have been there bled away, the space warping into something new, something wrong.

"Gabriel, the door..."

"Is the least of our problems." I nodded toward the far end of the archives, where the air had begun to ripple and fold in on itself, like reality was being peeled back, one layer at a time.

It heaved, then tore, and The Keeper stepped through the gash, his movements fluid and unrushed.

He looked human; tall, with the kind of pale, ageless face you'd expect from old money and older secrets. His eyes, however; those gave him away. Flat black pools that reflected nothing. Those voids locked onto Serena.

"Selene ap Myrddin," he greeted, his voice smooth and clinical. "I knew if I waited long enough, you'd end up exactly where I hoped you'd be."

I stepped in front of her, gun raised. "You can keep waiting."

The Keeper didn't acknowledge me. His flat black eyes looked at Serena with something too measured, too precise to be mere curiosity. "You should not exist," he murmured, almost to himself. "And yet here you are. Intact. Unclaimed. A wild thread in the tapestry." His head tilted, and a slow, knowing smile spread across his face. "Do you have any idea how long I have waited for you?"

My trigger finger twitched. "She belongs to no one."

I could feel the magic crackling in the air as she raised a shaking hand, the reality of the room bending in response. "You want me in a case, you pale fuck?" she growled, eyes burning with emerald fire. "Come and try."

That was the moment I knew she'd fight till her last breath. Even when the odds were bullshit, even when logic screamed at her to run, she'd stand her ground like a goddamn cliff daring the tide to try its best.

And fuck me if I wasn't about to do the same.

I'd been here before, in another life. A desert. A compound. Hostages. Screams. Blood on my hands. We thought we'd made it. We thought we'd snuck in quiet and clean.

We hadn't.

The room had exploded, first in bullets, then in flame, and the kid we'd come to extract was crying, his voice too small to carry over the noise of death. I'd dropped everything to get him out. Took three rounds to the vest for it. Thought I'd die with him in my arms.

I didn't. But I still remembered the way his pulse fluttered, like a moth trapped in a cage.

That's what Serena felt like now. That same fight-or-die burn, except now I wasn't rescuing a child. I was standing beside a woman made of starlight and shadow, and I'd be damned if I let anyone cage her.

The Keeper was watching her like a biologist studying a rare specimen. I'd seen that look. Cold. Detached. Planning how to dissect without damaging the integrity of the "subject."

He didn't see her.

He didn't fucking *see* her.

He didn't know the way she snorted when she was annoyed, or how she held her breath when she cast, like the world itself might hesitate with her. He didn't know what she'd already given up. He didn't deserve to know.

She belonged to no one, least of all me. I was beginning to realize, though, that I belonged to her. So, I braced myself for hell, because whatever she was about to do? It was going to be big, and I wasn't leaving her side. Not now.

Not ever.

I'd fought demons. Watched men die for less. But this?

This was the first time I felt like I might be about to watch someone break the world. I wasn't afraid.

I was ready.

The Keeper smiled. "As you wish."

He moved with the kind of speed that overwhelms the synapses, there one moment, impossibly close the next. I fired

124

twice, center mass, and watched the bullets slow and stop inches from his chest, suspended in air like insects in amber.

"Tedious," he murmured, plucking one from the air and examining it with mild interest. "I expected more creativity from the Necromancer's Daughter's ... companion."

Riot lunged, his form shifting as he moved into something ancient and hungry, all teeth and shadow. The Keeper merely gestured, and Riot froze mid leap, suspended in a shimmering field that crackled with cold energy.

"A fascinating familiar," the Keeper noted, circling Riot's frozen form. "I'll add him to my collection as well. A matching set."

"I'm nobody's exhibit," Serena snarled. The temperature in the room plummeted, and I watched frost crystalize along the edges of the shelves. A strange liquid light began bleeding into the edges of her fingers.

I knew that look in her eyes. I'd gotten really familiar with it over the last 48 hours. It was the one that said she was about to do something incredibly brave, incredibly dangerous, or both.

I was betting on both.

The Keeper tilted his head, studying her with those bottomless eyes. "How delightful! You're going to use your gifts." He sounded like a professor witnessing a particularly promising experiment. "I've catalogued countless different manifestations of the Necromancer's lineage, but yours, my dear, yours has always been the most intriguing."

"Serena," I warned, but it was too late.

She thrust her hand forward, and reality *screamed*. The air didn't just ripple, it *fractured*, splintering like glass under too much pressure. For a split second, I saw too much, layers of what should be peeling away to reveal what should not exist. The pressure in the room dropped, my ears popping, my vision flickering like an old film reel trying to skip to the right frame.

"You shouldn't be able to do that," The Keeper said, his voice no longer quite so smooth. "Not without training, not without..."

"Without a guide?" Serena finished, her voice strained but steady. The tear widened. "Turns out necessity's a hell of a teacher."

The Keeper stepped back, his perfect composure slipping. "You're channeling raw potential without proper conduits." His eyes sharpened. "You'll burn yourself out in minutes."

"Minutes is all we need," I said, moving to Serena's side. The air around her crackled with power that raised the hair on my arms and tasted like ozone on my tongue. The bubble holding Riot broke, and he hit the ground, disoriented but alive.

The Keeper's attention turned to me, his expression one of mild surprise, as if just remembering I existed. "You should be honored. Few get to witness the birth of a true necromancer."

"Shut...the fuck...up..." Serena panted. I could feel her trembling beside me. Too much power. She was pulling too much power, too quickly. The luminescent edging on the folder in her arms was creeping up her skin like veins of light. "Gabriel - get ready to run."

The Keeper's expression became something more intrigued than anything else. "Fascinating," he murmured. "You're channeling through the documents themselves. You're using your own file as a conduit." His smile was all wrong with too many teeth. "I've never seen anything quite like it."

"That's kind of the point of a collection, isn't it?" I spit. Blood was trickling from Serena's nose now, a thin crimson line that matched the red of her hair.

"Grab Riot," she whispered. "When I say run, GO."

I nodded, holstering my admittedly useless weapon and grabbing Riot, hoisting the woozy dog into my arms, then over my shoulder. I wrapped one arm around his middle, holding him in place, then wrapped my other hand around Serena's bicep.

"The Menagerie does not release what it claims," the Keeper said, his voice soft and certain as death itself.

Serena's laugh was cold and sharp. "Good thing I'm not asking permission to leave, then." She gestured, and the tear widened into a jagged, vibrating wound.

"RUN!"

We ran.

But the Menagerie wasn't done.

The tear in reality writhed like a wounded thing, its edges fracturing further, raw light bleeding from the split. Serena clutched the folder like it was the only thing keeping her tethered to this plane.

The ground buckled under us, stone curling like dead leaves. I stumbled before I managed to catch myself on a half-melted railing that screamed like a living thing.

The Keeper was close. I didn't dare look back.

"Faster!" Serena shouted, but her voice cracked, raw and thing. She was burning out.

We reached the edge of the tear, and I shoved her toward it.

"Go!"

She hesitated, looking back, and that was the mistake.

A hand shot out of the darkness, fingers like needles, and caught her wrist.

I moved before I thought, slamming into the shape that shouldn't exist. My knife buried into nothingness, its face, maybe, or its throat. It didn't matter. I screamed something incoherent, tore her free, and pulled her through.

The world on the other side slammed into us like a runaway train.

My vision went white.

The sound cut out.

Everything collapsed.

And then—

We hit solid ground.

I rolled, taking the impact on my shoulder, curling around her. Riot skidded across a slick floor, yelping once, then scrambled to his feet. The tear snapped shut behind us with a sound like bones breaking.

Silence.

My ears rang. My lungs heaved. I could feel my pulse pounding everywhere at once.

She was shaking in my arms, not crying, not speaking, just trembling. Her breath came in short, rapid bursts.

"We made it," I whispered, trying to make it real.

She didn't answer.

And that was when I realized she was still holding the folder, still clutching it, even as her body gave out.

It was covered in blood. Her nose still dripped red.

"What did we give it?" she whispered, staring at her hands.

"What do you mean?"

"It never lets you leave for free, and I can't remember what it took."

CHAPTER EIGHT

CONGRATULATIONS! YOU ARE THE CHOSEN ONE! TRY NOT TO DIE.

Gabriel

T HE WORLD REASSEMBLED AROUND us, the pieces slowly forming into something recognizable.

Stone beneath my knees. Blood on my hands. Serena slumped against me, her breath hitching, the black folder clutched to her chest like a lifeline. Riot growled low, circling once before placing himself between us and the shadows. The air buzzed, hot and thick, like we'd stepped out of one nightmare and into the next.

I shifted my weight, checking Serena with a glance. She was conscious—barely—but not speaking again, not yet. Her skin was cold and slick with sweat. The nosebleed that had started when she unleashed her power had soaked the front of her shirt.

"Red," I said low, trying to ground us both. "Come on. Say something." I cupped her face in my hands, forcing her to look at me.

She blinked slowly, like her eyes were trying to refocus. "We made it."

"Yeah," I said, scanning the jagged alley that surrounded us. "But where the hell are we?"

The space flexed, not quite stable, the walls shivering, the shadows too sharp at the edges. Noctis had lost track of her when she tore that rift, but it was catching up. I could feel it in my bones.

Riot let out a warning snarl.

Serena's fingers twitched around the folder. "Gabriel."

"I know."

I pulled her up gently, wrapping one arm around her waist, trying to ignore how light she felt. "We need to get out of here. Now."

She didn't argue.

We ran.

The streets of Noctis blurred around us in flickering layers, each one more unstable than the last. This wasn't just the city watching; it was the city hunting. It was adjusting, like we were a glitch in its system it didn't quite know how to parse. I hated how well I knew this place.

I hadn't been born in Noctis, but the city didn't care.

The first time I'd set foot inside the veil, something in the ground hummed like it recognized me. Not in welcome—Noctis doesn't do welcome, but with a kind of bone-deep recognition, like it had my name already written somewhere beneath its skin.

My babushka used to tell stories about places the world fought to forget, cities that remembered bloodlines better than names. I'd never believed her. Not until the first mission that had dropped me here and the streets whispered, *"Ah. You're back."* I never found out why the city knew me, but it did.

I had that same feeling now.

Riot took the lead, weaving through side alleys with military precision, his shoulders hunched and low. Every once in a while, he'd look back to make sure we were still upright. I appreciated the concern, because we were still far from steady on our feet.

Serena didn't stay upright for long.

Her knees buckled halfway through the second block. I caught her before she hit the pavement, one arm wrapping around her shoulders, the other clamping around her back. She was burning up. Not feverish; she'd been magically scorched, like something inside her had been hollowed out and set on fire.

"I'm fine," she muttered, even as she sagged into me.

"You're about as fine as a fucking tire fire," I growled. "Come on."

We ducked into a side corridor and paused beneath a half-collapsed overhang, broken bricks and rusted signage casting long shadows. I braced her against the wall, giving her a second to breathe.

Her head tipped back, eyes fluttering shut for a moment too long.

"Hey," I said, soft but sharp. "You with me?"

"I said I'm fine."

"Right. And I'm the fucking Easter Bunny."

That earned me the ghost of a smile. "You'd look terrible in pastels."

"Not my color," I agreed. "But if you pass out again, I'm carrying you bridal-style and making loud declarations of love the whole way."

Her lips twitched. "Fuck, you're a menace, you know that?"

"I've been told."

She shifted just enough to stand on her own again, jaw clenched. "The old station's four blocks west. There's an old ward line we can use to cut through."

"Great minds think alike, Red." I slung her arm over my shoulder again. "We just need to get there before the city gets bold."

We moved. Slower now, but steadier. Noctis didn't try to stop us this time, but I could feel the city thinking about it.

I swore that if it made a move I'd burn it down brick by fucking brick.

The abandoned train station still stood where I'd left it. That wasn't a given in this city.

Noctis had stopped pretending to have normal transportation a long time ago, so the station had been left behind. Not because it wasn't useful, but because it wasn't wanted. If a destination wasn't in the middle of somewhere appalling, then the trains simply decided they weren't interested in going there.

We crashed through the broken doors. The moment we crossed the threshold, the air inside settled. The station exhaled, the way old things do when someone finally remembers they exist. Serena slumped onto a rotting bench, still gripping the black folder with her real name on it. Riot pressed against her legs, growling low, watching the entrance.

I gave them thirty seconds. No more. Then I knelt in front of her.

"Talk to me."

She didn't argue, and I moved to sit beside her, sending up a brief prayer that the bench didn't collapse under my 230 pounds. It wobbled, but stayed mostly intact. She opened the folder.

The second she did, the air stretched thin, then snapped back into place. I felt it. So did Noctis.

Serena exhaled slowly, scanning the first few pages. I read over her shoulder. It was there, laid out almost clinically. The damning evidence of how the Bone Lords coveted her as a keystone. How the Hollow Vein viewed her as a way to unravel the very soul of this blighted city.

She turned the page. More details. More horror.

"The Bone Lords don't just want me back," she muttered, and her breath hitched. The muscles in her throat worked like she was swallowing something sharp that didn't want to go down. Her fingers tightened around the folder, white-knuckled, like letting go would send her spinning into the void. "They want me bound to Noctis permanently. Like," her voice broke, "like a living anchor. A damn supernatural battery."

She swayed, just a fraction, and I caught her wrist, steadying her before she even knew she needed it. Her skin was cold, pulse thudding fast against my fingertips. Her breathing had gone shallow, her pupils too wide.

"Serena," I said, low and firm. "Breathe, baby."

Her eyes flicked up to mine, and whatever she found there seemed to steady her. She rubbed her temple, trying to process. "If they bind me the way they're planning, I won't just be *in* Noctis; I'll be part of it. My power will be woven through the city itself. It'll function through me."

I stared at her. "So you'd be... what, Queen of the Nightmares?"

She exhaled a humorless breath. "No. Property of Noctis. Forever."

The words sat heavy between us, thick as a storm rolling in.

I saw it, hell, I *felt* it, the slow suffocation she was trying to put into words. Not just being stuck here, but becoming this place. Noctis breathing through her lungs, her thoughts dissolving into its shadows, her will stripped down to instinct and hunger and the city itself.

A prison without walls. A body without a mind.

I clenched my jaw, forcing down the sharp, useless rage clawing up my spine.

"Eternal slavery with cosmic immortality benefits," I said, keeping my voice steady despite the cold fury building in my chest. "How generous of them." My gut twisted. "Yeah, not on board with that."

Not now, not ever. Not her.

She let out a humorless laugh. "Yeah? And how exactly do you plan to stop that? Magic anti-delete button?"

"Was thinking more bullets, but sure, we can explore options."

She huffed, then went quiet. I could see the gears turning behind her eyes. She'd always known she was hunted, but this? This was something else entirely.

Her fingers brushed over a diagram that seemed to shift under her touch, lines rearranging themselves into patterns that hurt to look at. The page was filled with calculations, formulas written in a language that would look like mathematics if numbers could scream.

I frowned at the page. "Any idea what this means?"

She traced a finger over the impossible equations. "I think it's a binding ritual. The formulas describe how to anchor a person to the dimensional fabric." She turned the page and looked at the diagram that covered the paper.

The diagram spanned the whole sheet: a concentric ring structure with a human silhouette at the center—female, inked in blood-red pigment that had dried into the fibers like it had been *soaked in,* not written. Glyphs circled the silhouette's head, heart, and spine, each one jagged, geometric, like they'd been drawn with a blade. There was no grace here. No natural arcana. Just raw, surgical precision.

Tiny notations in the margins cataloged the conditions needed for anchoring:

"Temporal stasis ideal. Primary vessel must be conscious for root initiation. Identity destabilization preferred."

Below that, a long sequence of numbers and coded language. It read like a grim theorem written by someone who'd never met a soul they wouldn't dissect.

And at the very bottom—stamped in wax, still faintly warm to the touch—was a line of text written in Bone Lord's internal dialect:

"The Vessel must not love the city. The Vessel must not love anything. Only then can it be forced to hold."

Her voice dropped. "They've been planning this for a very long time. Look at the dates."

I shifted closer, my shoulder pressing against hers. The dates stretched back decades to long before Serena was born.

"They didn't just want any Necromancer's heir," I said slowly. "You were engineered for this."

She swallowed. "My father...he knew. He always knew. This was his plan. This was why I was born." She shuddered. "I was never meant to be anything more than a tool."

She looked up at me, and the pain in those green eyes nearly broke me. "I was never meant to be a person. In a world where the city constantly rewrites the rules, I was meant to be his instrument so that he could *be* the only rule."

The words landed between us like broken glass, sharp edges slicing deep. For a long moment, she just sat there, staring at the ground, shoulders shaking faintly. When she finally looked up, the ache in her eyes knocked the breath from me. It wasn't anger, not yet. It was something rawer, something brittle and fragile, a loss that went far deeper than fear or fury. It was a wound so old, so well-hidden, she'd almost convinced herself it wasn't there anymore. Until now. I reached for her hand without thinking, my fingers closing around hers. I expected her to pull away, but she gripped back with surprising strength, like I was the only solid thing in a world of shifting shadows.

"Bullshit," I said, my voice rough. "You are not a tool, Red. You are not a keystone, not a fucking battery. It doesn't matter what you were meant to be. What matters is what you are, and you're a whole hell of a lot more than a damn power source for this hellhole."

"But I'm not, am I? I'm Selene ap Myrddin. The Necromancer's daughter. His greatest creation." She spat the words like poison. "Everything I thought I was. It's all just a lie."

"No." I shifted to face her fully, curling one hand around the back of her neck and using the other to force her chin up, to make her eyes meet mine. "Your name doesn't define you. Your damn DNA doesn't define you."

I let my thumb caress her jaw. Her gaze softened, searching mine like she was searching for something real, something that wasn't fate or prophecy or nightmare. Something electric passed between us, a current that had nothing to do with her powers and everything to do with the way her pulse jumped under my fingers.

"Then what does?" she whispered.

"Your choices," I said firmly. "Every time you could have given in but chose to fight. Every time you could have used your power to hurt, but didn't. You look at a world that's trying to own you and tell it to go fuck itself. That's who you are, Serena."

Her eyes locked on mine, wide and vulnerable in a way that cut through all the bullshit. That indefinable something passed between us again, charged by the heartbeat I felt hammering under my fingers.

I should have let go. I didn't.

Her lips parted slightly, and she leaned in. Not much. Just a breath. Just enough for the air between us to turn thin and charged. It felt inevitable.

I could close the distance. Just a tilt forward, a fraction of space, and...

A loud, pointed grumble shattered the charged silence between us. I glanced down to find Riot standing inches away, his gaze flicking pointedly between us, the folder, and back to us again. He looked for all the world like a disappointed parent catching teenagers sneaking out. If spectral hellhounds could look smug, Riot had perfected it.

"Seriously?" I growled under my breath. Riot's innocent tilt of his head wasn't fooling anyone, least of all me.

I sighed, and tapped the folder, not quite believing I'd been cockblocked by a dog. I pointed at the Hollow Vein. "And these psychos?" When she looked back at the folder, I gave Riot a glare. He gave me one right back.

She exhaled. "The Hollow Vein?" She shook her head. "They don't want control. They think Noctis is a wound, something unnatural that shouldn't exist."

I leaned back against the bench, rubbing my jaw. "And they think you are the infection keeping it alive?"

Her hands clenched into fists. "Not as such, but they do think I'm the cure. They don't just want to kill me, Gabriel." Her voice went quiet. "They want to erase me completely."

I held her gaze. "What happens if they succeed?"

She hesitated. Then, softly, "Noctis falls."

The shadows stretched around us, not moving, but not exactly still either. I swore the ground rippled beneath my feet. Serena clenched her fists, and her fingers flickered, just for a second, like reality was deciding if she should still be here.

"And if Noctis falls..." I let the thought hang between us, heavy with implications neither of us wanted to voice.

"If they pull me out of the weave," she said, "if they un-make me, Noctis collapses, and if Noctis collapses, so does everything keeping the normal world intact. Reality tears, the boundaries collapse. Not just here, but everywhere. The normal world gets ... infected. All the nightmares that Noctis keeps contained would spill out like pus from a lanced abscess."

I grimaced at the imagery. "And you believe that?" I asked, watching her face carefully. "That Noctis would just collapse if you were gone?"

Serena's hands shook as she turned another page in the folder. "I don't know what to believe, but the point is THEY believe it. The Hollow Vein has been researching this for decades, maybe longer." She pointed to a diagram that looked like a twisted family tree with her name - her real name - at the center. "They think my father bound part of Noctis's essence to his bloodline when he created me. That I'm the last thread holding it together, and if they pull it, they can tear it all down." She swallowed. "What if they're right?"

"Well, shit," I muttered. "Guess I can't let you die, then."

She blinked, like she hadn't expected that reaction. "That's your takeaway?"

"Red, I've had a really long week. I'm not emotionally prepared for reality collapse right now."

A startled, breathy laugh escaped her. It was small and weak, but it was real.

Good. She needed that.

I leaned in. "Besides, what kind of guy would I be if I let you get unmade? That's bad form. Total betrayal of my reliable badass mercenary aesthetic."

She rolled her eyes, but the tension in her shoulders eased, just a little. I nudged her knee with mine. "Yeah, Noctis is a nightmare, but tearing it apart could make things worse. And I don't like worse."

She huffed. "Could've led with that."

I smirked. "Would've been less fun."

143

"You have a warped idea of fun, Gabriel."

"So I've been told." I kept my tone casual, but I hadn't missed the way she'd looked at me. I hadn't missed the way her body had angled toward me, seeking to lean on someone, just for a minute. It was about time she realized that there was no way in hell I was letting her carry this alone. Not as long as I was breathing.

She shook her head at me, but her hands weren't clenched anymore. She was still holding on. I tapped the folder. "So. That's what they want."

Serena turned another page, slower now. Her eyes narrowed. "Wait."

She held it up, showing me the heading:

"Internal Report: Subject 0A Acquisition Planning–Redacted Level 4."

My eyebrows rose. "Oh good. A redacted top-tier file. Those never mean anything horrifying."

Most of the text was slashed through in thick black glyph lines, but a few fragments remained:

...confirmed resonance lock via Veil-Seer contact...

...Subject's trajectory narrowed to three viable zones in Sector 13...

...Veil-Seer insists instability increasing. Timeline must compress...

I frowned. "Sector 13? That's the old cathedral district, right? Around Sanguine? The one nobody wants anymore. That's Bone Lord territory now."

Serena nodded. "Too many collapsed boundaries. You can't walk a straight line through it without ending up somewhere else."

I scanned the page again. "So this Veil-Seer. They're the reason they've been able to tail you so precisely?"

"Looks like it." She tapped a line further down.

...target relocation likely by tether, not trail. Continue extraction prep.

Repeat consultation with Veil-Seer before phase gate attempt...

"Tether," I repeated. "So they're not tracking you like a bloodhound. They're tracking you like a balloon on a string."

Serena exhaled slowly, fingers tightening on the edge of the paper. "It would take someone very specific to do that. And very powerful."

I glanced at her. "Someone you know?"

She hesitated. "There was a Seer who worked with my father. They never gave a name. They called him the Oracle Below. Male. Quiet. Dangerous. He didn't speak unless it was through symbols."

"Cryptic. I like him already."

She gave me a dry look. "He vanished after my father died. No one knew if he'd been taken out or just... slipped away. Some people said he went mad."

"Think this is him?"

"I don't know," she admitted. "Could be. But if Hollow Vein has someone like that on lockdown, they're not treating him as a partner. He's a tool. A locked box they only open when they need answers."

"Which means if we find him..."

"We might get one shot to break him out," she finished.

She flipped the page. A crude schematic. Lines of ley signatures radiating from a central point. Sector 13 again. One spot circled in red, stamped with the HV clearance glyph.

"That's a location," I said. "An active one."

"It's a weak point," Serena murmured. "A place where the walls between here and everywhere else are thin."

She paused. "That's how the Seer's working. He's not scrying. He's listening through the cracks."

I looked at the line of red ink under the glyph. One word had been left un-redacted: **"Containment."**

I met her eyes. "That doesn't sound like someone they're working *with*."

"No," she said, jaw tightening. "It sounds like someone they're afraid will talk."

She closed the folder gently, almost reverently. Then looked up at me.

She exhaled. Then, "We need to find this Seer. We need to know who told them where I was, and how they plan to do what they plan to do. Find out how they found me to start with, and how they keep finding me now."

I nodded. "Agreed."

Outside, a ripple moved through Noctis. The city had made a decision.

I heard it before I saw it. A subtle, shifting pressure in the air.

I grabbed Serena's arm. "Someone's coming."

Riot let out a low, rumbling growl.

Serena gripped the file tighter, just for a moment, then stuffed it in the backpack that had somehow managed to stay with her. She looked up at me. "Then let's go."

We headed toward the front, but we'd barely cleared the crumbling ticket booth when the station's main entrance shattered inward. Glass and twisted metal sprayed across the floor like shrapnel, forcing us to dive behind a row of ancient lockers. The sound echoed through the space, bouncing off vaulted ceilings and decaying walls.

"Always with the dramatic entrances," I groused, pulling my sidearm. "Just once I'd like to meet someone who knocks."

Serena pressed her back against the lockers. "In Noctis? Good luck with that."

A sound skittered across the cracked tile floor.

Not a footstep. Something softer. Wet.

Serena stilled. Riot's ears flattened, his growl dropping into an unnatural register.

"Tell me that's not what it sounds like," I muttered.

But it was already too late.

The shadows near the ruined entryway moved, then *unfolded.*

A figure rose out of the floor, a half-formed silhouette coalescing from ash, bone fragments, and wire. It had a face, or tried to. My face. Just enough to be wrong.

"Fuck me," I hissed. "It's a mimic."

Serena's hand went to her side, pressing against her bruised ribs. The dive behind the lockers must have jarred them. "That's not just any mimic. Look at its core."

She was right. Embedded in its chest, flickering behind translucent ribs, was a pulsing green orb. Hollow Vein tech. A caster core, used to store magic like a battery.

I raised my weapon. "So it's not just copying. It's recording."

Glyphs shimmered along the mimic's damaged frame, pulsing with a sinister rhythm. Hollow Vein tech, and now whatever we'd said, whatever Serena had revealed, was already being echoed back through invisible lines, carried along arcane frequencies, straight into the ears of those eager to exploit it. Each flicker of the embedded caster core meant more data siphoned, more secrets weaponized. As if to confirm it, the mimic tilted its head and opened its mouth.

Serena's voice came out. "I'm not afraid of you, Gabriel."

I felt my stomach twist.

Serena flinched, just a second, then she shoved herself upright. "Not mine."

"Sure sounds like you."

"Yeah," she snapped, "but I don't sound like a fucking *echo*."

The mimic lunged.

I fired instinctively, bullets ripping through shadow and wire. The mimic twisted mid-air, half of its shoulder exploding outward in a spray of something black and bubbling. It landed wrong, limbs bending too far, but it didn't stop.

It adjusted.

Riot leapt forward, his body warping mid-jump into something larger, more spectral. He collided with the mimic in a tangle of claws and shrieking static. They crashed through a row of lockers.

Serena was already moving, sketching a glyph midair with her bleeding palm. "Distract it!"

"I'm working on it!"

Serena's fingers traced rapid, precise symbols through the air, blood smearing her palm as she shaped the glyph into a complex snare. Magic flared brilliantly around her, arcs of energy crackling like lightning, briefly illuminating the ruined station in flashes of stark white. Her eyes glowed faintly silver, defiant and furious. Riot darted through the shadows, his spectral form twisting and snapping, driving the mimic into Serena's carefully woven trap.

I darted to the side, drawing its attention. The mimic straightened, its half shattered face flickering as it tried to become mine, then Serena's, then some twisted amalgamation of both. Its mouth opened again.

"Don't leave me behind," it said in my voice.

Serena's glyph ignited. The mimic screamed.

Magic tore through the air like shrapnel. For a second, the mimic lost cohesion, its form stuttering like a corrupted image, but it reformed faster than I expected.

"Not good," she muttered. "It's absorbing ambient spells. It's learning."

"Then we stop teaching it," I growled.

I dropped my gun—it was useless against this thing anyway—and pulled my blade. Noctis steel. The kind that didn't give a shit about data or cores.

The mimic charged.

I met it halfway.

Steel bit through wire, tore through shadow, but the thing was fast. It ducked and twisted like it had rehearsed this moment. Probably had.

It slammed its fist into my ribs. I felt something crack, but I shoved upward, slicing through its throat. Black mist sprayed out like vaporized oil. It shrieked again, but the pitch dropped. It was losing power.

"Serena!" I shouted. "Now would be a good time for something impressive!"

She was already chanting, low and fast. The glyph she'd carved twisted, spiraled, and sank into the mimic's core.

Its body spasmed.

The shadows imploded inward, the wire collapsing into itself as the core began to overload. Riot yanked me backward just as the mimic exploded.

No fire. Just *pressure,* like being hit with a scream at point-blank range.

I hit the floor hard, rolled, and came up coughing.

Across the debris field, Serena was braced against a pillar, blood on her hands and face, the sigil she used still glowing faintly in the air behind her.

Riot limped over to her, nudged her leg. She let out a breath, dropped to her knees, and scratched behind his ears.

"You okay?" I called, dragging myself upright.

She didn't answer right away. "That thing was transmitting," she finally said.

Yeah, I was afraid of that."

She held up a shard of the mimic's chest plate, etched with Hollow Vein glyphs, fine enough to be circuitry. "That wasn't just a scout. That was a beacon."

I swore under my breath. "They know where we are."

"No," she said, looking up. Her eyes burned with something hard. Fierce. "They *think* they know where we are."

I crossed the space between us, crouched beside her. "What's that mean?"

She looked at me, blood-smeared, shaking, but steady. "We're done running."

I blinked. "Say that again?"

Her jaw clenched. "We find the Seer. We find the leak. And then we go to war."

I stared at her for a long beat.

Then I nodded. "Good."

She stood, legs wobbling just once. Riot pressed against her side. I reached for the bag and slung it over my shoulder.

Serena looked out at the jagged doorway, at the city beyond it.

"Let's make them afraid for once."

And we walked into the night.

CHAPTER NINE

SET THE PLACE ON FIRE AND RUN-STANDARD OPERATING PROCEDURE

Serena

T HE SECOND WE HIT the streets, I knew we were in trouble.

Not because of Noctis, though I could still feel it watching. The city coiled around me, a predator always waiting for the right moment to strike. That was nothing new.

This was worse.

This was everyone else.

The people in the streets weren't just whispering anymore. They weren't faceless echoes, or empty reflections of Noctis's hunger. They were real, and they were staring at me. Everywhere we turned, eyes tracked us. Conversations stopped as we passed, replaced by low murmurs, quick glances sharp as the honed edge of a straight razor. A ripple moving through the crowd, like something had shifted in the unspoken rules of Noctis.

Gabriel noticed it, too. His stride never faltered, but I caught the way his shoulders tensed, his hand shifting closer to his weapon.

"We need to keep moving," he murmured, voice low.

I forced my legs to keep up with him. "What's happening?"

His jaw tightened. "Word travels fast here. Too fucking fast."

Then I saw it. A woman's fingers danced with a flickering token as she leaned against the side of a rusted-out hover cab. The gleam of a silver coin in a merchant's palm, disappearing into a pocket as he turned away from us. The smirk from a passing man, like he already knew what was coming.

A sickening inevitability settled in my gut.

My bounty had been posted, and now, every single person in Noctis had a reason to see me as prey, even if they didn't know *why*.

"Shit," I whispered. "They're carrying contract tokens."

Gabriel just kept moving. We turned a corner, cutting into a narrow alleyway, and for a second, I thought we'd lost the crowd. The alleyway twisted, the walls pressing closer until the sky was a mere sliver overhead, jagged and sharp like a wound torn in fabric. Beneath our feet, stones shimmered faintly, slick with something that looked too much like blood to be water. I resisted the urge to examine it closely.

Riot's growl vibrated through my leg, the low warning rumble making my skin prickle. He could sense what Gabriel and I were too distracted to notice, a shift in the heartbeat of the city. As I glanced at the shadowed alcoves, eyes glinted back at me, faintly luminous and not entirely human. Figures skittered away as we passed, murmuring words in a language that grated against my ears like broken glass.

"What are they?" I asked Gabriel, my voice barely above a whisper.

"Ghosts, mostly," he answered quietly, eyes scanning every dark crevice. "Souls that Noctis wouldn't release. Sometimes people who couldn't let go themselves. They aren't dangerous on their own, but if someone harnesses their hunger..." He left the rest unsaid, a warning loud enough on its own.

A woman's voice whispered from the shadows, smooth and sharp. "Selene. Welcome home."

I jerked around, heart thundering, but saw nothing. The shadows writhed, mocking my fear.

"Ignore them," Gabriel murmured, voice gentle. "They feed on reaction."

Easier said than done. My name echoed softly behind us, whispered like a prayer or a curse, over and over. The alley stretched endlessly, defying logic as reality bent itself to Noctis's whims. Even here, my father's legacy haunted me, his name woven into the city's fabric, his crimes etched into its bones.

Gabriel's hand found mine, squeezing gently. I returned the pressure, letting his strength anchor me as we pressed forward, the whispers fading but never fully disappearing.

A figure stepped out of the shadows ahead of us. A woman: tall, her presence that took up too much space, even in a city where reality could stretch to make room for whatever passed through. She wore a coat of deep, iridescent blue, too clean for Lowtown. The high collar framed a sly smile that belonged to a woman who never lost a fight she wanted to win. I felt as much as heard Gabriel's soft hiss.

She stood before us like a dagger unsheathed, and I felt a deep, unsettling pang of familiarity. Not in her face or her stance, but in the manner of someone utterly unafraid to wield death as casually as conversation. It was a chilling echo of my father. Long buried memories clawed their way to the surface: images of the cold disinterest with which he'd torn souls from bodies, the detached calm he'd maintained as he manipulated lives like pieces on a chessboard.

My skin crawled. Every step I'd taken to outrun him seemed meaningless here. His legacy lived in this city, in these bounty hunters who thrived on cruelty disguised as necessity. The dark, poisonous legacy of Myrddin coiled around my throat, squeezing tight.

For a split second, panic welled in me, the kind of pure terror that reduces everything to fight or flight. My fingers twitched at my sides, the air around me vibrating subtly with latent energy. Gabriel's hand brushed against mine, just briefly, a silent promise that I wasn't alone. It was a lifeline thrown into a stormy sea, grounding me.

Breathe.

I forced air into my lungs, the rush of adrenaline slowing to a simmering boil. Gabriel's presence steadied me, but the fear lingered, an icy whisper threading through my veins. *You're just like him.*

It wasn't true. It couldn't be true. The thing was, in Noctis, truth was a fluid, dangerous thing.

As her twisted smile widened, I made myself a silent vow: whatever happened next, I would not become the monster my father had tried so hard to create. Even if Noctis itself seemed determined to make that choice for me.

"Azrael Voss," Gabriel said, stepping subtly in front of me to draw her eye.

"Do you know her?" I questioned quietly.

"Pretty much everyone who's been here the past five years or so knows her. Noctis's premier bounty hunter, if you can call her that. Bounty hunters work for money. She hunts for sport."

She flipped the silver contract token between her fingers, letting it catch the dim neon light. "Don't be fooled, sweetie," she purred. "The money's nice, too. Pretty things are expensive." She turned to look at me. "Selene ap Myrddin," she said smoothly. "Fancy running into you here."

My pulse slammed against my ribs.

Gabriel's stance shifted, subtle but lethal. "That name doesn't belong to you."

Her eyes gleamed as she held up a silver token. "Doesn't it?"

And then she moved.

She came at us in a blur of motion that defied physics. Gabriel moved with practiced efficiency, shoving me behind him as he drew his weapon. He cleared the holster, but her foot was already connecting with his wrist, sending the weapon skittering across the pavement. She dodged his strike, dancing just out of his reach, knowing he didn't want to move too far away and leave me vulnerable.

"Always the protector, Gabriel Cade," she taunted. "Did you honestly think I wouldn't get in on this game?"

I'd seen Gabriel tense before, seen him brace for a fight, but this was different, the way I felt his body go still. He wasn't preparing to win. He was preparing to get us out.

Azrael Voss was too comfortable. Too at ease. She had the weight of inevitability wrapped around her like a second skin. That lazy, knowing smile carved across her face like she'd already caught us, even though we were still standing free.

It pissed me off.

Gabriel moved first.

It was subtle, almost too subtle, his hand shifting toward his waistband like an instinct. Like a snake sensing heat, Voss tracked the movement instantly. Her eyes flickered, silver-blue, just for a fraction of a second.

And that was exactly what he wanted.

He didn't go for his gun; he couldn't since it was lying on the pavement behind me. His hand went to his belt instead, palming something small, flat, and unremarkable. I barely saw him activate it before he threw it low, skidding it across the ground toward her boots.

Voss didn't even blink. She was already shifting, weight rolling onto the balls of her feet, bored amusement still sitting at the edge of her expression like she had all the time in the world.

Then the charge flared hot, and for the first time, her expression faltered.

The air imploded.

I felt it before I saw it, a pulling, twisting sensation, like the alley was folding inward, like space itself had decided to rewrite the rules of distance and depth. For a split second, Voss didn't exist. Not gone, just far away, impossibly distant, even though she hadn't moved. The space between us crushed into nothing. The alley behind us stretched forever, swallowing its own shape, twisting into something endless.

I didn't wait for an explanation. Gabriel grabbed my wrist and said 'run'. So I ran.

We sprinted through twisted paths, every step echoing like a gunshot. Gabriel's face was a mask of careful calculation, eyes assessing our surroundings with laser precision.

"Are you alright?" he asked, as we dodged yet another shadowed figure lurking near the edge of the path, its eyes glowing faintly in the gloom.

"As alright as I can be," I replied breathlessly, chest heaving. I'd expended a lot of energy in our recent escapes, and the fatigue was catching up to me quickly, my legs threatening to give out at any moment. "Just keep moving."

He frowned slightly, slowing his pace. Riot surged ahead, leading the way with fierce determination.

"Don't do that," I snapped, noticing his shift in position. "I'm not helpless."

Gabriel shot me a look, equal parts annoyance and something softer, more vulnerable. "I never said you were helpless, Red. But you're exhausted, and I'm not risking you getting hurt again."

A surge of frustration rose within me, but before I could voice it, I stumbled. Gabriel's hand caught my elbow instantly, steadying me without breaking stride. His grip was firm, reassuring, and infuriatingly gentle.

"See?" he murmured, a hint of wry humor creeping into his voice. "This is why."

I huffed in irritation, but my heart betrayed me, fluttering at the careful way he guided me through Noctis's treacherous pathways. "Fine. Just...don't get yourself killed trying to protect me."

"Wouldn't dream of it," he replied, a slight smile tugging at his lips despite the seriousness of our situation. It was the reassurance I needed, even if I was too stubborn to admit it aloud.

We tore through the alleyway, Riot materializing from the shadows to run alongside us. The world around us was warping back to normal, like reality was a rubber band snapping into place. Gabriel's fingers dug into my wrist with bruising intensity, not apologizing, not slowing. I matched his pace, my lungs burning.

"What the hell was that back there?" I gasped, dodging a pile of refuse that might have been garbage, might have been something worse. In Noctis, you learned not to look too closely.

"Spatial disruptor," Gabriel grunted. "One time use only. Creates a temporary fold in local reality." He threw me a look. "It won't hold her long."

"How long is not long?"

"For Voss? Minutes. Maybe less."

"Oh, goody."

We cut through a narrow passage that shouldn't have been there. A crack between two buildings that widened as we approached, then sealed itself behind us with a whisper of old stone. Gabriel navigated Noctis's shifting geography like he'd been born to it, each turn deliberate, each choice made with the expertise of someone who'd spent a long time learning how to disappear. Gabriel veered left, shoving open the nearest door. I followed without hesitation, and Riot slipped in behind us.

We crashed into a bar that probably hadn't closed in twenty years: dimly lit, the air thick with the scent of cheap smoke and cheaper magic.

The bartender looked up, expression bored. Then he saw me, and his face shifted. I looked down, and caught a glint of silver in his palm.

Contract token.

"Fuck," Gabriel muttered.

I saw the way the other patrons had turned toward us, some moving too fast, too eager. Gabriel took my hand and pulled me back toward the door...

And found the bounty hunter standing in front of us again. Arms crossed. Sly smile still in place.

"That wasn't very nice back there," she said smoothly. "Why don't we talk?"

Gabriel reached into the small of his back, pulling another weapon. Seriously, how many did he have on him? "You're in my way."

Her smile didn't falter. "So shoot me."

Voss's eyes locked onto mine, amusement glittering like polished steel. Behind her, the chaos of the bar dimmed into insignificance. It felt as if a spotlight had narrowed onto just the two of us, the edges of my vision darkening until nothing else existed but the silent probability of violence.

"Tell me, sweetie," she drawled, stepping closer with a predatory grace, "did you really think you could run forever?"

Her words coiled around my mind, echoing with cruel familiarity. My father's voice slithered into my thoughts unbidden, his presence a ghost I couldn't exorcise. *"You can't run from what you are, Selene".* Anger flared hot and immediate, incandescent in my chest, warring with the bone-deep fear that he might have been right.

Gabriel shifted beside me, his stance radiating readiness. "Back off, Voss," he warned, his voice dangerously calm, lethal in its quiet promise. "You're biting off more than you can chew."

Voss tilted her head, regarding him with a mixture of curiosity and disdain. "Oh, I think I've sized up this morsel perfectly." Her eyes slid back to me, sharpening. "Does he know, princessa? Does he understand what you really are?"

My heart stuttered. Gabriel's eyes flicked briefly toward me, a shadow passing behind his composed expression. He'd seen glimpses, knew some truths, but did he grasp the full depth of what my bloodline meant? The way necromancy pulsed in my veins, eager and hungry, always waiting for a chance to rise and consume me? I swallowed hard, trying to push back the rising dread.

Voss's smile widened, reading my hesitation with devastating accuracy. "Ah," she breathed. "He doesn't. Not entirely. That's cute."

Gabriel's grip tightened on his weapon, knuckles whitening. "Careful," he warned softly, but the threat was molten beneath the calm exterior.

My stomach churned. The room seemed to tilt slightly, reality shifting subtly under my rising panic. I felt my magic shiver deep inside, a whispering seduction of power and safety. I only had to reach for it, embrace it, surrender myself fully. My father had always insisted power was the only true currency, the only protection, and in this moment, with danger pressing in from every side, it felt terrifyingly true.

Riot pressed against my leg, growling softly, sensing my inner turmoil. His warmth and steady presence tried to anchor me, but it wasn't enough. The magic roared louder, a drumbeat of temptation, swearing that I could crush Voss where she stood. I could end this threat permanently. All it would take was one moment of release, one act of surrender.

It would feel good, a dark part of me whispered. *You could finally stop running.*

I clenched my fists, nails digging painfully into my palms, fighting the seductive pull of darkness. Gabriel's presence beside me was solid, protective, real, a tangible reminder that I was more than my legacy, more than the bloodline that threatened to swallow me whole. I wasn't sure it was enough.

"You're shaking," Voss noted softly, mock concern dripping from her voice. "Afraid?"

"Not of you," I spat, my voice trembling with barely restrained rage and exhaustion—and fear, though I'd die before admitting it aloud. I lifted my chin, staring her down despite the storm inside me. "But you should be afraid of me."

She laughed, rich and amused. "Oh, sweetheart. You really are his daughter, aren't you? Threats first, action second."

Gabriel tensed at my side, ready to launch forward, but it wasn't his fight. It was mine, and as much as it terrified me, I was done being the hunted. Whatever came next, I would choose my path, no matter the price.

The bounty hunter sighed, tilting her head. "You can make this difficult, if you want. But I think we both know how this ends."

I smiled. A slow, sharp thing.

"Yeah," I said. "With you hitting the ground first."

I grabbed the nearest chair and threw it at her.

It hit nothing but air. Voss moved like smoke, her body twisting impossibly to avoid the chair as it shattered against the wall behind us. The patrons who had been eyeing those silver tokens suddenly remembered that they had lives they wished to continue living and dove for cover. Gabriel fired twice, the shots impossibly loud in the confined space, but Voss was already elsewhere, dancing through reality like it was made of tissue paper, the rounds splintering the wood paneling of the wall they hit.

"Cute," she said, and then she was in front of me, so close I could smell her, all winter frost and expensive perfume. "I do like it when they put up a fight." She circled me, her expression turning into something sharp and amused, and I turned to follow her. "I've been asked to bring you in alive," she called out, her voice carrying easily over the chaos. "Alive, they said. They didn't define it."

Her hand snapped out, and one razor sharp fingernail sliced my cheek. I heard Gabriel roar, saw him lunge, but she was simply too fast. She had something in her hand now, and she swiped the blood on her finger, my blood, across the top. It was a neural net, a weapon that would shut down my nervous system without leaving another mark on me.

"This doesn't have to get messy," she purred, then looked at the blood trickling down my cheek. "Well. Messier."

She pressed the switch, and I felt the cold pressure against my skin...

Riot materialized from the shadows beneath a nearby table, moving with the fluid precision of something ancient and predatory. His form blurred at the edges as his teeth closed on Voss's forearm.

She cried out, the first genuine reaction I'd really seen from her, and the device clattered to the floor. I scooped it up. Riot savaged her arm, head shaking, before letting her go and backing up to stand in front of me.

"Interesting pet," she said, eyes furious, sneer turned evil. Metallic blood ran down her arm where Riot's teeth had left huge tears in her skin. "I think I'll make a coat out of him."

I was done. I was so damn DONE. Gabriel was again preparing to get me out of here. Me? I was ready to fight.

I reached out, not with my hand but with something deeper, the thing that lived in my blood. I wrapped my hand around the cord that held her life force to her body, and I started to squeeze.

"You wanted to go toe to toe with a necromancer?" I smiled. "Let's dance, bitch."

Her eyes widened. The smirk was gone, replaced by something sharper. I felt her resistance, like trying to crush steel between my fingers. "Impressive," she said, her voice tight. "They said you were untrained."

I squeezed harder. "They lied."

She dropped to one knee.

"Turns out," I said, my voice eerily calm, even to my own ears. "I'm a quick study."

Gabriel's hand closed around my wrist. "Serena." Just my name. Soft. Almost pleading.

I didn't look at him, didn't look away from Voss as she kneeled, panting, silver blood pooling beneath her. The bar had gone silent, every pair of eyes locked on us, on me, on what I was doing. I could feel the power surging through me. It wasn't like before, not the wild, uncontrolled bursts of earlier. This was different. Focused. Deadly.

And it felt good.

Too good.

"Serena," Gabriel said again, his voice closer now, more urgent. "We need to go. Now."

I didn't move, just tightened my grip on that invisible cord, watching Voss's face contort. Her silver-blue eyes dulled, the light in them flickering like a candle caught in a draft. Another squeeze and she'd be nothing but an empty shell. Just one more heartbeat...

"This isn't you," Gabriel's voice cut through the haze. He moved closer, just enough that I could see him from the corner of my eye. "Don't let them make you into what he wanted."

The words hit me like ice water. I looked up, and my eyes caught my reflection in the cracked mirror behind the bar.

I looked like him. In my reflection I saw his cruel calmness, his calculated gaze staring back at me from my own face. I looked like the portrait of Myrddin that had hung in my childhood bedroom, the one that had haunted my nightmares. For one terrible second, I still didn't let go.

Then I did, so suddenly that the backlash knocked me into Gabriel. He wrapped an arm around me to steady me, while the other kept his weapon trained on the bounty hunter kneeling on the grimy floor. Voss coughed, that silvery blood spilling from her lips now, and when she looked at me, her eyes held something new. Not fear, exactly, but the way a hunter might look when she went hunting deer and instead found herself facing a wolf.

"You really are his daughter. I'll be damned," she managed, her voice hoarse.

The words slithered down my spine, turning me to ice. I forced myself to straighten. "I'm nothing like him."

The lie tasted bitter on my tongue.

Her laugh was a broken, ragged thing. "Keep telling yourself that, princessa. Keep telling yourself that."

Before I could answer, Gabriel's arm around my waist tightened, pulling me back. "Time to go," he said. It was not a suggestion. Riot moved with us, a shadow at my heels as Gabriel steered us towards a narrow service door behind the bar. The bartender made no move to stop us; he just watched, wide-eyed, the contract token forgotten in his palm.

"This isn't over," Voss called, her voice following us through the service door and down a cramped corridor reeking of mold and stale beer. Gabriel's arm remained tight around my waist, half-guiding, half-dragging me.

I didn't fight him. I couldn't. Not with my mind replaying what I'd just done, the way I'd reached into Voss and nearly snuffed out her life like pinching a candle flame. The worse part?

I wanted to go back and finish it.

"She's right," I said, my voice hollow as we burst through a rear exit into the sidewalk. His pace didn't slow.

"It never is, here," he replied.

I knew we would have to talk about what happened. I also knew it would have to wait. We needed to find a place to rest; we were exhausted, and hungry. Now that the adrenaline was ebbing, the toll that the magic had taken was becoming apparent. My steps slowed, and I stumbled. I'd have ended up face down on the cobblestones if his arm hadn't still been banded around my waist.

"I've got you," Gabriel murmured, shifting his grip to better support my weight. His eyes scanned the twisted street ahead of us, calculating, assessing. "We need to get off the grid, and I'm damn tired of lumpy mattresses and MREs."

"I'm fine," I lied, tasting copper in my mouth.

"You're not. That's the problem with magic. It doesn't just take from them, it takes from you, too."

His words hung in the air between us. I knew he was right. I'd felt the power surge through me, felt its voracious hunger, but I hadn't realized how much it had taken in return until now, when my legs felt like overcooked pasta and my vision kept whiting out at the edges. I let myself cling to him, trusting him to get us—somewhere.

He led us through a series of turns that seemed random, moving into a part of Noctis I hadn't seen before. The buildings here were older, their edges blurred like watercolor paintings left in the rain. Riot padded alongside us, his form still occasionally rippling into something more shadow than substance.

"Where…" my voice cracked, and I cleared my throat. "Where are we going?"

"Somewhere safe," Gabriel replied, his tone brooking no argument. "Or as safe as anything gets in this godforsaken place." He flashed me a rare grin. "If it's still there, it's a damn sight more comfortable than where we've been holing up."

I frowned. "I like the safe house," I argued. "It's…" I tried to find the words, but none seemed willing to apply for the job.

"I know, Red, I know. But you'll like this, too."

I looked at him. "Promise?"

The corner of his mouth quirked upward, just a tick, and it felt like a reward. "Cross my heart."

I tried to say something, but the world greyed out. The last thing I knew was Gabriel catching me.

CHAPTER TEN

THE CHURCH OF BAD DECISIONS WELCOMES YOU

Gabriel

T HE PENTHOUSE HADN'T CHANGED at all, every detail untouched by the time that had passed.

I paused before the keypad, awkwardly shuffling Serena in my arms so that I could key in the passcode I hoped still worked. I braced myself for alarms, snares, anything that might signal the place had been breached. Instead, the lock released with a soft click, and I pushed the door open. Riot trotted ahead, sniffing the air, and he gave a low, approving sound. No threats, apparently; he made for the couch and stretched himself out with a sigh.

The dozens of stasis spells that kept this place pristine were all in place, humming like a lullaby under the skin of the world. No dust, no decay, food still preserved in the kitchen like I had just stepped out for coffee and forgotten to come back. In a sense, I had. The scent of stasis magic hung in the air, clean and soft, like flowers sealed in wax, the faint charge of power undiminished by time. Every breath I took felt like a ghost brushing past my skin.

Five years and nothing had changed. Not the furniture, not the lighting, not even my fucking coat on the hook by the door. Time had stopped here. I hadn't.

I crossed the threshold like a thief, half expecting the place to reject me; *you don't belong anymore, you left us behind*. But the spells held. The silence held. And me?

I felt like an intruder in my own memory.

Five years ago, when Serena first ran from this city, I'd made my home here, as much as any place could be a home, then. When it was offered to me in payment for a job, I'd taken it. I'd eaten here, slept here—I wouldn't say I'd lived here.

Serena stirred in my arms, her breath catching softly. The sound cut through my trip down the memory hellhole.

This wasn't about me.

I carried her past the velvet sectional, every step echoing with memories I hadn't invited. I remembered what it had been like to live here: alone, always half-alert, never warm no matter how high I turned up the heat. I'd never brought anyone here. Not once. Looking down at her now, unconscious and bloodied but still glowing under the soft light, I realized this was the first time it felt like a *home*.

Serena was still unconscious, her breath feather-light against my collarbone. I could feel her heartbeat against her ribs, and the steady thump reassured me.

I set her gently on the oversized bed, tucked into the sunken bedroom. The sheets, kept fresh by the magic of the place, still smelled faintly of cedar. I pulled the blanket up to her collarbone and just stood there, watching her. Even now—after everything—she was fucking radiant. Messy hair, bruised and bloodied and pale, but still burning like a star.

I set her down in the bed I used to dream of dying in, and realized that I very badly wanted to live if she was there.

I was completely, utterly fucked.

"Watch over her, ok? I'm going to clean up." I should have felt stupid addressing the dog, but I didn't.

I could shower in less than five minutes, but I took ten, giving myself time to think. The problem was my brain wouldn't settle, wouldn't fix on anything but her. I rinsed, dried, and pulled on clothes from the wardrobe that used to be mine before I walked over to check on her. She was still unconscious, but it seemed more like sleep than anything else, her face relaxed in a way I don't think I'd ever seen it. Unable to stop myself, I reached out and brushed a curl away from her face.

She was so damn beautiful that it knocked the wind out of me. I let myself twist that garnet colored lock around my fingers before tucking it behind her ear and allowed myself the luxury of running the backs of my knuckles down her cheek. Long,

long lashes shadowed skin soft as sleep, those deep green cat's eyes shuttered. Her plush, clever mouth was slightly parted, and I ran the pad of my thumb over her bottom lip. Usually that mouth was full of some dry remark that made me want to pull her into my lap and kiss the sharp right out of her, absorbing all her hard edges until she melted into syrupy softness against me. She sighed and nestled into my hand, and I think my heart stopped beating for a minute.

I turned away before I could do something stupid and headed for the kitchen. The fridge unsealed with a hiss, revealing food suspended in stasis like living memories. I picked what I needed, breaking the preservation wards with a whisper and a breath, and got to work. Real food. Not rations, not a can of whatever we'd grabbed from a forgotten alley, but a real fucking meal. She deserved that, and I needed something human to hold on to before the past swallowed me whole.

The scent of searing meat rose in waves, grounding me. The kind of thing you take for granted in another life. The kind of thing you forget to miss until you're half-starved for something that doesn't come in a tin.

I flipped the steak, watching the sizzle bloom outward like a sigil. My hands moved on autopilot—olive oil, salt, a pat of butter that hissed as it hit the pan. Ritual. Not just of food. Of *presence*.

Because I needed this. Not just for her, but for me, too.

There were too many ghosts in Noctis. Too many whispers in my head reminding me I didn't belong here anymore, that I was just a weapon someone put on a shelf too long. But this? Cooking? This made me feel like a person again.

It reminded me of the little moments I used to have. After a mission. After a kill. Quiet, clean-up, steak and potatoes and blood that was never mine. Back when I still thought doing the right thing meant you deserved a future.

I looked toward the bedroom. She hadn't stirred. Not yet. Good.

Because I didn't want her to see how badly I was shaking.

This wasn't about the food. It was about control. About holding onto something real, something normal, in a place that wanted to devour that word whole. I needed her to have that, even if it was just for an hour.

A real meal. Something ordinary.

I plated the steak and potatoes like it mattered. Like I was feeding this meal to something sacred. I didn't want her to wake up to fear, to blood, to me sharpening a knife and looking like her past had finally caught up to her.

I wanted her to wake up to warmth.

To the scent of dinner.

To the smallest kind of mercy I could still offer.

I was halfway through dressing the potatoes when I heard the soft shuffle of bare feet.

"You cook, too? That's actual food? I'm not hallucinating from blood loss or something?" Her voice was thick with sleep and surprise.

I turned to find her leaning against the kitchen doorframe, the blanket I'd tucked around her now draped over her shoulders like a cape. There was a bruise blooming along her jawline that looked worse in the penthouse's clinical lighting. Her hair was tangled, but her green eyes were clearer now.

"There's a lot you don't know about me, Morrigan." I replied, uncorking a bottle of wine that I'd pulled out of the pantry. "Including my tragic history as a sous chef in Prague."

She snorted, the sound unexpectedly delicate. "Bullshit."

"Special Forces survival training," I admitted with a half-smile. "Food matters. Morale matters." I laughed. "That, and Babushka's lessons. Right after 'how to kill a vampire with a wooden spoon' and before 'proper etiquette when dining with demons'."

She didn't answer, just came closer and slid into one of the bar stools. "Smells like... normal."

"That's the idea." I waved in the general direction of the bathroom. "Why don't you go clean up while I finish this? There's plenty of hot water, and you'll feel better if you're clean." I handed her a glass of wine to take with her. "If you want, there are some of my shirts and sweats in the wardrobe in there. Everything is clean." She hesitated, then gave me a nod, taking the glass and heading for the bathroom. I stood, not moving, until I heard the water come on.

I finished plating the food in silence and setting a glass of water next to her plate. I put down a plate of steak and a bowl of water for Riot, and waited.

It was a bare fifteen minutes before she returned, hair damp and curling, one of my T-shirts covering her to mid thigh. I pointed at the food. "Ribeye, potatoes, broccoli. Eat."

She did. Slowly at first, then like she hadn't eaten in days. We ate in silence, two people pretending the world wasn't actively trying to kill us.

"So," Serena said finally, setting down her fork with a gentle clink against the china. "This place is yours?"

I snorted, glancing around at the sleek, minimalist decor that practically screamed money. "Do I look like I shop at designer furniture stores?"

"You look like you sleep on a cot with your boots on," she replied, a ghost of a smile playing at her lips, and even that small expression felt like a victory. "But we both know appearances can be deceiving, yeah?"

"It belonged to an old contact." I gathered our plates, needing something to do with my hands. "Someone who owed me. Someone who won't be coming back to collect." I carried the plates to the sink. "His daughter gave it to me in payment. I wasn't sure it would still be here, intact, but needs must as the devil rides." I turned on the sink, rinsing the plates. "For once, we got lucky."

She stood and crossed to the floor-to-ceiling windows, staring out over the warped skyline of Noctis. The starlight above throbbed like a migraine. She didn't move.

"It felt good," she said softly.

I looked up. "What did?"

"What I did to Voss." Her voice was steady, but I could hear the thread unraveling under it. "I liked it. That control. That power. I liked watching her kneel." She turned then, eyes hollowed out with self-loathing. "Does that make me him?"

"No." My voice came out rough, edged with steel. I crossed the room, stopping just short of touching her. "You are not him. You are not a tool, not a keystone, not a fucking weapon for someone else's war. You're a person. With a choice."

She stared at me for a long moment, the green of her eyes catching the fractured light of the city. Behind her, a building folded in on itself like a paper crane, its windows blinking out one by one.

"A choice," she repeated, testing the word like it was foreign. "That's funny. I don't remember having many of those lately." She sighed, and the exhaustion on her face nearly broke me. "All my life, I thought I was making choices. Turns out that every decision, every path, all of them were leading me right back here. Like a fucking rat in a maze."

I leaned against the window frame. "That's the thing about mazes. Once you know the pattern, you can break the walls."

"Poetic," she said dryly. "Is that another Special Forces skill? Metaphorical wall-breaking?"

"No. That was pure Gabriel Cade bullshit." I smiled, and for a moment, she almost smiled back.

"I almost killed her, Gabriel."

"You didn't."

"But I wanted to."

"So did I."

That startled something in her. Her breath hitched, and I stepped in close, lifting a hand to brush back a damp curl of hair that was clinging to her cheek.

"You are not your father," I said. "You are not what they made you. You are what you choose to be, Red. And right now?" I let my fingers linger against her cheek. "Right now, you chose mercy. Even when every ounce of rage in your blood was screaming for vengeance."

Her eyes searched mine, looking for the lie, for the platitude. Finding neither, she leaned into my touch, just slightly.

"I've seen enough people break to know what it looks like when someone doesn't," I said, tracing the edge of her bruise, feather-light. "You bent. You didn't break."

Something shifted in the air between us, like reality holding its breath. Serena's gaze dropped to my mouth, and the world narrowed to just this, to her warmth under my fingers, the soft exhale of her breath.

"I'm not sure I can trust myself anymore," she admitted, voice barely audible.

"Then trust me, Red. I've got you." I let my hand wander into her hair, cupping the back of her head and tipping her face up. "I'll always have you."

"Even knowing what I am? What I could become?"

The question hung between us, fragile as spun glass. Her face was open, exposed in a way I'd never seen before, like she was offering me something precious and terrible all at once.

I'd seen monsters. I'd been one. I'd walked through villages where the only thing left standing was smoke and silence. I'd looked gods in the eye and walked away. I'd never feared a single one of them.

But her? She terrified me. Not because of her power, but because of the way she cracked something open in me, something I hadn't let anyone touch in a decade. She made me want things I'd buried in war zones, things like hope. She made me *hope,* and I hated hope. It always got people killed.

I'd risk it for her.

I didn't answer with words. Words were cheap in Noctis, where lies and texture and truth were just more currency to be bartered away. Instead, I closed what little distance remained between us, my lips finding hers with the inevitability of gravity.

She tasted like salt and copper, like the meal we'd just shared, the blood she hadn't quite washed away, like defiance and desperation, brightness and broken stars and something ancient clawing its way up from the beneath the weight of her own name. Her body went rigid for half a heartbeat before she melted against me, her fingers curling into the fabric of my shirt like she was afraid I'd disappear. Her mouth opened under mine and I was lost, gone in the firestorm of her kiss, her body pressing into me with all the fury and ache of everything she'd kept locked inside for too long.

I kissed her like it was the last time I'd get the chance. Like the world was ending—which, in Noctis, was always a safe bet. It wasn't a soft thing. It was teeth and tongue, breath and a sweet whimper that I dragged out of her by tugging sharply at her lower lip before licking into her and owning that smart mouth.

When her hands slipped into my hair, dragging her nails along my scalp, I hissed. The sharp edge of pain grounded me even as the fire between us threatened to burn me alive. Her touch wasn't hesitant; it was hungry. Claiming. And I let her.

I wanted her to write her name on every inch of my soul.

I hoisted her up without breaking the kiss, feeling her fingers fist in my hair like she needed to hang on or fall apart. I didn't know which terrified me more. A few strides took me into the bedroom, and I set her down at the side of the bed. I meant to pull back. I meant to ask her if she was sure, but when the backs of her knees hit the edge of the mattress and she pulled me down with her, I stopped thinking entirely. The world narrowed to skin and breath and the frantic rhythm of her heart against mine.

I kissed her jaw, the curve of her throat, the hollow where her pulse beat frantically beneath soft skin. Her breath caught when I sucked a mark into the delicate space beneath her collarbone, and I didn't stop, *couldn't* stop, until she was writhing under me, eyes gone dark with need. She made a sound low in her throat, half growl, half plea, and arched up, the rock of her hips against my cock making me groan. My hands moved with a reverence I'd never granted anything before, mapping the terrain of her ribs, the dip of her waist, the flare of her hips, like I was trying to memorize the shape of salvation. There was no hesitation in this touch. Only need.

I didn't just want her. I *ached* for her, marrow-deep and breathless. Every sound she made, every shift of her body beneath mine, broke open another part of me I thought had closed long ago. She was burning me alive, and I welcomed the fire. She was ferocious and vulnerable all at once, and if I'd had an ounce of sense left, I should have been terrified at how far gone I was for this woman.

I wasn't. I had no defenses left against her. So I did the only thing I could do; I pulled her to a sitting position and stripped her shirt off, then my own. She reached for me but I batted her hand away, snapping open the front clasp of her bra and ripping it down her arms and off. Any patience I'd once had had vacated the premises.

"*Krasivaya...takaya krasivaya*," I rasped. "You don't even fucking know what you do to me." I dragged my tongue over the swell of her breast, capturing her nipple between my teeth to flick it, over and over, with my tongue. I sucked, hard, and she arched off the bed, hands coming up to hold my head to her. I let go of her nipple with a pop, moving to suck a mark into the tender underside of one full breast.

Her fingers tangled in my hair, pulling hard, and I let her, loving the feel of her nails against my scalp. "Then show me," she whispered, her voice already wrecked. "Fucking show me, Gabriel."

My control snapped.

I yanked her underwear off in one hard pull and shoved her legs apart with a grip that promised bruises. I wanted to taste her. I needed to. I dropped to my knees at the edge of the bed and buried my mouth between her thighs like a man possessed.

She cried out, sharp and sudden, the sound filthy, her hips bucking as I sucked her clit into my mouth and groaned against her. She was already trembling beneath my mouth, slick and undone before I'd even truly begun. I devoured her like she was my last fucking meal, sliding one, then two fingers into her slick heat, searching for the spot that would make her shudder. She was so fucking tight and hot enough to scorch.

"Fuck—Gabriel—I can't," Her thighs clamped around my head, writhing against my mouth, and I grinned against her.

"Yes, you can," I growled before dragging my tongue up the length of her cunt. "You're mine tonight, Red. You'll take every fucking thing I give you. Be a good girl and fucking come on my tongue before you come on my cock."

I don't know if it was my words, or the sharp suck I gave her clit, but she obeyed. Her body arched in a perfect bow, pussy clamping on my fingers as she soaked my hand. I gentled her through it until she collapsed back on the bed, fingers easing their grip on my hair.

I kissed my way up her body to take her mouth, and she whimpered at tasting herself on my tongue. I reached down and tore at my jeans, pushing them off, settling back between her legs. I thrust against her once, twice, coating my cock in her wetness, grabbing her chin with one hand.

"Open your eyes, *zvezda*." Glazed green eyes opened.

"Tell me you want this."

She wrapped her legs around my waist, slipping her arms under mine to clutch my back.

"Tell me you're sure."

"I've never been this sure of anything in my life," she whispered, and that was it. I shoved inside her in one brutal stroke, and holy hell: tight, hot, perfect. She arched up, mouth falling open in a silent scream, nails clawing down my back.

I set a brutal pace, fucking her like I wanted to destroy everything that had ever hurt her, every lie they'd ever told her, every chain they'd tried to wrap around her throat. She met every thrust with fire in her eyes, not breaking, not bending, fighting with me for every ounce of pleasure like it was the only way to stay alive.

When I moved inside her, it wasn't just lust that drove me. It was fury. At the world. At her father. At every bastard who ever looked at her and saw something to be used, chained, consumed. I wasn't here to take; I was here to claim.

Mine.

I kissed her like a declaration of war, and she answered with a rebellion in her hands. We didn't whisper promises. We *devoured* them, fed them to the heat building between us until they melted into sweat-slick skin and ragged breath.

She wasn't fragile. She was forged, iron made flesh, and I worshipped her with every thrust like I could rewrite her history through the press of my body against hers.

And God, she let me.

I needed to be deeper. I flipped her over, dragging her hips up and slamming into her from behind, her moan sugar-sweet as she braced herself on the bed, hair tangled, sweat gleaming on her back. I watched her take me like she was made for it, her ass rippling with every thrust, the wet slap of skin on skin echoing through the room. I could feel her tense under me, feel her starting to clamp down on me.

"That's it, baby. Come all over my cock." She shattered again, sobbing my name as her legs shook beneath her, and I didn't stop. I couldn't.

"Say it," I growled, wrapping a hand around her throat and pulling her back against me, teeth at her shoulder. "Say you're mine." I needed to hear it.

"I'm yours," she gasped, voice breaking. "Fuck, Gabriel...yours."

That did it.

I slammed into her one last time and came with a roar, spilling deep, grinding my hips against hers until I felt her collapse beneath me, trembling and wrecked. I followed her down, dragging her against me, burying my face in her neck. We lay there, bodies tangled, breath ragged, skin slick with sweat and cum and magic and madness.

It wasn't just the orgasm that broke me; it was the sight of her, trembling and wild, marked by my hands, my mouth, my name. It was the fact that she let herself *go*. That she gave in. That she *gave me* this. It undid something in me that I didn't know I still possessed.

I wrapped my arms around her, not just to hold her close, but to keep myself from flying apart. The air was thick with lust and magic and something deeper, heat rising in waves off our bodies, and I realized I'd never felt more grounded in my life.

I'd spent years floating through kill zones and bloodstained negotiations, feeling like a ghost in my own skin. But now, now

I was here, anchored by the woman who turned and curled against my chest, her fingers still twitching with the last shudders of pleasure. I kissed her temple. Her cheek. Her jaw.

"I've got you," I whispered again, because saying it once wasn't enough.

She didn't say anything. She didn't have to. Her body molded into mine like it had always known the shape of me, like we'd just remembered something the universe tried to make us forget.

"I'll raze this city to the ground before I let them take you," I murmured against her ear.

She didn't answer with words, just curled closer, fingers sliding over my heart like she could feel every piece of it beating just for her.

The quiet after was its own kind of chaos. We lay tangled in sheets that smelled of sex and sweat and something ancient that clung to her skin like starlight. I combed my fingers through her hair until the long strands spilled across my skin like wildfire. I traced idle patterns on her shoulder, feeling the rise and fall of her breathing slow into something almost peaceful. The penthouse was silent except for the distant hum of the stasis spells and Riot's soft snoring from somewhere in the living room. Through the floor-to-ceiling windows, Noctis pulsed like a fever dream, buildings folding and unfolding, streets twisting into impossible geometries. Here, though, in this pocket of stolen time, reality held steady.

I hadn't expected this. Hadn't allowed myself to want it. But now that I had her, warm and real against me, I understood why men burned cities for less.

"You're thinking too loud," she murmured, her lips brushing my collarbone. "I can practically hear the gears grinding."

I huffed a laugh. "Professional hazard. Always planning the next move."

She propped herself up on one elbow, her hair falling in a curtain around us. The bruise on her jaw had darkened, a purple stain against her pale skin. I reached up to touch it gently, and she leaned into my hand like a cat.

"And what is the next move, Captain Cade?" Her voice was light, but those otherworldly eyes were serious. "Because as lovely as this interlude has been, Noctis is still out there and the Bone Lords still want to turn me into a battery. The Hollow Vein still wants me dead. And I'm still..." she hesitated, "whatever the hell I am."

"You're Serena fucking Morrigan," I said firmly, tucking a curl behind her ear. "Everything else is just the hand you've been dealt. It's what you do with it that matters."

Her gaze was measuring. "And what if I play the hand wrong?"

I sat up, pulling her with me, my hands framing her face. "Then I'll be there to pull you back. Every damn time."

She smiled, a fragile thing that broke and reformed in the space of a heartbeat. "That's a dangerous promise, Cade."

"I don't make promises I can't keep, Red." With that, I lay back, pulling her with me.

"I didn't think I could have this," she said softly. "Safety. Comfort. You." She kissed my shoulder. "But I want it anyway." She looked up at me. "It's terrifying, but so is everything else. At least this feels real."

"You've got me, *moya zvezda*." I whispered. "Sleep. We have a little time." And I meant it. I watched the city twist behind the glass of the windows, light folding in on itself like a dying star. Her fingers were tangled in mine even in sleep. Riot had returned from his couch snoring session to lay watch near the foot of the bed. Even he seemed subdued now, like he understood something sacred had just occurred.

I couldn't sleep. Not because I was restless, but because sleep would mean stepping away from this moment, and I wasn't ready to let it go. So I stayed there, tracing the slope of her spine with slow fingers, memorizing every inch of her again in the dark. Not as a soldier. Not as a protector. As a man.

Let them come. Let the city watch.

She was mine now, and I'd kill anything that tried to change that.

CHAPTER ELEVEN

PEOPLE WHO KNOW TOO MUCH SELDOM LIVE LONG. LET'S CHANGE THAT.

Serena

T HE MORNING AFTER, RIOT wouldn't look at us.

He'd taken one look at the bed, at the rumpled sheets and the absolute chaos we'd made of them, and emitted a disgusted huff, turning his back on us with the solemnity of an offended priest. His entire posture screamed betrayal. The only thing missing was a dramatic exit, but even he wasn't reckless enough to wander Noctis solo. Not while a bounty still rode my name.

Gabriel was still asleep, one arm heavy across my waist, his breath warm against the side of my neck. I could've stayed like that forever. I wanted to stay like that forever.

The sheets whispered their own story, however, and I knew he'd notice, eventually.

When he did, everything stilled.

He was sitting up halfway, the tension in his body a wire pulled taut. I'd slipped out to the bathroom to clean up, and he hadn't so much as twitched when I got up. It had made me hopeful I'd get back before he woke, but obviously that ship had sailed. His eyes were locked on the faint smear of red near the edge of the mattress, and when he turned toward me, his voice was low, raw.

"Red... was that... was that your first time?"

I didn't flinch, just nodded. "Yes."

He was quiet for a moment. Not the stunned kind, not the awkward kind, just... quiet. Like he was replaying every second of last night through a new lens and trying not to shatter under it.

"You should've told me," he said again, voice even rougher now. "Because I would've...fuck, I don't know. I would've slowed down. Taken more care. You deserved—"

"I know," I interrupted gently. "I know you would have. But I didn't want careful."

That got his attention.

"I didn't want to feel like something fragile, or like I was something that had to be protected. I just wanted *you*." I reached for him, threading our fingers together. "I trusted you. That's kind of the whole point."

His brow furrowed like he didn't understand, or maybe didn't believe. So I kept going.

"I've never trusted anyone like that before, Gabriel. Not enough to let them get close. Not enough to let them *see* me, let alone touch me. You think it was just about sex? No. It was about *you,* about choosing you. Letting you in." I took a breath. "And, dammit, it was about me, too, about choosing something for myself for once."

His eyes locked on mine, something both fierce and vulnerable behind the hazel. "You make it sound like I did something noble, Red. Like I earned that."

"You *did*," I said, without hesitation. "You don't try to own me. You don't try to fix me. You've never asked me to be less, or different. You stood by me, bounty, danger, fucked-up magic and all. I wanted my first time to be something, to be with someone, I chose for *me*. Not because I thought I was supposed to. I chose you because I wanted you."

He made a sound, something between a laugh and a curse. "Jesus. You're gonna kill me."

I smiled faintly, brushing my knuckles down his cheek. "Not planning on it." I dropped the blanket I'd wrapped around me, the corner of my mouth tilting up at the instant, unbidden heat in his eyes. I pulled him the rest of the way to sitting and climbed over him, knees on each side of his lean hips. His hands went to my waist, unthinking, and I cupped his cheeks in my hands. "The way you touched me...the way you made me feel?" I brushed my lips against his. "It was perfect."

His hands were gentle now, reverent. "When this is over," he said, "I'm going to date the absolute *hell* out of you."

That startled a laugh out of me.

"I mean it." His thumb traced slow circles against my hip. "Dinners. Dancing. Flowers for no reason. You deserve to be wooed, Serena. Not just fought for. You deserve to be loved."

There was nothing left to do but kiss him, so I did.

We couldn't stay.

With the bounty on my head, and the name Selene ap Myrddin hanging off me like a warning siren, every second above ground was a risk. There were no vehicles we could trust, no safe transit. No hovercabs or shadowrunners that wouldn't sell me out halfway through the route.

So we walked.

Noctis's underbelly was colder than I remembered, the kind of cold that settled in your bones and made your thoughts feel slow. Feral, like the city itself wanted to root around in your mind and pull out your worst fears to keep you company. The tunnels were wrong, etched with symbols that curled away when I looked at them, with floors that sloped toward unseen abysses. One hallway was filled with hanging lanterns that didn't cast light so much as remember it, their glow flickering with echoes of moments that didn't belong to us. I didn't ask. Gabriel didn't explain.

We passed a stairwell I knew hadn't been there when I left Noctis the first time. I stared a second too long, heart stuttering in my chest, because I remembered the arch beside it. I'd passed it a million times, back when I was escorted by my father's minions "for my own safety" through the city. It was rotted through now, the stairs cracked like broken teeth, the brass nameplate gone green with corrosion.

Riot caught my hesitation and leaned against my leg, solid and warm. Still not looking at me.

"You're really committing to this silent treatment, huh?"

He huffed, more air than bark. Still no eye contact.

"Look, I get it. You're scandalized. I'm not apologizing for having one night of something good in the middle of this shit show. And you could have gone in the kitchen."

His ears flicked back. I swear I caught the faintest glimmer of a snort.

"I'm going to buy you a sweater that says *Chaperone of the Year*."

"Make it a full set," Gabriel called back without turning. "He can match my *Perpetually Feral Mercenary* jacket."

Riot sneezed like we were both idiots, and trotted ahead, ears flicking in universal dog for *you disgust me.*

But he stayed close. Always close, even if he did level me with an atomic level side eye every chance he got.

Gabriel knew the way, navigating Noctis's underground through a network of passages not on any map, tunnels etched in stone that whispered old stories, routes only spoken of in curses or bribes. We passed abandoned sanctuaries built for gods long forgotten, broken staircases where time fractured at the edges, and hallways lined with runes too old to translate.

"You're sure Elaris will help?" I asked as we descended a narrow, spiraling staircase carved into a single monolithic slab.

"She'll help," Gabriel said. "But she never does anything for free."

"Welcome to Noctis," I sighed. "Business as usual."

The Observatory was exactly where I didn't expect it to be, hidden in the hollow heart of an ancient library that didn't exist anymore. Suspended in a moment between moments, it shimmered with quiet power, the air humming with the weight of what might have been.

Elaris stood at its center.

She looked like the edge of a blade that had never been dulled: tall, ethereal, her robes caught in currents of wind that no one else felt. Her silver hair was braided around her head, her eyes older than the rules of this place. When she looked at me, she didn't see Serena Morrigan.

She saw every version of me that never made it out alive.

"Selene ap Myrddin," she said, her voice like a cathedral bell, "and Gabriel Cade, you have brought your tether."

Gabriel's jaw tensed. "My what?"

"Thread-bound," Elaris said, lightly, as if that explained everything. "The Weave doesn't waste time with accidents. Your threads were tied long before you met."

I stared. "Serena Morrigan, and what does that mean?"

"As you like, Serena," she said. "It means the world remembers what you haven't learned yet," Elaris replied. "The Weave is not fate as you reckon fate. It is not prophecy. It does not choose." Her eyes met mine, calm and terrifying. "It *remembers*. That is why Noctis remembers, because the Weave is the living algorithm of time, bloodlines, and consequences. It is a loom where identity and possibility are the threads. Every decision, every lie, every name spoken in blood. It holds the record of every possibility and every eventuality. When enough threads tangle or tear, the pattern distorts."

My throat felt dry. "And then what?"

"Then the Weave tries to correct itself."

She turned away, already done with the moment, but the words lingered like a hook set deep. I'd felt it, that pull. I'd tried not to think about it, but I'd felt it. Not just to Gabriel, but to something larger. Older.

Riot growled, low and wary. Gabriel's hand hovered just off his weapon. No one moved.

"You've come for your bounty," she said, breaking the stalemate. "To lift it."

"Yes." There was no reason to beat around the bush.

"What will you offer in return?"

I pulled a tiny vial from my coat. Inside, possibility shimmered like molten silver. Not a memory. Not a soul. A future.

"A possibility," I said. "Of my own choosing."

She stepped forward, slow and elegant, and reached for it, her fingers just a hair too long to be human, the nails sharp. I hesitated, just long enough to feel the gravity of it. Then I uncorked it.

The moment the seal broke, the air changed.

A breeze that wasn't wind swept through the Observatory, rustling my coat, stirring the ends of my hair. The silver mist slipped from the vial moving like smoke with purpose, and I felt it pass *through* me, not just away from me. The magic brushed against something inside me—and for a breath, I *knew* what I was giving up.

Not a memory. Not a soul.

A life.

A version of me who never crossed paths with Gabriel Cade. A version who stayed hidden. Who never came to Noctis. Who never risked anything and who never loved anyone. That girl was safe. Untouched. Alone.

She would never exist now.

It didn't feel like a loss. It felt like burning a bridge I never wanted to cross.

The silver wrapped itself around Elaris's fingers, and when it disappeared, I felt something lift off my skin. The weight of the bounty, the echo of my name in every whispering shadow; it peeled away like dead skin.

And still, I kept my eyes on the space the possibility had vacated. Not in mourning, but in defiance. I had chosen this version. The one who would walk into hell for the man whose hand was still wrapped around mine.

I didn't regret it for a second.

The moment it touched her skin, her eyes fluttered shut. The silver mist coiled into her palm, vanishing like breath on glass.

When she opened her eyes again, something in her was brighter.

"It is done," she said.

The curse of my name, of what I might become, no longer echoed through Noctis with the same hunger.

"Cade, if I may have a moment?" Elaris's soft voice startled me, and I looked at her, then back at Gabriel. He gave my hand a squeeze and then walked off a few paces. They stood, with Elaris's back to me; I couldn't hear what she said, but I didn't miss the sharp way his eyes cut to me, then back to her. He nodded, then returned, and reached for my hand.

We turned to leave, but Elaris spoke one last time. "Be careful, Daughter of Ruin. A price paid in possibility always leaves a scar."

I heard it then. Elaris's words echoed behind us, but something else followed. Not a sound, but a sensation, like a shift in the air, a page turning in a book.

Correction pending. This version is unstable.

The words weren't angry, just—inevitable.

I froze. Riot did, too. Gabriel glanced at me, tension snapping like a drawn wire.

"What is it?" he asked.

I didn't answer. I couldn't explain it.

But the Voice wasn't gone. It had simply stepped back, waiting. Watching. I'd changed something, given up a future the Weave remembered, and now it was recalculating.

As we left the Observatory, I could feel her words settling into my bones. The weight of the bounty had been lifted, but something else had taken its place. A question. A warning.

Gabriel's hand was tight around mine, his thumb absently stroking my knuckles as we navigated back through the impossible architecture of Noctis. He hadn't said a word about what Elaris has told him, and I couldn't bring myself to ask. Not yet.

"What did you give her?" he finally asked as we emerged into a narrow alley where the buildings leaned so close they nearly touched overhead. They formed a jagged wound of sky above us. "What possibility?"

I didn't look at him. "One where I never came out of hiding."

Gabriel didn't move.

Just stared at me like he'd never seen me before. His hand tightened around mine, not hard, but with a kind of barely leashed tension that vibrated through every inch of him.

"You gave that up," he said, voice low and wrecked. "You gave up the one future where you were safe. Where you *survived* this. Where they never got near enough to ruin you. Serena, *why*?"

My heart stumbled. "Because in that possibility, I never met you."

His jaw worked, and when he finally looked at me, his eyes were wild and hurting. "I've spent my whole life trying not to want things I couldn't protect. And now you...you just..."

His free hand raked through his hair, rough and frustrated. "I've been trying to go slow. Trying to keep this thing from swallowing us whole, because it can. Because it already is. And here you go, giving up a version of yourself that was safe, because you never knew me in it?"

"That version was empty," I whispered. "I didn't want to be her. I never want to be her. I want this. I want you."

He exhaled shakily, like he couldn't hold it back anymore. "When this is over," he said, "I'm going to make damn sure you know what this means."

"What does it mean?"

His eyes burned. "It means I'm already yours. And I'm fucking terrified of how fast you became mine."

"I'd do it again. That possibility doesn't exist anymore. It can't." I smiled. "That's not a possibility I ever want."

He pulled me against him, his mouth finding mine with a desperate hunger that made my knees threaten to give out. I wrapped my arms around his neck and let him tell me without words what it meant to him.

We made it three levels deep into the tunnels before it hit me.

The thought came out of nowhere, a remembrance of last night that should have brought heat but dumped a bucket of ice water down my spine instead.

We hadn't used protection.

I stopped walking.

Gabriel did too. He turned to face me just as my stomach dropped, brows furrowed.

"We didn't..." I gestured vaguely, helplessly. "Last night. We didn't use anything."

He blinked once, then went completely still. "Fuck."

"Yeah."

"Are you...?"

"I mean, I have a contraceptive implant," I blurted. "It's good for another three years, but I didn't think about it in the moment."

He exhaled, some of the tension leaving his shoulders. "Okay. Okay. That's good. That's...fuck."

Riot gave us both an exasperated 'I told you it was a bad idea' look from ahead, then resumed sulking two steps ahead of us.

"I'm sorry," Gabriel said, rubbing a hand down his face. "I should've stopped. Thought it through."

"I didn't exactly hit the brakes either."

He glanced sideways at me. "For the record, I'm clean. I haven't been with anyone since my last test, which was a long time ago, and I always use protection." He reached up, brushed a hair out of my face. "Except with you. I didn't even think about it with you. You seem to be the exception to a lot of my rules."

That stopped me.

"You haven't? Been with anyone in a while, I mean?" It was pathetic how much that meant to me.

He shook his head. "No."

I studied him. "Why?"

He gave a quiet, almost embarrassed smile and dropped his hand to take mine. "I'm picky."

Behind us, Riot groaned. Loudly.

Gabriel didn't even turn. "We get it, fuzzball. You're morally outraged."

Riot sneezed in his direction and kept walking, ears flattening with exquisite disdain.

I muttered, "I think he preferred it when we were repressed."

"He liked it better when he was the only one in your bed."

"He was never in my bed. He got the foot of it."

Gabriel's smile tilted. "He was close enough."

"Jealous?"

"Fuck yes."

I laughed, the sound surprised out of me. It lingered in the tunnel like a dare, like hope. It felt dangerously close to joy, and in Noctis, that was as rare as mercy.

"I have a question," he said. "You gave Elaris a possibility, but back at the Veil Market, you gave Mira Dusk a memory. What, exactly, did you give her?"

I giggled. "Oh, it was a good one. She got the lovely, lovely memory of my bout with food poisoning from dodgy sushi."

He stopped, and the look on his face was priceless. "Morrigan, I think I might love you."

That was good, because I was pretty sure I was falling for him, too.

"Soooo....tit for tat time," I continued, as he turned and led us into what passed for a Main Street in this district of Noctis, a twisting thoroughfare where gravity seemed optional and vendors hawked impossible wares. "What did Elaris say to you?"

The tightening of his shoulders was small, but I saw it. He kept his eyes forward, his voice low. "That you're more valuable than either of us realize, and that there are people who have known exactly how valuable for far longer than we both realized."

"Fantastic," I muttered. "Yet another cryptic warning. My favorite."

Gabriel raised my hand, kissing my knuckles. "She also said I should guard you with my life. Not that I needed the reminder."

My lips twitched upwards. "So overprotective."

"So worth protecting," he countered, and the intensity in his eyes made my breath catch.

"We need to regroup," he said, after we'd worked our way deeper into the city. "Somewhere off the grid."

"I might know a place," I said, thinking of the tiny bolt-hole I'd discovered when I made my escape. "It's not much, but it's warded."

Gabriel raised an eyebrow. "You've been holding out on me, Red."

"A girl's gotta have her secrets," I replied with a smirk, "even from devastatingly handsome mercenaries."

"Especially from them," he agreed, a smile flirting with his lips.

The bolt-hole made his original safe house look like the Ritz; it boasted a closet with a sink and toilet, a mattress on the floor, and a rickety table with a single chair. I think it had once been a maintenance room of some sort, but since nobody ever actually did city maintenance, it had become this. I'd found it my third week running, when I was still running blind and terrified.

The wards, though, those were something else entirely.

"Not bad, Morrigan. Defensible. One entrance. Decent sight lines. And the wards, these are military grade," Gabriel murmured, running his fingers along the silvery runes etched into the doorframe. They flickered beneath his touch. "Where did you learn to cast these?"

I shrugged. "You'd be surprised what you can learn when you have to." I nodded at the bathroom. 'And it has running water." I thought for a moment. "Sort of. It's blue on Tuesdays."

Riot gave the space a cursory sniff, then settled down near the door, circling three times before settling with his back pointedly turned toward us. It was obviously the canine equivalent of sticking his fingers in his ears and humming.

"Still mad," Gabriel noted.

"He'll get over it." I dropped my bag. "Eventually."

Gabriel did a sweep of the space anyway, moving with that practiced, methodical calm that had to have come from spending years in war zones and worse. He tested the door, checked the corners, looked for magic that didn't belong. When he was satisfied, he finally relaxed; not all the way, but enough that the tension between his shoulders eased.

Riot decided he needed to check things next and sniffed the perimeter, snorting at the mattress before flopping down beside it with a sigh that carried a thesis-level dissertation of judgment. I dropped my pack and crouched beside him anyway, brushing a hand through his fur.

"You're still mad at me," I murmured.

He didn't look at me.

"But you're here. So I'm taking that as progress."

His tail gave the faintest twitch. A truce.

Gabriel was watching us when I stood. He arched a brow. "He always like this?"

"Only when I ruin his worldview."

He smiled, faint but real, and turned back to the table. He pulled out a chair, glanced at it, then stayed standing instead, laying out a tiny map he'd produced from one of his many inner pockets. A mechanical pencil followed. A military man's habits: precise, prepared, and quietly competent.

"Why do I feel like you're about to build a war plan with that tourist map of Noctis?" I asked.

"Because I am?"

I laughed softly, moving into the room. And in that moment, seeing him in the glow of too-bright runes and dust-heavy air, something in my chest loosened.

I sat down on the mattress, ignoring the puff of dust that accompanied the action, and pulled my boots off. "So, I can move around Noctis again, sort of, as long as nobody looks too close. We still need to find the Seer, though, and we have no idea where to begin to do that."

"Not exactly true," Gabriel said, folding his long form into the single chair. "Elaris gave me that piece of information. She owed me for a job I completed for her years ago. Not enough to buy you free of the bounty, but enough to get that tidbit of information." He stretched his legs out and sighed. "The Hollow Vein took over the old subway station near the eastern edge of the city, at Sanguine and 42nd, according to Elaris. They've been keeping the Seer...his name is Silas, by the way...there for weeks, forcing visions from him."

"Sanguine and 42nd is deep in Bone Lord territory. How'd the Hollow Vein set up shop there? At least, how did they do it without causing the sort of turf war that would set this entire city on fire? While we're at it, how in the hell do you force a vision from a seer?" I asked, frowning, rummaging in my bag for some of the MREs I'd shoved in there. God, I could still taste that steak from last night.

"Painfully," Gabriel rumbled. "And as far as the turf war, that's the other interesting part. They've got protection from someone higher up the food chain, someone who's got the Bone Lords looking the other way."

"So, we're going to break into the stronghold of the cult that wants to use me to unmake this whole city, a stronghold that happens to sit right in the middle of the territory of the *other* faction that wants me, rescue the Seer they've been torturing, find out everything he knows about, well, everything, and somehow get out alive?"

"That's the plan."

"It's a terrible plan. Can we make a new plan? Maybe one that involves running away? Maybe to someplace warm, with those fruity drinks with the little umbrellas in? I've never had those."

Gabriel laughed, the sound warm and rich in the tiny space. "We could, but they'd find us eventually. And they'd probably hurt a lot of people looking."

I sighed, closing my eyes. "I know. I just...wanted to pretend for a minute."

The chair creaked as he got up and crossed to me, crouching down to my level. His hand cupped my cheek, thumb brushing my skin. "I know it's a lot, but we've got something they don't have."

I opened my eyes. "What's that?"

"Me," he said simply. "And you. Together."

The faith in his voice made something in my chest tight. I leaned into his touch, savoring it.

"And the world's most judgmental dog," I added.

Riot's ears twitched, but he maintained his stalwart protest, and Gabriel's smile turned wicked.

"Think we could scandalize him further?" he murmured, sliding his hand into the hair at the nape of my neck and tugging to tilt my face up farther.

"Probably," I whispered, a frisson of heat sliding up my spine. "Let's see."

Gabriel let me push him down, his smile, equal parts cocky and dazed, curling at the corner of his mouth as his back hit the thin blanket. He didn't try to flip us or take control. Instead, he just gave the control to me.

My fingers unbuttoned his shirt, tasting each bit of skin I uncovered, and his breath caught. His hands hovered at my hips, light and reverent, like I was something holy. When I made my way back up to kiss his throat, slow and possessive, he groaned my name like it broke something in him. His hands worked to get me bare, and then returned to my hips: guiding, not controlling, letting me move on him as I wanted.

He was so reserved everywhere else, always, but under me? For me?

He was open. Bare. Beautiful.

When I moved lower, kissed lower, took more, his hands gripped the sheet like it was the only thing anchoring him to reality.

"*Bozhe moi*," he whispered, voice wrecked. "*Malen'kaya zvezda ... ty moya ...*"

God, I loved it when he spoke Russian, when the words slipped past his lips without translation, like his body forgot

212

how to lie. Every time he hit that edge, every time I gave him something he couldn't name, the language just spilled out of him. I hoarded every syllable like treasure, even though I didn't understand a word.

No one else had ever seen him like this; I knew this for certain. No one else had ever had this of him. They'd shared his body, but he was giving me so much more. By the time he finally shuddered beneath me, eyes locked on mine like I was the only thing in his world, I was shaking too.

He looked wrecked, and God, he was gorgeous, hair mussed, lips parted, chest heaving. I curled up against his side as his breathing slowed, his arm tucking around me like instinct.

Riot made a noise from his corner like a scandalized librarian at a smut convention.

I didn't even look. "He's going to need therapy."

"He's going to need a new religion," Gabriel muttered sleepily, voice slurred from bliss. "You're going to kill me."

"Not yet," I whispered, kissing the pulse at his throat. "But maybe someday."

He huffed a soft laugh, and then sleep claimed him.

I stayed awake a long time before I joined him.

CHAPTER TWELVE

SOME MONSTERS WEAR
FRIENDLY FACES

Gabriel

THE QUIET PRESSED IN from the corners of the bolt-hole, crept between the cracks in the wards and wound itself into the tight coil of muscle between my shoulders. The kind of silence that came before something broke. I was waiting for that break.

I counted the exits. Two: one through the front, shielded with enough glyphs to hold back a small army, and one through the crawlspace vent behind the sink. That one might buy us fifteen seconds if we needed to vanish. My weapons were laid out beside the mattress. My blade. Two pistols. One spare magazine. One fallback charm that wouldn't work if we were cursed, which, let's be honest, we probably were.

Riot was near the door, where he had retreated in theatrical protest, his dramatic sign echoing across the room before he'd thrown himself down with a huff that said 'this is why we can't have nice things'. Alert but pretending not to be, his chin on his paws, ears angled toward the hallway. He wasn't snoring. That was how I knew he was still listening.

I should've still been asleep; she'd pulled my soul out with nothing but her hands and mouth and the fire that lived just under her skin. It should have rendered me damn near unconscious.

But the kind of sleep I needed, the bone-deep, dreamless kind that might let me forget the number of lives I'd taken, or the way Serena had gone still under my hands when Voss dropped to her knees? That didn't exist for me right now. It felt like too much of a luxury when the woman in my arms had sacrificed a part of herself again for the sake of getting us one step ahead in a game that kept changing the rules. Silence always left room for ghosts, and there were a ton jostling for space in my head. So, I did what I always did when silence closed in and memory came knocking.

I took inventory.

I waited for the enemy.

And I kept my damn eyes open.

Serena slept curled into me like she'd always belonged there. She had tucked her head under my chin, her breath steady against my chest. One arm splayed across my stomach. I tightened my arm around her, just slightly. She didn't wake, only exhaled deeper and shifted closer, chasing my warmth like she knew it was hers.

God, I was so gone for her.

I'd never met anyone like her, someone who could look at a nightmare and smile like she had fangs of her own. Someone who stood at the center of the chaos with fire in her bones and still found the strength to care. To choose mercy.

To choose me.

I pressed a kiss to her hair, inhaling the wild mix of ozone, cinnamon, and starlight clinging to her. There was something elemental about her, like holding a storm, like chaos in a bottle. Something you could never own, only be lucky enough to survive. But right now, with her body tangled with mine and her breath ghosting over my skin? She didn't feel like a storm.

She felt like home, and that was the problem.

Because Elaris hadn't just told us to be careful; she'd warned us that someone close was helping the ones chasing us. Not just watching, but feeding them. That kind of betrayal wasn't theoretical anymore. It was tactical.

From the moment we entered Noctis, someone had been anticipating our every move. One ambush? Bad luck. Two? A grim coincidence. But three, four, five? That was coordination. We hadn't even lasted fifteen minutes in Seattle before the Collectors descended. No tracking glyphs, no scrying residue. They'd just... known.

Mira Dusk had hinted eyes were already on us, that the bounty had made the rounds before we even stepped through the gate. The Bone Lords, the Hollow Vein, factions that'd slit each other's throats on principle, were moving in sync like they'd rehearsed it.

That wasn't luck.

That was intel. Precise and terrifyingly accurate, and the more I turned it over in my mind, the more one name kept rising to the surface like oil slicking over water.

I started building the map in my head. Not the kind with roads and coordinates, but the kind built from patterns. Triggers. Chains of consequence.

Seattle: We hadn't been in that bar fifteen minutes before the Collectors showed up. Not stalkers, not scavengers. Collectors. The kind you don't send unless you already know what you're going to find. No scrying wards on the building. No tracking glyphs on Serena; Riot would've smelled them. So how the fuck did they know where to be?

Veil Market: Mira Dusk said they were already watching, that the price on Serena's head was already in circulation. The Bone Lords and the Hollow Vein both knew her face, her name, and enough of her movements to beat us to half our destinations.

The Menagerie: The Vesper might've been a wildcard, but the security? It wasn't random. We had triggered the defenses at a vault we only found because of a person that very, very few people had reason to connect to Serena. One person, in fact.

Post-Vault: Even the tunnel Elaris gave us, something deep, warded, and older than anything in Noctis, had signs of activity. Someone had been there. Recently. Dust had been disturbed, like someone had been through very recently, and there was a residual shimmer. A fucking fallback egress shouldn't have shown signs of recent activity.

The safe houses: They weren't compromised, not technically, but we hadn't stayed in one longer than 24 hours because I couldn't shake the feeling something was off. Like the air was too still, like someone was waiting just outside the frame. I'd told myself it was paranoia, but some old survival instinct knew not to trust them. Not anymore. The only people who even knew which safe houses I still had in rotation?

Me and Moshi.

It was too much. Too many points on the map. Too much precision.

Not coincidence.

Deliberate. Patterned. Controlled.

And it had all started with that first meeting.

Moshi had brokered it. Quietly. Discreetly. One name, one location, no preamble. Just a nod. A tilt of his head. A single line: *"You'll want to hear what she has to say."* At the time, it felt like a favor. Like Moshi was doing what he always did, positioning people like chess pieces on a board only he could see. No questions. No conditions.

But it wasn't until after Elaris said *someone close was feeding them* that the switch flipped, and I started retracing every step. Once I did? The convenience of that first meeting with Serena, and how fast the Bone Lords moved in after it, suddenly looked a hell of a lot less like strategy and a lot more like the result of surveillance.

Moshi hadn't just known *of* her. He knew who she was. Who she'd been. Who she could become. *Where she was.* If he'd passed her name along knowing all of that, knowing what the Hollow Vein and the Bone Lords wanted from her, then this wasn't just betrayal. This was orchestration.

The worst part was that I hadn't seen it sooner.

I wanted to believe he was still the man who walked me out of that crater in Berwick, the man who'd held the line while I tried not to bleed out and refused to let me die just because the mission had gone south.

The hell of it all was, this city didn't make you into a monster all at once. It did it slowly. One compromise at a time.

Maybe the man who helped Serena disappear, who gave her a new name, a new life, who helped her rebuild after she clawed her way out of her father's legacy, had believed he was doing the right thing.

But the man selling her out to the Hollow Vein? The Bone Lords? The ones who wanted to cage her, use her, bleed her dry until she wasn't even a person anymore?

That man wasn't her friend. That man wasn't my ally.

And if he thought he could hide behind old debts and plausible deniability, he hadn't been paying attention to who the fuck I was.

The thought twisted something in my chest. I wanted to believe otherwise. I wanted to believe that the man who first sent me after Serena had done it because he knew I could keep her safe—not because he knew so well how I operated that it was effectively leading her right out into the open.

But the breadcrumbs were too perfect.

He knew how the city worked. He knew every one of my safe houses, every shadow, every gate that led in and out. He'd built a reputation on discretion, on silence, on playing all the sides just enough to never fall to any of them.

Serena had barely made it through the doors of Noctis before they were on us. Contracts had circulated faster than gossip. Collectors had been sent to retrieve her like she was already theirs. The Hollow Vein, the Bone Lords—factions that couldn't agree on the shape of the sky were suddenly working in sync, moving like they knew her route.

Someone was feeding them.

And who else knew?

Who else had the maps, the contacts, the fucking *trust*?

Fuck.

I closed my eyes and let the scenario play out.

I walk into one of the old meeting dens in Noctis. Moshi's already there. He smiles like he always does: charming, unreadable, too smooth by half. He offers a drink. Something expensive. He says, "Let's not be hasty, Gabriel." And then?

I kill him.

That's how it always ends in my head. Doesn't matter if he confesses, deflects, or tries to spin it like he'd been offering her protection. Doesn't matter if he tells me it was never about her, never personal, just another deal on another day. The ending is always the same.

Blood and silence.

Moshi wasn't a soldier. Wasn't an operative. He didn't get his hands dirty unless he had to, and even then, only long enough to wash them with someone else's ruin. The first time I met him, I was deep in a black op the Pentagon swore didn't exist, one that crossed the Veil into territory that should've been a myth. And Moshi? He was the civilian asset. The name passed to me through encrypted channels, the one who could "open doors and arrange safe passage," which was code for: *he knows how to get you into Noctis without dying.*

I never asked how the U.S. government knew about him. Never asked how many times they'd used him before. I was a weapon back then. Point me at the target, pull the trigger. Leave the questions for someone else.

But Moshi always knew more than he let on.

And now? Now he knew Serena's every shadow. Every fear. Every crack in the armor she'd spent years building, because he'd helped build it. He'd held her hand as she became someone new. What if that had been a setup all along?

What if the whole thing was just another carefully placed piece on his board, or an ace up his sleeve? Had Serena been a move in his long game this whole time?

I wasn't sure which would be worse: that she never saw it coming.

Or that I didn't.

I buried my hand in Serena's hair, grounding myself in the feel of her, ignoring the bile rising in my throat. I didn't want to believe it. She didn't deserve to believe it.

He'd been her anchor once. The first hand that helped her build a new identity after she fled, the one she trusted when she had no one else. If I told her what I suspected, that the man who'd once helped her become Serena might also be the one selling Selene out to the highest bidder? It would break something in her.

She wouldn't let it show. Not to me, not to Riot, not to anyone.

I'd see it in the quiet spaces, though. In the way she'd go still when the world wasn't looking. I'd see it in the way she'd start to question every step that led her here. I wasn't sure she could afford that fracture. Not now, not with everything that was coming.

I brushed my thumb over the freckle just under her jaw, marveling, like I always did, that someone like her could carry so much power, so much pain, and still curl herself into the arms of a man like me and hand me her trust.

God, she *trusted* me.

And I hadn't earned it. Not yet. But I would.

Because whether she wanted to admit it or not, she wasn't alone anymore. She wasn't a tool. She wasn't a keystone. She wasn't a war waiting to happen.

She was mine. My grip on her tightened, just for a heartbeat, and she made a soft noise, nuzzling into my throat, and my breath caught. I closed my eyes, because now I had to be the one to put the blade in her back. If Moshi had betrayed her, if he'd carved her open and sold the pieces one by one, I couldn't keep that from her. Not even to protect her.

But god, it wouldn't just hurt her, it would damage her.

Moshi wasn't just a friend. He was the one who helped her stop being Selene. The one who gave her a name that didn't come with blood in its mouth. The one who taught her how to move without flinching, how to build a life out of ashes. If he'd sold her out? It wouldn't be anger that wrecked her.

It would be *doubt*.

Not in him. In herself. In the choices that led her here, in the people she'd let in.

And if she started questioning that?

She'd start questioning *me*.

I could take the hit if she turned away from me, but I wasn't sure she could afford to stop trusting herself. Not with the whole damn city trying to unravel her from the inside out.

I'd tell her. I had to tell her. Soon.

But not tonight. Tonight she got a few hours of rest. A taste of security. My arms. She'd earned that.

And for once in my fucked-up life, maybe I'd earned her, too.

If Moshi had betrayed her, if he'd sold her out to the Bone Lords or the Hollow Vein, I'd find out. And I'd deal with it.

Quietly. Permanently.

But for now?

I kissed her temple, whispered the words I didn't quite know how to say out loud to her yet. *You're safe. I've got you. I'm not going anywhere.*

I wouldn't stop until every goddamn enemy in this city had learned that the price of touching her was what I'd do to them.

CHAPTER THIRTEEN

WOW. BETRAYAL. GROUNDBREAKING.

Serena

IN NOCTIS, SILENCE WASN'T peace, it was pressure. It means something had gone still that shouldn't have, and now the city was waiting to see if you noticed.

I noticed.

Gabriel sat in the lone chair near the door, cleaning a knife he hadn't used, because his hands needed something to do. Riot was curled against the wall, pretending not to listen while absolutely listening. Me? I was lying on the mattress, head on my pack, staring at the ceiling like it owed me an explanation.

It didn't give one.

"Say it," I muttered.

Gabriel didn't look up. "Say what?"

"Whatever's been pacing the inside of your skull for the past hour. You're chewing on something; I can hear your mental teeth grinding."

He paused just long enough to make me uncomfortable. "I don't think you're going to like it," he said, sheathing the knife with a finality.

"Tell me how that's different from basically anything else," I retorted.

Gabriel sighed, leaning forward to rest his elbows on his legs. "Every time we move, they're waiting. Everywhere I take you, they're not far behind. The Collectors showed up when you'd only been in that bar in Seattle for 15 minutes. Maybe less." His heel tapped, the only outward sign of his agitation. "Someone's feeding them information. Someone who knows where we're going before we get there." He chewed on his lower lip for a second, then continued, "This is more than Seer intel."

I sat up slowly. "Are you saying what I think you're saying?" A name surfaced in my mind before he even answered, and I hated it. There had to be another explanation. Didn't there?

"That someone's selling you out? Yeah, Red, I am." His eyes met mine, hard and sharp as flint. "And I've got a damn good idea who it is."

"Moshi." The name left my lips like a curse, not a question.

Gabriel nodded once, the motion tight and controlled. "He's the only constant, Serena. The only one who knows how I work, where I'd go, where *you'd* go."

I wanted to argue, wanted to tell him he was wrong. Moshi had helped me bury Selene ap Myrddin, had helped me build a new life from the ashes of my old one. Now? Now I wondered if he'd handed out shovels to everyone else, too.

"I need proof." I looked at my hands. "I won't act on suspicion alone. He was there for me, Gabriel," I said, and I hated how my voice broke. "He was there for me when I was alone and broken and terrified. I won't—I *can't*—confront him unless I have proof." I looked at him, silently begging him to give me an alternative, any alternative. "He was my only friend."

Even as I said it, I could feel memories shifting in my mind. Moments I'd trusted Moshi suddenly looked...wrong. Different. Music remembered in the wrong key.

Gabriel rose from the chair and crossed the room, dropping to the mattress next to me. "There's someone who might know. An old contact of Moshi's that runs a contract den in the Glass District, from before he went respectable. Man named Thorn. He and Moshi have history."

"What kind of history?"

He snorted. "The kind that leaves scars. He owes me a favor, and he hates Moshi more than he hates most people. If Moshi has been selling information, he'll know. And?" Here Gabriel gave a predatory little smile. "Moshi has no idea I know him, let alone have done business with him."

Three hours later, we were moving through the Glass District, where reality refracted like light through a cracked prism.

The buildings here were impossibly tall, their surfaces mirrored or transparent, depending on the angle and the moment. Reflections walked beside us that were a half step too slow, a gesture too exaggerated, or had eyes that followed us independently of their owners.

"Don't look at them directly," Gabriel murmured, his hand at the small of my back. "The reflections get ideas."

"I know the Glass District, Gabriel," I chided, though I appreciated his concern, his protectiveness, far more than I wanted to admit.

"Yeah, but the Glass District doesn't know you," he countered. "Not as you are now." He had a point.

"You bring me to the nicest places," I muttered, and Gabriel laughed softly, leaning down to brush a kiss against my temple. "When this is over, Red, I promise you, I'll take you to that beach with the fruity drinks."

"The ones with the little umbrellas in?" I asked.

"The ones with the little umbrellas in."

We wound our way through the twisting streets, the pavement shimmering like liquid glass beneath our feet. Navigation in the Glass District was less about knowing where you were going and more about knowing what you were looking for. Landmarks were unreliable, and the streets rearranged themselves when you blinked.

"Thorn's place should be just ahead," Gabriel said, nodding toward what looked like a cracked mirror standing alone in the middle of an intersection. "The Contract Den of the Broken Reflection."

"Subtle," I quipped.

As we approached, the mirror seemed to grow, expanding until it was the size of a doorway. Our reflections stared back at us, but they weren't right. My hair moved in a nonexistent breeze, Gabriel's reflection had eyes that were bottomless white, and Riot glowed with a cold, blue light. Gabriel reached out and tapped a complex pattern on the glass. The surface rippled like water and then parted like a curtain. Beyond was darkness, broken by floating orbs of amber light. The three of us stepped through together.

A sign hung in the air before us, the letters constantly re-arranging themselves into different warnings: "Contracts bind more than words" followed by "No refunds for the foolish". The ceiling soared impossibly high, draped with crystalline chandeliers that caught the amber glow from the entry lights and scattered it in dizzying patterns across the walls. Dozens of small tables dotted the room, each occupied by a pair of people hunched over black parchment. Their whispers created a constant susurration like waves against a shore.

"Don't make eye contact with the scribes," Gabriel warned under his breath. "They're always looking for new clients."

A tall, rail-thin man with skin like polished turquoise approached us, his pristine suit a perfect match for the shadows that seemed to follow him. His hair was stark, snowy white, arranged in Marcel waves. "We don't offer services to walk-ins," he said, voice like gravel wrapped in velvet. "Appointments only."

Gabriel smiled, the expression not reaching his eyes. "Tell Thorn that Gabriel Cade is calling in his marker."

The man's mahogany eyes widened fractionally before his face settled back into practiced neutrality. "Wait here." He disappeared through a doorway that I was sure hadn't been there just seconds ago.

Minutes dragged by like hours, and the ambient whispers of deals being struck were a dissonant undertone around us. Riot pressed against my leg, his hackles raised.

"Easy," I murmured, running my fingers through his fur. Gabriel stood with deceptive casualness, but I knew better. His weight was balanced on the balls of his feet, his right hand hovering near the weapon at his belt.

"Cade." The voice came from everywhere and nowhere before a doorway shimmered into existence. A figure stepped through. "I thought I felt the temperature drop."

Thorn was not what I expected. He was short and round, with laugh lines around his eyes that didn't match the hardness in them. His skin was covered in what looked like tattoos, but they moved, shifting across his skin like ink in water. Most disturbing were his hands; the fingers were too long, too thin, tapering to points that looked sharp enough to draw blood.

"Thorn," Gabriel acknowledged with a nod. "Been a while."

"Not long enough for my taste." Thorn's gaze slid to me, and I felt the weight of his assessment like a physical pressure. "And what have we here? This isn't your usual type of companion, Cade."

His eyes raked over me. "You're smaller than I imagined. Quieter. I expected someone... sharper." His gaze flicked briefly to my throat. "She ever tell you how her father used to make his protégés bleed? Just to test how much shadow they could hold?"

I stiffened. Gabriel's hand twitched toward his weapon.

Thorn smiled wider. "Ah. There she is." His smile revealed teeth that were just slightly too sharp. "Yes, I know exactly who you are, Serena Morrigan. Or should I say..."

"Finish that sentence, and I'll finish you," Gabriel cut in, his voice dropping to that dangerous register that made even Riot's ears flatten.

Thorn laughed, a surprisingly melodious sound. "Still the same Cade, all teeth and loyalty." He gestured toward the shimmering doorway that he'd emerged from. "Come. We shouldn't discuss such delicate matters where the walls have ears. And mouths."

We followed him into a room that felt surprisingly normal; stuffed bookshelves, a rug beginning to border on threadbare, and a cart with a healthy selection of liquor. A black desk dominated the center of the room, a couple of leather armchairs in front of it.

"So," Thorn said, settling behind the desk. "You're in the market for information. What makes you think I'm inclined to give it?"

Gabriel sprawled in one of the armchairs, owning the space. "The fact that I saved your miserable life in Whispers Deep," he replied evenly. "The debt you swore you would faithfully repay."

"As you say. What's so important that you'd cash in your one favor?" Thorn asked, steepling those disturbing fingers.

"Moshi," Gabriel said simply.

Thorn went very still. "What about him?"

"I need to know if he's been selling information," Gabriel said without preamble. "Specifically, information about Serena."

Thorn's eyebrows rose. "My, my. Trouble in paradise?" His gaze shifted to me. "Moshi has always been rather protective of his investments. What makes you think he'd sell one of them out?"

"That's not a denial." My voice was flat.

Thorn leaned back in his chair, his tattoos rippling across his skin. "No, it's not. It's quite the opposite." His smile was shark cold. "Moshi has been selling information for decades. It's his primary business model, after all. The real question is who he's been selling it to, and what that information contains."

I felt something in my chest crack. "And do you have the answers to those questions, or are we wasting all our very valuable time?"

"Moshi has been enterprising lately. More than usual," he said, eyes never leaving mine. "The Bone Lords aren't the only ones he's been feeding information to."

I swallowed the bile that rose in my throat. "Who else?"

"The Hollow Vein." Thorn's voice was quiet, almost apologetic. "They've been particularly interested in your movements. Willing to pay premium rates."

The room seemed to tilt. Gabriel's hand found mine, steadying. Everything I feared, confirmed.

"You're lying," I said, but my voice lacked conviction.

"Oh, my dear, I wish I were. Moshi and I have our differences, but even I didn't think he'd sell out to those fanatics." He reached into his desk, pulled out a bottle and glass, and poured himself a drink that he downed in one gulp. "You want proof? I can do better than words."

He rose, those too-long fingers tapping a pattern on the wall behind his desk. A hidden compartment slid open, revealing a small safe. After working the combination, he withdrew a leather-bound ledger.

"Moshi keeps meticulous records," Thorn explained, placing it on the desk. "Don't ask how I came by this copy. I'm not in the mood to divulge." He opened it. "Every transaction, every scrap of information sold, and who bought it." He flipped through pages and pages that were filled with a script that I knew all too well. "Moshi may be a treacherous bastard, but his penmanship is impeccable."

Gabriel and I leaned forward. Each entry was carefully dated, the information categorized by value and buyer. My stomach twisted as I scanned the pages, finding entries that could only be about me.

Subject S, location update: Seattle address. Payment: 5,000 BL

Subject S, anticipated route through Noctis. Payment: 8,000 HV

Subject G, known safe houses and contacts, with relation to S. Payment: 3 artifacts from the Alabaster Collection.

Subject S, known power limitations disclosed to HV. Payment: future considerations

Each entry was a knife to my chest.

"He's been playing both sides," Gabriel muttered, his voice a dangerous growl. "Selling to the Bone Lords and the Hollow Vein simultaneously."

"Two factions," I said quietly, eyes scanning the entries. "One wants to sanctify me. The other wants to erase me. And it looks like Moshi sold tickets to both."

Gabriel's jaw clenched. "They're not working together. They're racing."

"And I'm the finish line," I murmured.

Thorn watched me with something approaching sympathy. "Moshi never could resist having both hands in the pot. It's why we parted ways." He cocked his head. "You think this is just a man being greedy," Thorn continued, swirling the liquid in his glass. "But it's deeper than that. Moshi doesn't just trade in secrets; he's part of the infrastructure. The factions trust him because the city does."

I frowned. "The city?"

"The Weave," Thorn said. "The way magic threads through Noctis? It recognizes Moshi. Not as a spellcaster, or a prophet, but as an interpreter. He can feel when a truth matters, and when a lie will bend a timeline. He doesn't just know what is said; he knows exactly what it is worth, and who will pay."

Gabriel went still.

"That's how he's lasted this long," Thorn added. "Not because he's feared. Because he's needed. You don't chisel out a keystone because you don't like the shape of it. You use it until it cracks." He looked at me, something unreadable passing through his expression. "Moshi is cracking. You just didn't hear it until now."

I traced my fingers over an entry from three days ago, reading it softly aloud. "Subject S, emotional vulnerabilities. Payment: 15,000 from HV." My throat closed.

He hadn't just sold my location. He'd sold my weaknesses, traded things I'd confided to him during late nights when I'd been at my most vulnerable. I'd thought I was talking to a friend, a mentor, a protector. Instead? I'd been giving ammunition to the very people who wanted to either use me or dissect me.

The room blurred, and I realized I was trembling with rage. The air around me crackled with energy, the lights flickering. Riot pressed against my legs.

Gabriel's hand squeezed mine, an anchor in my storm. "That son of a bitch," he breathed, rage matching mine simmering beneath his controlled exterior. "He's been with you every step of the way, Red. He helped build your new identity..."

"And then he sold it to the highest bidder." I laughed bitterly. "Or bidders, in this case." I looked up at Gabriel. "Every weakness, every hiding place, every damn thing I ever trusted him with." My magic sparked, sharp and uncontrolled. The lights flickered overhead, and the shadows shivered along the walls like they knew what was coming.

I couldn't breathe. I couldn't *think*.

Riot pressed harder against my leg, whining low, his fur bristling with static. Gabriel wrapped his hand over mine, warm and solid, an anchor in a sea that wanted to swallow me whole.

The fingers of Gabriel's other hand tightened around the ledger. For a second, I thought he might snap and throw it across the room. Instead, he slammed it shut with a violence that startled even Thorn. "We have what we came for," he said through gritted teeth, his voice barely tethered.

"Indeed you do," Thorn said, refilling his glass. "And now my debt to you is paid, Cade. I trust we won't be seeing each other again any time soon."

Gabriel laced his fingers with mine. "One more thing, Thorn. We were never here."

Thorn spread his hands and nodded in agreement. "I wouldn't dream of letting that little tidbit slip. The fallout from you confronting him will be worth more than anything he could offer me."

"You're quite the friend," I said dryly.

"I'm no one's friend, my dear." He raised his glass in a mocking toast. "Do give Moshi my regards when you discuss these matters with him."

As we left the Contract Den, the Glass District had shifted again, with the buildings having rearranged themselves like a deck of cards being shuffled. I barely noticed. My mind was consumed with Moshi's betrayal, each thought sharper than the last.

"I want to kill him," I said, my voice so calm it frightened me.

Gabriel didn't even try to talk me down. "I know."

"No, Gabriel, I don't think you do." I stopped walking. "He was the one who found me when I managed to break free from my father and run. He was the one who helped me build Serena Morrigan from the ashes of Selene ap Myrddin. Gave me the name Morrigan like it was a blessing, and all the while, he was already calculating how much I was worth to someone else. He held me while I cried, Gabriel. He told me I was safe."

My voice broke on the last word, and Gabriel pulled me against his chest, his arms wrapping around me like steel bands.

"All that time, he was selling pieces of me to the highest bidder," I whispered into his shirt. "Every secret. Every fear. Every weakness."

"We'll make him pay," Gabriel promised, his voice a rumble I could feel as much as hear. "But we need to be smart about this."

I pulled back, wiping angrily at my eyes. "How?"

"Moshi doesn't know we've found him out. That gives us a tactical advantage. He's expecting you to contact him eventually for help, not for a confrontation. "I fucking hate that he made you cry, *malen'kaya zvezda.*" He looked like he was going to say something else, but then stopped.

"I'm not crying because he hurt me. I'm crying because he'd convinced me I was safe." I sniffed. "What...what does that mean? What you called me."

"Little star," Gabriel murmured, his eyes softening. His accent slipped out, something that only happened when his emotions ran high. I'd heard it the night he made me his. "I've never seen you really cry before," he continued, his thumb brushing my cheek once more before he stepped back a fraction, giving me space to pull myself together without completely letting me go. "I want to kill him just for that," he said, and something warm unfurled in my chest, despite everything.

We stayed in that embrace a moment longer than we should have, given our surroundings. The Glass District wasn't a place for vulnerability.

"So what's the plan?" I asked, stepping back and squaring my shoulders. "We can't go after the Seer until we deal with the Moshi issue; we would 100% be walking into a trap. I'm not sure it's one we could get ourselves out of."

Gabriel's eyes tracked the movement of a reflection as it slid along a nearby window. "We approach this like any other op. Preparation, positioning, execution."

"It sounds so simple for something that will inevitably go tits up at the first opportunity," I muttered dryly, and he chuckled.

"Nothing simple about it, Red," he said, guiding me down a side street as a group of Glass Walkers—locals who'd spent so much time in the district that their skin had become reflective—drifted past. "But we do have one critical advantage."

"Which is?"

"Moshi thinks he's still the puppet master." Gabriel's smile was cold. "He has no idea his own strings are showing."

"We can't just walk up to his door and confront him? Can we?" At this point, I didn't know.

"Actually, that's exactly what we're going to do. But on our terms, not his. Moshi has a weakness; he can't resist playing the game. If you reach out and tell him you need his help, he'll bite."

"And then what?" I asked, my voice steadier.

"We make him pay." Gabriel's voice was so soft it was almost a caress. "For every bit of information, every secret, every moment of peace he stole from you."

I nodded, and let Gabriel lead us back to my bolt hole.

The journey back was tense; we took a different route, doubling back twice, cutting through alleyways that appeared at will. Whose will was anyone's guess. Gabriel was on even higher alert than usual, and couldn't blame him. Every shadow felt like it might be reporting back to Moshi.

Once we were back, Gabriel began methodically checking and cleaning his weapons while I paced. Riot tracking my movements with worried eyes.

"He knows all my weaknesses," I said suddenly, stopping mid stride. "Every single one."

Gabriel looked up from reassembling a sleek, black, rune-engraved pistol. "He doesn't know your ace in the hole, though."

"I have an ace in the hole?"

He set the pistol down and rose, crossing the small space to share mine, so close I could feel the heat off his body. "He doesn't know about us." The words hung in the air between us, charged with something neither of us had put a name to yet. "Not how it is now. He thinks I'm still just the hired gun." He reached up to tuck a loose curl behind my ear. "He has no idea what I'd do for you."

Something in my chest tightened. "What would you do for me, Gabriel?"

"Anything." He bent, lips brushing mine. "Everything."

My heart thudded against my ribs as we stood there, suspended in a moment that felt both inevitable and impossible. When he spoke again, his voice was soft. "He doesn't know what you're capable of when you're cornered." His hand cupped my cheek. "And he sure as hell doesn't know what I'm capable of when someone threatens what's mine."

"I'm falling for you, you know," I murmured. His smile was a light in the void.

"That's good to hear, Red, because I'm already there."

CHAPTER FOURTEEN

THANKS FOR THE KNIFE, IT LOOKS GREAT IN MY SPINE.

Gabriel

W E WALKED IN SILENCE, boots crunching over shattered glass and half-melted sigils. The air felt wrong, like it was waiting to inhale.

Serena didn't speak. She didn't need to. Her shoulders were squared, her jaw set. She moved like someone headed toward a reckoning, not sure if they'd walk out whole.

I'd seen this kind of silence before. War zones. Graveyards. Inside your own head, when the ghosts get loud.

"I ever tell you about the time I tried to summon a cab in Noctis?" I said, because I was terrible at letting tension go unpunched. It's a gift.

She glanced at me. "Pretty sure that's not a real sentence."

"It was a real mistake. Signal was dead, no taxis in sight. I figured I could rig a minor summoning. Something fast. Obedient. Maybe a nice spectral Vespa."

Serena raised a brow. "And?"

"I got a three-legged goat demon who wanted to discuss Nietzsche and eat my phone."

She blinked.

"Actually quoted *Thus Spake Zarathustra* while chewing through my charging port. Then he got bored and teleported into a poetry slam. I think he's still out there, winning awards."

Her lips twitched. Almost a smile. Almost.

"I was new to Noctis," I added. "Didn't know how the place worked yet. Thought I could brute-force it into something normal. Contain it."

She looked at me with an eyebrow raised. "You tried to contain a city that eats time?"

"I was optimistic," I said. "Or maybe just stupid."

We passed the remnants of a sigil burned deep into the pavement. Looked like it had once meant protection. Now it just whispered *too late.*

She glanced sideways. "Tell me how you came to speak Russian. Your name isn't exactly Slavic. You have an accent sometimes, too."

I shrugged. "My grandmother. Russian Orthodox, born outside of St. Petersburg, when it was still called Leningrad. The kind of woman who thought cold weather built character and prayer was a weapon."

"She's not wrong on that last one. Are you close?"

"She raised me. My mom vanished when I was seven. No notes, no goodbye. Just gone. My babushka never talked about it. Just handed me and my sister each a set of prayer beads and told me to learn how to throw a punch."

"She sounds terrifying."

"She was. She also made the best chicken soup I've ever had. Called it resurrection in a bowl."

Serena didn't laugh, but something in her expression shifted. A soft flicker, quickly gone, before she continued, "You have a sister?"

I sighed. "Had."

"I'm sorry. You learned to fight young," she said.

"Didn't have much choice."

Another beat of silence stretched between us. The wind shifted. The air ahead of us pulsed with the wrong kind of magic. Familiar.

"You don't have to come with me," she said.

"Not a chance in hell I'm letting you do this alone."

Her mouth twitched again. "Even after the goat demon incident?"

"I've summoned worse," I said. "I've survived worse."

"You really think you're ready for Moshi?"

"I'm not ready for how this might hurt you," I said honestly. "But I'm ready for whatever comes after."

She looked at me then, and I'm not ashamed to say I reveled in it. She didn't give me the hard, calculating stare she gave enemies, nor the guarded assessment she gave strangers. This was a look she reserved just for me, and I drank it down like it was water in the desert.

"You always say things like that," she murmured.

"Like what?"

"Like you'd go to war for me."

"I would," I said, easy as breathing.

She didn't blink. "Why?"

I could have dodged, made a joke, shrugged it off. I didn't, though. I wouldn't lie to her. Not now, not ever.

"Because love doesn't always come with confessions and fireworks," I said quietly. "Sometimes it's just showing up, staying, and standing between someone and the worst thing in the dark."

Her breath caught, so faint I might've imagined it.

"I'm not asking you to fight my battles," she said.

"I know. You never needed me to do that. But I'm fighting beside you anyway."

Her gaze dropped, just for a second, like she was afraid of what I'd see if she looked too long. "Gabriel..."

"I'm not rushing you," I added, softer now. "I'm not asking for anything you can't give. But I need you to know I'm here for you. Because of you. Not orders. Just you. I'm all in, Serena. You go, I follow. You fall, I catch." I looked at her and let her see everything in my eyes. "You rise, I kneel."

The wind shifted again, tugging loose strands of her hair across her cheek. She didn't move to brush them away. I did. Her eyes closed when my fingers touched her skin. Only for a moment, but it felt like the world held its breath.

When she opened her eyes again, she didn't say the words. Neither did I, but they lived in the space between us, steady and unshakable.

The old apartment complex came into view, a blackened silhouette against the ash-colored skyline. The place we both knew he'd return to, if he was called. If she called him.

It wasn't just ruined; it was hollowed out, as if something had chewed through the bones of the place and left the skin behind to rot. The wards were long dead, peeled back like old paint. A haunted echo of whatever safety it had once offered.

And still, she walked in.

She stood just inside the perimeter, arms loose at her sides, but I knew the truth. The calm before a storm wasn't calm; it was inevitability.

Serena had burned a signal into the ground with a blade of shadow and ash, a symbol older than any network. This was Noctis, after all, and no one got service in the city of ghosts. The last time I saw a cell tower even semi-functional here, it was on fire and broadcasting opera in reverse Latin. Whatever magic ran this place didn't give a damn about data plans.

We knew Moshi would answer. We were right.

He came with no escort, no goons in Bone Lord colors. There were no hired hands in Hollow Vein regalia skulking in the shadows. It was just him. He stepped across the broken threshold, immaculate as ever in a dark grey suit, like he didn't know how to dress down even for his own ruin. His shoes crunched over scorched tile and glass, and he didn't flinch.

When he saw her, *really* saw her, however, he stopped, just for a second. That pause was enough; he knew we knew.

"I was wondering when you'd call," he said. His gaze flicked to Serena and nowhere else. "It was always going to be here, wasn't it?"

"It didn't have to be," she replied. "But this is where it ends."

He crossed the perimeter, then stopped. He still didn't look at me, didn't look at Riot, who stood behind Serena like an unsheathed blade. He only saw her.

"I didn't sell you out for money," Moshi said.

"Then explain the payments," I snapped, tossing the ledger across the ground. It landed hard against his shoe, the pages fanning out like an accusation. Bound in cracked black leather, the book was older than it looked, a relic from a time when transactions weren't just financial, they were spiritual. Blood for coin and secrets for silence. Serena had stared at it for a long time when we found it. Not because she didn't believe it was real, but because she knew it had to be.

Every line told a story. Names of Bone Lords. Hollow Vein lieutenants. Codes, amounts, locations. And buried among them? Her. The price of her blood, measured in favors and currency.

Moshi's mouth twitched. It was almost a flinch, but he didn't speak.

"I've seen a lot of ledgers," I said, voice low. "Cartels. Arms dealers. Politicians." I pointed to the pages at his feet. "I've never seen one that looked like this. You didn't just balance books. You made a map. A breadcrumb trail with a heartbeat."

Serena said nothing. Her eyes hadn't moved from the page with her name.

"You orchestrated a chase," I growled, "and then had the audacity to showcase your handiwork like it was art."

Still, he said nothing. He just stood there, too clean, too calm.

"This isn't just betrayal, Moshi," I said. "It's choreographed subterfuge. And don't tell me you didn't know what they'd do with the information you gave them."

That finally made him flinch.

"You knew," I said. "And you did it anyway."

"I didn't keep the money," he said, softer now. "It was part of the agreement."

"What agreement?" Serena asked, unmoved.

Moshi exhaled, jaw clenched like he was chewing broken glass. "A year ago..." Moshi's voice thinned, roughened. "Something started watching you." For the first time since he arrived, he couldn't look at her. "Not the Bone Lords. Not the Hollow Vein, either. Something else." He hesitated. "Something older."

I felt Serena still beside me. Even Riot went motionless, and the air itself knew better than to move.

"It didn't announce itself," Moshi continued. "No shadows. No whispers. Just... forgetting. I forgot your birthday. The one date I never missed. Then I forgot the first time I met you. Then your face as a child."

His voice dropped. "I started leaving myself notes."

"What kind of notes?" I asked, voice low.

"Phrases. Written in my own hand. *She matters. Don't trust the Vein. They want her dead.*"

Serena's expression didn't shift, but something in her posture braced.

"Then came the...fuck, I'm not even sure what to call them. They weren't dreams. They weren't visions. They were insertions. False memories with perfect teeth. And the worst ones..." He dragged a breath. "The worst ones came at night. Waking dreams stitched from truths that hadn't happened yet. They didn't just take knowledge. They fed me new things. Images.

Visions." He swallowed. His hands, for the first time, trembled. "I saw Noctis burning. The rivers turned to black oil. The sky cracked open like a rotten egg. And you..." His voice hitched. "You were already gone. No grave. No pyre. Just absence, a hole in the world where you'd once been."

Serena didn't move. She'd heard worse. Lived worse.

"I thought they were showing me what would happen if I protected you," he said. "That they wanted me to step aside, let fate handle it."

"But that wasn't it," I said.

He shook his head. "No. They were warning me. That without pain, you'd never become what you were meant to be. That if you didn't bleed, you'd never *awaken*. They said your power was sealed like a geode: beautiful, but useless unless cracked open. That without that brute force, the magic would stay trapped. But pressure?" He swallowed. "The right pressure fractures everything, and inside that fracture? Light. Rage. Power old enough to burn the world clean."

"Who is they? What did they look like?" I asked.

Moshi shook his head. "I don't know. Every time I tried to focus, they dissolved. A whisper under skin. A scent of something that didn't belong, like dried roses and old bones."

He paused and then said, "They called themselves The Voice. I don't know what that means. I do know they were ancient. *Are* ancient. Not Bone Lord ancient, not Noctis ancient. Much older, like they remember when the Bone Lords were nothing but men in caves playing with power they didn't understand."

Serena's fingers curled slightly, a flicker of power racing up her spine.

"I tried to resist," he said. "Tried to shield you. But their logic was perfect. If you stayed hidden, you'd die. If you faced them, you'd suffer, but you might live. And if you lived..."

"She'd become something else," I finished.

He looked at his feet. "I used to watch you at council meetings," he said to her, unprompted, his voice barely above a whisper. "Before you were old enough to speak. Before you knew what you were. You'd sit beside your mother and tilt your head like you were memorizing the shape of power. You were never afraid," Moshi said. "Not even when you should've been." I clenched my jaw, swallowing the sharp, unfamiliar taste of pity.

I felt her still beside me. Even Riot shifted, ears twitching toward him.

"They came to me," Moshi said. "Not with threats, but with timelines. With what happens if you die too soon. If you never awaken. If Noctis loses you before you become what you're meant to be. They never gave orders," he continued. "Just whispering consequences. Showing probabilities. What would break if you fall too soon. They said you weren't just part of the balance; you were the fulcrum. The thing everything else tilts around. If you live, the city holds. If you die early?" He looked at her with something like awe. "The weight shifts, and the whole system cracks."

He studied her like she was already gone. "They said you needed to be hunted. That power only surfaces under pressure."

"So you turned me into prey." Serena's voice was flat.

"So I made it easier for the predators to sniff around. I left breadcrumbs. Enough to chase. Not to catch."

My fists clenched. "You steered them."

He nodded. "I thought I was protecting her. That guiding the danger was safer than letting it find her on its own. I thought I could control it, but I was wrong. They moved so much faster than I anticipated. They were so much hungrier. They stopped following the rules. And I didn't know how to stop what I'd set in motion."

"You chose for me," Serena said.

"I did," he said, voice cracking. "Because I thought you deserved the chance to actually live. Even if it meant you had to suffer first."

"You took my name," she said. "Gave it away like it was a trinket. Like it wasn't sacred."

"I thought it would save you."

"You thought wrong."

She didn't yell. She didn't have to.

Moshi looked like he'd been flayed open. Still standing, but only just. "I saw every ending. They showed me every ending. Every single one. Except this."

"What changed?" I asked.

That's when he looked at me, and I felt it like a round to the chest.

"I sent you a hero," he said. "And he fell in love with you."

Serena didn't move, but I could feel her breath catch.

"I sent him to you," Moshi said, still talking to her, always her. "Because if I couldn't protect you anymore, someone had to."

I didn't need to hear anything else. I saw it then. In the way he held her in his gaze, in the things he never said. It hit me slow, like surfacing from deep water.

He loved her.

Not just in theory. Not in some abstract, professional way. Not with the kind of love I carried, wrecked and reverent, aching and alive. His was older, quieter, like a hymn forgotten in the bones. He loved her with the kind of love you bury so deep you forget it's there, until you realize it bleeds out in everything you do. And he'd buried it.

I saw it in the way his voice broke when he said her name, in the way he kept looking at her like she was the only constant in a world full of rot. He'd made himself a satellite and decided to orbit her, even if she never looked up to see him reflect her light.

This wasn't the kind of love that screamed or burned out loud.

He'd turned it into the kind of love that shows up in spreadsheets and decisions that don't make sense. The kind that destroys you when you realize the only thing you were trying to do was the one thing you failed at. It made me sick, because I understood it.

I don't think she ever knew. I don't think she was ever meant to. She didn't know because he made sure of it, and he never expected her to love him back.

He just wanted her alive, and that's what gutted me.

All the times I'd yearned to be close to her, for every reckless risk I'd taken to keep her breathing, I'd never once hidden what I felt. I couldn't. It poured out of me like blood, bright and reckless and full of teeth. But him? He'd built a temple out of silence and called it safety, made his love a locked room and convinced himself it was mercy.

That kind of love corrodes.

"You had no right," she whispered, her eyes burning into him.

"I know."

"I trusted you."

"I know that, too."

"I needed you."

He shut his eyes.

And there it was.

The silence that followed was a blade turned sideways in the chest.

Serena stepped back. "You're not my enemy," she said at last.

His head lifted, hope sparking.

"But you're not mine anymore either."

Serena stood firm, but something in her posture shifted. A quiet fracture beneath the surface. She stood straighter, but I knew what it cost her. There was always a cost. Her words had been the knife.

Now came the bleed.

Moshi didn't move. Didn't speak. Just stood there, frozen in the echo of what he'd already lost. He looked so damn hopeful, even in the face of ruin. Like not being her enemy gave him something to hold on to. Like being *nothing* to her was still better than being the one who broke her.

She turned from him, slow and deliberate. There was nothing else to say, and it felt like closing a door.

I'd seen her angry. I'd seen her terrified. I'd seen her vicious and vengeful and ruthless. I'd never seen her heartbroken. Not like this. She didn't lash out. She just let go, and somehow, that was worse.

Riot moved to her side, brushing his body against her leg like a living shield. He didn't growl or posture. He just stood there, anchoring her to the moment, like he knew she was seconds from slipping.

Moshi opened his mouth. Closed it again. There was nothing left to say.

I watched her breathe. One inhale. One exhale. Then another. That was how she survived this.

One breath at a time.

She started walking, and Riot followed. No fanfare. No dramatics.

Just a girl in a black coat, leaving a man in ashes.

Before I followed her, I turned to him. He didn't look at me until I spoke.

"You love her," I said.

He flinched. Like I'd struck him.

"I saw it," I said. "In the way you watched her. In every decision you made that started with her name and ended with her bleeding."

He didn't argue. Didn't deny.

"She doesn't know," I added.

"No," he said. "She doesn't."

"You think love gives you permission to make choices for her?" I said. "To shape her life without her consent?"

His eyes found mine. Hollow. Wrecked. "I think love made me a coward," he said, "and I used that cowardice to justify every sin I committed in her name."

I believed him, and it didn't change a damn thing.

"She won't love you back."

His voice broke on a whisper. "I know."

"Then why not walk away?"

His answer was barely audible. "Could you?"

I nodded. Not in approval, but in understanding.

"She doesn't need a hero, you know," I said. "She never did. But I'll spend the rest of my life becoming one, if that's what it takes to stand beside her. Not because I was sent. Not because she asked. Because somewhere between her silence and her fire, she rewrote me. She's in my blood now. In my bones. I breathe like it's a prayer to her. She's not my reason for fighting; she's the reason I can't stop. They can send every blade they have. I've already chosen my grave, and it's at her feet." I clasped his shoulder, once, and walked away.

And this time, he let me.

We walked.

Away from the ruin, away from Moshi, away from the name she hadn't claimed in years but that still lived carved into her memory.

Riot padded ahead, ears low, sensing the shift in her.

She didn't speak. Didn't breathe, it felt like. Then, when we were far enough that the wind swallowed the last of his presence, when the wards behind us went still, when she could finally believe no one else would see...

She screamed.

Not just rage. Not just pain. All of it, twisted into one sharp, brutal wail. She screamed like it had been trapped in her chest for years, rattling against ribs that refused to break to let it out.

It ripped out of her in a fury of claws.

She sank to her knees, fists curled into the dirt, shoulders shaking so violently I thought something in her spine might snap. I dropped beside her, but I knew not to touch her yet. She needed space to shatter.

She let out another scream, this one rougher, cracking as if her voice had given up halfway through. Then another. And then—

She broke.

No words. Just sobbing so deep it came from somewhere below language.

I had never seen her sob. I'd seen tears, but never like this, like it was being torn out of her. Not when we ran. Not when she was bleeding. Not when she talked about her father and the punishments he called love.

Now she wept like the little girl no one had saved, like the teenager forced to become a symbol. She sobbed like the woman who thought she had clawed her way to freedom only to realize the people she trusted had tied a leash around her throat.

I gathered her into my arms and held her as tightly as I dared. It still didn't feel like enough. Her fingers fisted in my shirt like I was the only thing keeping her from falling straight through the ground. Her breath hitched against my chest in broken little gasps, and all I could do was whisper her name and curse the world that made her carry so much.

"I've got you," I murmured, over and over, like saying it enough would make it true. "I've got you, I've got you, I've got you."

No one had *ever* had her. Not in the way she deserved, and I hated them for it. Every last one.

Her father. The Bone Lords. Moshi. The gods, if they were watching. The universe itself.

Anyone who had looked at this girl, with fire in her eyes and steel in her spine, and thought she could be used.

They didn't deserve her name in their mouths.

She didn't stop crying for a long time. When she finally did, she just curled into me like a dying star, still burning, still impossible to touch.

And I knew, I knew in my bones, that this wasn't the end of anything.

This was the beginning.

Whatever she became after this would not be soft.

Would not be forgiving.

The world should start running.

CHAPTER FIFTEEN

SOMEONE'S GONNA DIE, AND IT'S NOT GONNA BE ME

Serena

I DIDN'T REMEMBER STANDING up after I'd screamed my rage and pain to the sky and let Gabriel hold me while I broke. When the shaking stopped, and I found my voice again, we took stock. We needed to regroup, and I needed to breathe air that didn't choke me with grief. We'd headed west, and somehow ended up ... here.

The Hateful Hag was the kind of place that stuck to your boots. Low ceilings, a flickering green neon sign in the shape of a cauldron, and a bartender who looked like she could hex a man blind with a glance and probably had. Rumor was the bar got its name from the owner's ex-wife; the preserved head mounted above the shelves of cheap liquor suggested otherwise.

The bar was technically above-ground, but the windows were slatted and grimy enough to give it a permanent haze. Most of the patrons looked like regulars. Some of them might have been alive. None of them cared that I was wanted.

The bounty was gone.

For now.

I nursed a glass of something vaguely bitter and blue while Riot curled under the table, eyes half-lidded but ears alert. Gabriel had dragged two rickety stools to our corner table and was currently hunched over the remote he'd swiped. He was trying to get the battered TV above the bar to stop cycling through static and curse ads.

"Got it," he said triumphantly.

I looked up just in time to see the beginning of a hockey game flicker to life.

Seattle vs. New Jersey. Gabriel lit up like a spellfire fuse. "Oh, hell yes. Real sports."

I raised a brow. "You're into hockey?"

"You don't understand," he said, settling into the seat beside me like he was about to revere something holy. "I once watched the New Jersey pull off a triple overtime Stanley Cup playoff comeback from a hookah bar in Kandahar. It was magic." He took a quick swig of the questionable beer in front of him. "I played in college, too. I love this sport."

I sipped my drink. "Pretty sure that wasn't magic. That was probably a concussion."

He ignored me.

For a few blissful moments, he was just a guy watching a game, mouth slightly parted, eyes focused. Relaxed in a way I hadn't seen since Noctis started to eat itself from the inside out. And then—

The camera panned across the rink. Underneath the ice, something moved.

Gabriel leaned forward. "Wait, is that—"

A massive tentacle slapped against the inside of the ice, causing a spiderweb of cracks to race across the surface. Fans cheered wildly.

He blinked. "That's a real kraken."

"Might be."

The camera cut to the stands. Jersey's mascot stalked across the rafters, red eyes glowing, tail lashing. A patron shrieked as it lunged and pulled them into the shadows.

"That guy just got eaten," Gabriel said flatly.

I shrugged. "They'll respawn. Probably."

He slumped back against the booth, arms crossed. "This city ruins everything."

I almost smiled. "Welcome to Noctis."

He sulked into his drink, casting the occasional betrayed glance at the screen.

It was good to see him relaxed, even if only for a second. I took a minute and looked around; The Hateful Hag had more stories than chairs, and every one of them stared at us from the walls.

Between the bar's warped ceiling beams, I counted half a dozen relics mounted like trophies, everything from bone-carved scrying tools to a rusted cage that still smelled of brimstone. The shadows didn't just sit idle; they leaned in, like they were listening for secrets. Maybe they were.

Behind the bar, a raven skull hung from a chain above the cash drawer. Its eye sockets glowed faintly, and when the bartender moved too close, it hissed a warning, or a maybe a benediction. Hard to say. Probably both.

An old man nursed a bottle at the far end of the bar, his nails yellowed, skin cracked like tree bark. He glanced at me once and muttered something under his breath. I didn't catch the full sentence, but one word cut clean through the noise.

"Myrddin's."

He looked away quickly. Didn't meet my eyes again.

A shiver chased up my spine, but I didn't flinch. I didn't have the luxury. This was Noctis. You didn't survive here by showing your throat.

Still, I felt the bar watching me, *recognizing* me, not just as Serena, but as something older. My blood was never unknown, not here. Not with what my family had built, what my father had broken. I looked at Gabriel to find him watching me.

"Silas," he said finally. "We need to move on it. Tonight."

I nodded. "What do you have?"

He slid a slip of paper across the table; not parchment, but real paper. That alone was enough to make me sit up straighter. "This was in the ledger we took. Folded into the spine so I almost missed it."

The writing was small, slanted. I read it aloud. "Let no light enter the sanctum. Let no time mark the archive. The Hallowed Court keeps what the world cannot bear." A chill ran through me.

"You know it?" he asked.

"No, but it sounds like the stuff my father's Seer used to say."

Gabriel tapped the table. "The ledger marked Silas's last location: Bone Lord territory. Sanguine and 42nd. That confirms the intel we already have. The problem is that the ledger also notes layers of additional protections have been purchased for this very location, and those wards aren't Hollow Vein."

My stomach dropped. "Then whose are they?"

"Someone else. Someone that makes Bone Lords nervous." He hesitated. "Maybe the same thing that set Moshi on his path."

We looked at each other.

Gabriel leaned forward. "We get Silas out. Tonight. Before the Vein tries again, and before the Bone Lords decide they want him bad enough to make a run at him."

I nodded once. Riot growled low under the table.

"And if we can't get him out?"

Gabriel didn't answer. He didn't have to; when someone was in the hands of the Hollow Vein, extraction usually meant a body bag. If you were lucky.

On the TV, the hockey game had devolved into chaos. The kraken had erupted through the ice, tentacles whipping through the air as it dragged opposing players under the frozen surface. Jersey's mascot was leading a counter-charge, horns gleaming in the arena lights.

Riot uncurled from beneath the table, stretching with a soft whine that made his silver-and-smoke coat shimmer under the lights. His blue eyes found mine, and I saw something there that looked a lot like anticipation. He knew what was coming, and he was ready.

The bartender watched us go, her ancient eyes following me with recognition and something like pity. As we passed, she slid a small object across the counter.

"On the house," she rasped. "For the road." It was a small vial filled with a pulsing crimson liquid.

"What is it?" I asked.

"Insurance," she said simply. "For when the time comes." She nodded once. "Some of us remember, Princess."

Princess. Vex had called me Princessa.

"You know who I am," I said. Not a question.

Her face curled into what might have been a smile on a face that had seen fewer centuries. "I knew your mother. And her mother before her." She tapped gnarled fingers against the counter. "They never listened, either."

I slipped the vial into my jacket pocket with a nod of thanks. Its warmth seeped through the fabric like a living thing.

Night had fallen over Noctis, as much as it could in a place that existed in a perpetual twilight. Stars hung too close, watching us back as they arranged themselves in bizarre constellations. Gabriel checked his weapons, a ritual I'd come to find oddly soothing. Two guns, a couple of blades, and something that looked suspiciously like a hand grenade. All probably useless against what we were about to face, but I didn't have the heart to tell him that.

We moved through back streets that shouldn't have connected, past buildings that leaned in to listen to our footsteps. The closer we got to Bone Lord territory, the more the world seemed to resist us: shadows pooling too thick, streets doubling back on themselves when we weren't looking.

"You know," Gabriel said as we ducked under a fire escape that writhed like a tentacle. "Your mother...was she really..."

"Yes," I cut him off. "And no. The stories get twisted."

"Which stories?"

I sighed. "All of them."

He was quiet for a moment. Then, softly: "How did you get away from your father?"

I stopped walking. Not because I didn't want to answer, but because I needed a breath that was separate from the memories.

"I didn't," I said finally. "Not really. Not at first. He didn't just hold me. He *kept* me. He bound me to the throne with ritual and blood and sealed my power in a cage of his own making. He thought he could make me into something he could control."

Gabriel said nothing. Just waited.

"But one night," I went on, "something cracked. I don't know what did it. Maybe it was rage. Maybe it was fear. Maybe it was just that I finally stopped believing he was invincible."

"You killed him."

I nodded, eyes still straight ahead. "He wasn't just a tyrant. He was like me. Held death in his hand like a familiar thing." I exhaled, fighting to keep the memories from closing over my head. "This time, I did what he'd been trying to get me to do all along. I opened the door and let myself feel everything, let everything that was inside me out. I used what he gave me."

I looked at him. "I didn't even know if it would work, but it did. I tore his life from the inside out, ripped it out of him, and when it was done, I collapsed. I thought I died, too. I wanted to."

Gabriel exhaled slowly. "And then?"

"Then I ran. Spent weeks starving, hiding, trying to find a way out. My father had made very sure that the location of the roads out of this place was information that I never had access to. I finally found Moshi; he remembered me. He helped me. I thought he helped me, anyway." I took a deep breath. "As for my power, I didn't use it again. Not until coming back here. Not until you."

He didn't smile. He didn't speak.

He just reached for my hand, and held it until the street stopped trying to turn us around.

Sanguine was vile, even by Noctis standards. This was the heart of Bone Lord territory, where even the most desperate smugglers and black market dealers kept their distance. It smelled like old blood, and the air was like breathing through wet cotton. The intersection had formed at the junction where two realities bled into each other, where the veil between worlds was tissue paper thin.

Right at the center sat a structure that pretended to be a warehouse.

Even from a distance, the place breathed. Not like lungs, but like the gasses coming off something decomposing. The ground at the perimeter wasn't soil; it was bone dust and ash, compacted into something that looked stable until you stepped on it and it crunched. Magic clung to it like mold, sickly green and pulsing faintly underfoot.

I stepped closer; the runes etched into the building's side twitched when I looked at them. That wasn't a metaphor; they actually moved, like they were aware. It felt like they were trying to crawl off the surface and dig into my skin.

I took a breath and forced my hand toward the door. I knew it would recognize my blood, even if I didn't know why. A pulse of pain lanced through my palm, sharp and familiar. The runes flared white once and then dimmed to black.

No alarms. They knew I wasn't my father.

They just didn't care.

"This isn't right," I said, pausing at the very edge of the perimeter. "This place should be crawling with magic. It knows I'm not my father, but no sigils, no protection spells, no alarm triggers. It feels fractured, like someone's taken a hammer to a stained glass window and then tried to piece it back together in the dark."

Gabriel nodded, his eyes narrowed. "This is supposed to be a fortress, but there are no guards, and the wards seem weak. The usual Hollow Vein paranoia package is conspicuously absent. They might have been compromised." He pulled one pistol from his waistband; I noticed it was the one with runes on the barrel, and then said "The Bone Lords might have gotten here first. Head on a swivel."

Riot growled low as we crossed the perimeter. A sigil flared under his paw, then fizzled out. Gabriel scanned the doorframe, then gave a slow whistle.

"Whatever was here got rewritten," he murmured. "Not broken or corrupted. *Rewritten*."

"I really don't like this."

"You're not supposed to."

The interior was worse.

Inside, the laws of space had been put in a blender. Hallways ran into each other like Escher diagrams. Doorways led into identical rooms until they didn't. The lights pulsed like heartbeats. Sometimes, the walls whispered names.

Time bent here. I didn't notice it at first. It was just a flicker, a blink where the shadows jumped ahead of the light. Then another. A clock on the wall was melted, still ticking backward. Gabriel's shadow moved before he did.

I checked my watch.

It read thirteen o'clock.

"Gabriel," I said tightly. "We're time slipping."

He paused mid-step.

I caught a flicker of *myself* just ahead, turning a corner, coat flaring behind me. But I was still here.

Gabriel looked past me. "Serena. Did you just—"

"No," I said. "Not yet."

He didn't answer, just pulled a thin strip of silver from his pocket: woven wire, wrapped in a loop. A tether sigil.

"You think that'll help?" I asked.

"I think it'll help me remember where the hell we are. When the hell we are."

I took one last look at the walls. They were starting to breathe. Gabriel pressed a hand to the wall and flinched.

"What?" I asked.

"I forgot your name. Just for a second."

I swallowed. "Keep moving."

We reached what might've once been a security room. A dozen monitors, all shattered, sat on broken desks. One was bleeding; thick, dark red pooled beneath the console like it had come from inside the screen itself. Riot sniffed at it once, growled, and turned his head.

"Something got here before us," Gabriel muttered. "We need to keep moving."

I didn't argue.

Everywhere we went, there were signs of Hollow Vein tech—conduits, binding chains, reinforced sigil plates—but all of it had been overwritten. Not destroyed, not tampered with, just repurposed. Like something smarter had come in and decided it could do it better.

"I don't think the Hollow Vein is still in charge here," Gabriel muttered.

"No," I said. "But I think they think they are."

We hit the final hallway.

There were names carved into the walls.

Dozens. Hundreds. In every language I knew and several I didn't. Names of people I recognized from old Council meetings. Bloodlines. Some crossed out. Some still glowing.

Near the end of the list: mine. Not Serena. Selene.

It was fresh.

As we descended deeper, my memories became tangled: visions of other lives, other versions of myself flickering across my thoughts. Me as a queen. Me as a corpse. Me as something monstrous.

I grabbed Gabriel's hand, trying to ground myself in the only thing that mattered: I was still here. He was still here.

So was Silas. We found him suspended mid-air in a chamber that vibrated with silence. He was mid-scream, lips parted, eyes wide, body arched in pain.

He wasn't restrained.

He was paused, a moment stretched past its breaking point.

Gabriel swore. "They froze him in his own timeline."

"I can fix it," I said, voice shaking. "I think."

I reached inward, past the magic I had learned and into the power I feared. The same power I used when I killed my father, and when I almost killed Voss. It came to my call like a hound answering its master.

With a breath, I unraveled the stitch that had sewn Silas into his own timeline. The air shattered like glass, and Silas fell forward, gasping as if he'd been underwater for years.

His eyes locked onto mine. Bloodshot. Wild.

"They're rewriting the end," he rasped. "They found the threads. They cut the ones where you live."

Gabriel stepped closer. "What do you mean? Who?"

Silas trembled. "The Voice always has been. It's what's left. Of gods. Of power. It doesn't want you dead, Serena. It wants you changed."

"Into what?"

He looked at me, really looked, and whispered:

"Ascendant."

I felt something stir inside me. Something that remembered what I had been. What I could become.

I took his hand. "Then it's going to be very disappointed."

Silas's body went rigid, his eyes rolling back as he seized. Blood trickled from his nose, his ears, the corners of his eyes. His mouth opened, but the sound that came out wasn't human; it was a discordant static, like a radio caught between stations.

Gabriel caught him before he hit the ground. "He's crashing, Serena. Whatever they did to him..."

"I think it's timeline shock," I said, placing my hand on Silas's forehead. He burned. "Being held between moments, it's broken his mind. Or tried to." Silas went limp, and Gabriel hoisted him into a fireman's carry. Riot growled, hackles raised, as a tremor passed through the building.

"I think that's our cue to leave," Gabriel said. I turned to follow, then froze.

In the curved glass of a shattered observation window, I saw her. A reflection that wasn't mine. Same face, same eyes, but older, sadder. Her lips moved, forming words I couldn't hear.

"Serena!" Gabriel's voice snapped me back. "Time to go!"

We fled through corridors that twisted like intestines while reality unraveled at the seams. Riot led the way, his form shifting between dog and the much larger, more primal creature, as though holding on to his canine body took too much concentration.

Silas mumbled against Gabriel's back, fragments of prophecy tumbling from his lips. "The mother of gods...she's rewriting the ending...the Bone Lords are just vessels...the Hollow Vein cannot see..."

Then the walls *screamed*.

Not an alarm. A command. A call.

And the Hollowborn answered.

We saw movement first, shadows jerking against the angles of the hallway, too fast, too still. Then their forms coalesced into once human figures that now moved like something other, featureless faces now embedded with various pieces of tech. Hollow Vein soldiers. Archivists of agony, and now, they were coming for us.

"Gabriel..." I started, already raising my hands.

But he was already moving, dumping Silas unceremoniously on the ground at my feet. He reached into his jacket and pulled out a jagged, oil-slicked orb covered in teeth-like ridges. He yanked the pin, and the orb let out a low whisper. Then a hum.

Then it howled, and the hallway shattered.

The walls convulsed and split, reality cracking around the explosion like it didn't know how to hold shape anymore. The Hollowborn staggered, just for a moment, but it was enough.

Gabriel went in first.

Knives. Gun. Rage like holy fire.

He struck the first Hollowborn in what should have been the throat, but the blade passed through flesh like fog. The creature hissed, coiled backward, and opened its mouth too wide. A thousand voices poured out. Sobbing. Laughing. Screaming.

Gabriel kicked it square in the chest, slammed it back against the wall, and fired a shot into the base of its skull. *That* did it. The thing spasmed, crumpled, and disintegrated, leaving a plume of ash that smelled like burnt lavender and rotting fruit.

"Go for the base of the head if they get close," he shouted. "Sever the memory connection."

I grabbed Silas and hauled him down toward another corridor as three more Hollowborn spilled from the ceiling. Riot snarled, eyes glowing, fangs too long for his mouth. He lunged at one of them, dragging it down in a flurry of teeth and shadow.

Gabriel caught another mid-turn, slammed it into the floor with a grunt, and drove both blades through its chest. It screamed, not in pain, but in joy, like it had been waiting to die.

Two more flanked him.

They were faster than the others.

These weren't just Hollow Vein soldiers. They were Wardens. The difference was written in the way they moved, like they were guarding something sacred.

One lunged for Gabriel with a howl that split into three different voices, overlapping in a chorus of grief. He ducked the first strike but missed the second, and its claws raked down his ribs, tearing fabric and flesh.

"Gabriel!" I shouted, dragging Silas back as Riot leapt between us and the nearest veil-draped monster.

Gabriel didn't stop moving. He gritted his teeth, slammed an elbow into the creature's face, or where its face would have been if it'd had one, and stabbed upward with both blades. It shrieked and disintegrated in a plume of black ash.

But he was bleeding; I could see the shirt going dark over his ribs, the torn flesh showing through the rips.

I turned to the last Warden. It reached for me, long, spectral fingers tipped with rune-carved nails. I knew they didn't want to kill me. They wanted to contain me, and that might have been worse.

I felt myself split, my reality lurching as every version of me scraped against the inside of my skin. A queen in chains. A body in flame. A girl who never escaped.

They screamed through me, fighting for dominance, and I lost time. A full breath. Maybe two.

Riot surged forward, shifting mid-leap into something *divine*. He landed on the Warden with enough force to crater the floor. His eyes glowed gold-white, and his fangs were made of light and shadow both. It wailed once and collapsed into a puddle of rotted memory.

Gabriel stumbled toward me, blood soaking his side. "Serena—are you—"

"I'm fine," I lied, voice hoarse.

Riot stood between us, taller than he should've been. His back was arched. His body still shimmered. But his eyes found mine.

He was waiting for me to catch up to whatever I was becoming.

Gabriel panted, backing up to where I stood. "How many more?"

"Too many," I replied tersely, hoisting Silas against my side. He was small, shorter than I was, and so, so thin. His head lolled, but his eyes were open, unfocused and glassy. Pulling him along, we ran. Riot cleared a path ahead while the halls twisted impossibly, doorways appearing and disappearing like a deranged funhouse.

"Almost there," Gabriel gasped as we rounded another corner. "Just need to..."

The floor dropped out from under us, the ground simply ceasing to exist, replaced by a yawning darkness that pulled us in. We fell, tumbling through nothingness until we crashed into solid ground with a bone-barring thud.

I groaned, every nerve screaming as I pushed myself upright. We were in some kind of maintenance tunnel, the walls slick with something that glistened like oil but smelled like copper. Silas was sprawled beside me, his breathing shallow.

Gabriel and Riot were already on their feet, scanning the shadows as if expected the walls to leap out at us. I managed to get my legs under me and then hauled Silas up. His head lolled against my shoulder, skin waxy, mouth twitching with fragmented prophecy.

"Did we lose them?" I asked.

"No," Gabriel muttered. "But they lost us."

He looked up. The ceiling had sealed itself, smooth as bone. No seams. No sound. No way back. "The floor didn't collapse," he said slowly. "It let us go."

My chest tightened. We didn't say it out loud, but we both knew. Something—*someone*—wanted us out of that fight. Not because they cared whether we lived, but because they needed us for what came next.

Silas stirred, coughing violently. Blood splattered my sleeve, but his eyes fluttered open.

"Serena," he rasped, voice cracking like dried leaves. "They think you'll come *after*. But you're going to walk in *before*. You'll cut the thread before it's woven."

"What thread?" I asked, heart pounding. "What are they doing?"

"They've marked a girl," he said, shaking now. "One of their own. A vessel. They're going to bleed her into the roots of Noctis. Anchor her soul to the city's foundation. Bind death into stone."

Gabriel stiffened beside me. "A ritual anchor?"

Silas nodded weakly. "It's not sacrifice; it's succession. They want to crown a new god. One born of their blood. Your line is too wild to bend easily. Too old, but so incredibly powerful. But hers, hers is twisted enough to obey. It will buy them time to find you and break you."

"Who is she?" I demanded. "What's her name?"

He blinked slowly. "She doesn't have a name yet. That's part of the ritual. They'll carve it into her bones. Rewrite her from the marrow out."

He gripped my wrist, surprising strength in his skeletal fingers.

"You have to interrupt it, Serena. Not destroy it. Interrupt it. If the pattern breaks before the binding seals, the magic will collapse on itself. Years of planning, turned to rot. All their work will be wasted."

"Where?" Gabriel asked. "Where does it happen?"

Silas's mouth twitched.

"Underground. Where the city drinks. Where it feeds. You'll know it by the teeth."

Silas twitched once.

I froze.

His chest barely rose, but his eyes flew open. Not gasping. Not aware. Gone somewhere else. Seeing something I couldn't. "Selene?" he whispered.

I leaned in. "I'm here." But I don't think he saw me. Not really.

"Your mother... she wore light like a cloak. Her voice was...gods, I remember her voice."

My heart clenched. "What do you see, Silas?"

"She's at the edge," he breathed, his eyes wide, unblinking. "Telling you not to make the same choice. Telling you... you don't have to burn everything to be free." His eyes flicked to mine for half a second, in recognition.

"You look like her." A tear ran down his cheek. Then his head lolled again, this time for good.

I didn't cry.

Instead, I eased his body to the ground and pulled a small satchel from my belt. I unwrapped the cloth inside to reveal a pinch of iron salt, a sprig of wormwood, and a shard of obsidian etched with my blood. A death charm. Not for protection, but for peace.

I pressed the shard to his sternum and whispered the rite under my breath. It wasn't dramatic. It didn't glow. But the air shifted, just slightly, as if the world acknowledged what had passed.

"May the threads that knew you unspool gently," I murmured. "May what waits be kinder than what kept you."

The shard cracked down the center, and his body feathered into dust.

And that was that.

Gabriel hissed as he leaned against the wall, pressing a hand to his ribs.

"Let me see," I said, already pulling the pack off my shoulder with fingers that wouldn't quite stop shaking.

Gabriel gave me a crooked smile, the kind he usually wore before doing something reckless. "If you wanted to get me out of my shirt, sweetheart, you only had to ask."

"Please," I muttered, peeling his jacket back with a gentleness that felt foreign. "You're lucky I don't staple it shut just to spite you."

He swore quietly when I pulled the fabric away. The wound was worse than I'd thought. Deep gouges had been clawed into his side, jagged and raw, blood seeping slow and steady from torn muscle. His ribs were scored like something had tried to carve its name into his skin and didn't quite finish the sentence.

"You should be unconscious," I muttered, forcing my voice flat to keep from unraveling.

"Been worse," he said, breath tight. "Felt better."

The skin around the gouges was already starting to swell, the edges hot to the touch. I cleaned it with water from the canteen, then doused it with the alchemical glue I'd appropriated from our first safe house. It fizzed on contact, hissing like it had a grudge. Gabriel's breath caught, sharp and sudden, then he clenched his jaw so hard I heard it grind.

"Hold still," I ordered, fingers pressing the edges of the wound together, sealing them as best I could.

"I *am* holding still," he bit out. "This is me being agreeable."

"Could've fooled me."

He let out a strangled laugh, then winced again as I wrapped gauze tight around his ribs. My hands were slick with his blood by the time I finished. His blood, on my hands.

I sat back on my heels, chest rising too fast, trying to find air that didn't taste like copper. "You're an idiot," I said, too quietly. "A beautiful, bleeding idiot."

He leaned forward—slowly, because even that much movement obviously hurt. But his eyes were steady. "Still breathing, though," he murmured. "Still here."

I kissed him.

Not softly. Not sweetly.

I kissed him like I was staking a claim, like I could rewrite what had happened if I just pressed hard enough, long enough, deep enough. I kissed him to show Death it couldn't have him, not today. I needed to feel his pulse against mine, needed to remember he was real, that he hadn't slipped into one of the timelines that kept trying to steal him away.

He kissed me back without hesitation, like he'd been waiting for me to stop pretending we were anything less than fate, like he was trying to rewrite our story with his lips and tongue and his hands on my face, callused thumb brushing the corner of my mouth, guiding me closer until I could barely remember which breath was mine.

I pulled back until I could rest my forehead against his. I could feel the heat of his skin, the slow drag of his breath, the iron and incense of our shared magic hanging between us like smoke.

"You are forbidden to die," I whispered. "You hear me?"

He nodded, voice gone hoarse. "I hear you."

"You promised to date the hell out of me," I said, still too breathless. "And death doesn't get you out of that. It just makes it awkward."

Gabriel gave a rough, broken laugh. "Noted."

I helped him up. Riot padded ahead, ears pricked in anticipation of the next threat.

We didn't know what came next. But I knew one thing with absolute certainty. They wanted a god?

Then they were about to find out what it meant to make one angry.

CHAPTER SIXTEEN

THERE ARE THINGS WORSE THAN DEATH: LET ME SHOW YOU

Serena

T HE HOTEL WAS OLD. Not charming old, not haunted old, just old, worn down by the weight of too many lives passing through it. The lobby smelled like lemon cleaner and mold, and the elevator wheezed like it had asthma. The room had peeling wallpaper and a window that faced nothing but fog, but it had a bed, and Gabriel needed rest.

He didn't say it. Of course he didn't. He bled silently, moved like nothing hurt, packed the wound on his ribs with practiced hands and gritted teeth. I'd seen the tremor in his fingers when he thought I wasn't looking. I saw the way he hesitated before lowering himself onto the edge of the mattress, his whole body locking like a structure bracing for collapse.

He'd done too much for me already.

So I let him sit. Let him breathe. Let him think, just for a minute, that we were safe here.

We weren't, of course. Safety was a luxury that we didn't have the coin for. I crossed to the window, parting the thin curtains with my fingertips. The fog outside was unnatural. Weather was never just weather, not in Noctis. It was a mood, a warning, sometimes even a weapon.

"You should sleep," Gabriel said, his voice rougher than usual. I went without a word into the bathroom, filling a cup with tepid tap water. I carried it out to him, watching him drain it without even a grimace. He sighed and leaned his head back on the cracked headboard, and I took the moment to just look at him.

The dodgy fluorescent lighting did him no favors, highlighting the bruise blooming across his cheekbone, the dark circles under his eyes. He was still the most beautiful thing I'd ever seen.

"That's funny, coming from you," I said, trying for lightness and missing. "When's the last time you actually slept?"

He gave me a half-smile, eyes still closed, and my heart stuttered. "Tuesday, maybe? What month is it?"

God, I loved him so much it ached.

Riot curled himself into a cinnamon roll on the carpet, chin on his paws, breathing in a slow, steady rhythm. He was watching both of us. Waiting. I think he knew what I was planning.

I moved back to the window and perched on the sill, knees pulled up, staring out at the endless grey. My fingers itched to draw a sigil, to carve a ward into the glass, to *do* something. I didn't. The city knew where I was. This room, this moment? It was a pause, not a shield.

Gabriel let out a breath like it hurt to keep it in.

"So," he said, low. "You going to tell me what you're thinking?"

I didn't answer. He turned his head toward me. Not sharp. Not angry. Just... waiting.

"You heard Silas," I said finally. "They're going to use this girl as an anchor. Bleed her soul into the roots of Noctis." I shivered. "They will sacrifice her to buy enough time to keep coming after me." I looked at a bead of water running down the outside of the window. "They will destroy her, because of me." I glanced at him. "He told me I needed to interrupt the ritual."

"I know what he said." His voice was tight. Controlled. "But you are not responsible for what they plan to do, and you don't have to stop it alone."

"There's no time to rally support. No time to call anyone else in." I gave a despairing laugh. "If there was anyone to call in. I don't know who's on my side anymore, outside of this room."

"Then I'm coming with you."

"Gabriel..."

"Don't do that," he snapped sharply. "Don't soften it. Don't start with my name like it's a salve."

"I don't want to fight with you." My voice was perilously close to pleading.

"Then *stay*."

I turned toward him slowly. "You know I can't."

His jaw clenched. "You mean you won't." I didn't answer, and he pushed himself upright. "Like hell you're going without me." He winced, then continued. "You think I'll let you walk into a ritual designed to kill without backup? Without a plan?"

"I *have* a plan."

"Bullshit. Your plan is martyrdom with lipstick."

That stung. "This isn't about self sacrifice. It's about stopping them, and I'm all out of other options."

He stood too fast and his whole body flinched from it, pain chasing up his spine. He gritted through it like he always did. Stubborn, reckless idiot.

My idiot.

"You think I followed you this far just to watch you die?" he growled.

"I think if you follow me into that ritual, you'll never walk out."

"I don't care."

"Well, I do!" The words ripped out of me louder than I had intended. Riot stirred near the door, but didn't rise. I breathed hard, swallowing the panic in my chest. "I've already lost too much, Gabriel. I won't lose you too."

"And you think I could survive losing you?" His voice dropped to something ragged. "You think I'd come out of that intact?"

I didn't answer.

"I can't do this," he said, softer now. "I can't watch you walk into something you know might kill you. Not without trying to stop it, and you know why."

He closed the distance between us.

"I chose you," he said fiercely. "Not the mission. Not the prophecy. *You.* I would've chosen you in a quiet life, in another city, in any damn version of this world. You were never a detour. You were the destination."

My breath broke.

"I know," I whispered. "And that's why I have to go. Because if I stay—I'll stay."

Gabriel exhaled like I'd stabbed him. He turned away, shaking. I could see the way his hands trembled. Rage, pain, something deeper. I crossed the room until I looked up into that beautiful, stricken face. His hands reached out, pulling me close, and then his mouth was on mine.

He kissed me like I was already gone, and I could taste his despair on his tongue, feel it in the way his hands shook.

I kissed him like I'd never stop missing him, in this life or the next.

The next minutes were a soft blur. He undressed me like I was a revelation, his touches slow and reverent. No fire, no rush, just warmth. Just aching tenderness and hands that knew the shape of my skin like scripture.

I memorized the way his muscles moved under my hands, the taste of the hollow of his throat, the way his beard felt against my palms as I cupped his face to kiss him like he was the oxygen I needed to live.

I helped him ease onto the bed, careful of his side. His breath hitched when I touched the bandage. I kissed the skin just above it.

"I'm here," I whispered, letting my mouth drift down, over the jut of his hipbone. He let me explore, let me do what I wanted, and I could feel the little tremors chasing through him as he forced himself to lie still. I curled my hand around his cock, stroking once, twice, taking pleasure in watching his neck arch back and his mouth fall open. I lapped at him, tasting salt and something uniquely him, and then slid him slowly into my mouth.

I didn't know what I was doing, having done this to him only once before, but he didn't seem to care; his hands came up to tangle in my hair, a quiet "Oh, fuck, baby" whispering out. He didn't shove my head down, but held onto me like he was grounding himself, and I closed my eyes, committing this to a memory I'd carry into hell. For long minutes I took him apart with my mouth, learning what made his breath catch, made him curse, made the muscles in his thighs shake.

"Baby...shit, you have to stop...I need to be inside you," he gritted out, tugging on my hair, urging me up his body. I let him, allowed him to pull me up until he could take my mouth, hands more urgent now, settling me over him, rocking my slickness over his cock. I let out a soft gasp as he positioned himself at my entrance, his eyes locked on mine. Even now, even like this, he waited for my consent, and I gave it by tilting my hips and sliding down his length. I could feel him straining beneath me, muscles taut like a man trying to hold back the tide, and I realized he was giving me time to adjust. Then his hands found my hips, and he started to guide me.

The world narrowed to just this, to just us: the drag of him inside me, the soft groan he made when I clenched around him. The way he breathed my name like it was a prayer to something holy.

I began to ride him in earnest, and his eyes never left mine, even when pleasure tightened his features. One hand traced upwards, cupping my breast, thumb teasing my nipple, before coming to rest at the hollow of my throat.

I'd never been more exposed, and I'd never been so happy to be seen.

I leaned down to kiss him, changing the angle, crying out against his mouth when he hit something inside me that sent sparks shooting up my spine. He swallowed the sound, his other hand sliding between us to find where we were joined, his thumb circling my clit with devastating precision.

"That's it, *moya zvezda*. Let me see you." There was something raw in his eyes, and I wanted to burn this moment into my soul.

He sat up, suddenly, wrapping an arm around my waist. He crushed my breasts against his chest, grinding me against him, the rough hair at the base of his cock teasing my clit. "*Ya nikogda tebya ne otpushu,*" he murmured. "I'll never let you go."

And just like that, something opened.

The world around me cracked like glass, and for a single, staggering moment, it was like flipping through static on an old TV, the dial turning too fast. Futures blurred across my vision, sharp and too bright.

A kitchen soaked in golden light. A child with wild black curls laughing as Riot—older, softer—rested his head on her lap. Gabriel barefoot at the stove, humming something I couldn't hear. My hands on my stomach. A ring on my finger. Whole. Happy. The image throbbed, vivid and warm. And then it changed...

Ash raining from a fractured sky. Me, standing on broken stone, a crown of smoke on my head. Gabriel on his knees before me, eyes hollow, hands red. The city burned behind him, and my name echoed from the flames like a hymn. I had survived. I had won.

But everything soft in me was gone.

The visions snapped out as suddenly as they came, leaving me gasping. Gabriel's arms tightened, and I clung to him as if I could anchor myself in just this one version of us where we still had time.

Pleasure coiled tightly at the base of my spine, and when he bent me back over his arm to take my nipple in his mouth, my world shattered. He held me through it, whispering praise against my skin.

"God, you're so damn beautiful," he breathed, and I could feel him still hard inside me, still waiting. "I want to see this forever."

Forever. The word sliced through me like a blade.

I kissed him fiercely, desperately, rocking against him with renewed purpose. His breathing grew ragged, his rhythm faltering as he got closer. When he came, he buried his face in my neck, my name a broken sound. I committed every sensation to memory: the heat of his release, the way his arms tightened around me, the slight tremble in his powerful shoulders.

We stayed like that, tangled together, his heartbeat gradually slowing in tandem with mine. Neither of us spoke.

What was there to say that wouldn't tear us apart?

I felt him finally start to lose the battle against pain and exhaustion, saw his eyes flutter closed. Then I whispered the charm. A soft one. Old. The kind that smells like lavender and feels like safety. His chest rose. Fell. Rose again.

Peaceful.

I kissed him one last time.

"I love you," I whispered. "I love you so much."

Riot rose as I moved to the door. I crouched beside him and touched his fur. "I need you to stay with him," I said, though it was yet another knife in my heart. "Keep him safe. Keep him here."

Riot's blue eyes held mine with that unnerving keenness, and he tilted his head, as though he was considering the merit of my request.

"Please," I whispered. "He'll try to follow me. You know what waits for me. You know what they'll do to him." I threw my arms around his neck and buried my face in his ruff. "I'm going to try to come back. I don't want to die. But if I don't return, he'll need you." I felt the tears I tried to hold back slip out, wetting the fur around his neck. "I love you so much. You've been my best friend; now I need you to be his." He ducked his head into my chest, and I knew he would stay. "Thank you. Thank you for loving me."

I stood. Straightened my coat. Shouldered the weight of the city.

And walked into the dark.

This wasn't surrender.

It might be sacrifice, but for him, I would make it.

Every. Single. Time.

CHAPTER SEVENTEEN

TIME TO DISASSOCIATE LIKE A QUEEN

Serena

NOCTIS NEVER SLEPT.

It vibrated beneath my boots like a live wire, humming with half-truths and simmering with the taste of old blood. The fog had thickened into a living thing, clinging to buildings, coiling through alleys, whispering across windows as if it was searching for someone to blame. The lights above me flickered in no discernable pattern, casting long shadows that never quite moved when I did.

The city was shifting. It always did before something broke.

My feet found the path easily. Not because I knew it, but because Noctis did. The city always remembered where pain had been promised, and tonight, it was leading me to the threshold.

Every step was too loud. I walked like I belonged here. Maybe I did.

The first memory struck without warning—sharp and sudden.

Riot, still gangly, his coat more shadow than shape.

We'd been hiding in a squat with a busted ward line, half-starved, too loud. Something got through. A man with no scent, no voice, and no soul. I froze.

Riot didn't. He launched himself at the thing like a blade forged in loyalty, fury given form. No plan, no thought, just instinct. They hit the wall hard, and Riot yelped when claws raked his side, but he didn't stop. He bit and tore and howled until the thing dissolved into ash that tasted like static.

I screamed. I think I screamed.

He limped back to me, bleeding from a dozen cuts, and collapsed at my feet. I dropped to my knees, hands shaking, trying to remember healing sigils I hadn't mastered yet. I couldn't recall them exactly, just fragments, impressions burned into the back of my mind like the echo of my mother's voice. But memory didn't need to be perfect in Noctis. It just needed to be real. Magic flows to memory, and mine was drenched in fear, in fury, in love. I'd burned too much, too fast, and the magic had scraped thin along my nerves, resisting the shape of the spells, but the Weave stirred anyway, trembling beneath my skin, like it was remembering, too. There was nothing elegant about it, just desperation and instinct. Riot had needed me whole, and I was already coming apart. He didn't growl, didn't flinch at my clumsy efforts, just pushed his head under my palm like he was reminding me we were still here. That I wasn't alone. Power taken leaves a scar. Power given? It leaves a bond, one that threads deeper than blood and doesn't unravel just because it hurts.

He was barely more than bones and fury back then, all limbs and teeth. I'd found him two weeks earlier, half-starved, curled behind a dumpster in a part of the city where even the rats walked in pairs. He'd looked at me like he already knew me. Like I was his.

That night, as I tended to him the best I could, I realized he wasn't a pet. He was a piece of me I hadn't known was missing.

I blinked hard and kept walking. I let the memories call my power to me.

My father's hand on my cheek. Not gentle. Never gentle. His voice like broken glass. "You are the vessel, Selene. The vessel doesn't question. It contains."

I'd been thirteen, caught reading forbidden texts about reality manipulation, trying to understand what lived inside me. What made the shadows stretch toward my fingers when I was angry. Why dead things twitched when I cried.

The bricks here were scarred with failed warding: sigils half-burned and melted by something that refused to abide by normal magic. The street underfoot buzzed in my bones, like the leyline was holding its breath.

Moshi in the dark, the envelope in his hand trembling just enough for me to notice. "I got you a way out," he'd said. "Might not last forever. But it'll buy you space."

Inside: forged ID, travel papers, a name that wasn't soaked in prophecy. Serena Morrigan.

I held it as if it might vanish, like wanting it was the same as failure. "It's not real," I'd whispered.

"It doesn't have to be right now," he said. "You'll make it real."

I'd stared at it like it would vanish. Like it would bite. He'd just waited and held space for me to decide.

I'd never said thank you. Not really. I'd meant to, but then the moment had passed, and so did the chance.

Moshi hadn't ever needed power in the way that most people understood it. He didn't throw spells or trade blood. He could feel when a lie was too sharp, a truth was too heavy to speak. He called it thread-sensing, though I don't think even he knew what it really was. He'd used that to give me a chance, give me the right documents and the right exit before it slammed shut.

I turned a corner. The wind shifted, bringing with it the smell of blood, ozone, and something metallic I didn't want to name. My skin itched.

A room. A cold drink. A moment that didn't hate us.

Gabriel had bandaged a shallow slice on my arm with careful fingers and quiet swearing. When he was done, I said something sarcastic. He told me I was lucky he liked me. I laughed. He didn't, but then he'd handed me the last square of chocolate from his pocket. We didn't talk. Just sat, shoulder to shoulder, watching the sky bruise with stars. He pressed against me like he forgot we weren't allowed to want things. I didn't lean away.

"You know," he said after a long moment, "I felt it the first time I touched you."

I turned slightly, but he kept his eyes on the stars.

"Didn't know what it was. Thought it might've been adrenaline. Or proximity. But it wasn't." He flexed his hand, like the memory was still there. "It was like...I'd been snapped into place. Like something in the Weave caught both our threads and said 'finally'."

I swallowed. I'd felt it, too. That pull. That impossible familiarity.

"Why didn't you say anything?" I asked.

"Because it scares the shit out of me," he said. "And I don't scare easy."

I was getting close.

More memories, one flickering behind the other, like a tv switching channels:

Blood on my hands. A circle of salt and bone. My father's voice: "You will be the conduit."

Gabriel's voice: "I chose you. Not the mission. Not the prophecy. You. I would've chosen you in a quiet life, in another city, in any damn version of this world. You were never a detour. You were the destination."

Riot's fur between my fingers when I thought we wouldn't make it through the night.

My father's hands on my throat, his smile all teeth and shadows as he whispered, "The vessel doesn't run."

Gabriel's eyes in the half-light, seeing me even when I didn't want to be seen. He'd been cleaning my finger after I'd burned it resetting the wards on one of our safe houses. Because I was his, even if he hadn't said it yet.

We'd only known each other for a few days, but time's a liar when you bleed beside someone, when they guard your back without question. When someone sees every ruined, jagged part of you and stays anyway, things move in ways that don't make sense to people who live safe lives.

I hadn't meant to fall for him, but somewhere between gunfire and silence, I had. For a few moments more, I let myself remember.

The way he always handed me water first, even when he was dehydrated.

The muttered Russian curses that turned into endearments when I touched him.

The instinctive way he reached for me in sleep.

The way he stared, awestruck, when I came apart for him, like I was holy.

The way his body trembled under my hands, undone but never afraid.

How he kissed me as if it hurt to breathe without me..

I used to think love was the first thing they took from you before you dared to hope. Love was dangerous. Love made you hesitate. Love meant soft things with sharp edges that could be used against you. My father told me once, in a moment that almost passed for honesty, that love was the key to destroying a target. You hit it where it cares, and it's easy to make it bleed.

Gabriel didn't ask me to bleed for him. He didn't need me soft. He never once flinched from the jagged pieces of me..

I never planned for him. I'd never factored anything like him into the equation of my life. I thought he was just a soldier, at best a shadow and at worst a distraction. And then, somehow, he became all the things I never thought I'd want. A heartbeat that matched mine. A body that knew how to shield without smothering. A voice that said my name like it was something sacred rather than cursed.

Now I wanted. God, I *wanted*. A future. A life. Something quiet and warm and real. I wanted to argue about toothpaste caps and eat bad takeout on floors that hadn't been hexed. I wanted to be *selfish*.

Noctis didn't allow for selfishness, and I didn't get to be ordinary.

Not yet.

But dammit, he made me want to live long enough to get there.

Glass crunched beneath my boots with each step, ground into dust and memory. Noctis was changing faster now, buildings stretching like taffy, windows elongating into hungry mouths. The fog parted before me, not out of respect but out of anticipation for what was to come.

A fissure split the street up ahead. The altar wasn't visible yet, but the magic pulsing through the concrete told me I was close. My skin burned as the power in my blood remembered what it meant to be used.

I stopped in the middle of the street.

"You're not subtle," I told the city, my voice steady despite everything inside me that wanted to run. "But then, you never were."

The wind answered with my father's laugh.

This wasn't Bone Lord magic. It wore their face: runes, chains, sigils etched in cruelty, but the frequency was wrong.

This ritual wasn't their show. They were just the theater. The architects of death. The Bone Lords had built the house, but the Hollow Vein had written the script. I wondered if any of them knew who had been the head architect of their uneasy detente.

Because The Voice? She watched. That was all. I didn't think she necessarily wanted me to be here. Not because she had mercy, but because she needed me alive. Ascended, maybe. Changed, but not erased. She wasn't going to stop it, though. She wanted to see what I would do.

I thought of the little girl again. That child with curls like a halo and Riot's head in her lap. The sunlight through the window. Gabriel's bare feet. My ring catching the light.

I wanted that. I wanted it so much it felt like a prayer lodged in my chest.

I had to survive this, somehow, but I wasn't sure there was any future where that was possible. I didn't have a full plan, just threads of one.

The ritual needed three things: A vessel. A seal. An anchor point.

I couldn't save the vessel, not yet, but maybe I could unmoor the anchor. Break the loop. Disrupt the leyline harmonics. Twist the city's roots out of sync. I had magic. I had blood. I had power this city hadn't burned out of me yet. I could offer something beyond sacrifice: interference.

Enough to make the ritual crack, to shove my hand into the gears before it finished.

Gabriel's voice echoed, unbidden.

"Don't do this alone."

I shook it off, but my fingers trembled.

I could still feel him, his hands gripping my waist, calloused and careful like he didn't trust the world not to break me. The smell of smoke and worn leather. The weight of him in the dark, solid and real in a way that defied every lie I'd ever believed about being unlovable.

He hadn't asked me not to go. He hadn't begged. He'd just looked at me like I was worth everything.

I closed my eyes and felt the phantom press of his lips to my shoulder. A touch meant for memory, not survival. and I almost turned around. Almost.

I didn't get to have that. Not yet. Maybe not ever. Still, his voice lingered in the back of my mind like a promise I didn't know how to keep, but I was determined to find a way.

"If you're the reckoning, I'll be your shield. Even if it kills me."

I wanted to scream at him. For loving me. For giving me something to lose.

Instead, I walked faster.

What I was about to do...It might break me. Probably *would* break me. Maybe worse.

But if it could buy even one second of delay, enough time for someone else to tear it all down? Then it was worth it. Even if that someone wasn't me. I didn't know who it would be, but there had to be someone, right? Somewhere?

The final stretch of road unspooled before me, straight as a blade. The ritual site loomed in the distance: an old chapel, broken and hollowed, beating like a heart made of stone. Its doors stood open. Waiting.

I blinked, and the world shimmered. For one breathless instant, I was there, and wasn't here.

I stood in the same chapel, but it was intact. Light poured through stained glass windows that were clean and bright. Children laughed somewhere behind me. Riot lay curled by the altar, and Gabriel sat on the steps, laughing with that wild-haired little girl.

She turned and looked at me, a smile splitting her face. "You're here!" she cried out, and turned to run toward me.

My breath caught, and the vision snapped like overstretched thread.

I stumbled, gasping, back into the present, heart pounding, skin cold.

I didn't know if that was a memory of the future or a lie designed to hurt, but it shook me, because part of me believed it. All of me wanted it.

I placed one hand against the chapel's ward line. It didn't reject me. It didn't welcome me, either; it just *knew* me. It knew what I was. What I carried, and what I might become.

I could still turn back, but I wouldn't.

This wasn't surrender.

It would be sacrifice, if it had to be, and I would make it.

For Riot.

For Gabriel.

Hell, even for Moshi.

For the future I hadn't dared dream of until now.

Even if it killed me.

Especially then.

I stepped forward.

The chapel shuddered as it recognized me. Not just the shape of my magic, but the weight of what I was about to do. The air turned viscous and cold. A dozen sigils flared around the archway, all burning violet, all flinching at my touch like they hadn't expected me to come willingly.

Then, like breath drawn through teeth, it opened. The pressure vanished, the veil parted, and I stepped through.

Nothing tried to stop me, which meant it might already be too late.

Behind me, the door closed with the softest click. I didn't look back. For a moment, just a breath, I imagined Gabriel standing there, Riot at his side, blood on his knuckles, and rage in his eyes.

I imagined him whispering my name one last time.

Not my title nor the name I'd been given by the man who engineered my existence.

Serena. The name of the girl he loved.

I forced my feet to move and walked forward into the shadow and wrongness as if I was still whole, like the world hadn't already started to rewrite itself in my wake.

I wasn't ready, but I was here.

It would have to be enough.

CHAPTER EIGHTEEN

OH LOOK, THE DOG HAS LORE

Gabriel

I WOKE TO ONLY the sound of my own breathing.

The bed beside me was cold, not just empty, but *cold*, like the absence had settled in for a while. I reached out, my hand grazing the sheet where she should've been. Her side of the bed held the shape of her body but none of her warmth. My fingers curled, clutching at nothing. The knife beneath the pillow was still there along with the one under the mattress and the one in the drawer. All untouched.

That's when I knew.

She was gone. She wasn't missing, she hadn't been taken. She'd *left*.

And I had *slept through it*.

I don't know how long I sat there. It was long enough for the cold to feel like it was mine, as if it had started inside me and spread outward, sinking into the sheets, the air, the bones of the room.

I told her she didn't have to run. I said it like a promise, like words could build a wall strong enough to keep her. She had slipped past it anyway: silent, deliberate, like she'd memorized the cracks and knew exactly where to escape.

A breath caught in my chest and wouldn't move. The stillness was too complete; even the dust was holding itself back. Part of me wanted to believe she'd be back, that maybe she'd just gone out for air. I knew that wasn't true, though. I'd seen this kind of absence before. It was the kind of emptiness that means *gone* and not *missing*. That kind that doesn't come back.

She hadn't left anything behind but the shape of her, and that, God, that hurt more than I thought it would.

The panic hit like a blade under the ribs, sudden and merciless. My breath caught somewhere in the back of my throat and stayed there, choking me on my own disbelief. I stood up too fast, head spinning, the slashes across my ribs pulling tight with pain. That's when I felt something clinging to me: magic. Residual, but recent. A thin sheen of charm dust shimmered in the morning light, glinting like betrayal on my skin.

She'd used a sleep spell. A gentle one; she'd put me under with care.

I stumbled away from the bed, feet tangling in the sheets. The sigil she'd drawn on the doorframe last night was smeared, edges bleeding into the wood grain. The windows still held the faint gleam of her warding, but the hum was dead, like the whole room was waiting to exhale.

"Serena?" I called, even though I already knew.

I turned in a slow circle, dread curling in my stomach. Her boots were gone. Her coat. Even the stupid ring she twisted on her thumb when she thought too hard was missing from the nightstand.

She'd gone prepared. She'd planned this.

And I—

I had kissed her hours ago, held her like she was mine, *looked her in the eye and told her she didn't have to go alone*—and she went anyway.

I stood in the middle of the room and let the world crash around me.

There was a flash of the night before: I could still feel her fingers in my hair, dragging slow nails across my scalp as she kissed me like the world wasn't ending. She'd curled into my side after, murmured something about the stars being too quiet. I told her she was imagining it. That she was safe.

She had nodded against my chest and lied with her silence.

I didn't even know I was crying until I tasted salt on my lips. My body didn't know whether to scream or shake or go still. I clenched my hands into fists and slammed them against the wall once, twice, until the skin split and the pain registered.

The worst part was knowing she'd done all of it to protect me.

I staggered back, heart in my throat, fists clenched. "You idiot," I muttered. "You brilliant, stupid, beautiful idiot."

I couldn't stay here. Couldn't sit in the echo of her absence.

And that's when I saw him.

Riot. Sitting at the edge of the room like a statue. Like he'd been there for hours. Waiting.

His eyes were different. Not the bright, curious blue that Serena swore meant he was paying attention. These were deeper, older, reflective in a way that had nothing to do with light.

"You stayed," I said, voice hoarse.

He nodded once. I didn't imagine it.

"She told you to guard me."

Another nod.

"And you did."

He blinked slowly.

"But you're not going to stay now."

This time, he stood.

I remembered the first time I saw him fight, really fight, at the Veil Market after we met with Mira Dusk. Serena had barely blinked before Riot had launched himself into the fray. No hesitation, no command, just this impossible fury, something primal and wrong and ancient in the way his body moved.

It wasn't a dog I saw that night. It wasn't even a familiar. It was something that came from before there were even words to describe what he was.

I remember Serena kneeling afterward, when we got someplace that we could take a breath. She'd embraced him, shaking, whispering something to him I couldn't hear. He'd pressed his head into her ribs like he was a penitent at prayer. Like he needed her breath to keep existing.

He fixed me with those uncanny eyes.

And then? I heard him speak.

At first, it wasn't English. It wasn't *language*.

It didn't come from his mouth. Instead, it scraped across the inside of my skull, a blade dragged through memory. It echoed with weight, tones stacked atop one another like voices through time, like thunder with opinions. My vision doubled. The room flickered.

Then, as if someone tuned a dial, it shifted. And Riot said, in a voice that wasn't a voice:

"She is not alone."

I staggered back a step. "You—what the hell—you can *talk*?"

"I always could," he said simply, as if a dog talking to me wasn't supposed to feel like the world was cracking open.

"You've always been able to talk?"

"Yes."

"Then why didn't you?"

He tilted his head, silver fur rippling like it was trying to remember being something else. "Because she needed me quiet. My silence gave her space. She didn't need prophecy or advice. She needed loyalty. She needed unconditional love."

"You let her go."

"She asked me to stay. So I did. Until the moment you opened your eyes." His eyes shimmered. "But you are awake now. The spell is broken. My obligation ends."

"She's walking into a death trap. And you—"

"I never planned to let her walk alone," he interrupted. "But I couldn't leave until you were ready."

"Ready for what?"

"For the truth."

He stepped toward the door, but I wasn't done.

"What are you?"

He looked back.

"I am what was made for her," he said. "Not with spell or blood, but with need."

"That's not an answer."

"No," he said. "It's a beginning."

My chest hurt. "I don't have time for riddles."

"I'm not a riddle," Riot said calmly. "I am the thing that watches. The consequence of too many timelines burned. I am the one who rises when the others fall. I am the fail-safe."

"Of what?"

"Of *her*."

And then, strangely soft, "You think she's breaking fate. But fate has been trying to break *her* for years."

He walked toward the door.

"Are you coming?" he asked without turning back.

"Do I have a choice?"

"Not a good one."

I moved.

The street outside didn't look like the one we had arrived through. The sidewalk breathed under my feet. Inhale, exhale, a low rhythmic thrum pulsing through the stone like the city was trying to sync its heartbeat to my own.

A newspaper blew toward me, pages flickering fast. It stopped at my boots, the headline morphing between three different versions of the same tragedy, each one dated tomorrow. I didn't bend to pick it up.

Riot padded forward like none of this was new. Maybe for him it wasn't.

To the left, a building split down the middle with a crack that shimmered in distinct realities. One side was brick and rot. The other? A cathedral in full bloom, windows flickering with stained glass portraits of a girl who looked too much like Serena.

I didn't look closely.

Not when the posters on the wall started bleeding through time, shifting from **Missing Persons** flyers to **Obituaries**, then to **Wanted** signs with her face and mine.

I reached for the wall to steady myself and jerked back.

It was warm and breathing, too.

Riot glanced at me over his shoulder. "Don't touch the city," he said, voice grating like iron against bone. "It remembers pain better than people."

Noctis had rearranged itself overnight: buildings folding inward, lamplight bending like gravity was drunk. I smelled blood on the air. Ash mixed in the concrete. The edges of the world curled as if the city was tiring of pretending to be a city.

"She's at the old chapel," Riot said.

"What the hell is she doing?"

"They started the ritual. A binding. They were going to use a girl, just some nameless soul, to anchor a spell to the city. A stall to buy them time to find Serena. Silas told us this. The Bone Lords want her tethered," Riot continued. "Threaded into the city's bones. They'll sanctify her if they have to. Make her eternal. The Vein? They'd rather cut her thread loose and let Noctis collapse. Obliteration is still a kind of freedom."

I stared at him. "So they both think they're helping."

"Helping," he echoed flatly. "The way fire helps by cauterizing a wound, maybe. Both factions want her, but neither knows what she truly is."

"And?"

"She plans to take the girl's place."

My stomach dropped. "She *what*?"

"She is stepping willingly into the circle. She's planning to poison the spell from the inside."

I pushed my legs faster. "She's going to get herself killed."

"She knows that's a possibility." He gave me a look that didn't belong on a dog's face, sharp and so fucking aware. "I've seen what happens when she dies," he said.

"And?"

"I'm not letting it happen again."

"Again?" I whispered, the word hanging in the air like frost. "What do you mean 'again'?"

Riot's ears flattened as he started trotting, forcing me to keep pace. My legs felt like lead, still heavy from the sleep spell, but adrenaline pushed me forward.

"Time isn't linear in Noctis," he said, voice ricochetting against the walls of my mind. "It pools. Eddies. Creates currents that double back on themselves. I've seen her die seventeen different ways."

"Jesus."

"He might be the only one who can help you here."

The surrounding buildings twisted, windows watching with too much interest. A shadow peeled itself from an alley and slithered away when Riot glanced at it. The air tasted like copper pennies and old smoke.

"Seventeen times," I repeated. "And you remember all of them?"

"Memory is the only constant." Riot paused at an intersection where three streets met at angles that hurt to look at. "I was designed that way."

"Designed? By who?"

"Her mother."

I nearly tripped over a crack in the sidewalk that hadn't been there a second before. "Serena's mother is dead."

"Yes." Riot's voice was matter-of-fact. "That's what made me possible."

He veered left down a street that shouldn't have connected to where we were. I followed, fighting the vertigo that came with Noctis' spatial inconsistencies. We cut through what used to be a train station, but the tracks had teeth now, and the rails whispered old names that made my skin crawl. A figure tried to block our path, something tall, wrapped in rust and shadow, but Riot didn't slow. He bared his teeth, and the thing unmade itself.

"Everything's coming loose," I said.

"No," Riot corrected. "Everything is waking up."

We moved in silence for a while after that.

The city dimmed. Sounds grew strange, and my shadow started moving a little too slowly behind me. Riot's reflection in a storefront window didn't match his real posture. One version looked at me. The other looked at something I couldn't see.

I looked at the buildings around us. One wall was covered in overlapping symbols: Bone Lord sigils, etched clean and orderly, now defaced by erratic Hollow Vein spirals. Not painted but carved, gouged so deep the wall itself bled shadow.

This wasn't vandalism. It was war. The city wasn't decaying; it was dividing, factions fighting for the same corpse. And Serena? She was the pulse they were trying to claim.

"This place," I said, breath catching, "I think it remembers us."

"It remembers *her*," Riot said. "It never forgot."

"What's the chapel?"

"Old ground. Pre-Veil. It was a site of convergence, where timelines used to stitch together before someone cut the thread."

"Someone?"

"The Voice. The first one. Or maybe the last. It's hard to tell, sometimes."

We turned another corner, and the chapel came into view in the distance, crooked and slouching, carved out of obsidian and malice.

"I thought the Voice was a person," I said.

"It was," Riot replied. "Once. But it made itself into an idea. A prophecy that could move. That could *change*."

"So, what? It wants Serena to replace it?"

"It wants Serena to conform, to become the version of herself that the Voice has seen. The girl who obeys fate."

I stared at the jagged steeple looming ahead. A sense of wrong clawed at my chest.

"And if she doesn't?"

"Then the story burns."

The deeper we ran, the worse the city got. Walls flickered in and out of existence, and signs bled ink down their glass. The sky split twice and stitched itself back together. Whatever stability the gods had built into this place, it was being undone, piece by piece.

We turned the last corner.

The chapel stood like a wound at the edge of a broken plaza. Broken teeth made of stone spires jutted out at random angles. Light spilled from the open doors, thick and sickly, oozing with too much intent.

Seven hooded figures lay scattered around the periphery of the opening, their bodies twisted at unnatural angles, throats glistening wet and dark, and I felt a stab of pride.

That's my girl.

We forced our way in, past the residual warding. Inside, the ritual had metastasized.

The circle was massive, old glyphs written in Bone Lord scrawl, but overwritten by something else. Vein work, living chaos written in arcane symbols. It crawled along the stone as if it had a heartbeat of its own.

At the center stood Serena.

She stood as the anchor. Barefoot. Bleeding. Power coiling around her like a noose. Her eyes were closed. Her hands raised, magic sparking wild and vicious as she held the spell in check. Blood streamed from her palms, feeding the circle. Feeding her sabotage.

"She's rewriting it," Riot whispered. "She's swapping the logic. Inverting the bind. Feeding the Vein false prophecy, twisted history. She's using her bloodline to *corrupt the core*."

"And if she fails?"

"She doesn't get a second chance."

I stepped forward. I didn't know what I was doing, I just knew that every atom in my body was screaming to get to her. The magic pushed back. I hesitated. Just for a breath, a fraction of a second, but it was enough for every doubt to crawl back in. Every moment I'd failed someone, every mission that ended in body bags and regret. Every person that I hadn't been fast enough to save. Riot said there were seventeen times he had watched her die. I didn't remember them, but my bones knew the truth of what he said.

She had walked into this alone because she thought I'd stop her, because she knew I'd try to drag her back. Because she didn't want me to break for her.

I wasn't trained for the kind of war where love made you reckless, where sacrifice looked like the only person you couldn't afford to lose.

I looked at her, standing in that storm of blood and defiance, and the realization hit me like the shockwave from an IED.

I wasn't here to save her.

I was here to stand with her, even if it killed me.

I was here to be hers.

I kept walking. I crossed the last line of the circle and stepped into the center, and the world screamed. Not with sound, but with pressure.

The glyphs beneath Serena's feet ignited. The entire spell structure surged inward, collapsing like a dying star. The ritual had realized it was losing her, so it struck back, fast and violent, trying to complete the ritual by force.

Serena staggered.

Her knees buckled.

Magic lashed out from the glyphs, clawing at her bones. Her spine arched and her mouth opened, but no sound came. It was trying to finish the bind, to rewrite her into the city, to make her something that could never leave. She was losing. I reached out, my hand wrapping around hers.

And everything changed.

The ritual shuddered.

Paused.

The anchor built for a single soul now sensed two, entwined and defiant. It reached for balance, for compliance. Found none. There was no logic for this kind of love, and it had not expected this. It hadn't expected both of us, bound by whatever it was that had wrapped itself around our hearts and fucking welded them together.

The ritual howled through the lines. It tried to throw me out, but my love, my magic, whatever you want to call it, locked onto hers. It didn't flare. It didn't burn.

It *held,* solid and unyielding.

A second heartbeat, a steady rhythm beneath the chaos.

Serena's eyes flew open.

She gasped, and for a moment, I saw the full weight of the ritual reflected in them. Her skin was cracked with glowing threads. Her hands bled freely, the blood hissing where it touched the glyphs.

But she was still in there, and now she was not alone.

Her magic surged one last time, surgical in its precision. She took everything she had left, all the corruption she'd fed into the ritual, all the false logic, the mirrored prophecy, the name she refused to let them write, and pushed.

With my hand in hers and my presence inside the circle, our bond tore through the ritual's core.

The glyphs fractured.

The altar cracked.

The tether snapped taut, reaching out like a final tongue trying to taste her soul, and Riot *moved.*

He launched into the circle, body streaked in firelight and shadow, something half-formed and holy, all muscle and righteous anger. His mouth opened wide and he bit the tether clean in half.

The ritual broke with silence that hit like thunder. Every glyph died. Every thread went dark. The air collapsed inward like a held breath released.

And Serena collapsed with it, straight into my arms. She was breathing.

Alive.

Still herself.

It had worked. She'd corrupted the ritual, broken the anchor, and destroyed the cult's foothold, but she'd nearly let it take her to do it.

I cradled her, shaking, overwhelmed by fury and awe and something far more dangerous:

Pride. Because she'd walked into that circle ready to die, and still chose to win. I held her until her breath smoothed out. Not all the way, but enough to know she was still fighting, even now.

Her lashes fluttered against my cheek. Her lips moved, but no words came out.

"Shhhh," I whispered. "You've done enough. You're allowed to survive this."

Riot circled once, then growled low. Not at us, but at the air. At the shift. The ward line surrounding the chapel began to retract. Magic, old and broken, slithered off the stones and returned to the dirt.

"They'll come soon," Riot said. "Whatever wasn't watching before, it is now."

I stood, one arm still around her shoulders, the other bracing her knees. She didn't weigh much. She should've been heavier, but instead she was all sharp edges and aftermath.

We made it to the chapel doors. My legs shook. Riot's paws dragged like he was burning off the last of whatever power had let him destroy the tether. We stepped out into the gray light.

And froze.

Two figures waited at the edge of the steps.

One was Moshi.

The other...I blinked, heart skipping. "I know you," I said.

The woman smiled. Same long coat. Same coiled braids. Same cool, unbothered energy I remembered from the Hateful Hag.

"You gave Serena something," I said slowly. "In a vial."

"A preservation charm," she said. "One of mine. For what was coming." She looked at Serena in my arms. Her smile didn't soften, but it gained weight. "Looks like she needed it."

"What are you doing here? HOW are you here?"

She nodded her head at Moshi. "That one called. Said that I might be useful."

My arms tightened around Serena instinctively. I turned to Moshi. I shifted Serena's weight, managed to pull my gun. I aimed it at his chest.

"You've got ten seconds to tell me why I shouldn't put a bullet in you."

Moshi didn't flinch.

"I'm here because Serena called me," he said. "Not with a spell. Not with a threat. Just... hope. She thought I might still have a soul." He cleared his throat. "She sent me a message. She said thank you. I had a feeling she was going to do something incompatible with her health."

Riot stepped between us. Not hesitating. Not aggressive. Just there.

"She believed he could come back from it," Riot said quietly. "She knew what he'd done, and she still gave him the chance."

"She gives everyone too many chances," I snapped.

Riot looked up at me. "She gave *you* one."

I didn't lower the gun, but I didn't pull the trigger either.

Not yet.

The bartender tilted her head, looking at Riot with a strange familiarity. "You're her mother's, aren't you? Made for her."

Riot didn't answer.

Didn't have to.

She turned her gaze back to Serena.

"I knew her mother, Rhiannon," she said. "And Brianna before her. This one carries all of their fire, and all of their weight."

She stepped forward, hand hovering over Serena's shoulder but not touching.

"She has more work to do," she murmured. "And she's going to need more than rage and instinct to survive it. She's going to need *you.*" She gave Serena one last look and then shifted her attention to me.

"Name's Edda," she said. "You remember me from the Hag. I've got a back room still under stasis, and a protection ward no Bone Lord's cracked in thirty years." She turned her gaze to Riot. "You're burning too fast. You need to rest."

Riot didn't argue. He just nodded once, gruff and tired and proud.

"We can't stay long," I said. "They'll be hunting us the second they regroup." I sighed. "I'm not even sure which they that was back there."

Edda shrugged. "Then you better rest fast and think faster."

She turned without waiting for approval, already walking. She didn't look back. Just trusted we'd follow.

Riot fell in step beside her.

I shifted Serena in my arms. She murmured something, so quiet I couldn't catch it, her fingers twitching like she was reaching for something in a dream. I shifted my arm so I could reach her hand, and her grip closed weakly around my thumb. Moshi stepped closer, hands lifted in something that wasn't quite surrender.

"Let me carry her," he said. "You're still bleeding."

I turned my head slowly, and he froze. "No."

"Gabriel—"

"You so much as *breathe* wrong near her," I said flatly, "and I will end you."

He blinked. "I'm trying to help."

"Great. Help by walking ten paces behind and keeping your redemption arc to yourself."

He opened his mouth again.

I smiled without humor. "Or I'll make sure your second betrayal ends with pieces of you very suddenly all over this street."

Riot let out a low huff that might've been laughter.

Edda just muttered, "Boys."

And we walked.

Noctis felt heavier now. The ritual had peeled away another layer, and the city wasn't bothering to pretend anymore.

"Why the Hag?" I asked, nodding toward Edda.

"She built it," Riot said before she could answer. "Before the Veil, before the Courts. She's one of the last true neutral anchors."

Edda gave him a sidelong look. "Flatter me and I might actually make you soup."

"I don't eat soup," Riot replied. That was a lie; I'd watched him scarf down an MRE, and I was pretty sure I'd seen him swallow a rat once.

"You will eat this soup and you will like it and be grateful."

She led us down a corridor that shouldn't exist, past a mural of a woman with white wings and empty eyes. My stomach turned as we passed. I recognized the shape of her jaw. Her hair. The tilt of her shoulders.

Serena. In another life. Or another death.

Edda caught the glance. "It's not a prophecy," she said. "It's a warning."

The Hateful Hag appeared around the corner like it had grown out of the bricks. From the outside, it looked the same—battered wood, rusted signs, and a faint flicker of purple fire in the lantern overhead. But the air around it was different. Cleaner, like stepping out of a storm.

Edda pressed her palm to the door. It opened without a sound.

"Inside," she said. "Before the scent of thwarted prophecy and blood brings scavengers."

We filed in. The place was empty, tables cleared, chairs stacked in shadow. The back room was already prepared: dim, safe, warded in runes that made my bones hum. A couch lay beneath a glowing line of protection glyphs, freshly painted and still steaming.

I laid Serena down as gently as I could.

She didn't wake.

Riot hopped onto the couch beside her, curled protectively at her side.

Edda lit a bowl in the corner. The smoke rose lavender and sharp. It sank into the corners of the room like it was stitching the ward together. "We'll be safe here," she said. "For a little while."

Moshi lingered by the door, looking like he didn't belong anywhere. He didn't, not really, and for the first time he couldn't make that an advantage.

"You're lucky she's unconscious," I said to him.

"Why?"

"She'd already have hexed your balls off."

He snorted. "Wouldn't be the first time she tried." He looked at Serena, regret dragging his mouth down. "I never wanted this for her."

Riot opened one eye. "And yet you paved the path that led her here."

Moshi didn't argue. I also noticed that neither he nor Edda seemed surprised that the dog was talking. That was a question I found I really wanted an answer to.

"Make yourself useful," Edda said to him. "Boil water. Find some clean cloth."

Moshi vanished into the kitchen without a word.

I sat on the floor beside Serena. Her breath came easier now. Her fingers had stopped twitching. I reached out and brushed the hair from her face. "You're not done yet," I murmured. "You made it through the fire. Now you have to survive the smoke."

Riot shifted beside her. "She heard you," he mumbled.

Edda sank into a battered chair across from us, legs crossed, gaze sharp. "This changes everything."

"I know." I twined my fingers with hers. Her hands were so small, long fingers tipped with short nails that had once been varnished a pale pink. They were chipped and torn now.

Edda looked at Riot. "You're still burning too fast."

"I'll hold." He laid his head back down, muzzle resting on her legs.

"For how long?"

"As long as she needs me to," he said, and closed his eyes.

The silence that followed felt like the closing of a door.

Outside, the city creaked like it knew a reckoning had arrived. Inside, I closed my eyes and held onto her hand like it was the only thread still tethering the world to what mattered.

A.L. RICHARDS

CHAPTER NINETEEN

TEAM TRAUMA, ASSEMBLE

Gabriel

SERENA SLEPT LIKE SOMEONE bracing for impact. Her body had gone still, but she rested like her bones remembered battle and didn't trust the quiet. Riot lay pressed against her side on the battered couch in the Hateful Hag's backroom, muzzle tucked near her ribs like he could keep her tethered to this world through sheer force of will.

I sat on the floor beside her, knees bent, hand still stained with blood that wasn't mine. Across the room, Edda sealed the final sigil at the door with a flick of her wrist. Smoke curled up around the threshold, sharp with iron and ash. Wards meant to hold against a siege were locked tight into place, at least until the Vein came looking.

"We'll stay hidden here," Edda said, her voice rough with exhaustion. "For a little while, anyway."

I didn't answer. My attention was still on Serena. I watched her breath rise and fall in shallow pulses, like each one had to fight its way through her chest. The lines of her face were drawn tight with strain even in unconsciousness.

Her breath hitched again, and I tensed at how shallow and slow it was. I found myself counting the seconds between each rise and fall of her chest, like if I kept track I could keep her tethered here. Beside her, Riot didn't move, but his gaze flicked toward her, his body curled protectively like a second set of ribs.

I'd seen soldiers like this before, after blasts, after blood, after what came too close to death to call what came next survival. They looked fine, mostly. They were breathing, their bodies whole. It wasn't until later that you could tell the soul had gone quiet in them. Like it was listening, waiting to decide whether it would come back.

Serena looked like that now, and it gutted me.

She wasn't a soldier, but she walked straight into the line of fire anyway. She stood in the path of something meant to shatter her and didn't blink. Now, though, I wondered if this time it had been too much. Her body was here, but I wasn't sure all of her had come back with it.

"Breathe," I whispered again, even though she was. "Come back."

If she didn't, I didn't know what I'd do with the part of me that went with her.

Even here, listening to her breathe, I couldn't stop seeing the moment the ritual ended, couldn't stop hearing the crack of broken marble underfoot. I could still feel her going still in my arms, like someone had turned out all the lights inside her at once.

The air had smelled like scorched bone and hot metal. Spellfire had clung to everything, sticky and buzzing. The walls were still humming with residual power, runes half-lit like they didn't know which reality they belonged to anymore. She had looked at me, just for a moment, and dropped. I'd caught her before she hit the floor, and even then, I could feel it, that her body wasn't empty, just *locked*. It was held in place by some goddamned metaphysical fail-safe her ancestors probably built in. It wasn't just a collapse, or a reset. It was containment, but what exactly it was holding, I wasn't sure.

I'd carried her through the wreckage like I'd done it before. The others—Moshi, Riot, Edda—were watching for cult stragglers, holding the line, but all I could hear was the absence of her breathing. It wasn't gone, but it was so shallow that it was just barely there.

I had kicked open a sigil gate with my heel, had shattered the edge of a binding circle and let the old protection ward flare once, then fizzle. My hands were already bloody by then, and I couldn't tell which part came from her, or me, or something else entirely.

The worst part of it was when she didn't stir when I called her name. Not once. That was when the panic hit, followed by this sudden, brutal certainty that if I lost her now, there would be no revenge worth having that would make me want to go on without her.

It wasn't just about protecting her anymore.

I'd known that when I'd woken up at the hotel, after she was already gone, the bed cold where she'd lain, Riot curled up at edge of the room like a sentry who knew his duty and hated what he'd been asked to do. She hadn't left a note, just quiet spells woven into the walls and one whispered charm to keep me sleeping while she walked away.

I should've been furious. I *was* furious. Underneath, though, was the raw understanding that she'd made that choice not because she didn't trust me, but because she loved me enough to keep me out of it.

That's what shifted everything.

I didn't want vengeance. I didn't just want to protect her. I wanted to stand beside her and be chosen back. I wanted her to come back to me, not because she had to, but because she *could*.

And if she couldn't?

I was going to tear the Weave apart until I found the thread that still held her.

It wasn't even about love, not really, though there was plenty of that. It was about right. The bone-deep, blood-sworn certainty that I was meant to follow her out of that place. That whatever came next, it had to have her in it, and if I needed to, I would lay waste to this world until it made room for her to stay.

Moshi stood in the corner like he wasn't sure if he was allowed to exist anymore. I didn't look at him. Not yet. I just ignored him, choosing instead to focus all my attention on the little bundle of woman on the couch.

"You made it through the fire," I murmured again, brushing a curl from Serena's cheek. "Now find your way back through the smoke."

Riot's ears flicked. For a long time, he didn't speak.

"I don't know what I'm becoming," he finally said.

It wasn't his usual voice. Not the sarcastic snap or smug mutter he wore like armor. This one was lower. Raw.

"I was made to carry her forward. That's not new." His eyes, bright and unblinking, stayed locked on Serena. "But this... this isn't like the others. Something's different. I'm not just remembering. I'm changing."

Edda turned, the lines around her mouth deepening. "Into what?"

Riot hesitated. "I don't know. She's not repeating the cycle. She's writing a new one. I'm part of it, I just don't know what part." He shifted, ears twitching like the past had a sound only he could hear.

"There was a time," he said slowly, "when she died with a prayer on her lips."

Edda stilled. Even the wards seemed to pause.

"I think it was the ninth life," Riot continued. "She had white hair that time. A scar across her palm she could never explain. We lived in a monastery built on top of a collapsed fracture. People came from all over thinking the place was sacred. They weren't wrong, but it wasn't the kind of holy anyone wanted."

He turned his eyes toward Serena, gaze soft as wool and twice as heavy. "She bled out on the stones behind the altar after fighting off something they tried to crown in her place. I curled around her as she died behind that altar, pressed my body against hers so the stone wouldn't be the last thing she felt, and she whispered, 'Make it count.' Then she closed her eyes and never opened them again. I dragged her body past the gates and let the river take her bones."

Edda murmured something that sounded like a name, but Riot kept going. "They burned the place down after. They said it was cursed. I thought that would be the end of it, but then she woke up somewhere else. New name. New face. Same soul." He exhaled slowly.

"I used to think I was just the tether. The thing that dragged her back each time the world tried to bury her. But this time..."

He looked down at his paws. "I don't feel like I'm just carrying her forward. I feel like I'm becoming part of the story."

His voice dropped even lower, almost reverent. "She's not rerouting fate anymore. She's making a new one. And I can't tell if that means I'm more real... or if I'm something else entirely."

He looked at me then, dead serious. "But I know this: I don't want to start over again." His voice in my mind was so, so serious. "I was created to follow her across timelines. To survive her deaths and pull the thread into the next life. But she's not dying this time. She's not resetting. That rewrites me, too."

"You were built to endure her endings," I said quietly.

He nodded. "And now she's building a beginning."

His voice dipped into something that bordered on awe. "She makes me want to stay."

Riot sat blinking slowly, like the air had thickened in his lungs. When he finally spoke, his voice was almost too soft to hear. "You know what scares me?" he asked. "It's not the change. It's that I want it."

His gaze flicked to the door, the wards, the blood-streaked floor. "All my lives, I've been the reminder. The memory that won't die. The dog that follows her down every ruined path. I've watched her burn. I've watched her break. I've dug through rubble with my teeth just to find pieces of her."

His voice wavered. "But this time, I dream. I sleep. I taste food. I feel things. Not echoes. Not reflections. Actual things." He looked at his paws again. "I think I'm becoming real. I know this isn't a human fairy tale. There's no Blue Fairy. But I can feel it."

In the hush that followed, I understood the truth of his words. He wasn't afraid of forgetting what he was. He was afraid of finally being something new, and losing her anyway.

I understood exactly how he felt.

Edda listened quietly, but then her mouth tightened, her gaze flicking to Moshi like she wanted to spit out something she'd been holding for years.

"You know what one of the worst parts is?" she said, not looking at either of us, but fixing her gaze on Moshi like a laser. "He's done this before."

Moshi didn't move. He stood like someone already halfway erased. Hands limp at his sides. Shoulders slightly hunched, not from fear, but from habit, guilt worn so long it had calcified into posture. I watched his jaw clench, a vein pulsing at his temple. Whatever Edda's words stirred in him, he didn't fight back. He didn't defend himself. You could only take so many hits like that and keep standing. But Moshi didn't sit down. He didn't ask for forgiveness and he didn't try to justify what he'd done. He just absorbed it like someone who'd been preparing for this reckoning for a long time.

I didn't trust him, but I understood the look in his eyes. It was the same one I'd seen in mirrors I'd wanted to smash. The look of a man who didn't know how to fix what he'd shattered, but was willing to be turned into a tool anyway if it meant there was a chance.

I didn't know if that made him brave or just desperate, but I was beginning to think it didn't matter.

"Not like this," Edda continued, almost to herself, looking back down at Serena. "Not with her. But with Rhiannon."

That got my attention.

"She never told her daughter," Edda said. "Of course she didn't. But Brianna knew."

The names landed heavy. Serena's mother and grandmother, the ones whose legacy still bled through half the wards Edda used, who had vanished so completely that even the city didn't whisper their names unless it had to.

"She and Rhiannon worked together for decades. Always in pairs. One would raise the wards, the other would bait the trap. They were vicious, brilliant, bound by blood and ambition. But when the Voice came whispering through the fracture points, when the first prophecy shifted, Moshi broke." She turned to him then. "Didn't you?"

Moshi's hands curled into fists. "I didn't know what I was giving them."

"You knew enough," Edda snapped. "You knew Brianna was missing. You knew Rhiannon was half-dead trying to hold the splintered threads together, and you still handed them the cipher."

"Tell me," I said. "Start with the cipher."

Edda folded and unfolded the cloth in her hands. "It wasn't just a code. It was the key to everything Brianna and Rhiannon had woven into their original protections. Glyphs, songs, knots of power that they tied to the earth itself. They used it to bend the prophecy around her like a shield." She reached out with the cloth and wiped a smudge of dirt from Serena's face. "She was never just a girl. She was a convergence."

I felt my jaw tighten. "Convergence of what?"

"Of every thread that The Voice tried to sever." Edda's voice went quiet. "The first prophecy back before...whatever that thing is...touched it and twisted it into a war cry didn't name her as a weapon. It named her as fulcrum. A living knot.

"Brianna said fate wasn't a line, but a braid, a thousand possibilities tangled together. Selene was the point they all knotted around."

I didn't speak. I couldn't.

"She wasn't meant to be used. She was meant to be the one to choose, to choose which thread to pull, which world to save, which possibility to make reality. So, they gave everything they were to wrap the original prophecy around her so that the inner core of what, of who, she is would be safe. Then *he*," and she glared at Moshi, "gave the key to undoing it to her father."

"I didn't know!" Moshi snarled, finally showing a spark of life.

"You knew it mattered! You knew Rhiannon died to keep it hidden, and you gave it away anyway!"

"I thought I was protecting her!"

"You keep saying that," I said. "I'm not sure you know what those words mean."

Edda pointed at him, and he actually flinched. "Brianna died trying to keep the original prophecy intact. Rhiannon died trying to keep Selene free. You? You gave Myrddin the only thing that could undo everything they tried to do."

Edda turned back to the table, dropping the cloth in her hands onto the table. "The reason I didn't kill him back then is the same reason I'm not stopping him now. Guilt is a better chain than loyalty, and because Rhiannon said something to me, just once, after Brianna disappeared." Her voice dropped, gravel-thick. She said, "'There's no version of this where we all make it. So pick the one that gives her a future.'"

She looked down at Serena, still unconscious, curled like a blade that hadn't decided who to cut yet. "That's what we're doing now. Picking the version. And this time, I don't care what we have to burn to keep it."

Serena stirred, just a flicker of movement. Her fingers curled faintly, like her body was still cataloguing loss and demand and what came next. Her breath hitched, and then smoothed. Riot shifted beside her, his body an anchor. She took a deep breath, and her eyes fluttered open. She looked at the ceiling, then at me, then sat up slowly, as if it hurt to remember how to move.

"Talk," she said. "Tell me everything. I need to know *everything*."

Edda stood. "Where do I start? What your mother and grandmother suspected—that fate has been repeating itself, spiraling through bloodlines and bone—that part you already know."

Serena nodded once. "And?"

"You weren't supposed to win," Edda said, voice low. "You weren't supposed to kill him. That was never the plan. In the story they were writing... whoever *they* is...you were the container. The sheath. You were meant to hold power, not wield it. That was what your father intended, what he'd been maneuvered to work towards. That was what your mother and grandmother tried to subvert."

Serena didn't react, but I saw the way her spine stiffened.

"The Voice doesn't care who ascends, not really. It only cares that someone does. Someone who fits the pattern, who can be manipulated. You were meant to be a stepping stone, a tool for ultimate control."

"And I wasn't," Serena said flatly.

"No," Edda said, with something like pride. "Because Rhiannon lied."

She reached into her pocket and dropped an object onto the table: a length of red thread, knotted in thirteen places, humming with stored magic. "She told them she was raising a vessel. She wasn't. She was raising a queen."

Serena reached toward the thread, fingers pausing just above it. For a second, she didn't touch it, just stared at it like it was vibrating at a frequency only she could hear. Then she brushed it lightly, and something in her went utterly still, as if she were listening.

I watched the breath catch in her throat, the way her lashes fluttered like a wind had passed through her without moving the air. She didn't speak, didn't attempt to explain. Her hand curled slowly, withdrawing from the thread like it had burned her with memory.

When she finally looked up, her eyes were both sharp as a new blade and so much older than before.

"I watched them do it," Edda said quietly. "Rhiannon and Brianna. Side by side. Always in lockstep. You couldn't split them if you tried."

She didn't look at us. Her fingers hovered over the knotted thread on the table, like it still remembered the weight of the choice they'd made. "Everyone talks about Rhiannon like she was the fire, the wild one, but they forget who taught her to burn. Brianna was quieter. But gods, she was the one you had to watch. She didn't scream her warnings; she sang them. In lullabies, in stories, in the way she braided your hair or salted the doorframe. Everything she touched was layered in purpose."

Serena didn't move, but I saw the shift in her expression. Recognition. Remembrance.

"She was the one who started it," Edda said. "She found the theory, the idea that fate wasn't a line, but a braid and that if you could follow the twists back far enough, you could find the place where everything converged. She thought that place was a person. She thought it was *you.*"

Serena's voice was soft. "I thought it was my mother who believed that."

"She did," Edda said, "because Brianna made her believe it."

She turned her eyes on Serena, ancient and burning. "They raised you together. Don't let the story cut Brianna out of it. Rhiannon was the fire, but Brianna was the forge. She built the tools. Drew the first blood. She sacrificed her own name to keep yours intact."

Serena's brows knit slightly. "No one talks about her."

"Because she asked us not to," Edda said. "She told us if she became a symbol, they'd twist her. Some would turn her into a prophecy, others would use her as a cautionary tale, or worse, a martyr to use as leverage."

I asked the question I knew Serena didn't want to. "How did she die?"

"She didn't," Edda said. "Not completely. She offered herself to the city as a trade. She was a sealing knot, tied in blood and will. She said, 'Write me out, and I'll make room for her.'"

"You mean she—"

"Some part of her lives in the cracks," Edda said, "In the spell that still shields Serena from full recursion. In the wards that never fall, even when they should."

Riot looked at Serena. "That's why so much of this city keeps your secrets, even when so many work to drag you into the light."

Edda nodded. "Because someone else already paid the price for its silence."

Serena swallowed. "I need the truth," she said, face hard. "Not the grief, not the legacy. I want to know how my mother ended up with *him*. How I came from that. How, if they were trying to stop him, she ended up having a child by him."

Edda was silent for a long time. Long enough that I thought she wouldn't answer, but then she spoke.

"She made the decision herself."

Serena blinked.

"There was no coercion. No ritual rape. No glamour fog. He didn't force her, not in the way you're thinking. Rhiannon saw what he was trying to do, what he was building. She saw his experiments. The deaths. The bodies that couldn't hold what he wanted to anchor."

Edda's mouth twisted. "He was looking for your bloodline. And if he didn't get it from her, he was going to take it from someone else. Someone younger. Weaker. More breakable."

"She did it to stop him," Serena said, voice hollow.

"She did it to control the story," Edda corrected. "To take the one thing he couldn't fake: your blood. Our blood." Serena's eyebrows raised at that, and Edda nodded. "We're related, somewhere in there. The lines get muddled, but we share an ancestor somewhere." She sighed, then continued, "Anyway, Rhiannon got to him first. Played the part he wanted, gave him the illusion of control. She let him think it was his idea. And then, when she was carrying you, she started weaving protections into you so deep he'd never see them until it was too late."

Serena's hands clenched.

"She knew he'd never love you," Edda said. "She knew he'd try to mold you into a tool. But she also knew one truth he never accounted for."

"What truth?"

"That you'd be hers. That her love would forge something he could never break."

The words hit like a ward line breaking. Serena sucked in a sharp breath.

"She built you from his bones and her blood, and she made damn sure that whatever part of you came from him would never be stronger than the part that came from *her*. She didn't just carry you; she designed you to survive him, grown in the depths of a mother's love for her child."

I didn't know Brianna, and I'd barely known of Rhiannon. I'd only heard the echoes. Now, though, looking at Serena, I saw the magic they left in her veins, a war cry disguised as inheritance.

Hearing Edda, I was struck by how much of them Serena truly carried.

Rhiannon was fire. That part was easy to spot. I saw her in Serena's sharpness, her ferocity, the way she never flinched when things turned bloody. She was the strike, the spark, the blade drawn before you even realized a fight had started.

Brianna was the quiet danger, the kind you didn't see coming until the ground gave way. I saw *her* in the details. The salt lines along every windowsill. The way Serena checked every lock twice, not for paranoia, but for ritual. The stories she carried in her silence. The softness that wasn't weakness but strategy.

Together, they'd built something monstrous and beautiful: a girl born from bloodlines that never broke, shaped by women who knew the stakes and chose to love her anyway.

Serena had always moved like someone used to standing alone. But now I understood: it wasn't because she'd been abandoned. It was because she'd been *loved*. Their love had given her the strength to hold her ground, even if she held it alone.

She didn't just carry their legacy. She was the weapon they left behind, not to follow a twisted prophecy, but to break it.

More than that, I knew exactly why they'd done it.

Because if anyone could crack fate at the spine and demand a better ending?

It was *her*.

Edda stepped closer, voice lowering. "Your mother made herself the firebreak. And when Myrddin realized what she'd done, he tried to rewrite it. Tried to lock her away. Brianna got her out. Not alive, but out."

Serena's expression didn't shift, but her magic did, flickering faintly across her skin like old lightning remembering how to burn. "She left you not because she was afraid," Edda said. "But because it was the only way for you to win."

Serena didn't cry. Didn't flinch. She looked down at her hands, and for the first time, she didn't seem angry about what she'd inherited. She seemed almost...reverent.

"She chose me." Her voice was quietly incredulous.

"She *loved* you," Edda said. "And with that love, Rhiannon and Brianna built a resistance."

And from the way the walls pulsed behind her words, I knew: the city had never forgotten Serena. It had just been waiting.

Serena looked down at the thread on the table, then at Edda. "What happens if I don't ascend?"

"Then they'll force someone else to. They'll crown her. Rewrite you and collapse the rupture."

"And if I let them come," Serena said, voice soft, "but give them the wrong ending?"

"Then we have a chance."

Moshi shifted. I looked at him for the first time in what felt like hours.

"I know everything you said before," Serena said without looking at him. "But I need to know why you're still here."

He opened his mouth, closed it, tried again. "Because I want to help."

"No," she said. "You want to matter. Those aren't the same."

He stood stock still.

"You still have a purpose," she added. "If you're willing to be used."

His jaw tightened. "What do you want me to do?"

She rose from the couch. Riot moved with her, like a shadow trailing light.

"You're going to be bait."

Even Edda blinked at that.

Serena crossed the room until she stood in front of Moshi. "They don't completely trust you, but they don't distrust you, either. You'll let them think you're still compromised, that you're still their man."

"And then?"

"Then I close the door," she said.

He swallowed. "You'll really use me."

"I'll use anything I can," she said. "You're not special."

Moshi didn't answer. Just nodded once and stepped back into the shadows.

Edda moved to the shelf and pulled down a brittle roll of parchment bound in rusted wire. She unrolled it across the table with deliberate care.

It wasn't a map in the traditional sense, with lines and streets. It was a memory of the city: what it used to be, what it wanted to become, and all the places in between. Points glowed faintly, like dying stars.

"These are the fractures," she said, "where the rules break. Where time skips. Places where the city forgets itself."

"I've seen one," I said.

Edda looked over. So did Serena, her head tilting slightly like she wasn't sure whether to ask or listen.

"Wasn't part of the mission," I said. "We were running recon near what we thought was a collapsed sanctum. Third sublevel, no known enemy activity, and no, I'm not telling you what the US Army was doing in Noctis. It was just leftover energy and half-dormant symbols. I stepped into a hallway and walked thirty feet. Turned a corner. Walked thirty more. When I turned again, I was back at the first corner. Same bloodstain. Same dust."

Serena frowned. "A loop?"

"Not quite. The third time around, there was a girl walking toward me. About ten, wearing a crown made of nails. She never blinked. Just kept whispering, 'You're early.'"

"Shit," Riot muttered.

"I tried to leave. Burned a door into the wall with C4. It opened into another hallway, this one full of portraits. They were all of me. Not just military. Childhood. Things that hadn't happened yet."

Serena's voice was quiet. "How did you get out?"

"I stopped walking like a soldier," I said. "Stopped trying to track time. I told the space I wasn't afraid to forget myself."

"And it let you go?"

I nodded.

Serena leaned over the map. "Which one can I collapse?"

Edda pointed to a jagged sigil that glowed faintly with residual magic. "Here. It used to be an office, then a market, then a sanctuary. Now it's just a hole. Nothing stays. No one remembers it's there until they're standing in it."

"Perfect," Serena said.

"You'll need anchors," Edda said. "False ritual markers. Blood signatures. Something to make the pattern believe it's already started."

"I can fake compliance," Serena said. "I've been doing it my whole life. I'll feed them the thread myself. But when they come for it?" She met my eyes. "They'll find teeth."

We spent hours planning, Edda marking the anchor points. Riot vanished into the city to check each one. Moshi memorized his route and the way he'd let the Bone Lords think he was leading them somewhere sacred. I added my own layer: sabotage patterns from my time in the field. Fail points, triggers, with every step timed to Serena's pulse.

I didn't just mark exits and fallback zones. I built rituals into the floorboards of our plan, layered beneath the warding lines—subtle, quiet spells of collapse, keyed not to her failure but to her refusal. If they caught her, if they tried to cage her again, I'd lay waste to the whole goddamn story before I let them take her back.

I used grave wax and the last of my soulstone filings, stamping the seals with her blood and mine. I finished the spells with interlocked runes no one but I could read, symbols I hadn't touched since I left the service, since I swore I'd never run ops like this again.

One of them would lock the fracture point in on it-self—folding the recursion inward, crushing anything caught inside it.

The second would light the sanctuary with fire from beneath, a silent blaze laced with spiritbane. It wouldn't kill them, but it would strip the magic from their bones long enough to make them *hurt*.

The third was the one I didn't tell her about. It wasn't destruction.

It was extraction.

It was a failsafe designed to grab her soul if they separated it from her body, to pull it out of their hands and bury it in the only place they couldn't reach.

Me.

The warding took hours to etch. I carved it into shell casings, the lining of my boots, the cloth over my ribs. I painted it on the inside of her coat while she slept for a few precious minutes, her body still trying to recover from the ritual she'd poisoned.

Where this was concerned, it was better to ask forgiveness than permission.

Behind me, the others worked in silence. Moshi practiced his trail, perfecting the staggered glance over his shoulder that said "almost caught." Edda reworked the binding thread, muttering to the air in four languages. Riot was nowhere to be seen, but I knew he was doing his recon out in the city.

And Serena...

She stood by the shattered mirror in the corner, watching herself with a look I couldn't quite read, like she already knew which parts of herself she'd have to leave behind to make it out.

I closed the final loop, sealed it with a whisper, and pressed the ward into my palm until it cut.

I would wade through entire fields of brimstone to carry her out of this fire. That was my vow.

And when it was all laid bare, when the plans were scrawled across the floor and the wards were burning low, we were alone again, Edda having disappeared to tend to the bar, Moshi having left to begin to lay the trail that would lead them to us. Serena stood by the window, backlit by the dying streetlight outside, the glow staining the edges of her hair in copper. She didn't move when I stepped behind her, just let the silence settle between us like something sacred.

"They're going to come," I said quietly.

"That's the plan."

"They think they've already won."

She didn't laugh. "They think they're writing my story." She turned then, eyes sharp and steady. "They forgot something."

"What's that?"

She reached for my hand. "I'm the one holding the pen."

I gripped her fingers tight.

"We have to burn their version of the story," she said.

I didn't hesitate. "Then we salt the ashes."

She didn't look away from me. Not right away. Just stood there, fingers curled around mine, steady in the silence.

"I don't know how this ends," she said quietly.

"I do," I answered.

She raised a brow.

"You survive."

The corner of her mouth lifted, just slightly. "That simple, huh?"

I hesitated. Just for a breath. Then: "I love you."

She stilled.

I didn't backpedal. Didn't soften it. Just kept my voice low, sure. "I know it's insane. I know this is a war zone and we're stitched together with trauma and borrowed time. But I'm saying it anyway, because if you're walking into hell again, I want you to carry that with you."

Serena blinked slowly, like the words had landed in places she didn't know were waiting. She didn't say it back. She didn't have to.

She stepped in close, pressed her forehead to mine, and whispered, "Then I won't let go."

"Neither will I."

I kissed her like a vow.

CHAPTER TWENTY

PLEASE HOLD WHILE WE FUCK EVERYTHING UP

Serena

T HE BACK ROOM OF the Hateful Hag smelled like old beer and older magic. Dust clung to the ceiling beams like the cobwebs had made peace with being cursed. Someone had carved protective runes into the table legs and then scratched through them. The wards on the door didn't hum, they hissed, and the floor creaked under too many memories. Somewhere in the rafters, something unseen moved, too slow to be a rat, too light to be human. A sound like teeth clicking echoed once, then stilled. The air pressed against my skin like it wanted to peel it away and wear it. Not hostile really, or hungry. It felt like it was curious and wanted to take me apart to find out how I worked.

I didn't flinch. The Hateful Hag was full of old things that had stopped being things and started being something else. It watched us; a mirror caught our reflections, but only two of us were real. The third figure flickered. Wrong height. Wrong face. I didn't look again.

Gabriel sat on the battered desk. He hadn't said a word about the way he winced every time he moved. Neither had I.

Riot shoved the door open with his shoulder and staggered inside, looking like the city had tried to chew him apart and spit him back out. His coat was streaked with soot and blood, one flank scorched with a line of magic that pulsed like a fading heartbeat. His blue eyes, when they found mine, were full of storm clouds. I knelt beside him. He looked at me, and I knew he didn't want me to touch him yet, not till the magics clinging to him had dissipated.

"They are already moving." His voice slid into my skull like smoke through a crack in the wall. "Not separately. Together."

I still wasn't used to the fact that my dog could talk to me, but I hadn't been surprised, either. Nothing much surprised me anymore.

Gabriel, still half-slumped on the desk, straightened like a wire had been pulled tight. "What do you mean together? Bone Lords and the Vein?"

Riot shook his head, slow and deliberate, then leaned into my side like he didn't trust the floor to hold him.

"Maybe? Or not exactly?" He shook his head, like he was trying to jostle his thoughts into some sort of order. "The orders aren't theirs anymore. I saw one of the Vein wearing a face it hadn't earned. It wore a man like a suit. And the eyes didn't blink."

Gabriel's voice dropped. "So it's coming. The Voice."

"No." Riot's mental tone hit like a cold snap. "It's not coming. It's already inside. It's not controlling them, it's rewriting them."

I felt it then, and I realized the monster wasn't outside the door. The call was coming from inside the house.

"They believe it, though." I said. "Whatever it is. They think they're choosing."

"They *are* choosing." Riot's head dropped against my lap. "You know how Noctis works. Something can't be taken, it can only be accepted if freely given. They chose this. They think this ends with a crown. On *your* head. At least the Bone Lords do."

I grabbed a pillow off the worn couch, sliding it beneath Riot's head, then stood, every nerve ringing like a hammer on an anvil. "A crown?"

"They think you're the throne."

Gabriel's jaw clenched. "So we're not just fighting cults. We're fighting a rewrite of reality."

My gaze snapped to Riot. "Has The Voice revealed itself?"

He didn't answer right away. "I don't know," he finally answered. "It started as whispers. Then it started writing. Now? It's not whispering at all. It's speaking through them."

"And they don't even know," I whispered.

"No, they know. They just think it will end well for them. They think it's fate. That's what makes it dangerous."

Gabriel looked between us, tension radiating off him like heat. "What if we're in the story, too? What if this—this trap we're building—what if it's part of the plan? The Voice wants an Ascendant. What if this is the path to make you one?"

I didn't answer, because I'd already thought of that, and I hated how much sense it made.

I brushed ash from Riot's fur, fingers slow and deliberate. His body trembled like a dog coming down from a lightning strike.

"We're not ahead of this," I murmured. "We're already inside it."

Gabriel looked at me like he wanted to argue, but Edda's arrival kept him silent.

The round table in the bar's warded cellar looked like it had been dragged out of a forgotten war, with burned edges and bloodstains worked into the grain. Someone had carved a chessboard into the surface and then gouged out half the squares like they'd lost one too many games. Edda stood by it, red thread looped twice around one wrist. She didn't ask if we were ready. She just started talking.

"They've begun aligning sigils over fracture sites. Vein and Bone Lords both. Sanguine, the Kline Rift, the Dry Market vaults. That's not resource control; that's ritual staging. They're not allies," she added before Gabriel could speak. "The Bone Lords build scaffolds. Shrines to try to contain her. The Hollow

Vein usually just burns it all down. But they both want her in the center of the wreckage. The only difference is what they want to do once they get her there."

Gabriel frowned. "So... a stalemate?"

"No," Edda said grimly. "A race. And she's the finish line."

Gabriel planted both hands on the map. "We don't stop them by fighting every location. There aren't enough of us. We pick the one that matters, the deepest fracture, and build a recursion trap. One entrance. No exits." He pointed. "We'll use false anchor points here, here, and here, sigils keyed to collapse on activation. They'll think they're writing an ascension rite. We let them believe that. We let them drive themselves into position."

Edda raised a brow. "And then what?"

Gabriel didn't smile when I answered. "Then we rewrite the ending." I continued, my voice quieter. "I'll stake my soul to the center of it. They want a vessel? I'll let them think they have one."

Moshi stood near the shadows, hands clasped behind his back like he hadn't betrayed us, like the guilt hadn't carved new hollows into his face. He stepped forward before anyone could speak, but not with a plan. He didn't pull out a strategy. He looked at me, not as the leader, not as the name they all wanted to crown or kill. Just me. And his voice, when it came, was smaller than I remembered.

"Do you still drink rose tea with honey? The one your grandmother used to make?"

I froze. For a second, the thread in my palm pulsed. That memory wasn't in the files. It wasn't tactical. It was mine.

"I haven't had that in years," I said quietly.

Moshi nodded. "You used to curl your hands around the cup like it was armor. You'd sip it during council meetings, when your father was razing someone's life to the dregs and you didn't want anyone to see your hands shake."

He didn't look at anyone else. Just me. "I used to brew it for you. When you were too proud to ask."

A breath caught in my throat, just for a second.

It didn't change what he did, but it reminded me that once, a long time ago, someone had remembered that how I liked my tea, and in a world full of knives, that memory cut the deepest.

It didn't make forgiveness easy.

But maybe...*maybe*...it made it possible.

One day.

He cleared his throat. "I can walk them in," he said softly, looking at the others. "They'll still trust me." He looked at me, and for the first time, there was no calculation in his gaze. Just weight. "Just promise me there's a way out."

The room went still. No one answered, not because we didn't want to, but because we couldn't.

Edda's jaw flexed. "You know no one can promise that."

Moshi closed his eyes. "That's what I thought."

Gabriel folded the map, the motion sharp. "We need more than sabotage. We need chaos."

Edda hesitated. Her fingers flexed once, and then she whispered a word I didn't recognize. The temperature in the room dropped ten degrees.

"What are you doing?" Gabriel asked, his brows drawn together.

"Calling the ones I probably shouldn't." I didn't know if she sounded apologetic or defiant.

The wards flared once, a slow, aching chime, and then the Saints arrived.

They didn't knock.

Mother Salt came first, barefoot and crusted in grief, her presence making the floorboards warp beneath her. Her long skirt dragged like seaweed, trailing salt and bone fragments that hissed when they hit the ward lines. One of the dice on her belt bit her finger when she reached for it. She didn't flinch. She bled into the pouch like it was an offering.

She smiled at me without warmth. "Your blood smells like the tide before a storm." Then she dumped the dice across the map. The runes squirmed, shifting. A location. A threat.

"I brought the wound-reader," she announced. "Tell me where the city bleeds."

The Archivist of the Silent Bell followed, her arrival more sensation than sound. The air grew *thin* around her, like she'd stepped through a dimension that wasn't quite finished printing. Scrolls spilled from her sleeves, living skin inked with timelines that moved when you blinked. The bells at her throat didn't ring, they thrummed a warning to reality: *You've been recorded.* When her eyes found me, the floor swayed.

"This is not prophecy," she said. "This is a translation error. I am here to correct it." She turned her head, slow and deliberate, and fixed her gaze on me. "You are not in the story you think you are." Her voice was full of static.

Saint Knuckle slouched in with a shrug like damnation bored him. He looked like a war crime in thrift store denim. The ward line flared as he passed, and he flipped it off with two fingers and a grin. "Nice place. Hate the ambiance." He popped a cigarette into his mouth and looked at Gabriel. "If this goes sideways, you owe me a drink. And a resurrection."

Gabriel didn't answer. Neither did I.

Then came Brother Hexane. Or part of him.

He existed in frame skips, like he was being projected through a stuttering machine. He wore a coat covered in sigil-burn scars, and the dagger in his hand quivered like it hated being held. "Don't lie to me," he said to no one in particular. "This place remembers lies."

One last shimmer. Then silence.

A shadow crawled up the back wall, shifting like a ripple through oil. A fifth presence, but it never stepped forward.

Gabriel looked at Edda. "I thought you said four."

"I did," she murmured, eyes not leaving the ripple. "But apparently the Saints don't count the same way we do."

Gabriel exhaled. "I hate this."

Edda didn't blink. "I hope to every deity ever this isn't a mistake."

Mother Salt smiled. "Darling. *Of course* it is. That's how we know it's going to work."

The Archivist stepped closer. Her eyes never left mine. "You want to understand what you're fighting?"

I nodded once.

Her next words didn't feel like speech. They felt like revelation.

"The Voice is not possession. It is not prophecy. It is narrative revision. It does not take control; it changes the page. The Bone Lords think they're ascending, the Vein think they're consuming, but the truth of it is none of them are in control. The Voice doesn't need to dominate them. It needs them to believe the wrong story."

She reached across the table, touched a blood-smeared sigil.

"It rewrites memory. Identity. Fate. Every lie they tell themselves becomes true if they say it in the right place, at the right time, and enough followers believe it."

She looked back at me.

"You are not the girl they think you are, and you are not the god they want to make."

A breath caught in my throat.

"What am I, then?"

The Archivist tilted her head.

"You're the blank page." She straightened slowly, the red seals on her wrists cracking like ice under pressure. One of them split. Ink poured down her hand, but it didn't drip. It climbed, curling around her knuckles like it was trying to write its way free.

"You thought the Voice wanted your death," she said, low and even. "It doesn't."

She looked down at the map again.

"It wants your choice."

That hit differently. It wanted me to agree to playing the role it dictated?

"What does that mean?" I asked, throat tight.

She didn't blink. "It has rewritten countless timelines to find the version where you say yes. It has bent belief, history, even love. It gave you enemies to kill, mentors to lose, friends to grieve. And when that wasn't enough?" She looked up, sharp. "It gave you purpose. A reason to fight. A reason to rise."

She turned her hand. The ink was gone. Her palm was covered in runes that looked suspiciously like mine.

"The Voice does not want to break you. That never worked."

I felt the air shift. Riot growled once, deep and low.

"It wants to inspire you."

Gabriel stepped forward. "To do what?"

The Archivist's answer came soft as smoke. "To write the story it cannot."

She looked at me again.

"The Voice is not building a god to rule. It is building a god who believes she made herself."

I don't remember Edda handing it to me.

Maybe she didn't. Maybe I just looked down and there it was, curled in my palm like it had always been waiting.

The red thread was still warm, frayed where it had been bound and broken and tied again.

Edda had worn it like a tether. Now it was mine.

The room behind the bar was quiet in the way of aftermaths. Dust hung in the air like breath that had nowhere left to go. A single bottle of blood-bright gin sat unopened on the sideboard, the wax seal untouched. I could feel the place watching through the walls, curious and silent. I was never sure what it wanted.

I sat and let the thread unwind in my hands.

It shouldn't have felt like anything. It was just fiber, but holding it was like touching the perimeter of a truth I hadn't dared step into. It wasn't a ward or a spell. It was a story that wanted to be finished, and now it had found someone who might just be able to do it.

Maybe.

I ran the thread through my fingers, slow and deliberate, watching the light catch where the fibers split. Edda had used this to stitch magic into torn places, to bind meaning where none was left. To hold the line, like the women who had woven it had done.

I wasn't sure I knew how to do any of that, and maybe that was the point.

The Voice didn't want me broken; it wanted me to believe I'd already won. It wanted me to stitch a crown from the thread and call it resistance, to claim power like it was rebellion. It wanted me to rebuild the city in my name and believe I'd saved it, not because it needed a ruler, but because it needed an author. It needed someone who would write the ending it had already whispered through every loss, every prophecy, every choice that felt like mine but never really was.

My hands trembled as I wrestled with every version of myself I had survived being, and with every one I had already buried.

I thought of Rhiannon's voice, sharp and wild, a feral song. Brianna's hands in my hair, her low, soothing humming weaving magic along with my braids. Moshi's betrayal, still aching like a bruise that would never quite fade.

I thought of Gabriel asleep beside me, his chest rising and falling like the only truth I wanted to believe in.

I thought of Riot, scorched and trembling, still choosing to stay, like he had in every other reality that I couldn't remember but that he was cursed to carry.

I thought of the girl I used to be. The one who thought survival was the end of the story. That love was weakness and that choosing yourself meant standing alone. The girl who thought her power was a curse. The one who still ached for her mother's face, her grandmother's voice.

That girl would've looked at this thread and laughed.

That girl was dead, along with so many versions of myself.

I tied the thread around my wrist. One loop, then two. Tight enough to stay.

"I don't know how to win this," I whispered.

The thread didn't answer, but it shivered once against my skin, like it knew that wasn't the point.

"I'm not what they want me to be."

Another beat. Steady. Sure.

I could hear the Archivist's words echoing behind my ribs. *It wants your choice.* Not a sacrifice, and not a martyrdom, but a story.

And not just any story: a good one, the kind of story that made survival look like victory, that made the prison look like the palace. A story that made the crown feel earned.

That wasn't the story I came here to write, and if I had to tear the ending out by the roots, if I had to become the villain of their sacred text, the ghost in their gospel, then so be it.

"I'll be what I need to be." I swallowed. "You didn't get to finish the story," I whispered to the thread, to the women who had woven it, to Edda who had guarded it. "So I will."

I stood.

And for the first time in a long time, I didn't feel like I was walking into someone else's ending.

I felt like I was writing the beginning of my own.

I didn't look up when the door opened, but I didn't need to look to know who it was. The slight drag of a heel, a remnant of an old injury she had yet to talk about. The scent of rosemary smoke.

Edda.

She didn't speak, just set something on the table beside me: an envelope, worn at the edges, sealed with wax that was cracked, but intact. I just stared at it.

"Brianna and Rhiannon's last gift," she said finally. "They made me promise. 'Only when it is her choice, Edda. Only when she is past surviving and ready to live.'" She patted my hand, and slipped back into the bar.

My hands shook as I picked up the envelope, the paper starting to yellow with age. I broke the seal, and pulled out the pages.

The letter inside was written by two people—Rhiannon's sharp, spiky handwriting crowding the margins, Brianna's elegant cursive flowing across the page like a river.

I didn't read it all at once. I let my eyes drift, line to line, letting the voices rise up between the strokes. Letting myself *feel* them again. Not as ghosts, not as echoes, but simply as mine.

Selene, my girl—

You were never meant to be soft. That's not what we gave you. That's not what the world needed. You were meant to be sharp. Wild. The knife that sings. The wind that does not ask for permission.

And gods, you were beautiful, even as a baby. Even when you screamed the walls down. I used to call you my war cry. You were all fire and fists before you could walk. I was terrified. And proud. So proud.

I didn't want you to be like me.

I wanted you to be better.

And you are.

You'll stand at the edge of the world one day, my love. You'll think you're alone. You'll think you're ruined. And I need you to remember—being broken is not the end. It's the beginning of something they can't tame.

You don't owe them forgiveness. You don't owe them grace. You don't owe them survival.

You owe yourself *everything.*

I wish I could see what you've become. I know it's fucking glorious.

— Rhiannon

My beloved—
I *hope you read this in your own time. I hope no one gave it to you before you were ready, because this is not a letter for survival. It is a letter for living.*

You are not cursed, my darling girl. You are chosen. Not by fate. Not by prophecy. But by us. We chose you. We loved you into being. And everything in you—the wildness, the rage, the gentleness you hide, the ache that never leaves—it is holy.

You do not have to become anything more than you already are. You do not have to earn love. You do not have to burn to be worthy.

You are already enough.

I wish I could brush the hair from your face one more time. I wish I could hold your hand and tell you all the stories we never had time to finish. But if you are reading this, it means you have lived. It means you have made it through the fire, even if the flames are still chasing you.

Let them call you dangerous.

Let them call you queen.

Let them tremble when they speak your name.

But never forget—

You are loved. Beyond death. Beyond time. Beyond every story they tried to write without you.

— Brianna

And one last thing, sweetheart—

If anyone tries to use your name like a leash, cut them down. You belong to no one but yourself.

We love you.

We love you.

We love you.

Let them come.

Let them try.

We'll be behind you—always.

The tears came quiet. Not a flood. Not a break. Just a release. Not because I was sad, but because something inside me had finally let go, something that had been clenched so tightly for so long it had forgotten how to feel anything but the ache of holding on.

I folded the letter with careful hands, pressing the paper flat like I could still feel their fingers on it. I tucked it into my jacket, close to my heart. I didn't put it there for safekeeping. I put it there for strength.

The door creaked open behind me, and Gabriel slipped into the room. I felt the air pause, my body knowing his presence before my mind caught up to it.

I loved him. I loved him beyond reason, beyond thought, with something feral and furious and all-consuming.

"They're ready," he said softly. His voice carried the weight of a soldier who'd seen too many last stands. "The Saints are setting the outer perimeter plans now."

I nodded. "And Riot?"

"Resting. Edda's working on the burn. Says it's nasty, but she can patch him up." A hesitation. "He's worried about you."

"Everyone's worried about me," I said with a half-smile that I know didn't reach my eyes. "It's quite exhausting."

Gabriel moved closer, slow and careful, like he wasn't sure how close I'd let him get.

"You don't have to do this alone," he said. "Not anymore."

"I know." I paused. "Knowing doesn't make it easier."

He gave me a wry smile. "Didn't think *anything* about you came easy."

"Oh, I'm very low maintenance," I said dryly. "I just come with a little light generational trauma and a tendency to implode timelines."

He chuckled, stepping into reach now, his hands sliding into his pockets like he was holding himself back from touching me.

"You forgot the part where you're the hottest apocalyptic variable I've ever been lucky enough to survive."

I blinked. "You're not surviving *me*, Gabriel. You're part of this."

His gaze softened, and I looked at him—really looked. The worn edges. The weight he carried. The steadiness he offered without asking for anything in return.

And finally, I let myself say it.

"I love you," I said. Quiet and sure. "I love you, and I'm going to fight like hell to make it out of this. Not just to stop them, not just to finish the story, but to *have* a story. A story with you."

He didn't freeze. Didn't falter. He just smiled.

"Good," he said. "Because I already staked my soul on you. Thought it was best to be efficient."

I laughed, cracked and real, my voice catching halfway through. "That sounds on brand."

"You're so full of it."

"You're so dramatic."

"Do *not* start," he warned, leaning in, his mouth brushing the corner of mine.

I turned my head, letting my lips find his like iron bending to true north.

Slow. Certain. Not an ending.

A promise.

When we pulled apart, the bond between us sang low and fierce beneath my skin. Not magic, but something deeper and older. The thing that has bound two souls together since the beginning of time.

"I'm ready," I said.

Gabriel nodded once, steady as gravity.

"Then let's go fuck everything up."

CHAPTER TWENTY-ONE

DEATH CULTS AND CHILL

Gabriel

T HE FIRST DRUMBEAT OF war was a footstep.

Not Serena's. Moshi's.

He walked alone through the broken artery of what used to be 7th and Marlow, a stretch of intersection so warped by magic it didn't remember its own name anymore. Broken glass glittered in the gutters. Forgotten sigils glowed faintly on street signs like bruises under skin. The city didn't hum; it held its breath.

The cultists followed.

Bone Lords in ceremonial bone-etched armor, some bare-chested and painted with blood, some masked in iron veils, led the march. Behind them came the faithful by the dozens. Maybe by the hundreds. They didn't march; they processed, chanting, a dirge and a hymn wrapped into one. Their voices echoed off the buildings in patterns too exact to be human.

From the other side came the followers of the Hollow Vein, covered in robes and laden with profane tech. Hollowborn held the outer edges.

From the rooftop, I could see the shape of the trap as they marched toward the neon crossroads. Three main arteries converging on the fracture zone, a place that had once been a place but was now a memory glitch wrapped in concrete. Edda's binding net was already humming through the gutters, strung between lamp posts, sewer lines, ghost wards.

If Moshi had a plan, it wasn't glaringly obvious. The information broker moved with the casual confidence of a man out for an evening stroll, not someone walking into the jaws of death. His expensive shoes clicked against pavement that rippled like water, leaving momentary footprints of silver light.

Riot crouched beside me, ears twitching.

"They're stepping into it," he said. "Just like she said they would."

"She better be right about more than this," I muttered.

"She usually is."

Below, Moshi dropped to one knee in the center of the intersection, his hands raised in mock surrender. Ritual submission. A pageant of guilt. His face was turned down, but his back was straight, defiance written in his posture. The Hollow Vein's advance guard reached the first trigger point. One of the Bone

Lords raised a banner, a spiral of blood and thread, and the cultists screamed.

Edda flinched beside me. "It's coming."

"How do you know?"

"I don't," she said. "The city does." I took a breath, and then the world shuddered.

The sky didn't darken; it cracked, as if something behind it had leaned too hard on the wrong reality. Light spilled through in bands. Red. Silver. Something colder than white.

And then—her.

Serena stepped onto the street like it had always been hers.

I knew that walk. Purposeful. Resolute. It was the walk of a woman who had decided to stop running.

She wore black, from her jeans to her shirt, her practical leather jacket catching the light on silver buckles. She'd pulled that mass of fiery hair into a tight braid, putting the lines of her face on full display. Power radiated from her in waves that made the air shimmer like heat over the desert, trailing from her fingers in tendrils that writhed and snapped.

She walked through the line of cultists as if they were already ash. Every eye turned. Every chant faltered, because the prophecy shimmered in the air above her, and it recognized her.

"The heir approaches!" someone screamed, voice cracking with religious fervor. "The bloodline returns!"

She was the lie they had written into power, and that lie just walked into the center of the page.

My eyes never left her as she approached Moshi. I could see her lips moving, but whatever she was saying was meant for him alone. His shoulders tensed, then relaxed. A group of Collectors shifted to allow their leader to step forward.

"Daughter of Myrddin," he called, voice echoing unnaturally. "You walk willingly into judgment and transformation. You have come to accept your part."

Serena looked down at her nails. "I have decided to decline the honor."

The threads she'd planted flared, sigils lighting up one by one like trap points in a ritual gone sentient. I gave three short whistles, pitched to carry.

Riot stood.

Edda took a deep breath, her fingers tracing patterns in the air that left faint blue trails.

Serena didn't flinch when she reached into her pocket and pulled out a knife that she dragged along her forearm. She raised one hand, swiped the blood onto her fingertips, and said, "This is the version where you take your prophecy and choke on it." She dropped to one knee and slammed her bloody hand into the street.

The blazing net surged to life, sigils keyed to her blood blazing along the streets in geometric patterns that burned themselves into the eye. She did more than trigger the net, though. She began inscribing something deeper into the world. Her blood was more than ink. It was correction. She wasn't following the script. She was editing it.

And then?

Hell began.

The trap didn't just close. It snapped, and everything moved.

Moshi didn't wait. He bolted to his feet and surged forward with a blade I hadn't even seen him draw; crude, hooked, old enough that the blood on it looked baked into the metal. He didn't run.

He killed.

He cut the first Bone Lord low, from groin to throat, before the bastard could even raise his weapon. A second tried to block him, but Moshi flared a counter-sigil off his arm and flash-fried the man's eyes. He gave no mercy. He wasted no motion. This wasn't a man praying for forgiveness. This was the man the shadows whispered about. This was the man who wielded a blade made of regret.

A Bone Lord recognized him. "Koru'el's creature." The voice rang out across the field, thick with loathing. "We sheltered you in the temple. And you—"

Moshi didn't hesitate.

The cultist brought up a glaive too slow. Moshi sidestepped the arc, ducked low, and opened the man's gut with a single clean sweep. There was no flourish, just a quick, clinical execution.

Blood steamed on the pavement.

"You didn't shelter me," Moshi said flatly, voice like old parchment catching fire. "You used me. You all did."

Another came at him: female, younger, faster. He caught her wrist mid-strike. Held it. Hesitated. For one breath, his mask cracked.

She gasped. "You taught me the bone wards. You said—"

"I said a lot of things." He twisted, disarmed her, and drove his blade through her ribs. "None of them were true." She crumpled.

Moshi staggered back, eyes wild, blood streaking his face where a counter-sigil had nearly blown back.

"Do not," he hissed to no one in particular, maybe to himself, "do *not* make me a martyr."

He vanished into the smoke, carving sigils as he went.

Mother Salt walked barefoot through ash and memory, dragging seaweed and bone behind her like ceremonial chains. Her hair hung in damp clumps, tangled with brine and nettles. Salt crusted her lips. Her eyes had no whites. She didn't sprint. She didn't fight.

She grieved.

The first cultist to step in front of her raised a blade. She looked at him, voice low and drowned. "Tell me what you stole."

He hesitated, then dropped to his knees, weeping. "Her name. I took her *name.*" Mother Salt touched his forehead with two fingers soaked in sorrow, and he fell. Not dead, just *undone.*

She turned to the next. "And you?"

"I—" He tried to lie.

The ground cracked beneath him. She didn't need to raise her voice.

"Salt remembers," she whispered, and the city wailed with her.

She never stopped walking.

The Archivist of the Silent Bell hovered inches above the ground, wrapped in scrolls that fluttered like dying birds. Her face was veiled in static, her hands inked in recursion loops. She moved like punctuation; where the sentence of battle faltered, she corrected. Reality bent like parchment beneath her steps.

A cultist cast a shield. She deleted the outcome before it happened.

A Bone Lord stabbed a Hollow Vein soldier, caught up in bloodlust, slashing out at anything. The Archivist paused, reversed three seconds, and let the man sidestep the blade, only to delete his page a second later.

She was editing the field.

Her gaze swept past me, and for one breath, I saw my own death. Quick. Quiet. A different outcome. Then it vanished, and she moved on.

Brother Hexane twitched through the veil of linearity, glitching at the edges. His coat burned and re-stitched itself with every breath. He made it to Serena's left flank, blade jittering in his palm like it hated being held.

"Prophecy," I heard him rasp. "Prophecy lied."

She didn't answer.

"Don't say yes," he warned, slicing a ward in the air that bled black light. Then he vanished again and reappeared in front of a collector, whispering, "Your truth is brittle." The collector laughed until the bones in his chest folded inward.

Hexane didn't laugh back.

The Fifth Saint, a crawling shadow, counted.

One too many.

Always.

And every time they counted, someone disappeared.

Even the Archivist looked away.

Riot broke mid-air.

He didn't shift; he fractured. The leash Rhiannon had sealed him with shattered like bone under pressure, and the thing beneath the familiar was finally, fully unleashed.

He hit the ground on four legs, but they were too long, too jointed in the wrong places, as if the idea of a hound had been redrawn by a fevered god. His body stretched and expanded, doubling in mass with each breath. His paws split at the ends, claws erupting like knives made of wrought iron, curved for rending, not running.

Fur sloughed off in patches. What replaced it wasn't skin; it was sharpened metal, overlapping plates like natural armor fused to war-forged purpose. His spine arched high, each vertebra tipped with a jagged blade. Spikes protruded down his back like spears erupting from a corpse.

His tail lashed once, and took a piece of the pavement with it.

Eyes, way too many eyes, opened across his head and shoulders, burning like live coals, pupils vertical, molten, intelligent. His mouth split twice, once at the jaw, once again further back. When he roared, it wasn't just sound, it was memory made violent, a howl that summoned every fear you had ever buried. It clawed at your thoughts and dragged your nightmares to the surface while it whispered your worst moments back at you.

He took a step forward and the ground cracked beneath his weight.

The cultists faltered, and even the Bone Lord Collectors hesitated. One screamed something in a lost language, something that might have been a prayer.

Riot grinned, an impossible, fanged grin that split his face in too many directions at once, and then he charged. I'd seen horrors before: war machines, summoned revenants, even a soldier who kept fighting for six minutes after losing half his skull. But this? This wasn't horror. This was myth dragging itself into the world through a beast that used to wear a dog's shape. Riot wasn't just unleashed. He was remembering, and whatever he used to be, it wasn't built for mercy. Iron claws hit bone and split it like paper. Serrated teeth, layered and unforgiving, ripped a Hollow Vein war priest clean off the ground and crushed him mid-scream.

Blood sprayed.

Metal gleamed.

The Saints saw him, and bowed.

Not out of submission, but out of recognition, because whatever Riot had become?

It was something older than monsters, and it had finally remembered what it was made for.

The Fifth Saint was standing closer than I'd realized, right at my shoulder, their shape flickering like a shadow that hadn't picked which body it belonged to yet.

They didn't look at me. They didn't speak aloud, but I heard it anyway.

"One step left," they whispered. "Two hearts break. Three truths bleed. Four threads burn. And then—none."

I turned, but they were already counting again, softly, to themself...

To the fracture.

The numbers didn't line up with anything I could see, but a chill rolled down my spine. I wasn't sure if I wanted to know what came after "none."

I looked back at Serena, and for the first time, I wasn't afraid of what she was walking into; I was afraid of what she might be when she came back.

The battle continued, and so did I.

I stayed low and moved fast, one eye on the rooftops, the other on the binding lines Edda had strung like tripwires through the gutters. Cultists surged forward in waves, not mindless, but driven. Someone had a tactical mind in their ranks. I adjusted accordingly.

Three on the left. One raised a sigil to flare. I shot him first; a center mass shot, clean kill. His body jerked and the sigil burned out mid-cast. The other two flinched and I didn't wait; I took out the knee of the one closest and dropped him, screaming, to the pavement. The last one tried to retreat. Smart, but useless. I double-tapped and pivoted without watching him fall.

My second magazine was already half empty.

Edda screamed from above, the sound short and sharp before it cut off. I moved.

Up ahead, a Bone Lord had broken from the others and was pushing toward her position. His staff burned with white-hot runes. If he breached her circle, we'd lose the net before it sealed. I raised my Glock and fired, but the runes flared and absorbed the round. Fuck. I adjusted, crouched, and aimed lower. I fired again, trying to overwhelm his shielding.

Knee. Shoulder. Hip.

The third shot landed. The fourth dropped him. The fifth was insurance.

I sprinted forward, grabbed his fallen staff, and tossed it into the seeping edge of the binding line. It sparked, caught, and hissed out in a puff of sulfur and smoke.

Behind me, another cultist screamed my name. I spun, got off one round, and my slide locked. Empty magazine.

He lunged, and I had just enough time to meet him with my blade. We crashed hard. He was bigger, stronger, but it didn't matter. I hit him in the throat with my hilt, twisted, and drove the blade into his side. Up, not in, through the ribs. He gurgled and went limp.

I stood, breathing hard. My ribs ached and my hands shook from fatigue and adrenaline.

One mag left, loaded with rune bound hollow points. I didn't have time to count how many enemies were left in front of me.

I counted how many people still stood behind me, loaded, and kept moving.

Pain hit fast across my left shoulder. Shallow, but deep enough to burn.

I hadn't seen him. The cultist came in low from the debris line, curved blade held backward. Smart angle. Even smarter timing. If I'd been half a second slower, he'd have gutted me.

I wasn't, though, and he didn't.

I staggered back, kicked him off balance, and planted two in his chest before the scream even reached my throat. Then I clamped a hand to the wound and hissed through my teeth.

The heat of it told me it wasn't fatal, but it would slow me down. And slow wasn't an option, not now. Not with Serena walking into prophecy with nothing but her blood and her will to protect her.

I kept moving. Kept firing.

The pain sharpened everything—sounds, shadows, shifts in movement. My body wanted to fold, to favor my left side, to retreat. I didn't let it. I forced my stance wide, sucked in one brutal breath, and pivoted to cover Edda again.

Blood soaked into my shirt. Every step sent another bolt through my side where the claw marks down my ribs had re-opened.

Good.

Let it hurt.

Let it remind me why we were here.

A pair of Collectors broke through the southern line. I caught the first with a headshot, then spun and dropped the second at the knees. They screamed something about a false heir. I didn't bother answering.

Another tried to flank Edda; I shot through his casting arm and finished him on the rebound.

Saint Knuckle landed beside me mid-roll.

"You're finally using the toys," he said. "Proud of you."

"Cover left."

"I got you, soldier boy."

He cracked a Bone Lord's helm with his elbow as I dropped two more with precise shots. Tactical. Clean. Efficient. We moved like we'd trained together for years.

Saint Knuckle used a cultist's corpse as a bat to take down another. His coat was smeared with runes and blood, and his grin never slipped.

"Gabe!" he shouted. "This is still easier than Prague!"

"I wasn't in Prague," I shouted back.

"Exactly!" he said, delighted. He punched through a summoned horror like it owed him money and tossed me a new magazine from God-knows-where as my last one ran dry. I caught it. Loaded. Kept moving.

A fresh wave came in fast: four, maybe five cultists, flanking hard from the south corridor. I didn't have the angles, but Knuckle did. He dropped one with a boot to the throat and caught another mid-lunge, slamming him against a half-collapsed wall.

"Back to back, soldier boy!"

I pivoted, covered his blind side, took two out with precise shots to center mass and head.

One made it through. Too close. I spun, caught their blade on mine. Knuckle reached around me and cracked their skull with a bone flute.

"Why do you *have* that?" I panted.

He shrugged. "They gave it to me when I died."

I didn't ask.

We exhaled in sync. Watched the smoke rise between us.

"Still easier than Prague?" I asked.

"Eh. Fewer demons in the plumbing here."

We split without speaking, each covering a corridor. The rhythm didn't need words anymore. We just moved.

The fracture waited.

Bullets don't last forever. I knew that going in. Knowing, however, and feeling it run dry in real time are two different things entirely. Every round I fired had weight now. They kept coming. A cultist with half her face branded in sigils lobbed a hex across the binding line. I dove, rolled, came up firing. Her hex missed; My shot didn't. She dropped with a scream that didn't sound entirely human.

I didn't look long. Couldn't afford to.

Edda was down again, coughing blood. Riot was ripping something apart twenty feet to my right. Knuckle was laughing like this was a party, and somewhere beyond that, I could hear the Saint chanting numbers that made my skin crawl.

The plan was holding. Barely.

I pivoted and caught another center mass on approach, one shot, two, and drop. And then it hit me.

This wasn't like Kandahar, not exactly, but it rhymed. I remembered the silence after the IED. The way my hands had shaken even after I'd saved the kid. The smell of copper in my nose and the taste of ash in my mouth. The way the world kept going, even when someone was screaming just off to the side. I remembered the way the dirt turned to glass in the blast radius and the smell of burning plastic and bone, indistinguishable at the edges. A shoe, small, pink, untouched by blood, rested alone in the rubble. The silence afterward had felt like the world itself had gone deaf. I'd kept moving anyway. Saved the kid. Buried the rest.

I hadn't thought of that particular day in years. But right now? Right now it lived under my skin like a second pulse.

A Bone Lord charged, broke through the line. I barely dropped him in time.

I crouched low, checked my ammo. Three rounds.

I stood up fast. I raised my gun, found my breath, and picked the next target. Kept going.

Then Serena passed me.

She didn't look back. Didn't speak.

She just walked. A Hollow Vein fanatic ran in, screaming, raising a serrated blade toward her back, and she didn't turn, trusting me to have her. I had his throat opened up and blood running into the gutter before her next breath.

Another Bone Lord stepped into my path; this one was older, robed in black, face half-covered in gold-plated bone. His armor was ceremonial, but the way he held that blade? Pure soldier.

He didn't charge. He waited.

"I know you," he said, voice like gravel dragged over ash. "You were the one they couldn't break. The soldier who refused to kneel."

I didn't recognize him, but something in his stance made my pulse spike.

"Didn't break then," I said. "Not planning to start now."

He moved first, fast. I barely brought my blade up in time. The clang of metal rang through my bones. He pressed close, strength behind every strike.

"You're not chosen," he growled. "You're just in the way."

"Then move me."

We locked again. His weight pushed me back until I kicked low, broke his stance, and drove an elbow into the hollow of his throat. He stumbled. I shot him point-blank in the knee.

He screamed and dropped, but even on the ground, he fought, swiping upward, blade grazing my leg.

It burned.

I didn't give him a second chance. I drove my knife through his ribs, up beneath the sternum, angled toward the heart. He spasmed once and went still. I stood, panting, blood slicking my gloves.

"You're right," I said to the body. "I'm not chosen." I looked for Serena.

"I'm hers."

The net shimmered beneath her feet. The prophecy bent around her shape. The Saints stood behind her like a procession.

And every Bone Lord on the field *knew*:

They'd already lost.

Edda collapsed, blood slicking her palms. She looked up, teeth red. Her eyes were unfocused, one pupil blown wide. Blood trickled from her left ear, soaking into her scarf, and her fingers spasmed through sigil patterns even as her body rebelled. The magic laced through her veins looked like wire pulled too tight. I saw her mouth a word that didn't exist in modern language.

The binding net flared in response, every line thrumming like a harp string made of static and nerve endings.

She wasn't casting anymore, she was channeling, and it was killing her.

"Don't burn your thread too early," she whispered. I wasn't sure if she meant the net or herself.

Then louder, as if she were answering someone none of us could see:

"I know what Rhiannon said. I'm not her. I don't need saving." Her hands shook harder. Blood ran from her nose now, too vivid against pale skin. "But if she fails, I burn. You all do."

Her gaze locked on Serena across the battlefield.

"So don't fail, Rhiannon's daughter, or you'll take us all with you."

Then she collapsed forward onto her hands, spine arched like a snapped bowstring, and kept working.

"Serena—" Edda's voice carried, despite it all.

Serena turned slightly. Just enough.

"Finish it."

Serena nodded, and walked the rest of the way into the fracture.

The fracture was a tear in the world, as if reality had never been stitched quite right and now the seams were pulling loose.

I didn't see it at first. I was too busy shooting, bleeding, calculating, but when Serena had neared the edge, I'd felt it, deep in my gut, in my boots, like the earth beneath us couldn't make up its mind about what gravity was supposed to do. The air had turned cold and humid at the same time, like breathing through stone dust and ozone, every breath tasting like the moment before a lightning strike.

Sound warped. Shouts from across the field came too slow. A scream from the left reached my ears before the cultist's mouth had even opened. And light...God, the light. It didn't shine. It bled. Pale and endless, veined with static.

I caught myself staring and forced my eyes back to Serena. She didn't flinch. Didn't slow.

She walked like the world didn't scare her. Like it owed her.

The factions weren't fighting anymore.

The Bone Lords stood to one side of the shattered plaza, robes like flayed parchment, sigils glowing soft and slow. The Hollow Vein clustered opposite, half in shadow, half in motion, bodies flickering like thoughts caught between dimensions.

They watched her walk. They didn't strike. Didn't speak.

They weren't allies, just aligned temporarily. They knew what was coming. Knew she was the axis now.

One side wanted to bind her. The other wanted to break her. Both knew they couldn't touch her until she stepped into the heart of it on her own.

Let her rise, the Vein whispered. *Then end her.*

Let her bloom, the Bone Lords thought. *Then sanctify her.*

They would devour each other after, but first, they'd wait for her to *become.*

That's when the whisper started. Not in my ears. Behind my eyes. Low and constant...not a voice, but something watching.

It wasn't looking at me.

It was looking at her.

Riot, still monstrous and gleaming, bounded forward and stopped cold. His spines bristled. One massive paw lifted, mid-stride, and hovered in the air like he was caught between instinct and memory.

I met his eyes, one of the bigger ones, burning like a coal rimmed in molten steel. It locked on me, just for a second. And I saw it.

Recognition.

Like he knew how this story ended, and didn't want to see it again.

"Not this time," I whispered. Didn't know if I meant him or me or her, but it didn't matter. He lowered his paw and stood watch as she walked in.

He knew this place. Or something like it.

I didn't, but I understood the message in my bones.

Whatever waited in that fracture, it hadn't been summoned.

It had been waiting all along for this one woman.

Edda limped up, blood on her teeth, hands trembling, but still moving, still channeling. Her eyes didn't leave Serena, even as her body faltered.

"She's not casting," she rasped.

I turned to her. "What?"

"She's not casting, Gabriel. She's editing."

The word hit like a shot.

"She's inside the fracture," Edda whispered, eyes wild, reverent. "That place was built from converging timelines, knotted prophecies, failed rituals, all trying to overwrite each other. A glitch in the Weave. It's raw narrative space. Anyone else steps in there, they burn, but her?"

She shuddered, hands spasming through another sigil as her voice dropped to a whisper.

"She's Myrddin's blood, and Rhiannon's fire, and Brianna's knowledge. She isn't following the story. She's rewriting it."

I stared at Serena, silhouetted against the impossible light. "I don't..."

"She's not fulfilling the prophecy," Edda said, breath ragged. "She's replacing it."

Serena was not a weapon. She was not a sacrifice.

She walked into the fracture like a sovereign, and when the world held its breath, it was because it knew: She was overwriting the story, line by line, god by god, and the fracture welcomed her.

I'd seen the Archivist rewrite moments on the battlefield. Serena rewrote meaning.

I should've said something.

When she'd passed me, I should've reached out, kissed her, *anything*. But that wasn't what she needed, and maybe it wasn't what I needed either, because all I could do was watch.

The fracture pulsed once, like it breathed her in, and the air around us stilled.

I saw the Saints halt mid-step.

I saw Edda's hands go limp.

Riot didn't move.

All I could think was, if she's writing the last line, I'll burn the rest of the book to make sure she survives it.

CHAPTER TWENTY-TWO

I DID NOT CONSENT TO AN ASCENSION ARC

Serena

T HE TRAP SNAPPED SHUT behind me.

The moment my blood hit the fracture, everything screamed. Not with sound, but with shift. The ground reeled, like it was trying to remember what it used to be before the gods carved through its spine.

Behind me, the world exploded.

The recursion trap ignited across the ritual site, each anchor point erupting into sigil flame, catching cultists mid-step, mid-prayer, mid-belief. One of the Bone Lords collapsed instantly, his body already unraveling from the inside. Another tried to run and was yanked back by a Saint's chain, his mouth still moving like he thought he could finish an invocation, but he couldn't.

Gabriel's gun barked three times in rhythm before he dropped into a crouch behind a fallen altar slab. Saint Knuckle dove over it, laughing like he'd waited centuries for this exact apocalypse, a chain-wrapped fist lighting up as it connected with the face of a Vein high priest. The sound that followed didn't belong to any human throat.

Somewhere to my right, Riot moved like a shadow caught on the wind, no longer bound by the shape that had caged him. He was huge now, his eldritch form shimmering with an otherworldly wrongness that made the Vein devotees hesitate just long enough for him to tear one in half with iron claws.

And still, the ritual fought to live.

The fracture beneath me howled in refusal, like it didn't want to be healed, like it had tasted ascension too many times and still hadn't decided whether it hated it. Threads of narrative lashed at my feet; the spell wanted to wrap me in the version it already thought was true. The one where I was crowned. The one where I said yes. It always wanted more—wanted to remake me, rewrite me, hollow me out so it could wear my skin and call it fate. Power taken leaves a scar; I'd rather bleed on my own terms than let them carve me into something I never chose.

I didn't move.

"You've stepped into the fracture willingly," the priest rasped. His voice cracked like parchment, wet and unraveling. "You know what that makes you."

I didn't turn. "Yeah," I said. "It makes me the end of your story."

The cult surged. Another wave of believers poured from the east entrance, faces half-masked, blood-scrawled, their feet pounding through ash and bone. Edda caught them first, her red-thread net erupting upward like a web made of blade-light. The front rank dropped, screaming. The rest scrambled.

I stepped deeper into the fracture. It wasn't a floor anymore. It was a mouth.

I felt it peel itself open beneath me, threads writhing, stories coiling. Every one of them trying to name me. Vessel. Heir. God. Ascendant.

"No," I whispered.

The word didn't echo. It sank, and the spell trembled.

Somewhere above me, the shape of the crown began to form—bone-laced, blood-spun, heavy with inherited expectation. I let it. I let them build their fantasy for one more breath. One more beat.

And then I reached up and crushed it.

The crown splintered, power cascading in all directions. Magic lashed out, looking for someone else, anyone else, to anoint. It found nothing. No vessel. No god. No willing volunteer.

Only me. I stood at the heart of a dying ritual, holding nothing but the ragged remains of my name. And then? I let that go, too.

"Selene ap Myrddin," I said aloud. My true name.

It shook the fracture. The magic shuddered, hungry, eager. The Weave didn't just offer power. It tried to shape you with it, shave down the edges, recode the marrow, make you into something easier to name. I'd spent my life dodging definitions. Rewrite the self, risk becoming unknown to fate; that's the danger, but it's also the freedom. They couldn't shackle what they couldn't predict. So, I called up my name, my legacy, my heritage...

And then I severed it.

"I am not yours," I said. "I am not your god. I am not your queen. And I am sure as hell not your vengeance."

The threads split. Every line of prophecy screamed, and the story broke wide open.

It broke in colors I didn't have names for. The spell didn't just collapse; it fractured backward through time, peeling apart the scaffolding of every version they'd ever tried to make of me. I saw them. Each one, split across the smoke of what had been a ritual: fractured girls made of prophecy and pain. One wore a crown of bone. One had no mouth. One held a blade too heavy for her arms, eyes hollowed out from trying to carry a world that never wanted her.

Each one stared from the folds of the undone spell, their faces stitched with threads that had never been their own. I knew, without asking, that they were the versions I'd refused. The stories that the fracture still held like old drafts, annotated in someone else's blood. One reached toward me, her hands cupped like she was holding something. I saw teeth in her palms. I saw hope.

I knew these weren't memories. They were warnings.

The fracture had tried to make them true. The spell had eaten them when they faltered, swallowed them whole, and called it sanctification. It had tried to write me like it had written them: obedient, obedient, obedient. A vessel with a name and no voice. It hadn't succeeded.

I stood at the center now, the last draft it had left. And I was holding the quill.

The smoke bled upward, carrying something older than magic, trying to reassemble itself around the bones of a god who hadn't consented to live. But I wasn't trying to just survive this time.

I was trying to end it.

I stared into the shape of the girl who still wore a crown. The bone circlet cut into her skull. Her mouth was stitched shut. Her eyes were wide and wild, like she had never known anything except the moment before sacrifice.

"I'm sorry," I whispered. And I was.

Not because I pitied her, but because I recognized her.

The spell tried to take that from me, too. Tried to bury it in light. In submission.

I gripped the memory with both hands and made it mine.

I wasn't their vessel; I was the storm. I was the rupture in their script. This wasn't destiny. This was choice, and I was making it.

When the crown shattered above me, taking the spell screaming in reverse, it unmade itself as it spiraled inward. Everything the cult had written, everything they'd poured into the trap, all the blood they spilled to thread it together; it all went wrong.

Because I said no.

Because I didn't consent.

Because I broke my name open like a lock and refused to step into the shape they built for me.

A raw silence punched through the chamber. The chanting stopped. The howling cut short. Even the magic fell still for a single, breathless second as if the entire city had to look, and I showed it what I was.

My power surged. Not the sweet, neat lines they'd traced out for me. It didn't rise. It wrapped itself around everything like tentacles and pulled. Every thread of the ritual, every splinter of worship, every echo of belief; they all turned and collapsed inward, pulled toward the only thing still standing at the fracture's heart.

Me.

I opened my hands. I didn't cast. I didn't scream. I took.

The Vein came first, their tether lines snapping free from the bodies they'd rewritten. The essence beneath peeled away like rotten paint, revealing the hollow, desperate things they'd become. Their magic poured toward me like smoke too thick to breathe. I inhaled it anyway, took it into my lungs and let it burn. The seam didn't just resist. It fought me, like reality itself was warning me to stop, that I was too close to the edge. Another pull, and it might not be the magic that tore. It might be me.

I kept going.

The Bone Lords followed. Their masks cracked as their anchors faltered, their spell work imploding mid-chant. I saw one claw at his own chest, trying to contain the backlash. Another kneeled like he thought submission might save him.

It wouldn't.

I didn't devour them. I didn't destroy them. I claimed them. I unstitched their borrowed futures and tore out the lines they'd carved into other people's bones. I dragged every scrap of prophecy and consumption into the wreckage of the crown they'd tried to place on my head.

They wanted an ascendant, but they got a reckoning.

The fracture writhed beneath me. Noctis groaned like a beast waking up beneath a ruined cathedral. The walls blurred at the edges, reality rippling like heat off scorched stone. I felt the city trying to make sense of what I'd done. It flickered through versions of me—vessel, god, queen, saint—and couldn't find a match.

So I gave it a new one. I reached deeper. Into the city. Into its bones, into the place where my mother's magic still whispered and my grandmother's will still held. Into that braid of memory and madness that had built Noctis into a fortress of recursion where instead of solutions, there were only more problems.

And I rewrote the core.

I could feel the blood-magic bindings still woven into its frame, the rites that demanded bloodlines to power the wards, the sacrifices that kept the cycle spinning. The choices that were never really choices.

I unhooked them, one by one. I burned the contract signed in ancestors' blood. I pulled the wards off the bones of the dead. I cracked the altar of lineage and rebuilt it from ash, and then I bound the city to something else.

Choice.

Not legacy. Not lineage. Not prophecy.

Will.

The spell didn't know what to do with that. The threads snapped and re-knit, growing panicked and wild, clawing through versions of the story that had never been told. The fracture howled like it wanted to reject me, but I wasn't standing in it anymore. I owned it. I felt it try to rewrite me. I felt it reach for another crown. Another name.

And I refused again.

"No gods," I whispered, power roaring around me.

"No thrones."

I clenched my fists, and every binding in the chamber cracked.

"No fate but what we make."

For a moment, I thought I heard her voice.

Just a whisper, brushed through my ribs like a breath too old to belong to this life. *"If they hand you a cage and call it destiny, break the bars and rename it."* I didn't know if it was Rhiannon or Brianna. Maybe it was both. Maybe it was me.

The spell stuttered like it heard it, too, like that truth didn't fit inside the story it had been trying to tell. Threads twisted upward, searching for the shape of an ending they could understand, but none of them knew what to do with a woman who said no and meant it.

I saw one flicker catch; an echo of my first life, or maybe just the first time I bled willingly for someone else. A shattered corridor. A girl with her hand pressed to a lover's wound. Blood everywhere, and behind her, a man screaming as the sky split open and I said no then, too. That memory didn't belong to this body, but it was mine all the same. And holy hell, it burned.

I was starting to understand. This wasn't about thrones. It was never even really about power. That was just the bait. The crown was only a bribe dressed in gold and worship, meant to make me forget the cost.

What the fracture feared most wasn't rejection.

It was indifference. It couldn't control what it couldn't name, and I wouldn't give it anything it could use. Not a scream, not a title, not even a moment of longing.

It didn't feel like triumph. It felt like standing still after sprinting through the inferno and finding, impossibly, that you were still whole.

The spell broke, and this time, it didn't rebuild.

The city screamed, and then it breathed.

Not the ragged gasp of something dying, nor the desperate rattle of old magic trying to reassert itself. This breath was clean. Slow. New.

I stood in the hollow where the fracture had lived, the ground still glowing faintly beneath me.

The ritual was gone, not broken, but completely *undone*. The recursion loop no longer spun on blood. The altars no longer whispered names I hadn't chosen. The throne had crumbled, and I hadn't fallen.

The fracture had poured everything into me. It had given me every story, every version, every prophecy sharpened like a knife, and I hadn't let it crown me. I'd held it, and then I'd refused to accept what it gave me.

I opened my fingers slowly, unsure what I'd find. A thread rested in my palm. Thin. Red. Not thirteen knots. Not the old tether.

This one was clean, untouched and unwritten. For a second, I couldn't breathe. A stillness braided from generations of women who had refused to die before they'd finished their part of the story settled over me.

I felt them then.

The scent of rose tea on old wood, the hush of salt shaken on a newborn's brow, a lullaby sung in a voice I didn't know I remembered. I saw hands moving in the dark, drawing ward lines not to keep something out, but to keep me in. Safe. Small. Oh, so loved.

A vision flickered behind my eyes: Brianna, years younger, fingers quick with a red thread that shimmered in the candlelight. She was singing under her breath, and the words were old. Older than Noctis. She sang words about the shape of power, about what you choose to protect when the world won't protect you.

I was a sleeping baby in that memory. And she was crying. Not because she was afraid, but because she already knew.

Rhiannon stood nearby, a blade strapped to her hip. She wasn't crying. She was watching her mother bind a spell into the tiny braid behind my ear. She was learning. Preparing. Every part of her had already decided: if this child lives, she will never be alone. And gods help the world when she learns how to fight.

I came back to the present with my hands trembling from recognition.

They'd given everything so I could make a choice they never had.

And now I would.

Around me, silence rippled through the wreckage.

Then footsteps. Fast. Familiar. For one awful second, I thought maybe I'd misjudged the cost. Maybe I'd cracked the spell wide open but left my body too far behind. The silence had shape now, like it might decide not to give me back, might hold me just a few moments too long, and Gabriel would arrive to find only the echo.

I didn't even have to turn to know he was coming. I felt him before I saw him.

I felt the weight of him in the world, guns still warm, coat streaked with ash, blood that didn't belong to him soaked into his cuffs and blood that did belong to him staining elsewhere. His footsteps were heavier than usual, not because he was hurt, though he was, and I needed to tend to that, but because he'd spent the last ten minutes bracing for the kind of loss that doesn't leave survivors.

He thought I was gone, and still, he ran toward what he thought might be left of me.

Gabriel hadn't wanted me to go into the fracture alone. I hadn't let him argue. I thought he'd stayed behind because he trusted me, but now I knew. He'd stayed because someone had to keep the rest of the plan intact if I failed.

I think it broke him to do it. I think he'd been ready to blow the whole plan up if I didn't walk out.

There was blood on his collar when he rounded the corner. Dirt streaked on his jaw, his gun still in his hand. His eyes found me, standing, breathing, *real*, and something in his body folded.

I watched the moment it hit him, the moment his brain caught up with his eyes, the second that hard, tactical stillness cracked down the middle like a fault line.

And he ran.

Not toward a threat, but toward me.

Not because I was powerful.

Because I was his.

"Serena!"

I looked into his face just as he reached me, and for a second I thought he was going to stop. Ask if I was hurt, maybe make sure it was over. He didn't do any of that. He wrapped both arms around me and pulled me into his chest like he wasn't sure I was real.

I felt the tremble in his breath before I heard it. "You're still here," he whispered. "You're still..."

"I told you I wasn't going anywhere," I said, voice rough, words muffled against his chest.

"Yeah," he muttered, pulling back enough to look me over. "But I've seen enough rituals to know that 'rewriting reality from inside a fracture' is probably a one-way trip."

"You think I'd let a city take me out?" I smirked, the joke too sharp at the edges.

"I think you just made yourself the most dangerous thing still breathing."

He was probably right.

Around us, the Saints were picking their way through what was left. It was just the memory of a battlefield now, crumbling at the edges. The false priests were gone. The cultists had vanished, not in death but in undoing. The magic had rejected their contracts. Knuckle dropped onto a chunk of broken street like it was a barstool, dragging on a cigarette that hadn't been lit in at least five minutes.

"Well," he said, eyes glittering with chaos. "That was dramatic."

Mother Salt exhaled hard through her nose and walked past him without answering. She paused at the edge of the fracture site, bare feet sinking into the upturned dirt.

"It's done," she said. "But it's not over."

I looked toward her. "No."

Because it wasn't.

The city had stopped spinning on stolen bones, but it hadn't chosen its future yet. That part wasn't mine to write. I'd only cleared the page.

Riot approached next, his body still limned in the faint shimmer of the form he'd taken during the battle. Not fully eldritch beast, not quite dog, but something in between. He came to my side and pressed his head into my hip, not speaking, just being. I buried one hand in his scruff and held.

"You stayed," I said.

"You let me," he murmured. "This time, you let me."

His voice was quiet, but full of something that felt like wonder.

Behind him, Edda approached, her coat ragged, spellthread clinging to her like smoke. Her eyes met mine, tired and too full of knowing.

"Well," she said. "You didn't ascend."

"No," I said. "I declined the honor."

Her lips curved. "And you made the city listen."

I didn't answer. She was wrong. I didn't *make* it do anything. I gave it the chance. And it chose.

The fracture closed behind me without a sound.

No quake. No flash of light. Just a long, slow exhale as the wound in the world sealed itself, sighing with relief. Even the city had finally grown tired of bleeding.

I watched as the ground settled, the edges of the rupture pulling inward, not quite returning to what they'd been, but forming something new. A scar, maybe, but at least not a prison.

We hadn't won through domination. We'd won by refusing the script, and now the city was beginning to remember itself without a crown.

The Saints didn't linger. They didn't gloat. They didn't speak prophecies into the dust. Mother Salt bent once and placed something at the edge of the collapsed fracture: a tiny glass vial filled with seawater and ash. A tide offering, a reckoning paid.

The Archivist's scrolls re-wrapped themselves around her arms, the ink curling back into place as she stepped into the wind. Her eyes brushed mine, sharp and full of static. "You're not a god," she said.

"No."

"But you are the ending."

I didn't flinch. "Not quite."

She tilted her head, considering. "I liked it when you were the fire. Before the coronation."

"What coronation?" I asked.

"Oh. Not yet." She inclined her head, and then she turned, her shadow bleeding into the rest.

Knuckle wandered past like he'd missed his stop on the way to hell and wasn't mad about it. "You ever feel like reality owes you a beer?"

"Constantly," I muttered.

He winked. "Glad we're in agreement. Don't fuck it up." He clapped Gabriel on the shoulder and walked off.

Brother Hexane didn't say goodbye. He flickered at the edge of the square like a badly skipped reel and vanished between breaths. The fifth Saint, still unseen, rippled once along the wall and faded.

Edda stood apart from the others, watching me.

I walked over slowly, Gabriel and Riot trailing behind. Her eyes met mine, unreadable.

"So," she said. "What now?"

I looked down at the new thread still wrapped around my fingers. No knots, no path laid out. Just infinite possibility.

"I don't know," I said honestly. "Maybe... nothing. Maybe we just live."

She nodded, once. "That's harder than it sounds."

"Tell me about it."

She stepped forward and reached into her coat. When she pulled her hand out, she was holding a slip of parchment. Charred around the edges. Still warm.

"She left this," Edda said.

My pulse kicked.

I took it gently, expecting prophecy.

Instead, I found a recipe.

Rose tea. Honey. Salt. A little citrus zest to cut the bitterness. The handwriting was delicate, familiar, and braided through memory were my grandmother's words: *Just because it hurts doesn't mean you stop tasting the sweetness.*

My throat tightened. Gabriel touched my back, steady and quiet.

I looked toward the city. Noctis hadn't grown quiet. It had just grown still. Listening. Waiting. Not for a command, but for a choice.

It would not be ruled again, but it might be loved.

"Come on," I said softly, folding the parchment.

"Where to?" Gabriel asked.

"Home," I said.

The word tasted different now. Not like surrender. Not like hiding. Just... steady.

I turned my face to the wind as we walked. Noctis didn't roar, but it didn't whisper, either. It breathed, soft and low, the way a city might if it had lungs and had only just realized they were still working.

The streets were littered with the debris of a war few would understand: sigils melted into stone, salt lines cracked by refusal, the broken teeth of a ritual that never earned its sacrifice. Even the ruins felt quieter now. Not because they weren't dangerous, everything here would always be dangerous, but because the danger no longer had a script.

A shop window caught our reflection as we passed. Me. Gabriel. Riot trailing just behind. For the first time, we didn't look like survivors. We looked like a beginning.

I kept the thread in my hand and let it trail through my fingers, a thread with no destiny tied to its end. Just possibility, and a future that I could make.

The city saw me now; not the fractured girl in exile, not the daughter of tainted bloodlines. Not the vessel. Just Serena. Just a woman who refused the ending she'd been handed and destroyed a crown to prove it. And I swear—I heard it breathe my chosen name back.

Gabriel bumped my shoulder gently with his.

"You okay?" he asked.

"No," I said. "But I think I will be."

He nodded, as if that was enough. And maybe it was.

Riot made a low sound in his throat. The kind that meant he was listening to something far away, but not afraid of it. He caught my eye, but didn't speak. He didn't have to.

Whatever came next—we'd decide it ourselves.

I took one last look over my shoulder, half-expecting the scar in the street to wink open again, but it didn't. The wound was real, but so was the healing.

And then we turned away from the site of my unmaking.

Toward home.

Whatever that would mean now.

"Wait a minute," I said, stopping suddenly.

He turned to look at me, brows drawn together, "What?"

"Do we actually HAVE a home?"

CHAPTER TWENTY-THREE

GUESS WHO'S SOUL BONDED NOW?

Gabriel

W E DIDN'T TAKE THE most direct route.

It wasn't about caution. Those days were gone, or at least shelved under "check again tomorrow." No, this was something else.

She walked, and I followed.

The city was still settling. You could feel it in the seams, old enchantments breathing different, old streets bending slightly where the pressure had changed, like Noctis was learning how to wear its new skin. We passed an alley where the air used to buzz with tether wards; they were gone now, just a clean line of moonlight cutting between buildings. I watched Serena glance toward it and keep moving, her fingers brushing a brick wall like she was checking for a heartbeat.

She was still quiet, but not in the way she'd been before, when she'd been guarded, half-buried, built of thorns. This was something looser, like she was finally in a body that fit.

That terrified me more than a little bit, because I didn't know what came next. I didn't know if she'd still need me.

She hadn't flinched once while unraveling a goddamn city.

No matter how long I looked at her, I kept finding myself whispering one stupid, gut-punched sentence in my head: she's still her. Not ascended, not rewritten, not some echo of Selene wearing Serena's face.

She was just Serena, and I didn't realize how scared I'd been that she wouldn't be until the fear started to drain and left me shaking.

She looked back then, catching me mid-thought. "You okay?"

I huffed a laugh. "Not even close."

Her lips quirked. "You want to lie about it?"

"Later," I said. "Maybe over something alcoholic and wildly overpriced."

"I'll hold you to that."

We turned down the outer causeway and the city opened up like a page peeling back to show its edits. The Veil Market was still there, but it was changed. Where it used to twist in on itself, a labyrinth of bargains you never meant to make, it had unfolded. No longer fractal, just streets. Vendors. Noise. People.

People who looked like they didn't know whether to celebrate or bolt, like they were waiting for the market to bite back.

It didn't.

One woman spotted Serena. Clutched the edge of her shawl like it might shield her from what she remembered. She hesitated, then bowed her head. Not in worship, but in recognition.

Serena didn't stop walking, but I saw the way her fingers twitched like she wanted to reach out and didn't know how. There was still so much to learn.

We passed a cart stacked high with carved talismans, no longer vibrating with Vein sigils. Someone had scratched them out. Replaced them with etchings that looked like doors. Choices. Symbols I didn't recognize, and didn't need to. They were new.

That was the point.

A little boy darted past us, chasing a blue light that wasn't attached to any magic I knew. He was laughing.

I'd never heard that in the Veil before.

I exhaled, slow and rough.

Serena glanced over again. "You're staring."

"Trying to decide if this is real."

"Define real."

"Stable. Functional. Not likely to dissolve in the next five minutes."

"Then no," she said, "but it's trying."

We turned again, cutting through a half-collapsed wall into what should've been dead space. I felt it before I saw it.

The Glass Menagerie, or what was left of it, sat there, carried to this part of the city by some wave of wild magic.

The structure had warped in the ritual backlash, its mirrored surfaces shattered. They'd turned inward on themselves, the recursion unraveling. No longer a trap, it was just a space. It was reflective and strange, but it wasn't lying anymore.

The structure had always shimmered with mirrors, illusions, twisted bends in space, but now half the walls had collapsed. The rest stood on cracked wards that no longer pulsed. The illusion was broken, the glamour stripped, and inside there were signs of the absolute chaos that had been unleashed.

Glass cases sat shattered. Sigils bled out. Walking through the fragments were figures: not illusions, not reflections, but p*eople*.

Some staggered, half-formed. Others wept. One crouched by the edge of a broken pedestal, hands pressed to their face like they didn't remember having one.

The exhibits were free, the Keeper's legacy gone. The bindings were undone.

Serena stood at the threshold; she didn't cross it. She just looked.

I did, too, and for a moment, I swore I saw him, *it*, what was left of the Keeper.

He lay curled in a heap of broken glass and bone, whispering to the shards like they might remember him. His mask, that unassuming face he'd always worn, was cracked open. Nothing sat behind it but dust.

"What happened to him?" I asked.

She didn't answer right away, then said quietly, "That kind of hunger doesn't survive choice."

The wind shifted. The Menagerie groaned.

And we turned away.

I caught my own face in one of the broken panes.

Tired. Bloodstained. Smiling anyway.

And Serena's behind me. Whole. I reached for her without thinking. Just my hand brushing hers, but she didn't pull away; instead, she laced her fingers through mine like we'd always done this. She didn't say anything.

Didn't need to.

The Menagerie shimmered behind us as we passed, its echoes fading like a house that had finally stopped telling old stories.

And still, the walk continued.

The path to the Whispering Vault was always crooked. Even when the rest of Noctis obeyed its geometry, that road twisted, a psychological trap as much as a magical one. Even if you didn't want to hear the voices, it made sure you did. Especially then. If you craved a truth you weren't ready for, it whispered lies with a voice that sounded like your own.

The last time, we'd had to board what passed for a train in Noctis, to reach the Vault. Now? Every path seemed to take us past what had changed, like the city was showing off its new clothing.

Before, even the ground hadn't been exactly what you expected it to be, but tonight, the path was clean. I realized it after a minute; my boots landed where I expected them to. No shift, no tilt, just stairs of cracked stone and silent arches. Still haunted, sure, but not *hungry*. The Vault had stopped devouring.

Its great door stood open.

That hit me harder than I expected. I stopped walking, the words catching somewhere between breath and memory.

Serena slowed. Turned back.

"Vault's never just open," I said, mostly to myself.

"No." She looked at it like she was watching an old enemy sleep. "It hasn't been. Not since before I was born."

"What does it mean?"

"That it's listening. For once, it doesn't think it knows better."

A breeze stirred the space between us as The Vault exhaled, and from somewhere inside, a sound rose. Not a whisper but laughter, light and unsteady, like someone had told a joke that almost didn't land.

We moved on. The Vault didn't call after us, not exactly, but as we turned down the next street, I heard something shiver in the air behind us. A single word.

Selene.

Serena didn't stop. She didn't even look back, but I felt the magic in that name break like a glass thread stretched too thin.

"The Vesper's still in there," I said.

"I know."

"What happens to them now?"

Her voice was quiet. "They wait for someone else's name." There was no glee in it. No triumph, just the tired truth of something left behind. We walked on, and the whisper didn't follow.

As we continued, I felt something unspool inside me. "I don't know what to do with this," I admitted. "I keep waiting for the price tag."

Serena's expression didn't shift, but her fingers twitched like she wanted to hold that thought between them and keep it safe.

"You don't have to do anything with it," she said. "You just have to stop looking for the knife."

I barked a laugh. "That's not how I'm built."

"I know," she said gently. "But maybe we get to rebuild, too."

I almost said something, about the way her voice sat under my skin now, like it belonged there. About how I hadn't felt alone, even when we weren't touching. It didn't feel like a confession; it felt like a fact, like the spell I laid down—my last-ditch fail-safe, the one built to rip her soul from the fracture and bury it in me—might have done more than I meant. Might have worked. Might still be working.

But it didn't feel like she was trapped in me. It felt like we'd met halfway, like her magic had reached out, touched the edges of what I'd made, and said yes.

Not because fate demanded it, but because she wanted it.

We lingered a moment longer. Then we kept walking.

The streets were unfamiliar now in ways that had nothing to do with architecture. Shops we'd passed a thousand times were suddenly lit differently. Wards peeled back. Doors open. People talking like they weren't afraid of being overheard.

Noctis wasn't safe, but it *was* free. Freedom might be its own kind of danger, but at least it was one you could choose for yourself.

We passed a woman with a burned-out Vein mark still etched into her forearm. She didn't cover it, didn't hide, just kept talking with the man beside her like the past was a fact, not a curse. A trio of teenagers darted out of a doorway behind us, paint-streaked and laughing, armed with buckets and stencil glyphs. The wall they left behind shimmered with something bright: new sigils I didn't recognize, pulsing like a heartbeat in sunlight.

It wasn't rebellion.

It was a rewrite.

Serena slowed as we reached a narrow street with broken stone pillars stacked like bones against the walls. She stared at a stretch of scorched brick. I didn't recognize it until I saw the sigil half-melted into the wall.

The Kline Rift.

This was where one of the false rituals had been staged, where a binding circle had cracked open in the first wave. Where people had died.

Now it was empty. Still.

I touched her shoulder. She didn't flinch.

"They'll rebuild here," she said quietly. "Not because I told them to, but because they can."

I didn't answer, because I'd never seen her look like this. Her expression wasn't victorious. It wasn't haunted. It was unburdened, and it finally hit me.

All that power. All that weight. She'd carried it through the worst kind of battlefield and come out the other side—

Still Serena.

I cleared my throat, because it suddenly felt too tight.

"I really thought I'd lose you."

She looked over. "You didn't."

"No. I mean..." I shook my head. "You said no to everything. Every god, every crown, every rewrite. You unmade the whole fucking spell. And then you stood there like the city had to answer to you."

She tilted her head. "It did."

"Right. Exactly. That's what scared the hell out of me."

She smiled, slow. "You thought I'd forget myself."

I met her eyes. "I was afraid you'd have to."

She stepped into me then, hand against my chest, face raised to mine. "Gabriel Rhys Cade," she whispered. "You idiot. I didn't come this far just to become something else." Her hands slid around me, curled up under my jacket, flattening against the plane of my back. "Not when being me finally meant I had someone to be me with."

I laughed, breath catching. "No. I don't guess you did."

And then we just stood there, in a city that wasn't trying to bite us, surrounded by stories that were still figuring out how to end.

For the first time since I'd stepped back into Noctis, I wasn't waiting for the sky to fall.

We ended up on a rooftop.

Not one of the ritzy ones with bottled ward light and imported moonstone benches, but an old half-busted landing above what used to be a black-market relic shop. The sign still dangled over the door: *SEMI-ETHICAL ARTIFACTS, MOSTLY CURSED, NO REFUNDS.* I liked the honesty.

We climbed up the back stairwell in silence, the soft kind that comes when you're done with the part of the day where everything has to mean something.

Serena reached the top first and let out a sound somewhere between a sigh and a laugh. I followed and found her already sitting on the edge of the ledge, boots dangling over the drop, eyes trained on the sky, which, notably, hadn't opened up to devour us yet.

Progress.

"You really picked a scenic spot," I said, flopping down beside her.

"You're welcome."

We sat there a while. Below us, the streets buzzed—not frantic, not afraid. Just moving, figuring it out in real time.

Serena leaned back on her palms, eyes half-lidded.

I tilted my head toward her. "So. Hypothetical question."

She glanced over. "This should be good."

"If I was hypothetically soul-bonded to someone now, like, say, a terrifyingly powerful woman who just rebuilt the metaphysical infrastructure of an entire city, what kind of benefits would that include?"

She made a thoughtful hum. "Free health care."

"Useful."

"Occasional nightmares. Blood rituals at sunset. Access to one very judgmental dog."

I looked around. "Where *is* Riot?"

"Shadow-stalking. He's in his 'this is fine, I'm just keeping an eye on everything forever' era."

"Ah. Eldritch helicopter parenting."

She snorted.

I nudged her knee with mine. "Okay, but seriously. Are we? Bonded?"

She gave me a side-eye. "Do you *feel* bonded?"

"I mean, I've been emotionally compromised since I met you, and willing to kill anything that looks at you sideways pretty much from day one. Is that a yes?"

"That's just how I know you're into me."

I laughed. I couldn't help it. "You're so astute."

"And you're lucky I didn't soul-bind you into a tree."

I gave her a side eye. "Wait, that was an option?"

"I had a whole diagram drawn up."

We fell back into quiet again, but it didn't feel final. Just full.

Eventually, she spoke again. "If something's changed, between us, I think it was always going to."

I turned toward her. "And if it hasn't?"

She shrugged. "Then we still get this."

"I think it happened anyway," I said.

Serena looked over. "What did?"

"The bond." I rubbed a hand over my face. "I laid the spell. You know that now, right? To pull you out if it all went to shit."

She nodded, slowly.

"But I think you pulled back. I think you met it with something. I think we built a bridge without realizing."

Serena was quiet for a long time. Then she reached for my hand again.

"Do you want it undone?"

I didn't even hesitate. "No. I just want it to be real, not another something fate forced on you."

She kissed the inside of my wrist. "Then it is."

She was still her. She was *so* her.

And maybe the bond, if it was real, didn't need a ritual. Maybe it was just this, this ache in my chest that eased when I looked at her, this gravity that hadn't let me walk away even when I should have. This *relief* that felt louder than any vow that she was here.

"Hypothetically," I said again, "what if I told you I don't care if we're bonded or not?"

"I'd say you're stalling for a kiss."

"You'd be correct."

She kissed me. Not a fireworks-and-prophecy kind of kiss. Not a magic-seals-it kind of kiss. Just warm and real and ours. When we pulled apart, she tucked her head against my shoulder.

I reached into my coat, pulled out a crumpled snack bar I'd forgotten was in there, and handed it to her without a word.

She unwrapped it, took a bite, and immediately grimaced. "This expired during the last moon cycle."

I nodded. "Yep."

"Tastes like sugar-coated regret."

"I was saving it for a romantic moment."

She shook her head. "We're going to need better snacks if this soul bond thing is going to work out."

"I'll check with Riot. I hear he's good with procurement." I kissed the top of her head, just because I could.

She smiled against my shoulder, and whispered so softly I almost didn't hear her, "Take me home, Gabriel. Take us home."

I didn't move right away.

Didn't speak. Didn't even breathe.

Because the way she said it—*us*—hit somewhere deeper than any spell ever had. It wasn't a plea, or a surrender, because God knows there wasn't an ounce of surrender in her. It was a tether, threaded in her voice, in the air, in the way my heart kicked like it recognized the shape of her. For a second, I felt it again, that flicker, like something inside me answered.

There was a hum behind my ribs, a resonance that wasn't mine alone. It wasn't compulsion, but connection, faint, steady, and unbreakable. I knew that feeling. I'd built it into the failsafe I carved in blood and wax and reckless devotion. I'd meant it as a last resort, a desperate way to keep her from fracturing into nothing.

I never expected it to hold if it hadn't been needed, and yet, there it was, warm and quiet and so very alive. It nestled there, fueled by the kind of love I'd never thought was possible.

She shifted beside me, eyes still on the sky. Her cheek rested lightly against my shoulder like she belonged there, and suddenly the whole fucking war felt worth it just to have this. To have her.

I cleared my throat, barely above a whisper. "Do you feel it too?"

Serena didn't ask what I meant. She never did, not when it counted.

"Sometimes," she said. "Like you're standing closer than you are. Like I could find you with my eyes closed."

I swallowed hard. "You could."

She nodded once. "Yeah. I think I could."

She didn't say it was magic. She didn't say it wasn't. She just let it exist between us, this quiet tether made of every choice we hadn't walked away from. Behind us, I caught the faintest scrape of claws on metal: Riot, somewhere in the shadows, making no sound beyond what he meant us to hear.

He was watching, as always, but not intervening, like the bond had been noted, logged and approved.

Or maybe just... *understood*.

Serena didn't move, and neither did I. The wind stirred her hair, brushing it across my collarbone, claiming the space between us as ours, and I let my head rest lightly on hers.

No vows. No rituals.

Just us.

CHAPTER TWENTY-FOUR

NOT QUEEN, BUT THANKS FOR ASKING

Serena

T HE MORNING AFTER SAVING the world didn't feel like victory.

It felt like raw skin and bruised bones, a shoulder I couldn't move without aching, and a faint pulse of something under my ribs that whispered: still here, still you, still breathing.

I didn't remember coming back to the penthouse. I remember telling Gabriel to take us home, but I don't remember the process of getting here. I hadn't even known where home *was*. I remembered the note, though, a scrap of parchment tucked under the front door ward, inked in Moshi's careful hand. *You'll find everything moved here. It felt right.* No signature, no flourish. Just that. A quiet act of service. I'd clutched it in my fingers for longer than I should've, pulse tight in my throat, because godsdammit, he'd survived. Despite everything, every betrayal, every memory that hurt more than it helped, he had made good on his promise, even when I couldn't give him one in return.

I was tired of losing people. I was grateful he wasn't another one.

The wards had welcomed us like we'd never left, but something had changed. The place felt cleaner, more ours, like the city had reshaped the penthouse itself in gratitude. The edges of Gabriel's boots were dusted clean in the closet. My jackets had been repaired. There were fresh sheets on the bed, cool linen that smelled faintly of cedar.

We didn't do much after getting inside.

No dramatics, no epic speeches, just the dull, wordless ritual of trying to be whole again.

We staggered into the shower first. Gabriel didn't protest when I hauled him in fully clothed, too caked in ash and blood to even think about waiting. I peeled his shirt away from the mess on his ribs, noting how he hissed, low and sharp. Burns, slices, bruising that tracked like someone had tried to write a curse into him by hand, all over his body. He'd spared nothing in protecting me.

He leaned against the tile, eyes shut, mouth twitching with a grimace he refused to let fall as I peeled him out of his clothes, and then me out of mine, tossing them into a pile in the corner. "Did I mention I'm too old to be a human shield?" he murmured.

"You're thirty-four," I said as I maneuvered him under the water, watching it sluice down his body in red brown streams. I reached for the bottle of shampoo and poured some into my hand, lathering up his hair, smiling when he closed his eyes and tilted his head into my hand like a cat.

"Like Indy said, it's not the years, it's the mileage."

I raised onto my tip toes and kissed the corner of his mouth anyway. "Still hot."

He didn't open his eyes, but the smile that curled on his lips was real, pulling me close.

After the shower, it was bandages, ice packs, and the slow process of closing the gashes on his leg and shoulder that had nearly taken him down. He let me work in silence, fingers flexing only when the pain caught wrong. I whispered old spells under my breath; not healing, not quite, but something older, deeper. Something that made the ache ease even if it didn't completely fade.

When we were clean, when we'd eaten the burnt toast and hard cheese I managed to put together from the still semi-stocked kitchen, we collapsed. No sex, no ceremony, just clean sheets, his arms around me and the world going still.

I hadn't moved since.

Sunlight edged through the curtains now, or what passed for it in Noctis, casting weak gold across the marble. The air didn't feel heavy anymore. No tension. No static. My head rested on Gabriel's shoulder. His fingers traced idle patterns along my spine, slow and gentle. I could feel the dull throb of his injuries, his body working overtime to repair itself, but he was here. Whole. Real.

"I thought I lost you," I murmured.

He didn't ask when, and I didn't ask how close. He just wrapped his arm tighter around me, like he was trying to make the space between us nonexistent. "You didn't," he said. "You won't."

I tilted my head to look at him. "I really went into the fracture without a backup plan, didn't I."

He snorted. "Last time I checked, you were the backup plan."

"I was the only plan."

A silence stretched between us, soft but weighty.

"This doesn't mean we're safe," he said. "Doesn't mean everything's over."

"No, but for now? This is enough."

He leaned in. Pressed his forehead to mine.

"I love you," I whispered.

A groan erupted from the hallway before he could give it back to me.

"Oh my gods," Riot grumbled. "Are you two soul-bonded now? I need my own apartment. Do you know what it's like trying to sleep in a warded penthouse with a soul bond flaring through the floorboards? You're like a living security system powered by sexual tension."

I buried my face in Gabriel's chest to stifle my giggles. He didn't even flinch. "You want me to draw you a floor plan for your new place?"

"I want noise-dampening glyphs," Riot snapped. "And a soundproofed dog bed. And possibly a restraining order against any future orgasm-induced magical feedback."

I bit my lip.

Gabriel grinned. "You're just mad you don't have a key."

"I don't need a key," Riot said, storming off. "I need earplugs. And a damn vacation."

The door slammed.

Gabriel turned to me, one brow raised.

We didn't rush; there wasn't any need.

His body was warm beneath mine, steady and familiar, ribs still bruised under the soft curve of my palm. My hand rose and fell with his breath, the pattern so rhythmic it felt like a lullaby. Like the city was holding still just for us.

Gabriel didn't speak. He just looked up at me. His thumb brushed the edge of my jaw, slow, like he wasn't touching to possess, just to remember. The curve of my cheek, the place where the ward-burn from the cathedral had healed, the line of my throat; they all received touches that felt reverent.

"You're staring," I said softly.

"You're here," he murmured. "And I still get to look at you. That seems worth staring at."

I flushed, stupid and soft in a way I only was with him. "You're terrible at compliments," I whispered.

He smiled. "I'm just out of practice. I'll get better now that I have a reason." His hand moved to my waist, patient and possessive, devout, touching me simply because I was his and he could. I shifted to sit up slightly, knees bracketing his hips, and caught his breath hitching at the sight.

We were still clothed. Well, mostly clothed: I was wearing one of his shirts, sleeves rolled, hem brushing my thighs. He hadn't put on more than his boxer briefs. It shouldn't have felt intimate. It shouldn't have felt like anything, but it did. It felt holy.

I braced a hand on his chest and leaned down slowly, letting my lips graze one corner of his mouth, then the other, then down to his jaw, where his beard scraped gently against my skin. He exhaled through his nose, a sound rough enough to make my pulse stutter.

"You trying to kill me?" he asked.

"Not unless you ask nicely."

He laughed, but it dissolved when I kissed him properly, deeper this time. No hunger. No rush, just heat curling slow and inevitable. The slide of his tongue over mine sent a lazy lick of heat down my spine that he followed with his hands

His hands slid up my thighs, slow and reverent. He didn't pull, didn't try to guide, just *touched*, like he still wasn't convinced I was real. I rocked forward slightly, just enough to feel the drag of friction between us, letting my clit ride along the ridge of his cock, and he groaned like it was too much and not enough all at once.

"You sure you're okay?" I murmured, nipping at his bottom lip. "You took a fair bit of damage."

"I've had worse."

I laughed. "Liar."

He grinned, breathless. "Okay. I've had similar. But this is a better kind of pain."

I sat up again, tugging at the hem of the shirt I'd stolen from him. I didn't rush. I just pulled it over my head slowly, the fabric sliding over my skin with a whisper, revealing inch by inch until I was bare before him, and ignored my own blush as I watched his eyes darken.

Possessive. Greedy. Worshipful.

"Serena," he breathed, and my name was like a blessing. I didn't let him finish. I leaned back down and kissed him again, pressing my chest to his, the rub of my nipples against the hair on his chest causing every inch of skin to spark like it had been waiting for this moment since the day we met. His hands found my back, fingers splaying wide, drawing slow circles against my spine like he wanted to memorize every vertebrae.

When I ground my hips down against his, his mouth dropped open with a sound I felt more than heard.

"You're evil," he groaned.

"I'm considerate."

"Debatable."

I grinned and rolled my hips again, this time slower, savoring the way his hands tightened on my thighs, the way his jaw clenched like he was hanging on by the thinnest thread.

"You're going to make me beg, aren't you," he said, voice rough.

"I haven't decided."

His eyes met mine—dark, wild, utterly undone.

"You're not going to win this game, you know."

I leaned in, lips brushing his ear. "I already did," I said, before I scooted down enough to pull his briefs off and leave him as bare as I was. I took a moment to just look. To watch him breathe, watch his skin flush. To feel him, alive and warm, hard between my legs as I crawled back up his body, his heart hammering under the hands I braced on his chest. I slid myself along his length again, feeling how slick I was, reveling in the clench of his hands on my hips and the way his head dropped back, eyes closed.

"Say it again," I breathed.

Gabriel looked like he might break. Not from pain, but from the sheer force of trying not to come undone. His hands were splayed across my hips now, thumbs stroking slow, reverent circles against my skin as I rocked against him, all rhythm and heat and maddening control.

I bent, and he kissed me like it was killing him not to lose it.

"I love you," he murmured against my throat, voice cracked and thick with hunger. "Do you know what you do to me?"

I shook my head, breath hitching. "Tell me."

His hands slid up, sliding past my waist and cupping my breasts like he could anchor himself with the shape of me. His fingers teased my nipples until I shuddered.

"You ruin me," he breathed. "You look at me like I'm not already yours, and I forget how to think."

I moaned, soft and helpless, the sound spilling from me before I could stop it. His grip tightened.

"Every time you touch me, I think 'thank fuck she's real'."

I bent down, buried my face in his neck, shaking.

"And when you ride me like this," he groaned as I rolled my hips again, taking him inside me, deep enough that his breath stuttered, "I can't believe I ever lived without you."

I felt the words sink into me like heat. Like hunger. Like magic I didn't need to cast.

I arched against him, needing more but not sure where to put it, this magnitude of feeling, only knowing that every part of me was tuned to the cadence of his voice, the edge of his praise.

"Gabriel..."

His hands slid to my thighs, spreading me wider across his lap.

"Look at me," he said, voice lower now.

I did.

"*Ty moya ved'ma.*" he rasped. "*Moyo serdtse. Moyo spaseniye.*" My breath caught. I felt something tighten low in my belly, sharp and sweet and aching.

He leaned up, brushing his lips against my ear, whispering in Russian again, syllables thick with reverence and need, and I nearly shattered just from the sound.

"You have no idea what you've turned me into," he said. "You could ask me for anything, and I'd kill for it, bleed for it, just to hand it to you."

I rocked against him again, harder this time, chasing that edge he'd drawn in words.

"And you think I'm the dangerous one," I gasped.

Gabriel smiled, slow and wicked. "You are," he said, "but I like living on the edge."

He surged up then, flipping us with a force that made me gasp as my back hit the mattress. His hands slid under my thighs, pulling me further under him, and he hovered above me like something feral with a soft mouth. He kissed down my neck, my collarbone, the inside of my breast, murmuring things in Russian I didn't understand but felt in my bones. He sucked marks onto my skin and I welcomed them.

He worshipped me with every inch of his body, with his words, with his soul, and I melted under all of it. His eyes stayed locked on mine as he pressed in slow, and I could feel the reverence in every inch of it. The careful control. The almost-violent need to make this good for me.

And it was.

God, it was.

The stretch of him, the heat, the grounding weight of his body and the way he watched me like I was a miracle unraveling beneath him—it shattered something soft and hidden in my chest that I didn't know I was holding. Didn't know it *could* break like that, and still be okay.

Gabriel cupped my jaw with one hand, his thumb brushing my lower lip. "You still with me?"

"Always."

He kissed me, deep, slow, consuming. His hips rocked again, and I gasped, clutching his shoulders like I needed to hold onto something real. Because I was floating, flaring like a spellfire fuse.

Burning.

He didn't fuck me like he was staking a claim. He fucked me like he already had me, like I was already his, and this was his right.

I gave it back to him, moved with him, met every thrust, wrapped my legs around his waist and dragged my nails down his back because I wanted to feel him lose control.

He gave me praise in ragged whispers. "Look at you. Look at what I get to touch. You're so beautiful, so damn perfect, and every inch of you is mine." Each word melted something deeper.

It wasn't just that I liked it. It was that I needed it, the affirmation, the devotion, the quiet, devastating truth of how completely he loved me. I had never felt anything like it.

His rhythm faltered just enough to tell me he was close, and I arched into him, hips rolling, matching him stroke for stroke.

"You gonna fall apart for me?" he whispered, lips dragging along my jaw. "You gonna let go?" He reached between us, fingers circling my clit in firm, expert strokes.

"Gabriel—"

"That's it," he breathed. "Take what I give you. Let me feel you."

My orgasm hit like a curse being lifted: full-body, blinding. Shattering. I cried out his name, magic flaring under my skin, and I felt him follow, hips snapping once, twice, before he groaned against my throat, every muscle going taut with release.

We collapsed into each other, trembling, slick with sweat and shaking with something that felt too big for just magic. He didn't move for a long time. Neither did I.

Eventually, his fingers found mine, twining gently.

"You okay?" he whispered.

"I think I forgot how to breathe."

He laughed, exhausted and wild. "Yeah. Same."

I turned my face into his neck, nuzzling him like it was the only thing that mattered. "I love you," I whispered. He held me tighter.

"I hope you realize," I murmured, "how lucky you are that I don't have girlfriends. I'd have to tell them about this."

"About the soul bond?"

"No. About the fact that you talk like that in bed."

He grinned against my temple. "Let them wonder."

I snorted. "Riot's already requesting noise-dampening wards."

"He should've put in for hazard pay."

We stayed like that, tangled and still, while the city turned beneath us, and for the first time in my entire life, I wasn't afraid of what came next.

I woke to the smell of eggs, the faint sizzle of something in a pan, and the distinct sound of a paper being aggressively slapped onto a hard surface.

I blinked against the light, sheets tangled around my legs, and groaned.

"Gabriel?"

"Kitchen," came the reply, followed by, "Riot, if you touch the butter again I swear to every minor god in this city—"

Another slap of paper. Another sigh.

I sat up slowly, sore in a very good way. My thighs ached. My voice felt rough. My neck bore the shadow of a bite that probably hadn't been meant to bruise but absolutely had, and still, the only thing I felt was light.

No magic clinging to my skin like static. No false prophecies. No weight I hadn't chosen.

Just a day, real and warm and full of possibility.

I dragged on his shirt from the floor and padded barefoot into the kitchen.

Gabriel was standing at the stove, hair still damp from a quick shower, wearing nothing but joggers and a self-satisfied smile.

He looked domestic. Dangerous. Unbothered by the apocalypse we'd just barely avoided. He handed me a cup of coffee.

Riot was perched on a barstool beside the island, glaring at a stack of pamphlets.

I blinked. "Are those... yours?"

Riot gave me a scathing look. "Welcome to the Mandatory Soul-Bond Recovery Protocol."

Gabriel snorted. "He printed them while we were asleep."

"He summoned them," I corrected, walking closer.

"Oh no," Riot said darkly. "I summoned the templates. I customized the content."

I picked up the top pamphlet.

"HEALTHY BOUNDARIES: How to Avoid Becoming a Two-Headed Psychic Disaster"

Below the title, a stick-figure illustration of two people tangled in a heart-shaped knot, with a dog in the background looking deeply unimpressed.

I laughed so hard I choked on my coffee. Gabriel thumped my back. "Ward interference and a Heimlich moment. Riot's gonna put us on a watchlist."

"Oh my God," I whispered. "This is incredible."

"There's a glossary," Riot said, nose twitching. "And a flowchart."

Gabriel leaned over and flipped to the centerfold. "There's a quiz."

"Are You Using Magic to Enable Codependence or Are You Just In Love: A Five-Point Checklist," I read aloud.

"Question one," Gabriel said. "Have you destroyed a major cultural institution together in the last seventy-two hours?"

"Check."

"Question two: Do you anticipate your sex life creating ward interference?"

"Oh, we already have," I said.

Riot groaned. "You two are going to kill me. I can hear your emotional bond now. Do you know what it's like living with a magical version of your foreplay? It's like being haunted by a really horny ghost."

I laughed. Actually, fully laughed.

Gabriel handed me a plate of scrambled eggs and toast. "We'll build you an apartment," he said. "You can even pick your wards."

"And your soundproofing," I added.

"I want a panic button," Riot muttered. "One that explodes your bed when things get too sentimental."

"You're just mad we didn't name the soul bond after you," I said.

He narrowed his eyes. "Name it after me and I swear I'll teach your future children how to bark in Enochian."

I nearly dropped my toast.

Gabriel sipped his coffee. There was a long, dangerous pause.

Then I turned slowly. "Children?"

Gabriel looked suspiciously neutral. "Hypothetically."

Riot looked delighted.

I put the plate down. "What hypothetical conversation was this?"

Gabriel held up his hands. "I'm just saying, if someone were to suggest that I wanted to ruin you in the domestic sense—"

"Gabriel."

"—I would say we've already started with the matching emotional trauma, so it's a natural progression."

I stared at him.

He smiled.

I walked around the island and kissed the smug right off his mouth.

The eggs got cold. Riot left in a huff, trailing pamphlets behind him like bitter confetti.

For the first time in what felt like my entire life, everything was exactly as it should be.

Gabriel pulled back. "Wait a minute. Why is Riot teaching our future kids how to *bark*?"

Epilogue: THIS IS WHY WE CAN'T HAVE NICE THINGS

Serena

S HIT NEVER STAYS QUIET in Noctis for long.

Even after the blood dries, after the bones stop humming and the fractures seal with a hush like a held breath, the city never sleeps. Not really. It just... tilts. Pauses long enough for someone to think it's safe to breathe, and then shifts the streets while you're not looking.

But for tonight, there's a hush. Not peace, Noctis doesn't do peace, but a kind of stillness. The kind that comes when the gods have finished rewriting the script and the stagehands are still sweeping up ash and prophecy.

I stand at the edge of the Veil Market, watching the stalls rebuild themselves from memory. The fabric drapes re-stitch with golden thread. Candles relight without touch. The merchants are slower now, more cautious, like they're waiting for the punchline. Or the next reckoning.

Somewhere down the block, a child with glass eyes is selling bottled laughter to a warlock with blood on his shoes. A woman made of wire and hummingbird wings is reading palms in reverse. And above us all, the stars blink like they're not quite sure they're in the right sky. A real night sky.

Noctis is healing, a month out from the insanity. It's doing it wrong, the way everything here does, but it's doing it.

Behind me, I hear Gabriel laugh.

He's sitting on the steps of what used to be a courthouse and is now a noodle bar, sleeves rolled up, a bowl of what might be noodles and might be something else in his hands. I think it's wiggling. Riot is sprawled beside him, head resting on one paw, chewing on a pamphlet titled *So You Accidentally Became Divine*. There's a bite taken out of "Divine."

I join them. Fold myself down beside Gabriel and lean into the steady warmth of his side.

"Still quiet," he murmurs.

"For now."

"Think it'll last?"

I snort. "In Noctis? Absolutely not."

He hums, fingers brushing my knee. "Good. I was starting to get bored." I look down at his right hand, at the interlocked band of three colors of gold—white, yellow, and rose. A matching one sits on mine. Right hands, in the Russian tradition.

I'd turned down being queen. But being his wife?

Yeah. That felt right.

He'd taken me to that beach, just as he'd promised, and we'd said our vows while standing on the sand. It had been just us and an officiant, and water so clear it held its own sort of magic.

And I got a drink with a little umbrella in it.

Fuck anyone who thought it was too fast; if you haven't been bonded by existential trauma and reality-warping rituals, you don't get to judge.

Across the street, someone screams. It's not urgent, just annoyed, like a barista out of oat milk mid-latte.

Riot perks up. "That's the third summoning gone wrong tonight. If one more amateur tries to bind a grudge spirit with hot glue and spite, I'm moving to the suburbs."

"You wouldn't last ten minutes," I mutter.

"I would THRIVE," he declares. "I'd join a gardening club."

"You hate flowers."

"I'd learn."

Gabriel shakes with silent laughter beside me. "He's been like this all day," he says, taking a bite of his noodles.

"He's earned it." I tilt my head. "We all have."

And maybe that's true. Maybe we survived the worst of it. The curses, the cults, the collapsing timelines. Maybe we bought ourselves a future, even if it came wrapped in scars and stitched with blood.

But Noctis is still Noctis, and I'm still me. The girl who rewrote the story. The weapon who learned how to love. The daughter of a god, the bloodline of a revolution, the witch who chose not to ascend but to live.

The storm will come again. I know that. The Voice is quiet, but not gone. The fracture is sealed but not forgotten.

But when it comes?

We'll be ready.

Gabriel rests his head against mine. "So what now, Serena Morrigan Cade?"

I smile.

"Now?" I say. "We live."

I still felt the weight of every spell I'd cast, but maybe that was the point. Power should be heavy. It should remind you that you're still carrying it.

Beneath our feet, the city hums. Waiting. Watching. Dreaming a little louder than before. He hadn't noticed, but just before we sat down, the steps outside the noodle bar shimmered. Not visibly, nothing showy, just a low, sympathetic thrum in the stone beneath Gabriel's boot.

I felt it. The Weave did too.

Not for me.

For *him*.

Like Noctis remembered something it hadn't realized was missing. Like it was waiting to see if he'd remember, too. Somewhere far below the Market—beneath the fractured streets and forgotten foundations—a thread twitches.

Not pulled.

Not cut.

Just... noticed.

The city doesn't flinch, but it remembers.

Ready for the next page.

Rose Tea With Honey

2 cups water

1 tsp dried citrus peel, chopped

1 tbsp dried food grade rose petals

pinch salt

honey

Boil the water, and pour it over the peel and rose petals. You can also use a tea ball. Add the barest pinch of salt. Steep for 5 to 15 minute, depending on how strong you like your tea, and add honey to taste.

Also by A.L. Richards

Coming Titles:

Blocked and Bewitched — a paranormal hockey romance —
Coming Winter 25/26

Blood and Brine — pirates and sirens in the 18th century
Caribbean

Revenant — Book 2 in the Blood & Magic series

If you enjoyed this book, please consider leaving a review! As an
indie author, reviews are life!

About the author

A.L. Richards has spent her career moving between the worlds of criminal psychology, library science, and education, always fueled by too much coffee. These days, she channels that energy into crafting stories full of courage, heart, and a touch of magic. She lives near the mid-Atlantic coast with her Viking (since her Valkyries had the nerve to grow up and start their own adventures), two cats and two dogs, one of which is a very judgmental Australian Shepherd. When she's not writing, she can be found painting, obsessing over hockey, and dreaming of the perfect gothic home library—rolling ladder very much mandatory.

You can join The Liminal Court at:

https://www.alrichards.com/

https://www.instagram.com/alrichardswrites/#

https://www.tiktok.com/@alrichardswrites

https://www.patreon.com/AuthorALRichards

Acknowledgements

How in the world do I go about thanking everyone who made this possible?

To my alpha readers: Aimee, Anett, and Casey. You took a terrified woman with a horrible case of imposter syndrome and convinced her that she did indeed have a story worth telling.

To Aimee: your work in editing this was more than I could ever have asked for. If you ever decide being a lawyer has gotten old, I think you should hang out a shingle as an editor. You made me a better writer, and I cannot thank you enough. I owe you Kraken tickets.

To my ARC readers: thank you for giving me a place on your TBR. I'm forever grateful.

To Blindlove: Your music was the soundtrack to this story for me. Thank you.

To Heather: I miss you every day. I wish I could hand you a copy of this and listen to you raz me about the spicy scenes.

To my parents: I love you. Please don't read this.

And to my Viking and my Valkyries: I love you more.